"Noël aims for the celebrity-hungry chick-lit crowd and scores. . . . Chick-lit gold."—*Kirkus Reviews*

"This is a suspenseful, scandalous, and consumable novel that is sure to gain instant fandom and leave readers eagerly awaiting the next installment. A must-have selection for older teens."—*SLJ*

"For readers looking for a breezy, glamorous look into LA's underworld, this is the page-turner for the job."—ALA *Booklist*

"Noël cycles among the stories of Layla, Tommy, Aster, and Madison in a gossipy, third-person narrative that makes for addictive reading."—*Publishers Weekly*

"Like a good celebrity, *Unrivaled* is mysterious and compelling and so gorgeous you won't be able to look away."
—Cecily von Ziegesar, author of the Gossip Girl series

"A glitzy, suspenseful, shamelessly addictive read."
—Margaret Stohl, #1 *New York Times* bestselling author of *Beautiful Creatures*

"*Unrivaled* will have you hooked from the very first page. Everything from the glitzy setting to the suspenseful plot is pure gold."—Jamie McGuire, #1 *New York Times* bestselling author of *Beautiful Disaster*

"*Unrivaled* reveals the dark, grittier side of fame and leaves the reader caught in a web of suspense and lies."
—#1 *New York Times* bestselling author Jennifer L. Armentrout

"Pulling back the curtain on Hollywood's nightclub scene, Alyson Noël's *Unrivaled* has it all—glamour, passion, scandal, and even a missing starlet. More please!"
—Kimberly Derting, author of the Body Finders series

"*Unrivaled* is addictive! With a killer cliff-hanger and twists around every corner, I couldn't stop reading this novel. Now I'm impatiently waiting for the second book in the Beautiful Idols series."—Anna Todd, bestselling author of the After series

# ALYSON NOËL

## A BEAUTIFUL IDOLS NOVEL

**KATHERINE TEGEN BOOKS**
*An Imprint of HarperCollins Publishers*

Katherine Tegen Books is an imprint of HarperCollins Publishers.

Unrivaled

www.epicreads.com

ISBN 978-0-06-232453-5

Typography by Erin Fitzsimmons
17 18 19 20 21    CG/LSCH    10 9 8 7 6 5 4 3 2 1
❖
First paperback edition, 2017

*For Jackie and Michelle,*
*my BFFs for too many decades to count!*

*All that glitters is not gold.*

—WILLIAM SHAKESPEARE

# PROLOGUE

# LOST STARS

Despite the crush of tourists storming the sidewalks year after year, Hollywood Boulevard is a place best viewed behind a pair of polarized lenses and lowered expectations.

From the string of sagging buildings in various stages of decay, the tacky souvenir shops hawking plastic statues of Marilyn in her windblown white dress, and the seemingly endless parade of addicts, runaways, and glamour-deprived transients, it doesn't take long before the sunburned, white-sneaker-wearing masses realize the LA they're searching for does not exist there.

In a city that feeds off youth and beauty, Hollywood Boulevard more closely resembles a former screen siren who's seen better days. The incessant sunshine is a harsh and brutal companion, intent on magnifying every wrinkle, every age spot.

Yet for those who know where to look (and those fortunate enough to boast a spot on the guest list), it also serves as an oasis of the city's hottest nightclubs—a sort of hedonistic haven for the young, fabulous, and rich.

For Madison Brooks, the boulevard was everything she'd dreamed it would be. Maybe it didn't look anything like the snow globe she'd had as a kid, the one that showered small squares of golden glitter over a miniature version of the Hollywood sign, but she never expected it would. Unlike those clueless tourists expecting to see their favorite celebrities hanging by their Walk of Fame stars, handing out autographs and hugs to all who passed by, Madison knew exactly what she'd find.

She did her due diligence.

Left nothing to chance.

After all, when planning an invasion, it's best to familiarize yourself with the lay of the land.

And now, only a few short years after exiting that grimy bus station in downtown LA, her face was on the cover of nearly every magazine, every billboard. The town was officially hers.

While the journey was far more arduous than she'd ever let on, Madison managed to surpass everyone's expectations but her own. Most merely hoped she'd survive. Not a single person from her former life expected her to rocket straight to the top. Ultimately becoming so known, so lauded, so connected, she'd command full, no-questions-asked access to one of LA's hottest nightclubs long after it had closed for the night.

In a rare moment of privacy, Madison strode toward the edge of the vacant Night for Night terrace. The heels of her Gucci stilettos sliding gracefully against the smooth stone floor, she pressed a hand to her heart and bowed toward the skyline, imagining those flickering lights as an audience of millions—cell phones and lighters raised in her honor.

The moment reminded her of a similar game she'd played as a kid. Back when she staged elaborate performances for a crowd of grubby stuffed animals with matted hair and missing limbs. Their dull, unblinking button eyes fixed on the sight of Madison dancing and singing before them. Those tireless rehearsals prepping her for the day those secondhand toys would be replaced by real, live screaming fans. She never once doubted her dream would become a reality.

Madison hadn't become Hollywood's hottest young celebrity by hoping, wishing, or depending on others. Discipline, control, and steely determination steered her ascent. Although the media loved to portray her as a frivolous party girl (albeit one with serious acting chops), beneath the salacious headlines was a young and powerful girl who'd seized control of her destiny and made it her bitch.

Not that she'd ever admit to such a thing. Better to let them think she was a princess whose life flowed effortlessly. The lie provided a shield that kept them from learning the truth. Those who dared scratch beneath the surface never got very far. The road to Madison's past was jammed with so many roadblocks even the most determined journalist eventually yielded defeat by writing about her unparalleled beauty—her hair the color of warming chestnuts on a crisp fall day (according to the guy who'd recently interviewed her for *Vanity Fair*). He also described her violet eyes as shadowed by a lushly dark nimbus of lashes used to alternately reveal and conceal. And wasn't there a mention of her skin being pearlescent or incandescent or some other descriptor that translates to radiant?

Funny how he began the interview as just another jaded journalist sure he could break her. Convinced that their vast age difference—she being eighteen, he hovering way past forty (ancient in comparison)—along with his superior IQ (his assumption, not hers)—meant he could trick her into revealing something regrettable that would send her career into a tailspin, only to walk away from their meeting entirely frustrated, if not a little infatuated. Same as all the others who'd gone before—each of them grudgingly admitting there was something different about Madison Brooks. She wasn't your average starlet.

She leaned deeper into the night, swept her fingers across her lips, and arced her arm wide, releasing a string of kisses to her imaginary fans flickering and gleaming below. So captured by the sheer unbridled giddiness of all she'd accomplished, she lifted her chin in triumph and released a shout so thunderous it blotted out the incessant soundtrack of traffic and sirens below.

It felt good to let go.

To allow herself, for one brief instant, to be as wild and untamed as she'd been as a kid.

"I did it!" she whispered to herself, the imaginary fans glimmering in the distance, but mostly to those who'd doubted her, even tried to thwart her.

The second time, she allowed the startling twang she'd long since abandoned to slip to the surface, amazed at how easy it was to summon that voice—another remnant of a past she could never fully escape. Considering the reckless way she'd behaved earlier, she wondered if she really wanted to.

The memory of the boy she'd kissed was still fresh on her lips. For the first time in a long time, she'd allowed herself to relax enough to let down her guard and be seen for the girl she really was.

Still, she couldn't help wondering if she'd made a mistake.

The thought alone was sobering enough, but a quick

glance at her diamond-encrusted Piaget gave her real reason to worry.

The person she was meeting should've been there already, and his lateness, along with the silence of the closed and empty club, was starting to feel far more eerie than liberating. Despite the warmth of the California summer night, she pulled her cashmere scarf tighter around her. If there was one thing that made Madison shiver, it was uncertainty. Maintaining control was as necessary as breathing. And yet there she was, second-guessing the message he'd sent.

If the news was good like he'd claimed, she'd put the nuisance behind her and never look back.

If not . . . well, she had a plan for that too.

She just hoped it wouldn't come to that. She hated when things got messy.

Curling her delicate fingers around the slim glass partition, the only thing separating her from a forty-foot fall, she lifted her gaze to the sky, trying to locate a single star that wasn't actually an airplane, but there's only one kind of star in LA.

While she usually fought to avoid all thoughts of the past, on that night, for that one brief moment, Madison allowed herself to drift back to a place where real stars were abundant.

Back to a place that had better stay buried.

A breeze curled past her cheek, delivering the sound of light footsteps and a strangely familiar scent she couldn't quite place. Still, she waited a beat before turning, stealing the moment to wish on a shooting star she'd mistaken for a jet, crossing her fingers as it blazed a wide and glittery arc across a black velvet sky.

It would all be okay.

There was no need to worry.

She turned, ready to face it, whatever *it* was. She was telling herself she could handle it either way—when a cool, sure hand slipped over her mouth and Madison Brooks disappeared.

ONE MONTH EARLIER

# ONE

# HYPOCRITICAL KISS

ayla Harrison could not stop fidgeting. First she sank down low in her beach chair, burying her feet deep into the sand, then she wiggled upright again until the canvas bit into her shoulders, before finally giving up and squinting toward the ocean where her boyfriend, Mateo, waited for the next decent wave. A tedious pursuit that never failed to supply him with an endless stream of happiness she could not understand.

As much as she loved him, and she did (hell, he was so cute and sexy and sweet, she'd be crazy not to), after spending the last three hours dodging the sun under her giant umbrella while struggling to write a decent piece that contained the right dose of humor and snark, she wished Mateo would call it a day and start the long paddle in.

Clearly he had no clue how crazy uncomfortable it was to sit for hours on end in the rickety, ancient beach chair he'd loaned her, and how could he? It wasn't like he ever used it. He was always out on his board, looking Zen and gorgeous and completely at peace, while Layla did all that she could to blot out the splendors of Malibu. The giant umbrella she hid under was just the beginning.

Beneath the bulky hoodie and the extra towel she'd placed over her knees, she wore a thick layer of sunblock, and of course she'd never venture outside without her over-size sunglasses and the crumpled straw fedora Mateo had brought back from a recent surf trip to Costa Rica.

For Mateo, Layla's ritual of blocking and shielding was futile at best. *You can't master the environment,* he'd say. *You have to respect it, honor it, play by its rules. It's madness to think you're in charge—nature always gets the last word.*

Easy to say when your skin is immune to sunburns and you were practically raised on a surfboard.

She returned to her laptop and frowned. Writing a cheesy celebrity gossip blog was a long way from the *New York Times* byline she dreamed of, but she had to start somewhere.

### Arrested Development

No, I'm not referring to the too-smart-for-network-what-were-they-thinking cult comedy (insert I'm-surrounded-by-idiots sigh), I'm talking about actual *arrested development*, people. The kind you can read about in your Psych 101 books (for those of you who actually read anything other than gossip blogs and Twitter feeds). The kind yours truly witnessed last night at Le Château, when three of Hollywood's youngest and hottest, but certainly not brightest, decided olives were for more than just aimlessly lolling at the bottom of a martini glass—

"You still at it?" Mateo stood before her, board tucked under his shoulder, feet sinking into the sand.

"Just doing some last-minute edits," she mumbled, watching as he dropped his board on the towel, swiped a hand through his sun- and salt-water-streaked hair, and unzipped his wet suit. He peeled it so far down his torso Layla couldn't help but gulp at the absolute speech-defying wonder of seeing her beautiful boyfriend bared and glistening before her.

In a town teeming with oversize egos, a surplus of vanity, and a cult of body-obsessed green juice devotees, Mateo's obliviousness to his natural good looks was so rare, most of the time Layla couldn't imagine what he saw in such a pale and cynical slip of a girl like herself.

"Can I help?" He reached for her water bottle, looking as though he'd like nothing more than to read her take on three martini-fueled A-list celebrities reenacting their former high school cafeteria hijinks by chucking olives at everyone around them.

Typical Mateo. He'd been like that from the first night she'd met him, just a little over two years ago, on her sixteenth birthday. Both of them had been amazed to discover they were born just a year and ten days apart, and yet their birthdays still managed to make them different (and mostly opposing) astrological signs.

Mateo was a Sagittarius, which made him a free-spirited dreamer.

Layla was a Capricorn, which made her ambitious and a wee bit controlling—if you believed in those things, which of course Layla didn't. It was just some weird coincidence that in their case was true.

She handed over the laptop and sank deeper into her seat. Hearing Mateo read her work aloud was her own personal version of crack.

It was good for her process. Helped her edit and hone. But Layla had enough self-awareness to know that when it came to her writing, she was the world's biggest praise slut, and Mateo usually found something nice to say, no matter how lame the content.

Water bottle dangling from one hand and Layla's MacBook Air perched on the other, Mateo started to read. When he reached the end, he looked at her and said, "Is this for real?"

"I kept an olive as a souvenir."

He narrowed his gaze as though trying to picture the celebrity food fight. "You get a picture?" He returned the laptop.

Layla shook her head, paused to make one small adjustment, then hit Save instead of the usual Send. "The Château is serious about their photo ban."

Mateo shook his head and drained the water bottle in one steady stream as Layla continued to ogle him, feeling more than a little perverted for reducing her boyfriend to a sweet piece of eye candy. "You going to send that?" he asked. "Seems ready."

She sank the laptop into her bag. "You know how I've been talking about starting my own blog, Beautiful Idols?" Her tentative gaze met his. "I'm thinking this might be the perfect launch piece."

He shifted his stance, played with the bottle cap. "Layla, it's a good bit." He spoke as though he was handpicking each word. "It's funny, and on point, but . . ." He shrugged, letting the silence say what he wouldn't: it was hardly the caliber of work she was capable of.

"I know what you're thinking." She rushed to her own defense. "But none of the crap I write about qualifies as world-changing news, and I'm sick of working for crumbs. If I want to go it alone, I'll have to start somewhere. And while the blog might take a while to really catch on, once it does, I can make a ton of money on the ad revenue alone. Besides, I've saved more than enough to hold me between now and then."

That last part was a hasty addition that might or might not be true. But it sounded good, and it seemed to convince Mateo, since his first response was to pull her out of her chair and into his arms.

"And what exactly will you do with all that ad revenue?"

She ran a finger over his chest, stalling for time. Her dream of going to journalism school in New York was something she hadn't yet shared, and to do so now would bring an awkward moment she'd rather avoid.

"Well, I figured the bulk of it would go toward the burrito fund."

He grinned, circled his arms at her waist. "The recipe for a happy life—you, decent surf, and a healthy burrito fund." He touched his lips to the tip of her nose. "Speaking of—when are you gonna let me teach you to surf?"

"Probably never." She allowed her body to melt against his, burying her face in the crook of his neck, where she inhaled a heady base scent of ocean, sun, and deeply rooted contentment—complemented by a top note of honor, sincerity, and a life lived in balance. It was everything Layla wished she could be, but knew she would never achieve, encompassed in one single breath.

Yet despite their enormous differences, Mateo accepted

her as she was. Never trying to change her or make her see things his way.

She wished she could say the same.

When he tipped a finger under her chin and lowered his lips to meet hers, Layla responded like a girl who'd spent the last three hours waiting for exactly that (she had). At first the kiss was gentle, playful, Mateo's tongue gliding with hers. Until Layla ground her hips against his, returning his embrace with a passion that saw him groaning her name.

"Layla . . . *jeez* . . ." The words were a blur on his lips. "What do you say we find a place to continue this?"

She curled her leg around his, pulling him closer, as close as her denim cutoffs and his wet suit allowed. Aware of nothing more than the heat spiraling throughout the length of her body as his hands slipped under her hoodie. So drunk with his touch she'd gladly drag him down to the warm golden sand and straddle him there. Luckily, Mateo had sense enough to pull away before she got them arrested.

"If we hurry, we can have the house to ourselves." His grin was loose. His eyes heavy and glazed.

"No, thanks." Layla pushed him away, quickly losing the mood. "That last time Valentina nearly walked in, the panic I experienced shortened my life by a decade. I can't risk that again."

"So you live to one forty instead of one fifty." He

shrugged, tried to pull her back to him, but Layla stayed put. "I like to think that it's worth it."

"Easy for you to say, Mr. Zen Master." It was one of her many nicknames for him. "Let's go to my place. It's free of little sisters, and even if my dad's in the studio, it's not like he'll bother us. He's really into his newest series of paintings, not that I've seen them. I'm just glad he's working. It's been forever since he last sold a piece."

Mateo cringed. Obviously he still wanted to be with her, but all it took was the mention of her dad for his own enthusiasm to wane.

"I can't get used to that." He busied himself with packing their stuff, pulling the umbrella apart, and sliding it into its bag. "It's too weird."

"Only for you. Don't forget Dad's a self-described open-minded bohemian who believes in free expression. And more important, he trusts me. And he likes you. Thinks you're a calming influence."

She cracked a smile. It was undeniably true. Then, tossing her bag over her shoulder, she headed for Mateo's black Jeep, where she plucked a flyer from under his wiper blades and read: *Promote with Ira Redman's Unrivaled Nightlife Company this summer for a chance to win an unbelievable cash prize.*

Her interest was instantly piqued.

She'd had her sights on journalism school in New

York since her junior year of high school, and while she was thrilled to have been accepted, there was no chance of attending when the staggering tuition, not to mention the high cost of city living, was like a brick wall blocking her way. And with her dad's current financial slump lasting longer than usual, asking him for help was out of the question.

While her mom could easily provide whatever amount Layla might need (correction: her mom's wealthy *husband* could provide; Layla's mom was just another Santa Monica zombie shuffling between Soul Cycle and Drybar), the fact was Layla and her mom hadn't spoken for years, and Layla had no plans to start.

As for Mateo—his job as a surf butler at some of the pricier beachfront hotels didn't pay much (not that Layla would accept his help if it did). Not to mention she'd yet to fill him in on that particular goal—mostly because he'd insist on joining her, and as nice as it would be to have him around, he'd only end up distracting her. Mateo didn't share her ambition, and sweet as he was, Layla refused to be yet another female who let a cute boy keep her from achieving her dreams.

She scanned the flyer again—a job like that could be just what she needed. The exposure to the Hollywood club scene would give her way better material, and who knew where it could lead?

Mateo leaned past her shoulder and tugged the flyer from her hands. "Tell me you're not interested in this." He swung around to better see her, his brown eyes narrowed as Layla bit her lip in response, unwilling to admit it was the most exciting thing to happen all day (other than that kiss on the beach). "Babe, trust me, you don't want to get involved in this." His voice was stern in a way she rarely heard. "The club scene is sketchy at best. You remember what happened to Carlos."

She dropped her gaze to her sand-covered feet. She was overcome with shame at having forgotten about Mateo's older brother, who'd OD'd right outside a club on Sunset Boulevard, not unlike River Phoenix collapsing in front of the Viper Room, except for the fact that nobody built a shrine in his honor. Aside from his immediate family, no one had even stopped to mourn. By the time Carlos died, he was so far gone the only friends he had left were drug dealers—none of whom bothered to go to his funeral. It was the greatest tragedy of Mateo's life. As a kid, he'd totally idolized his brother.

But what if this was the perfect way to honor Carlos— maybe even vindicate him?

She reached for Mateo, her fingers grazing his arm before falling back to her side. "What happened to Carlos was the worst kind of tragedy, because it could've been avoided," she said. "But maybe the best way to draw attention to

Carlos and other kids like him is to expose what really goes on in that world. A gig like this would allow me to do that."

Mateo frowned. She was going to have to try harder than that.

She stared at the flyer still clutched in his hands, knowing in her gut she was right. Mateo's resistance only made her more determined. "I hate our celebrity-worshipping culture as much as you do. And I totally agree the whole club scene is one major sleaze fest. But wouldn't you rather I do something to shine a light on all that? Doesn't that beat sitting around and complaining?"

While he didn't necessarily agree, he wasn't arguing either. A small victory she was happy to claim.

"I have no illusions I'll win the competition. Hell, I don't even care about that. But if I can just get in on the game, I'll have all the necessary ammo to reveal that world for the fraud that it is. If I can get just one kid to stop hero-worshipping those shallow, needy, undeserving assholes—if I can convince just one teen that the club scene is seedy, dangerous, and better avoided—then my job will be done."

Mateo gazed at the ocean, studying the horizon for a long while. Something about seeing him in profile, shadowed by the fading rays of the sun, softened her heart. He loved her. He only wanted what was best for her, including keeping her far from the world that had claimed his brother. But as much as she loved him, she would not let him win.

He lingered on the postcard-perfect view of the sun dipping toward the ocean before turning to face her. "I can't stand the thought of you getting mixed up in all that." He clenched his fist, causing the flyer to crumple loudly. "That whole world's a lie, and Ira has a well-earned reputation as the worst kind of scumbag who doesn't give a shit about the kids who've made him rich. He only cares about himself. They dumped Carlos outside and let him die on the street so they wouldn't have to call the ambulance and shut down the club for the night. Though you can bet they didn't hesitate to benefit from the scandal."

"But that wasn't Ira's club."

"It's all the same. Carlos was a smart kid, and look what happened to him. I can't let that to happen to you."

"I'm not Carlos." The instant she said it, she was filled with regret. She'd do anything to pull the words back from the ether and swallow them whole.

"Meaning?"

She paused, not entirely sure how to explain without offending him further. "I'm going in with a purpose, a goal—"

"There are other, better ways to do that."

"Name one." She tilted her chin, hoping to convey with a look that she loved him but they'd reached a dead end.

Mateo tossed the flyer into the nearest can and propped the passenger door open as though that was the end of it.

But it wasn't.

Not even close.

She'd already memorized the website and phone number.

She inched closer. She hated when they argued, and besides, there was really no point. She'd already made her decision. The less he knew about it going forward, the better.

Knowing exactly how to distract him, she ran her hands up the length of his thigh. Refusing to stop until his lids dropped, his breath deepened, and he'd forgotten she was ever interested in promoting Ira Redman's clubs.

TWO

# WHILE MY GUITAR GENTLY WEEPS

"C'mon, bro—you gotta weigh in. We won't leave until you do."

Tommy glanced up from the copy of *Rolling Stone* he'd been reading and shot a bored glance at the two garage-band wannabes standing before him. Four and a half hours into his eight-hour shift and he'd yet to sell so much as a single guitar pick. Unfortunately, these two wouldn't change that.

"Electric or acoustic?" they asked, voices overlapping.

Tommy lingered on a pic of Taylor Swift's mile-long legs before flipping the page and devoting equal time to Beyoncé. "There's no right or wrong," he finally said.

"That's what you always say." The one in the beanie eyed him suspiciously.

"And yet, you keep asking." Tommy frowned, wondering

how long they'd persist before they moved on.

"Dude—you are like seriously the worst salesperson ever." This came from the one wearing the Green Day *Dookie* T-shirt, who might've been named Ethan, but Tommy couldn't be sure.

Tommy pushed the magazine aside. "How would you know? You've never once tried to buy anything."

The two friends stood side by side, both of them rolling their eyes.

"Is commission the only thing you care about?"

"Are you really that big of a capitalist?"

Tommy shrugged. "When the rent's due, everyone's a capitalist."

"You gotta have a preference," Beanie Boy said, unwilling to let it go.

Tommy glanced between them, wondering how much longer he could put them off. They dropped in at least once a week, and though Tommy always acted like their incessant questions and attention-seeking antics annoyed him, most days they provided the only entertainment in an otherwise boring job.

But he was serious about the rent. Which meant he had no patience for bored little punks wasting his time, only to leave without buying so much as a single sheet of music.

The gig was commission based, and if he wasn't actively selling, Tommy figured his time was better spent either thumbing through unsold copies of *Rolling Stone* and dreaming of the day he'd grace the cover, or scouring the web for gigs—minimum effort for minimum wage, seemed fair to him.

"Electric," he finally said, surprised by the stunned silence that followed.

"Yes!" Dookie Boy pumped his fist as though Tommy's opinion mattered.

It was unnerving the way they looked up to him. Especially when he wasn't exactly living a life worth admiring.

"Why?" Beanie Boy demanded, clearly offended.

Tommy reached for the acoustic the kid was holding and strummed the opening riff of Deep Purple's "Smoke on the Water."

"Hear that?"

The kid nodded cautiously.

Tommy returned the guitar and reached for the electric twelve-string he'd been eyeing from the moment he started working at Farrington's. The one he'd be a lot closer to owning if one of these punks ever decided to make themselves useful and actually buy something.

He played the same piece as the kids leaned toward him. "It's louder, fuller, brighter. But that's just me. Don't go acting like it's gospel or anything."

"That was good, bro. You should think about joining our band."

Tommy laughed, ran an appreciative hand over the neck of the guitar before returning it to its hook. "So, which one you gonna buy?" He glanced between them.

"All of 'em!" Dookie Boy grinned. He reminded Tommy of himself at that age—a lethal mix of insecure and cocky.

"Yeah, as soon as he sells his MILF porn collection on eBay!" Beanie Boy laughed and ran for the door as his friend gave chase, shouting insults that weren't nearly as good as the one he'd been served.

Tommy watched them exit, the small silver bell attached to the handle jangling behind them, relieved to finally have some time to himself.

Not that he disliked his customers—Farrington's Vintage Guitar was known for attracting a pretty specific, music-obsessed crowd, but it wasn't exactly the job he'd envisioned when he first arrived in LA. He had some serious skills, all of which were going to waste. If things didn't pick up, he'd have no choice but to track those kids down and beg for an audition.

Aside from playing the guitar, he could also sing. Not that anyone gave a shit. His last attempt to book some steady solo gigs was a fail. The hundred or so flyers he'd plastered around town (prominently featuring a picture of him in faded low-slung jeans with his guitar strapped across his bare chest) gleaned only two hits. One from some pervert asking him to "audition" (the sick giggle that followed had Tommy seriously considering changing his number), and an actual gig at a local coffee shop that seemed promising, until his original stuff was quashed by the manager, who insisted he play nothing but acoustic covers of John Mayer's biggest hits for a full three hours. At least he'd managed to make a fan of the fortysomething blond who'd passed him a crumpled napkin with her hotel and room number scribbled in red, winking as she sashayed (no other way to describe it) out the door, sure that he'd follow.

He didn't.

Though he had to admit he'd been tempted. It'd been a bleak six months since he'd arrived in LA, and she was damn good-looking. Fit too, judging by the dress that hugged every curve. And though he appreciated her directness, and while her body probably really was a wonderland, he couldn't deal with the thought of being no more than an interesting diversion for a woman who'd grown bored with men her own age.

More than anything, Tommy wanted to be taken seriously.

It was the reason he moved halfway across the country with the entirety of his worldly possessions (a dozen or so T-shirts, some broken-in jeans, a turntable that once belonged to his mom, his prized vinyl collection, a pile of paperbacks, and a secondhand six-string guitar) shoved in the trunk of his car.

Sure, he figured it might take some time to get settled, but the shortage of gigs was never part of the plan.

Neither was the job hawking guitars, but at least he could tell his mom he was working in the music industry.

He turned the page of his magazine, only to see a full-page article praising the Strypes (fuckin' sixteen-year-olds poised to take over the world—making Tommy wonder if he'd peaked two years ago and missed it entirely).

When the door clanged open, Tommy was glad for the distraction, only to see some rich bastard who looked totally out of place among all the Jimi Hendrix, Eric Clapton, and B. B. King posters slapped on the walls. His designer jeans and T-shirt alone probably cost more than Tommy made in a week. Never mind the suede blazer, flashy gold watch, and spendy-looking loafers—most likely handmade by craftsmen in Italy—that probably cost more than all of Tommy's possessions combined, including his car.

*Lifestyle tourist.*

Los Feliz was full of 'em. Rich, wannabe hipsters, ducking in and out of the area's numerous cafés, galleries, and eccentric boutiques, hoping to glean a little street cred they could haul back to their Beverly Hills hood and impress all their friends with tales of their journey to the wild side.

Tommy frowned and flipped past the article. Reading about the Strypes was bringing him down.

Waiting for the customer to complete his obligatory

walk around, maybe even ask for a card (they made great souvenirs—proved you really were there!), was also bringing him down.

But unlike the Strypes, this guy would eventually pass through Tommy's life. Whereas every band in that magazine seemed to mock him, making him realize just how big a fail his move to LA had become.

Figuring he should exert a little effort and acknowledge the pretentious asshole invading his space, he started to speak when the words caught in his throat and he found himself ogling like the worst kind of groupie.

It was Ira.

Ira Redman.

The überconnected, big-shot owner of Unrivaled Nightlife, who also happened to be Tommy's father.

Though the father bit was really more a technicality. Ira was more of a sperm donor than an actual dad.

For one thing, he had no idea Tommy existed.

Then again, up until Tommy's eighteenth birthday, Tommy didn't know about Ira either. He'd believed the story his mother told him about his war-hero dad who'd died before his time. It was only by chance he learned the truth. But once he did, his fate was sealed. Much to his mother's (and grandparents', and ex-girlfriend's, and counselor's) dismay, he took the money he'd saved for college, graduated early from high school, and headed straight for LA.

He'd had it all planned. First he'd find a great apartment (a shithole in Hollywood), then he'd score an awesome job (Farrington's was severely lacking in awesome), and then, armed with all the details he'd gathered about his father courtesy of Google, Wikipedia, and an archived issue of *Maxim*, he'd track down Ira Redman and confront him like the independent, deserving young man that he was.

What he didn't expect was how completely intimidated he felt just being in Ira's vicinity.

Shortly after he'd first arrived in LA, he found and followed Ira, watching from the cracked windshield of the clunker that seemed cool in Tulsa and so offensive in LA that even the valet parkers sneered when they saw it. Tommy saw the dismissive yet entitled way Ira left his chauffeur-driven Escalade at the curb and strode into the restaurant like a man who consumed power rather than food. His grim, all-seeing gaze was cloaked in a calculated ruthlessness that immediately convinced Tommy he was out of his league.

The reunion fantasy that had fueled the drive from OK to CA instantly evaporated into the Los Angeles smog, as Tommy made his escape, vowing to make a name for himself before he tried that again.

And now, there he was. Ira Redman sucking down oxygen like he owned controlling shares in that too.

"Hey," Tommy mumbled, hiding his hands under the

counter so Ira wouldn't see the way they shook in his presence, though the tremor in his voice surely gave him away. "What's up?"

The question was simple enough, but Ira chose to turn it into a moment. An awkward moment. Or at least it was awkward for Tommy. Ira seemed content to just stand there, his gaze fixed like he was assessing Tommy's right to exist.

*Don't flinch, don't be the first to look away, don't show weakness.* Tommy was so focused on how *not* to react he nearly missed it when Ira pointed an entitled finger at the guitar just behind him.

Clearly Ira had decided to take a little time out from world conquering to indulge some latent rock star fantasy. Fine with Tommy, he needed the sell. But he'd be damned if Ira walked out with the beautiful twelve-string Tommy had mentally tagged as his own from the moment he'd strapped it across his chest and strummed the first chord.

He purposely reached for the guitar just above it, lifting it from its wall hooks, when Ira corrected him.

"No, the one right behind you. The metallic blue one." He spoke as though it was an order. As though Tommy had no choice but to do Ira's bidding, serve his every whim. It was unnerving. Degrading. And it made Tommy even more resentful of Ira than he already was.

"It's not for sale." Tommy tried to direct Ira to another, but he wasn't having it.

His navy-blue eyes, the same shade as Tommy's, narrowed in focus as his jaw hardened much like Tommy's did when attempting a piece of music he'd been struggling to interpret. "Everything's for sale." Ira studied Tommy with an intensity that made Tommy squirm. "It's just a matter of negotiating the price."

"Maybe so, bro." *Bro? He called Ira Redman bro?* Before he could linger on that for too long, Tommy was quick to add, "But that one's mine, and it stays mine."

Ira's steely gaze fixed on Tommy's. "That's too bad. Still, mind if I have a look?"

Tommy hesitated, which seemed kind of dumb, since it wasn't like Ira was gonna steal it. And yet it required every ounce of his will to hand the piece over and watch as Ira balanced it in his hands as though expecting the weight to reveal something important. When he strapped it over his chest and assumed some ridiculous, pseudo-guitar-god stance, laughing in this loud, inclusive way like they were both in on the joke, Tommy had to fight the urge to hurl right then and there.

The sight of Ira manhandling his dream had him sweating straight through his Jimmy Page T-shirt. And the way he dragged it out, pretending to do a thorough inspection when he clearly had no idea what to look for, made it clear Ira was putting on some kind of show.

But why?

Was that how bored rich people entertained themselves?

"It's a beautiful piece." He returned the instrument as Tommy, relieved to have it safely out of Ira's possession, propped it back against the wall. "I can see why you'd want to own it. Though I'm not convinced you do."

Tommy's back stiffened.

"The way you handle it . . ." Ira placed both hands on the counter, his manicured fingers splayed, his gold watch gleaming like a cruel taunt, as if to say, *This is the life you could've had—one of great privilege and wealth, where you'd get to harass wannabe rock gods and piss all over their dreams just for the fun of it.* "You handle it with too much reverence for it to be yours. You're not comfortable with it. It's a part *from* you, rather than a part *of* you."

Tommy pressed his lips together. Shifted his weight from foot to foot. He had no idea how to reply. Though he'd no doubt the whole thing was a test he had just failed.

"You handle that guitar like it's a girl you can't believe you get to fuck, rather than the girlfriend you've grown used to fucking." Ira laughed, displaying a mouthful of capped teeth—shiny white soldiers standing in perfect formation. "So how 'bout I double whatever it is you think you could pay for it?" His laughter died as quickly as it started.

Tommy shook his head and stared at his trashed motorcycle boots, which, in Ira's presence, no longer seemed cool. The treads were shot. The shank was gashed. It was like his favorite boots had suddenly turned on him, reminding him of the enormous gap yawning between him and his dream. Still, it beat looking at Ira, who clearly considered Tommy a fool.

"Okay, triple then."

Tommy refused to acknowledge the offer. Ira was insane. The whole scene was insane. He was rumored to be a relentless negotiator, but all this—over a guitar? From everything he'd read about him, the only music Ira cared about was the song that played during last call when he collected the money from his various clubs.

"You drive a tough bargain." Ira laughed, but it wasn't a real laugh. The tone was way off.

And it wasn't like Tommy had to actually look at him to know that his eyes had gone squinty, his mouth wide, his chin lifted in that arrogant way that he had. He'd seen plenty of photos of Ira being the inauthentic, entitled bastard he was. He'd memorized them all.

"So what if I quadruple my offer, hand over my credit card, and you hand over the guitar? I'm assuming you work on commission? Hard to pass on an offer like that."

Clearly Ira had pegged him for the rent-hungry wannabe he was, and yet Tommy still held his ground.

The guitar was his.

Or at least it would be just as soon as he collected a few more paychecks.

And while it was definitely a risky move to deny Ira Redman, Tommy watched as he finally gave up and exited the store as arrogantly as he'd entered.

Tommy clasped the guitar to his chest, hardly able to believe he'd almost lost it. If he could just make it through the next few months, he'd have enough saved to make it officially his. Sooner if he went on a hunger strike.

And that was how Ira found him—standing behind the smudgy glass counter, embracing his dream guitar like a lover.

"Farrington wants a word." Ira pressed his phone on Tommy, who had no other choice but to take it.

Who knew Ira and Farrington were friends?

Or better yet, who didn't know Ira had an in with the owner?

Fuckin' Ira knew everyone.

The conversation might have been brief, but it was no less humiliating, with Farrington ordering Tommy to sell Ira the guitar at the original price. There might also have been a mention about Tommy losing his job, but Tommy was already returning the phone, reducing Farrington's angry rant into a distant muffled squawk.

Fighting back tears too ridiculous to cry, Tommy forfeited the guitar. Hell, he hadn't even cried the night he'd said good-bye to Amy, the girlfriend he'd been with for the last two years.

He could not, would not, cry for a guitar.

And he definitely wouldn't cry over his father making him look like a fool, showing just how insignificant he was in the world.

Someday he'd show him, prove his worth, and make Ira regret the day he walked into Farrington's.

He didn't know how, but he would. He was more determined than ever.

With the guitar in Ira's possession (paid for with his Amex Black card, which probably had a gazillion-dollar limit), Ira shot Tommy one last appraising look before pulling a folded piece of paper from his inside jacket pocket and sliding it across the counter. "Nice try, kid." He made for the door, guitar strapped over his shoulder. "Maybe you could have bought it sooner if you worked for me."

# THREE

# REASONS TO BE BEAUTIFUL

Aster Amirpour closed her eyes, took a deep breath, and slipped beneath the water's surface until the bubbles covered her head and the outside world disappeared. If she had to choose a happy place, this would be it. Cocooned within the warm embrace of her Jacuzzi, free of the burden of parental expectations, along with the weight of their disapproving gaze.

No wonder she'd favored mermaids over princesses as a kid.

It was only when her lungs squeezed in protest that she sprang to the surface. Blinking water from her eyes, she pushed her hair from her face, allowing it to fall in long, dark ribbons that flowed to her waist, and adjusted the straps of her Burberry bikini—the one that took a month to convince her mom to buy, and then another month to convince her to let her wear it, and then only within the walled-in confines of their yard.

"All I see is four tiny triangles and a handful of very flimsy strings!" Her mother had dangled the offending pieces by the tip of her index finger, looking as though she'd been scandalized by the sight of it.

Inwardly, Aster rolled her eyes. Wasn't that the whole point of rocking a bikini—to display as much gorgeous young flesh as possible while you still had gorgeous young flesh to display?

God forbid she wore something that might be considered highly immodest within the confines of her Tehrangeles neighborhood.

"But it's *Burberry*!" Aster had pleaded, trying to appeal to her mother's own high-end shopping addiction. When it didn't help, she went on to add, "What if I promise to only wear it at home?" She eyeballed her mother, trying to get a read, but her mom's face remained as imperious as ever. "What if I promise to only wear it at home when I'm the only one there?"

Her mother had stood silently before her, weighing the merits of a promise Aster had no intention of keeping. The whole thing was ridiculous. Aster was eighteen years old! She should be able to buy her own stuff by now, but her parents liked to keep as tight a rein on her spending as they did on her comings and goings.

As far as getting a job and financing her own bikinis—Aster knew better than to broach that particular subject. Other than the rare exception of a random lawyer here, a famed pediatrician there, the females in Aster's family tree didn't work outside the home. They did what was expected—they married, raised a family, shopped, lunched, and chaired the occasional charity gala—all the while pretending to be fulfilled, but Aster wasn't buying it.

What was the point of going to those impressive Ivy League schools if that expensive education would never be put to good use?

It was a question Aster had asked only once. The steely gaze she received in return warned her to never speak of it again.

While Aster loved her family with all her heart, while she would do anything for them—heck, she'd even die for them if it came to that—she absolutely, resolutely, would not live for them.

It was too much to ask.

She inhaled a deep breath, about to take another plunge, when her cell phone chimed, and she shot out of the Jacuzzi so fast, she had to yank her bikini bottom back into place when the water threatened to drag it right off.

Seeing her agent's name on the display, she crossed her fingers, tapped the gold and diamond hamsa pendant (a gift from her grandmother) for luck, and answered the call, trying to convey a capacity for great emotional depth in a single *hello*.

"Aster!" Her agent's voice burst through the speaker. "I've got an interesting offer to run by you. Is now a good time?"

He was calling about the audition. She'd put her whole heart and soul into it, and clearly it had worked. "This is about the commercial, right? When do they want me to start?" Before Jerry could answer, she was envisioning how she'd break the news to her parents.

They were in Dubai for the summer, but she'd still have to tell them, and they were going to freak. She'd dreamed of becoming a world-famous actress since she was a kid, always begging her mom to take her on auditions, but her parents had other ideas. From the moment that first ultrasound revealed Aster was a girl, she was groomed to meet a set of expectations that seemed simple enough: be pretty, be sweet, get good grades, and keep her legs firmly crossed until she married the Perfect Persian Boy of her parents' choosing the day after she graduated college, only to start producing Perfect Persian Babies a respectable ten months later.

While Aster had nothing against marriage and babies, she was committed to delaying those dream stallers for as long as she could. And now that her big break had arrived, she was determined to dive in headfirst.

"This isn't about the commercial."

Aster blinked, clutched the phone tighter, sure she'd misheard.

"They decided to go another way."

Aster's mind raced back to that day. Hadn't she convinced the director that completely foul cereal was the best-tasting thing she'd ever put in her mouth?

"They're going ethnic."

"But I'm ethnic!"

"A different ethnic. Aster, listen, I'm sorry, but these things happen."

"Do they? Or do they just happen to me? I'm either too ethnic, or the wrong ethnic, or—remember that time they said I was too pretty? As if there was such a thing."

"There will be plenty of auditions," he said. "Remember what I told you about Sugar Mills?"

Aster rolled her eyes. Sugar Mills was her agent's most successful client. A no-talent pseudo celebrity discovered on Instagram thanks to the staggering number of people with nothing better to do than follow the daily adventures of Sugar's Photoshopped body parts. Because of it, she'd snagged some high-profile commercial eating a big sloppy burger while wearing a tiny bikini, which inexplicably led to a role in an upcoming movie playing some old guy's wildly inappropriate much younger girlfriend. Just thinking about it made Aster simultaneously sick and insanely jealous.

"I assume you've heard of Ira Redman?" Jerry said, breaking the silence.

Aster frowned and lowered herself back into the water, until the bubbles rose up to her shoulders. "Who hasn't?" she snapped, feeling more than a little annoyed at a system that celebrated girls like Sugar Mills and wouldn't give Aster a chance, even though she was a much classier act. "But unless Ira's decided to get in on the movie biz—"

"Ira isn't making movies. Or at least not yet." Jerry spoke like he knew Ira personally, when Aster was willing to bet that he didn't. "Though he is running a contest for club promoters."

She closed her eyes. This was bad. Very bad. She braced herself for whatever came next.

"If you make the cut, you'll spend the summer promoting one of Ira's clubs. Which, as you probably know, are frequented by some of Hollywood's biggest players. The exposure will be great, and there's money in it for the winner." He paused, allowing the words to sink in, while Aster fought to keep her disappointment in check.

She climbed out of the Jacuzzi. The heat of the water combined with the heat of her humiliation was unbearable. Preferring to finish the call barefoot, wet, and shivering, she said, "It sounds shady. And sleazy. And low class. And desperate. And just overall beneath me."

She gazed toward her house—an over-the-top, sprawling Mediterranean-style monument to her family's wealth with its tennis courts, covered loggias, big cherub-adorned fountains, and rolling manicured lawns. Wealth that would one day be hers and her brother Javen's, provided they followed her parents' strict and uninspiring plans for their lives.

She was tired of the way they tried to leverage her inheritance. Tired of the emotional turmoil they caused by insisting she choose between pleasing them and living her dreams. Well, screw it. She was done pretending. She wanted what she wanted and her parents would just have to deal. And if Jerry thought this was a good career move, then clearly it was time to cut ties and move on. There had to be another way. Someone to better guide her career. Problem was, Jerry had been the only agent out of a very long list who'd been willing to meet with her.

"You're wrong about Ira," he said. "He's a class act, and his clubs attract the cream of the crop. You ever been to one?"

"I just turned eighteen." She was annoyed at having to remind him. As her agent, he should've known that.

"Yeah." He laughed. "As if that ever stopped anyone. C'mon, Aster, I know you're not as innocent as you like to pretend."

She frowned, unable to establish whether he'd just said something completely inappropriate, or if he was just calling it like he saw it. She was used to the way men reacted to her. Even much older men, men who should know better. But apparently it would take more than smooth skin, long legs, and the kind of blessed bone structure that photographed well to earn her a SAG card.

"So, you're seriously trying to convince me that being a nightclub hostess will help my career as an actress?"

"Club promoter. For Ira Redman, no less."

"Why not just take pictures of my butt and post them on Instagram? It worked for Sugar."

"Aster." For the first time since the conversation began, Jerry was running out of patience.

Well, he wasn't the only one. But Aster was smart enough, and just desperate enough, to know when to fold.

"So, how does this work? You going to claim ten percent?"

"What? No!" He barked, like she'd said something crazy. As though that wasn't an agent's main role. "I know how tough it is to catch a break, and I really think you've got something, which is the only reason I signed you. This gig with Ira will get you in front of more influential people in one night than twenty auditions put together. If you truly believe the road to fame is beneath you, then maybe you don't want it as much as you claim."

She wanted it. She plucked a towel from a nearby lounge chair and wrapped it loosely around her. And while it clearly wasn't the same as scoring the lead role (or any role), she had to start somewhere.

Besides, Jerry was right; everyone knew Ira's clubs attracted loads of Hollywood types, and in a town full of gorgeous young girls, all of them fueled on the same dream of fortune and fame, this could be just the thing Aster needed to help her get noticed for the find that she was.

Trying to drum up a modicum of enthusiasm she didn't yet feel, she headed for the pool house and said, "Let me grab a pen so I can jot down the details."

# FOUR

# CELEBRITY SKIN

Madison Brooks sprawled across the plush velvet chaise tucked into the corner of her massive walk-in closet, sipping the freshly pressed green juice her assistant, Emily, delivered and wrinkling her nose at the dresses her stylist, Christina, pulled from an assortment of garment bags bearing the names of LA's most exclusive boutiques.

It was one of her favorite activities, in one of her favorite places—her closet serving as a sort of sanctuary from the incessant demands of her life. Every item—from the mirrored chests, to the soft woven rugs underfoot, to the crystal chandeliers dangling overhead, to the hand-painted silk wallpaper—was carefully chosen to exude feelings of unbridled luxury, comfort, and peace. The only thing even remotely out of place was Blue lying asleep at her feet.

While other starlets preferred their precious purse-size purebreds, for Madison, her scraggly mutt of indeterminate origins was everything a dog should be—solid, tough, no-nonsense, and a little rough around the edges. It was how she preferred her boyfriends too—or at least back when she was allowed to choose them herself.

If there was anything that surprised Madison about the inner workings of Hollywood, it was the approach to relationships as just another commodity—something to be bartered and arranged by a team of managers, publicists, and agents, or sometimes, the celebrities themselves.

The right pairing could raise an actor's profile in ways that were otherwise hard to achieve, ensuring endless publicity, a permanent place in the tabloids, and, more unfortunate, the annoyingly cutesy phenomenon of name blending. Problem was, most actors were so used to delving into character they'd actually start to believe they'd found the person they could not live without. The one who completed them. Or whatever movie line they'd been spoon-fed since they were a kid.

"I'm thinking this one would go well with those new Jimmy Choos." Christina dangled a cute color-block dress before her, but Madison didn't want *cute*. She wanted something special, not the same tired thing everyone else was wearing.

Her phone chimed, but Madison ignored it. Not because

she was lazy (she wasn't), or because she was pampered to a ridiculous degree (she was), but because she knew it was Ryan and she had no interest in FaceTiming with him.

Christina paused, but Madison nodded for her to continue, until the ever-faithful Emily swooped in, retrieved Madison's phone from the table, and in a tone of hushed excitement said, "It's Ryan!"

Madison fought the urge to laugh. Emily was a good assistant—solid, dependable—but her fangirl crush on Ryan made her impossible to trust. The less she knew about Madison's true feelings for Ryan, the better.

"Hey, babe." Ryan's voice was lazy and deep as his sandy-blond hair and sleepy green eyes filled up the screen. "I've been thinking about you all day. Have you been thinking about me?"

Madison watched as Christina and Emily crept from the room, closing the door behind them. "Of course." She sank deeper into the cushions and pulled a cashmere throw over her lap. Whenever Ryan was around, or even on FaceTime, she found herself reaching for a pillow, a blanket, whatever she could find to build a barrier between them.

"Yeah? And what exactly were you thinking?" He sprawled full length on the couch in his on-set trailer, his head propped with a cushion, his hand working his belt.

"You couldn't handle it," she said, her voice barely disguising her resentment for the way he always pushed her into doing things that made her uncomfortable.

It wasn't that she was a prude—far from it—and it wasn't like Ryan wasn't a fine piece of boy specimen—as the hot young star of a popular TV drama, Ryan Hawthorne was the fuel of countless teen fantasies. He simply wasn't her type, and no amount of publicity would ever change that. After putting up with him for the last six months, she was more than ready to end it. Her agent had other ideas and was actively campaigning for her to continue the charade until she inked her next deal, but he wasn't the one who had to kiss him, watch him chew with his mouth open, or fend off his constant need for FaceTime sex. The public canoodling had dragged on long enough. It was time for RyMad to die. Though it was important to time it just right.

"Oh, I can handle it." His voice was raspy, his breathing strained, as his fingers tugged at his zipper. In another half a second those pants would be gone.

"Baby—" She deepened her voice in the way Ryan liked. "You know Christina's here. Emily too."

"Yeah, so, send 'em on an errand or something." He kicked his boxers to his knees. "I miss you, baby. I need me some Mad time."

Madison cringed. She hated when he said things like *Mad time*—there was nothing sexy about it. There was also nothing sexy about seeing Ryan Hawthorne bared on her screen, despite what his millions of fans might think.

"But I still haven't found a dress for *Jimmy Kimmel* tomorrow," she cooed in a way she hoped was convincing.

"Does Jimmy have *this*?"

"Pretty sure he does." He was too far gone to notice she'd rolled her eyes.

"You always look good, baby." His voice was hoarse.

Madison muted the volume, absentmindedly fingering the scar on the inside of her arm—the only blemish on her flawless white skin. She was often asked about it in interviews, but Madison had a well-rehearsed answer for everything regarding her past.

She waited for Ryan to go through the motions, wondering how much longer she could put him off without him catching on to just how much she'd grown to despise him. Once it was done, she raised the volume and purred, "You have no idea how much I miss you." Not a total lie, she reasoned, since he clearly had no idea she didn't miss him one bit. "But now is not a good time."

He made no move to cover himself, even though she'd made it clear that round two would not happen on her watch. Though a second later he was pulling a T-shirt over his head, saying, "Rain check?"

That was the one good thing about Ryan—he had the attention span of a gnat, and his moods were easily changed. He was just about to nail down a time, when Madison smiled apologetically and pushed End.

She leaned against the cushions and waited. Emily and Christina were probably mashed against the door frame, eavesdropping. They'd check in soon enough.

"So . . ." As if on cue, Christina peeked into the room. Her blue eyes worried, shoulders rising to her ears. "None of them work?"

Madison blinked. Maybe those dresses weren't all as bad as she'd thought—surely at least one was a keeper?

Then again, why not pretend to hate them? It was good to shake people up. Make them try harder. Sharpen their game.

She scrunched her nose and shook her head. She had a long, hot summer of talk shows, movie promos, and photo shoots. Christina would have to exert a little more effort.

"From what I hear, Heather's dying to wear the black one," Christina said.

Madison crossed her legs and purposely nudged a still-sleeping Blue with her toes, amused by the way his ears perked up for a second before flopping down again. The thought of her annoying former costar brought a scowl to her face. Heather was always trying to promote herself through her connections, no matter how tenuous, to bigger celebrities, and Madison would never forgive herself for having fallen for it.

It was back in the early days when they'd first met. Back when she didn't really know anyone and was so grateful to make a friend in a town where she didn't have any, she ignored Heather's more alarming traits—her pathological competitiveness among them. Though as soon as Madison hit it big, her star blazing so bright Heather's was reduced to a flicker, the snide comments, thinly veiled insults, and fits of jealousy increased to where Madison could no longer overlook them. So she cut Heather off; visited her local dog shelter; found her new best friend, Blue; and never looked back. And yet, Heather still continued to stalk her, always tagging her on Twitter, or trying to copy Madison's every move, like there was a formula for success other than hard work, determination, and a little sprinkle of fairy dust. What a bore.

"Well, I think the only reason she wants it is because she thinks you want it." Christina turned toward the rolling rack and started closing the heavy bags so she could haul them back to her car—the sight of which made Madison feel a little sad for rushing the process.

After the fiasco with Heather, Madison hadn't made other friends. She had plenty of hangers-on, sure, but not a single bestie. The problem with girls (the nice ones, not the crazy ones like Heather) was they always wanted to delve too deep. To share and confide, to glean her innermost thoughts, explore the territory of their mutual mommy and daddy issues, and, unlike boys, they couldn't be dissuaded with sex (or at least not most of them); they demanded answers instead. It was the sort of intimacy Madison just couldn't risk. The moments spent trying on clothes and gossiping with Christina were as close as Madison got to girl bonding.

"Well, won't she be disappointed to learn I rejected it." Madison was determined to delay Christina's departure for as long as she could. "Unless we don't tell her. Might be fun to watch her try to trump me in yet another tireless round of *Who Wore It Better?*"

Christina grinned knowingly. She had a reputation for being the best, limiting her list of clients to the topmost members of the Hollywood elite. "I don't think that's going to happen anytime soon."

Madison's lips curved into a half smile as she nudged Blue again with her toes. "You've been here for over an hour and the only gossip I get from you is about Heather? Are you holding out on me?"

Christina shot her an alarmed look, and then seeing Madison was joking (well, kind of), she relaxed and said, "It's been a slow week. But I did hear something about a competition that Ira Redman's running. Have you heard about it? He's posted flyers all over town."

Madison shot her a curious look. She knew Ira the way she knew most people connected to the industry—through the party, charity, and awards shows circuit. Of course she was aware of his reputation as the nightclub czar of LA, everyone was, but most of their contact had been relegated to Ira trying to lure her to his clubs through flattery and gifts. For her last birthday he'd sent her a red Hermès Kelly bag, which cost three times more than the Gucci bag her agent had sent. She'd quickly unwrapped it, added it to her collection of designer handbags, and told Emily to send him a thank-you card.

"Anyway, it's something to do with promoting his clubs, but I have a friend on the inside who says you're on his list of gets. So prepare for a bunch of desperate kids trying to lure you in!"

Madison settled deeper into the cushions, a sigh of contentment escaping her lips. So what if her life was filled with suck-ups and sycophants—all of them handsomely paid to fluff her ego and laugh at her jokes? She was still the luckiest person she knew, living the kind of gilded existence most people couldn't conceive of. And wasn't one of the major benefits of being rich and famous the unfettered access to all the right things?

The right table in a crowded restaurant with a three-hour wait.

The right first-class seat on an overbooked flight.

The right VIP pass to any concert or sporting event worth seeing.

The right clothes arriving straight to her door for her to try on at her leisure.

The right team of people who kept her life running safely and smoothly, for which she paid dearly.

She'd worked hard for the privilege and saw no reason not to milk it.

If Ira Redman wanted to enlist a bunch of kids to flatter her, who was she to stop him?

"Come back tomorrow morning," she said, assuming Christina would move any other appointments she might have. "And bring me something pretty. I want to leave Jimmy speechless. Oh, and get me a list of those kids from your friend. I like to know who's stalking me."

# FIVE

# MENTAL HOPSCOTCH

Layla felt bad lying to Mateo, but really, what choice did she have? He'd made it clear that day at the beach exactly what he thought of the LA club scene. Admitting she'd decided to show up for the interview would only upset him. Besides, it wasn't like anything would ever come of it. Surely Ira would see she didn't fit in that world.

She steered her Kawasaki Ninja 250R toward Jewel, the club designated for the interview, about to claim a space that had just opened, when, seemingly out of nowhere, a white C-Class Mercedes swerved into her lane, forcing Layla to squeeze hard on the brakes. Her back wheel fishtailed wildly as she fought to keep control of the bike. Finally screeching to a stop and miraculously managing to stay upright, she watched in a mixture of frustration and outrage when the driver stole the spot right out from under her.

"Hey!" Layla yelled, her heart racing frantically thanks to the near-death experience. "What the hell?" She watched as a dark-haired girl in a tight black dress rolled out of the car with such arrogance and ease Layla was completely incensed. "That was *my* space!" she shouted in outrage. In a place where street parking was scarce, space snatching was a serious breach of common decency.

The girl anchored her sunglasses onto her forehead and glared dismissively. "How can it be your space if I'm in it?"

Layla stared in astonishment. So enraged she practically spit when she said, "Are you for real? You almost killed me!"

The girl shot Layla a derisive look, shook her long hair over her shoulder, and headed for the club. By the time Layla found another, less desirable space, the girl was long gone. She'd probably jumped the line and was already inside, while Layla slogged along with the rest of them, slowly wending their way toward the door.

She removed her helmet, ran a hand through her wheat-colored hair, and checked her reflection in the smudgy glass window, hoping her gray V-neck tee, shrunken black blazer, and tight leather leggings looked more rocker chick than Hell's Angel. Then she traded her heavy boots for a pair of designer knockoff stilettos she'd bought for the occasion and could still barely walk in.

Despite making a living reporting on the celebrity scene, she couldn't remember the last time she'd been inside a club. Most of her stories revolved more around the closing-time antics, when the celebrities spilled out the doors, swaying precariously on their Jimmy Choos as they made their way to their rides. Those drunken, unguarded moments provided loads of material. She'd learned that firsthand after nearly getting clipped one night by some B-list jerk driving a Porsche. When Layla used her cell to record the offense, the celeb went after her, and she sold the resulting coverage to TMZ in an act of revenge that inadvertently kick-started her freelance career.

It wasn't exactly the writing gig she'd dreamed of, but it'd gotten her through high school without having to rely on her dad, whose career as an artist was either feast or famine. And while she told herself she was doing her part to chip away at a world she despised, most of the time she felt more like a low-life paparazzi than an actual journalist. But, if this gig with Ira worked out, she could put all that behind her.

When she finally reached the door and the bouncer permitted her entry (the six people ahead of her weren't nearly so lucky), she was handed an application and a name tag to stick on her blazer, then directed to a photographer, who clicked the shutter so fast Layla was sure he'd caught her mid-blink. Still dazed from the flash, she was then ushered by yet another assistant into the Vault—Jewel's much-coveted, much-talked-about, legendary VIP section, which resembled the inside of a very plush jewelry box (as opposed to the actual bank vault Layla expected)—where she was told to wait.

Most people flocked to the front and center seats in an attempt to get noticed, but Layla headed straight for the back. Not because she was shy (she was), not because she was feeling intimidated (she definitely was), but because that particular vantage point allowed her to scope out the room, scrutinize her rivals, and determine who to beat and who to dismiss.

While she never got competitive over the usual things like being the prettiest girl in the room (the effort required to go from cute to pretty just wasn't worth it), or gaining the attention of the hottest boys (it was already done—Mateo was the hottest guy in town), when it came to nailing the interview, she morphed into a cunning strategist fixed on securing the job no matter the cost.

Of course the girl who'd stolen her parking space (Aster, according to her name tag) was sitting front and center, and worse, she didn't even blink or look away when Layla caught her openly staring. Her gaze remained focused, wide, and assured, and she brandished her startling beauty like a weapon meant to intimidate. So Layla did the only thing she could think of—she rolled her eyes and looked away, painfully aware she'd just time traveled straight back to junior high. Still, ignoring the mean girls was never an option. It hadn't worked then, it wouldn't work now. Girls like Aster had a loud bark, but Layla had a sharp, nasty bite. Aster would be a fool to underestimate her.

The rest of the crowd was pretty much a cross section of so many looks it reminded her of an *American Idol* casting call. There were goths, punks, metalheads, rappers, princessy blondes, a girl wearing pink cowboy boots and cutoffs so insanely short Layla wondered if she'd mistakenly wandered in looking for a bikini wax—all of them jockeying for attention. All of them completely clueless, in Layla's estimation.

"Hey, you're the girl with the bike, right?" There was enough of an accent to prove he wasn't a native. "I saw you ride up."

Layla's gaze roamed past a pair of destroyed black leather motorcycle boots and frayed jeans slashed at the knee, before pausing on a vintage Jimmy Page T-shirt that looked so overly laundered she couldn't help but wonder if he'd slept in it.

She shrugged in response. The weirdness with Aster had left her ready to hate on just about anyone who invaded her space, starting with this walking, talking indie-rocker cliché who'd probably never straddled a bike in his life.

"Mind if I sit here?"

"Whatever," she mumbled, overcome with shame the second she said it. It wasn't like her to act like such a snot. Still, she wasn't there to make friends, and she definitely wasn't there to make small talk with some LA transplant desperate for connection, and she couldn't think of a better way to get those two points across.

He lowered himself into the seat, settling into such a major manspread, one of his knees bumped against hers.

She sighed loud enough for him to hear. She had graduated from a snot to a colossal bitch, but she just didn't care.

"Sorry." He drew his legs in, which was better, until his foot started to jiggle.

She focused hard on her cell, doing her best to ignore him, but there was no use.

"Can you just—"

He followed the tip of her pointing finger to his bouncing foot.

"Oh. Guess I'm a little nervous." He laughed. "Which probably makes me sound really uncool, but there it is. So, how'd you hear about this?"

Completely out of patience, Layla turned to him and said, "Listen—can we not do this?"

"Do what?" His grin was slow, wide, and disarmingly open. And when her gaze met his, all she could manage was a sharp intake of breath. His eyes were the most intense shade of blue she'd ever seen.

She stole a quick glance at his name tag, *Tommy*, and fought to pull herself together. "Let's not chitchat, make small talk, or pretend to be friends." Her tone was harsh, way too harsh for the circumstance, but she was beginning to think she should've listened to Mateo and avoided this place.

"Your call." Tommy shrugged. Dismissing her so easily she couldn't help but feel a little incensed by that too. "Too bad, though. From what I've seen so far, friends are in short supply around here."

His words settled around her. And while part of her wished she could lighten up, another part, the part that was frustrated, insecure, and woefully out of her league, said, "Yeah, well, welcome to Hollywood."

# SIX

# LONG COOL WOMAN (IN A BLACK DRESS)

Five minutes into the ordeal was all it took for Aster to dismiss everyone in the room as a possible competitor. Nightclubs thrived on glamour and beauty—the unattractive need not apply. That single requirement was enough to ensure that Aster secured the top spot.

Still, Layla (Lila? She had to squint to read the name tag) could pose a threat. She wasn't nearly as pretty as Aster, but damn if she hadn't hesitated to call her on that unfortunate parking space incident. Aster hadn't even seen her until she was already climbing out of her car and Layla got up in her face. She'd been so agitated during the drive from Beverly Hills to Hollywood—alternating between *you can do it!* style pep talks and complete despair that she was fresh out of high school and had already sunk to this level—that when Layla went after her, Aster responded the only way she knew how—by acting like the worst, most haughty version of herself.

Everyone had a go-to defense. Some got angry, like Layla—some made jokes, like Aster's brother, Javen—and some acted like stupid arrogant peacocks. Well, it was done now. There was no going back. Besides, Aster had a feeling that deep down, Layla wasn't as tough as she seemed. As someone used to acting her way through most facets of life, Aster found it easy to recognize the trait in another. The game was equal parts illusion and distraction, but on Layla's part, it was poorly played.

For one thing, her shoes were 100 percent *not* Louboutins. The red on the sole was way off. Never mind the heel height. And the way she'd stumbled into the room like a newborn colt testing its legs—clearly she hadn't bothered to practice walking in them like Aster when she'd scored her first pair. Total rookie move. Even the biggest amateur knew you had to rehearse the role you wanted to play until you owned it so fully, you could no longer distinguish yourself from the fiction. Layla was out of her league. She might try to come off as strong and capable, but those sad knockoff shoes told the story of an imposter trying to inhabit a world she did not understand. And yet, clearly Layla was every bit as hungry and ruthless as Aster. Willing to play dirty if that was what it took, which was exactly why Aster focused on her.

Aster was an achiever, used to excelling at pretty much anything she set her mind to. Good grades, prom queen, class president—it had all been hers for the taking. But with her acting career failing to launch, she needed this job more than ever. The gig was sleazy, completely beneath her—but that was exactly the reason she needed to clinch it. If she couldn't succeed as a lowly nightclub promoter, then what would that say about her?

Ira took his place at the podium, and Aster wasted no time crossing her legs in a way that significantly hiked up the hem of her Hervé Léger bandage dress, hoping to draw attention to a healthy expanse of tanned and toned thigh, while also sending the message she knew how to play this particular game.

Dressed in dark denim jeans and a black shirt, Ira somehow managed to look as tall, assured, and commanding as though he were standing behind the presidential podium wearing a bespoke suit.

"You all share one thing in common," he began. "You were drawn to the idea of an epic competition, access to the hottest clubs, and, let's not forget, the promise of an enormous cash prize."

His gaze swept the room, and when it met Aster's, she could've sworn he held it just a little bit longer. Then again, it was entirely possible she'd imagined it. Ira was magnetic—time seemed to stop and start depending on where he directed his attention.

"Like you, I was young and hungry once." Ira shot them a well-practiced grin. "Back then, I would've jumped at the kind of opportunity I'm offering you."

Another dramatic pause. *Sheesh. Is everyone vying for a SAG card? No wonder it's so tough to book a job.*

"The rules are simple. Those who make the cut will be assigned a club to promote. At first you'll be working in teams, but don't think for a moment you can slack off and let the others pull your weight. I'll be watching. I'm always watching. I know everyone who walks through my doors, and I'll know whose efforts reeled them in." He reached for a bottle of water and took a slow, purposeful swig that seemed less about thirst and more about allowing time for his words to sink in. Ira was positioning himself as a sort of all-seeing, all-knowing sage, and judging by the sudden onset of shifting and throat clearing, it worked.

"Getting a good turnout at your club earns you points. And I'm not going to mince words, since we're all adults. . . ." Ira checked with his assistant. "They're all adults, right? You checked IDs?" The assistant smiled coyly. "In the world of nightclubs, the younger, the hotter, and the more famous your *gets*, the more points they're worth. The clubs are all eighteen and up—eighteen to party, twenty-one to drink. Obviously." He quirked a brow, allowed enough time for people to laugh, which of course they did, then went on to say, "Each week, the promoter with the least number of points will be eliminated, while the promoter with the most points will earn cash to spend on marketing and party planning for their clubs. The promoter with the most points at the end of the summer wins. And by 'wins,' I mean the winner will walk away with *half of all the cover charges collected by the clubs during the course of the summer.*"

The words were spoken in italics. Or at least that was how Aster heard it.

"The harder everyone works, the bigger the prize. The profits could be *huge* and they're for the winner to keep."

Blah, blah, blah. Aster couldn't care less about the cash. Sure it would be nice to buy her own Burberry bikinis, but it was the connections that truly interested her. Her agent was right—Ira's clubs attracted Hollywood's finest. She was beginning to wonder why she hadn't thought of it herself.

"Any questions?" Ira's tone made it clear that questions weren't actually welcomed, but just as Aster was raising her hand, having no idea what she would ask but determined to be noticed, that damn Layla beat her to it.

"What about the first week?"

Ira squinted, fiddled with the cap on his water bottle. "What about it?"

"Will we be given a promotional allowance to get started?"

"Only twelve will make the cut. No use talking details that won't apply to most."

Layla nodded, then shot Aster a squinty look.

Clearly she didn't give a shit about the answer. She just wanted the same thing Aster did, to get Ira to notice her in a sea of desperate wannabes too scared to speak up in his presence.

Yep. She was definitely one to watch.

SEVEN

# I CAN'T GET NO
# (SATISFACTION)

Tommy followed Ira's assistant into his office, trying not to stare too hard at the way her hips swayed in her little black skirt. From what he'd seen, all of Ira's assistants were smokin'. His dad was clearly living the good life.

"Mr. Redman, Tommy Phillips is here." Her voice was prim, but the intimate look that followed was all Tommy needed to know Ira was nailing her.

Well, at least someone in his family was having some fun. His mom had sworn off men long ago. Claimed to be perfectly happy keeping house with her bilingual parrot. And despite Tommy's good looks, in a showy town like LA it hardly compensated for the crap car, the shithole apartment, and the nearly empty wallet.

Tommy sat before Ira, wishing he'd taken time to prepare. He knew the importance of rehearsing for a gig, but when it came to the most important interview of his life, he hadn't so much as bothered to go over some possible responses to Ira's inevitable questions. And yet, nothing could've prepared him for the intensity of going one-on-one with Ira in a closed room with a pack of hot, clipboard-toting assistants standing by.

Ira leaned back in his chair and pushed his sleeves up his forearms, allowing a glimpse of the bracelet of small round beads that reminded Tommy of the prayer beads his mom always wore. It seemed like an odd choice for a man like Ira. Then again, most LA moguls liked to feign a spiritual side, claiming to adhere to a rigorous schedule of yoga and meditation before heading out into the world and obliterating competitors, entire companies, and anything else that got in their way.

Just above the bracelet was an expensive gold watch, this one a Cartier, as opposed to the Rolex of the other day. Probably had a whole collection of 'em—one for every day of the month—while Tommy relied on his cell phone to keep track of time. And if things didn't pick up, he'd be forced to hawk it on Craigslist.

This was a mistake—one of his biggest in a very long list. He should've left that stupid flyer in the trash where he'd originally tossed it.

"So," Ira said. "Tell me something about you that I don't already know."

Tommy hesitated, unsure what he meant. Did Ira recognize him from that day at Farrington's?

He forced his gaze to meet Ira's, wondering how he'd react if Tommy said, "Well, *Dad*, as it just so happens, I'm the long-lost son you abandoned."

Would Ira lose his cool? Have him tossed from the room?

Wasn't worth finding out. Or at least not today.

"Guess that depends on what you *do* know." Tommy practically dared Ira to remind him of how he'd nearly cried when Ira bought his dream guitar out from under him. He was guessing Ira was enough of a douchebag sadist to do it.

"You're hungry." Ira steepled his fingers and held them under his chin. "Otherwise you wouldn't be here. Question is, what are you hungry for?"

*Rent money, a shelf full of Grammys, to prove myself worthy and one day surpass your success in ways you never saw coming.*

Tommy shrugged and looked around the room. It was sleek, modern, minimal but expensive. Even the requisite ego wall, covered floor to ceiling with framed photos of Ira's various magazine covers, was tastefully done. "I like to win." Tommy shifted in his seat, then instantly regretted it. It made him look nervous, unsure of himself. He was, but it wasn't like he needed to show it.

"Who doesn't?" Ira frowned, the steeple collapsed, and his hands fell to his lap, where he fiddled with the tiger's-eye beads on his bracelet, as Tommy wondered if something from Ira's brief dalliance with his mom had managed to stick.

Tommy's mom was one of those new-age hippies (except she really hated that word—the beliefs dated back thousands of years, she would say). Not only did she believe in the healing power of crystals but also that everyone was guided by angels, that Love with a capital *L* could cure anything, along with a whole list of other stuff Tommy could never fully align with. She was the one who should've moved to LA. It would've been a better fit. Though if he remembered correctly, she might've said something about tiger's-eye being protective, guarding against curses and the like. All Tommy knew was on his first day of high school she'd slipped a similar stone into his pocket. By the end of third period he'd already lost it, and yet he still managed to survive those four years mostly unscathed. Though it made sense that Ira would need that sort of protection. A guy like that came with a long list of enemies just waiting to attack.

Tommy counted himself among them.

He picked at the hole in the knee of his jeans and waited for Ira to continue.

"Heard I caused you some trouble over at Farrington's?" Ira paused, waiting for Tommy to confirm or deny.

It was a test. Every moment with Ira was a final exam.

"He canned me." Tommy lifted his shoulders as though it was no big thing, but they both knew he was lying.

"You might think that makes me feel obligated to you." Ira studied his nails, not polished, just filed and buffed, keeping the *man* in manicure. "But that would be a mistake." He leveled his gaze on Tommy's. "I tend to take a more nihilistic view—at least where the more mundane social mores are concerned."

Was this guy for real? Did all of the interviews go like this—with Ira aimlessly pontificating like they both had all the time in the world?

And how the hell was Tommy expected to reply to a statement like that?

Ira was a major windbag who loved to hear his own voice.

Tommy was a man of much fewer words.

Clearly he took after his mother.

"You made a choice that day. You chose to act on your own and risk the consequence. All of our actions bring consequences. Getting fired was yours."

Tommy ran his tongue across his gums, flipped his boot on his knee, and messed with the gash in the shank. No longer caring if Ira saw the sorry state of his shoes, his finances, his life. Seemed like he'd blown the interview long before he arrived. It was Farrington's all over again.

The guy was completely devoid of an empathy gene. Great father figure he was turning out to be.

It was time to head back to Oklahoma, where people at least said what they meant and never made sport of other people's well-being. Back home, he didn't know a single person who behaved like Ira. They were good, down-home, solid, dependable folks. He couldn't believe he'd just used the word *folks*—but yeah, *folks* who would never so much as—

"—which is why you're not a good fit."

The room fell silent. Tommy had no idea what had just happened. "So . . . I'm not a good fit because you like to take a nihilistic approach, or because you got me fired so easily?" He scrambled to catch up.

"What do you think?"

Tommy shook his head. This was un-fucking-believable.

"For someone who claims they love to win, you haven't said a single thing to convince me."

"You don't even know me." Tommy stood, struggling to keep his cool. He wasn't good enough for the job, wasn't good enough to be Ira's son. He'd never felt as powerless as he did at that moment.

"Don't I?" Ira tilted his head, studying Tommy like he saw right through him.

"You have no idea what I'm capable of."

Ira shrugged and reached for his phone, which only

enraged Tommy more. He might be broke, down on his luck, but he didn't have to tolerate being treated like this, and he wouldn't leave without Ira knowing it.

"Just so we're clear—" He pushed his chair aside, nearly tipping it over. "The consequence of *your* decision will prove to be your loss, not mine."

He made for the door, pushing past the assistants scurrying out of his way, just as Ira said, "I'm beginning to wonder if you're right."

Tommy pulled the door open, still committed to leaving while he was somewhat ahead.

"You're my weakest candidate by far."

Tommy scowled. Ira was an asshole. An asshole who didn't know when to quit.

"But if you can learn to take that grudge of yours and use it to fuel your goals, as opposed to using it as your go-to excuse for remaining a victim, then you just might end up surprising us both."

Tommy turned. "So now you're quoting Oprah?"

Ira laughed. It was short, almost inaudible, but Tommy caught it nonetheless.

"Usually at this point, the groveling interviewee conveys a stream of gratitude they can barely contain."

"I don't remember groveling," Tommy snapped, wondering if maybe he was the one who didn't know when to quit.

"To your credit." Ira nodded. Dividing his attention between his phone and Tommy, he said, "Jennifer will lead you to the back room, where the other candidates are waiting. You'll need to remain there until the rest of the interviews are concluded, at which point you'll receive your assignments."

Tommy shook his head, trying to make sense of what had happened. Maybe Ira wasn't as bad as he'd thought. Maybe he just took some getting used to. Besides, all that stuff about Oklahoma was bullshit. People are people. Prone to do what they're prone to do. Geography had nothing to do with it.

"Oh, and Tommy?" Ira's eyes glinted with an emotion Tommy couldn't quite place. "I can see why you loved that guitar. My instructor says it's as good a starter instrument as any."

Another test. Ira was trying to rile him by inferring that his dream guitar was somehow inferior. But Tommy just grinned. Following Jennifer out the door, he said, "Glad to hear she's working for you."

# EIGHT

# TEENAGE DREAM

Of course Aster made the cut. She saw how Ira looked at her. Like most men who'd risen to a place of power, he appreciated the sight of a pretty girl. Probably even thought his success somehow entitled him to date her. Only in Ira's case, it wasn't just that.

As Aster sat across from him, she couldn't help but notice that while he clearly liked what he saw, it was more in terms of what her sexy good looks could do for his clubs (as opposed to him envisioning her legs wrapped around him, or whatever old men think about when they're fantasizing about girls who are far too young for them). His eyes conducted a thorough inspection, evaluating her physical advantages like any other commodity, while determining the best way to exploit them for professional gain, and it didn't bother her in the least. She'd survived enough disappointing auditions to know the score. This was the first time she'd nailed one.

She wondered if it had to do with his final question: *What makes you think you can win this thing?* All the while studying her with that deeply penetrating gaze of his.

For a few panicked moments she sat silently before him, trying to determine the best angle to follow. Finally deciding that Ira didn't seem like the type to honor humility, she met his gaze and said, "Next to me, everyone else is an amateur." Then she chased it with the sexy and confident grin she'd practiced earlier.

He'd gazed at her a good long time—enough for Aster to second-guess her answer. She was just about to say something to soften the boast, when he ordered his assistant to escort her into the next room.

What she didn't expect when she got there was the unlikely group who'd made the cut too. Of course that damn Layla was there, she'd figured as much. But Tommy she'd pegged as a wild card. She guessed he was cute—if you liked 'em low rent, anguished, and hungry. Aster did not. As for the rest, well, Karly was a surprise; then again, some guys (a lot of guys—most guys) really went for that sparkly, frothy blond look. The goth guy, Ash, made it, as did Brittney, the girl in cowboy boots and denim cutoffs so short they covered only slightly more ass than Aster's

Burberry bikini bottom. There was another guy, Jin, who was so skinny and pasty Aster figured him for a gamer or tech geek who rarely ventured outside, and an androgynous girl, Sydney, covered in loads of tattoos and piercings (or at least Aster *thought* she was a girl). Two of the guys, Diego and Zion, looked normal enough (well, normal for LA), which meant they looked like they'd strolled straight off the page of a Calvin Klein underwear ad. Cute, no doubt, but Aster didn't go for the overtly pretty types. Guys like that tended to spend way too much time thinking about themselves, and not enough time focusing on her. The final two looked wholesome, all-American. The girl, Taylor, was so fresh faced and healthy, she looked like she came straight from an equestrian lesson, while the guy, Brandon, was tanned with just the right amount of windblown hair, like he'd docked his yacht in the harbor and was waiting for his driver to whisk him off for dinner and drinks at the club.

Ira had cast a wide net of looks and ethnicities. Six girls and six guys—not a single one over the age of nineteen. Guess he wasn't joking when he said he was after a young, hot demographic of club goers.

Aster settled among them, making a point to avoid Layla, who she'd already deemed as the first to take down—and waited for what happened next. Unlike the earlier waiting room, this new room was silent. Probably because they were no longer potential comrades—they were now competitors out for the win.

She crossed her legs and massaged the tight muscles around her ankle and calf. It'd been a long day, and her toes were starting to ache after so many hours inside the take-no-prisoners Louboutin toe box. She snuck a glance at Layla, wondering if her cheap knockoffs hurt too, only to discover they'd been replaced with a pair of serious-looking black motorcycle boots.

"It's been a long and grueling day." Ira strode into the room, followed by his usual team of assistants. "Which should give you an indication of the level of commitment I expect. Though before you get too full of yourselves for having made it this far, let me remind you that not a single one of you is over nineteen—which makes you woefully inexperienced, despite what you think. Working for me will allow for the sort of real-life education you can't get at school. But before I continue, is anyone having second thoughts? Anyone want to back out?" He surveyed the room for a beat before continuing. "So, on to the logistics . . . there are legal forms to fill out. My assistants will guide you through the process. But first, you're probably wondering which clubs you'll promote."

Everyone nodded like they'd been wondering exactly that, Aster included. She had her heart set on Night for Night, the Casablanca-chic rooftop treasure. It was a perfect fit in every way—classy, sexy, and named after a cinematography technique used for night filming. She'd had a thing for Morocco ever since she came across a stack of her mother's old *Vogues* and spent the entire day staring at the spread of Talitha Getty wearing white patent-leather boots and a colorful coat, lounging on a roof with a mysterious man in the background. If Aster had to pick one single, defining moment that would shape who she'd hoped to one day become—it was that shot of Talitha Getty. She looked beautiful, pampered, exotic, and adored. Maybe even the slightest bit bored—but in a good way. Like her life was so full of lush adventures, she couldn't help but wonder if there was anything left to amuse her. She tapped her hamsa pendant for luck while Ira squinted at the clipboard his assistant held before him.

"Layla Harrison—you're promoting Night for Night."

Aster involuntarily gasped and shot a quick look at Layla, trying to gauge her reaction. But Layla just nodded, gave nothing away.

"Tommy Phillips—" When Ira's gaze centered on Tommy, Aster could've sworn she saw something pass between them. Something she couldn't quite read. "You're promoting Jewel."

If Tommy looked upset, it was probably because he had his heart set on the Vesper. It was gaining a reputation as a gritty underground club attracting top-notch musicians—a perfect match for someone like Tommy. Jewel was sleek and modern and attracted a high-end crowd—it was out of his league.

Ira made his way down the list, and even though she'd been keeping track, she couldn't stop from groaning when Ira's gaze settled on hers. She knew what was coming.

"Aster Amirpour—you'll be promoting the Vesper."

She shook her head as her hand shot up.

"Problem?" Ira looked at her

"I'd like to request a different club." There was no way she'd fit in at the Vesper, and someone as business savvy as Ira should've known that. She wondered if he was testing her, testing all of them.

Ira studied her for a long moment. "Then I guess you'll have to find someone to trade with." He left without another word, leaving his assistants to pass out the piles of legal forms.

Aster shoved the forms in her purse. She needed to get to the three other people who got Night for Night that she hadn't almost run over.

"It's Sydney, right?" Aster approached the girl who, from what Aster could tell, was wearing a full bodysuit of tattoos.

She was about to compliment Sydney on her septum piercing, anything to get on her good side, when Sydney snapped, "Don't bother. I already traded with Taylor." She turned away before Aster could react to the snub.

She headed for Diego and Jin on the other side of the room, but when she got there, they were already negotiating with Brittney and Ash, which left only Layla.

*Great.*

And on top of that, Layla was gone.

"Hey—Aster?"

She turned to find Tommy standing behind her.

"I was wondering if you were up for a trade?"

"Not unless you got Night for Night, which we both know you didn't." She raced for the door. Layla had probably already left, and Aster needed to reach her while she still had a chance. But when she replayed her words, she forced herself to turn back. She'd already made one enemy. She didn't need to start a collection. "Sorry," she said. "That was uncalled for."

"Won't argue with that." Tommy's face broke into a grin that made his eyes gleam. Maybe he was cuter than she'd first thought.

"It's just—I really want Night for Night."

"Well, Jewel's a closer match than the Vesper, no?"

Sure it was better, but better wasn't good enough. "Can you help me get to Layla?" she asked, hoping he'd made a better impression than she had.

He ran a hand over his chin and shot her a skeptical look. "Doubtful," he said.

"Would you be willing to at least try?" She gave him her

best grin, the one she saved for auditions and head shots.

"Depends." He folded his arms across his chest and shifted his weight to his heels, like he had all the time in the world. "What's in it for me?"

"The Vesper." She shrugged. "That's what you want, right?"

He studied her for a moment, then led her to the entry, where Layla was talking on her phone, until she saw Aster and Tommy and hastily ended the call.

"Can I help you?" She frowned.

Tommy hooked a thumb toward Aster. "I was thinking you two should meet."

"We've met—" Layla turned away. "She nearly killed me in pursuit of a parking space."

"And I want to apologize for that." Aster hurried alongside her.

"So, it's true." Tommy looked amused by the news.

"No, it's not true," Aster snapped. "I didn't even see her. It was all a big misunderstanding."

"Oh, you saw me." Layla whirled on her. "Don't even try to pretend like you didn't."

"No wonder you needed me to mediate." Tommy looked at Aster, shaking his head.

"Believe me," Aster said. "I'm already regretting that."

"Maybe so, but deal's a deal," Tommy reminded her. "I did my part, now you do yours."

"What deal? What's going on?" Layla glanced between them.

"Aster wants to switch clubs."

"Um, hello! I'm right here and I can speak for myself!" Aster shook her head. Maybe she should just stick with the Vesper; it would be better than dealing with this. But who was she kidding? It was a disaster in the making. Besides, she was still convinced this was all part of some weird game Ira was playing.

"Then why'd you ask me to help?"

"I asked you to help me find her, not to—ugh, just forget it, Okay? Listen." Aster faced them both. "Here's the deal. We all want each other's clubs. So I'm proposing we put our personal feelings aside and—"

"I don't want your club." Layla made her way out the door and onto a street crowded with tourists, as Aster and Tommy rushed to follow.

"You're seriously trying to tell me you want Night for Night? You wouldn't prefer Jewel?"

Layla stopped. "What's the difference? A club's a club."

"You can't be serious!" Aster cried, scowling at a guy wearing a Superman costume that looked ratty and decrepit under the glare of the bright summer sun. It probably smelled bad too. And yet there was no shortage of tourists willing to pay to take pictures with costume-wearing weirdos like him. Sometimes people completely boggled her brain. Layla included.

"Way to negotiate." Tommy laughed, which only annoyed Aster more, mostly because he was right. This whole thing was a mess, and it was all her fault. Something about these two pushed all her buttons. Normally she had no problem making friends and keeping her cool.

"There's a big difference," Aster said, determined to rein herself in. "And Layla, you're far more suited to Jewel."

"And why's that?" She folded her arms across her chest, guarding against whatever insult Aster might sling.

"Because it's sharp, modern, and eccentric. All the things Tommy's not, but you are."

"Oh." Layla seemed to visibly relax, if only a little. "So let me get this straight. Tommy wants your club, and you want my club."

"Yes." Aster stood uncertainly before her. Surely even Layla could see the logic in her plan.

"Well, good luck to you both."

Layla made for her bike, as Aster hurried alongside her and Tommy stayed put. "Just give me a minute," Aster called after her. "That's all I ask."

To her surprise, Layla stopped and looked pointedly at the time on her phone.

"Listen, I'm sorry for what happened earlier." Aster fought to catch her breath, the words hurried but heartfelt. "Truly. But if you'll just—"

"Tell me." Layla cocked her head and narrowed her gaze, and despite the way her features sharpened, Aster was surprised to find she was actually pretty. "If you'd gotten Night for Night, would you have tried to apologize?"

Aster took a moment to answer, unsure how to play it. "Honestly?" she finally relented. "Probably not."

Layla nodded, seemingly satisfied. "So, what's in it for me?"

Aster studied Layla, trying to determine why she was interested in Ira's contest. She assumed most people were after the money, but something about Layla told her it wasn't just that. Still, money was the only thing she could think to offer. "I'll give you my share of the first week's marketing money."

Layla rolled her eyes. "Please, you drive a Mercedes. A C-Class, but still a Mercedes. I don't want your money, I want something that will truly cost you."

Aster was shocked by the snub. A C-Class Mercedes beat a cheap bike any day, but whatever; Layla was trying to get to her and Aster wouldn't fall for it. "Name it," Aster said, ready for this to be over.

"I will. Just as soon as I think of something."

Aster's eyes widened. She couldn't be serious, could she?

Layla paused long enough for a foreign tour group to go by, their leader excitedly pointing out all the landmarks the locals never even bothered to look at. "I'll let you know when I decide," she finally said.

"I'm not comfortable with that," Aster snapped.

"That sounds more like your problem than mine." Layla shrugged. "And don't even think about trying to back out when payday comes around, because I *will* hold you to it."

Aster gnawed the inside of her cheek, a nervous habit she'd yet to cure herself of. "You're not going to ask for the soul of my firstborn child or something, are you?"

Layla rolled her eyes. "Why would I want your illegitimate mistake?"

Aster sighed. The girl was a nightmare. Who knew what she'd demand? Well, she'd deal with it later. For now she had Night for Night, and that was all that really mattered. "Guess you're representing Jewel," she said.

Layla shrugged like she didn't care either way, leaving Aster to second-guess the deal she'd just struck as she watched the other girl walk away.

"You convince her?" Tommy called, as Aster made her way back.

Aster nodded, wondering if she looked as shaken as she felt. "I feel like I just made a deal with the devil, but yeah, it's done."

"Hope it turns out to be worth it." Tommy squinted against the sun, eyeing her carefully.

She shrugged, clicked her key fob, and unlocked her car. Remembering her manners, something that had been in short supply all day, she looked over her shoulder and said, "Hey, Tommy—good luck with the Vesper."

"Good luck to you." He grinned.

The competition had officially begun.

NINE

# SUMMERTIME SADNESS

L ayla stepped out of the shower and reached for a towel at the same moment there was a knock at the door.

"I'll get it," Mateo offered, pausing a moment to grin appreciatively at the sight of Layla naked before heading down the hall.

She wrapped the towel around herself and pulled a comb through her hair. It looked awful, more neglected than usual, like the hair of an overstressed soccer mom who'd run out of Xanax. She should try harder. Maybe do something with the color. Though she doubted she would. It was bad enough she'd worn a pair of toe-numbing stilettos in order to look the part for the interview. If she started highlighting her hair, where would it end? Scouring Pinterest boards, looking for nail art ideas? She refused to be *that* girl.

Then again, Mateo had exhibited some major appreciation for the shoes. Especially when she'd kept them on well after everything else had come off. And lately, making Mateo happy went a long way toward alleviating her guilt over not telling him she was working for Ira. She wanted to. She just hadn't found the right time. But tonight she'd tell him for sure. It was her first official day on the job, and the last thing she wanted was for Mateo to discover the truth on his own.

She rubbed some moisturizer into her skin, letting the towel slowly drop to the floor like some kind of bathroom burlesque, winking salaciously at Mateo through the mirror as he returned with a large white envelope clutched in his hand.

She strained to make out the lettering, but Mateo's fingers covered the logo. "Did Publishers Clearing House finally send me that million-dollar check?" She laughed playfully, until she saw the hurt expression on Mateo's face and the laughter died on her lips.

Today was the day Ira was sending their first list of celebrity gets, which Layla assumed would arrive by email. It never occurred to her he'd opt for home delivery. And now her phone was chiming with incoming texts—most likely from her team wanting to strategize.

"You gonna get that?" Mateo struggled to keep his face

neutral as he nodded toward her phone.

She shook her head, reached for her towel, and quickly covered herself.

"What if Ira needs you?" he said when her phone chimed again.

She swallowed past the lump in her throat, searching for just the right words to explain, only those words didn't really exist.

"When were you going to tell me? Or were you ever going to tell me?"

"Tonight." She lifted her gaze to meet his, needing him to believe it.

"And how long have you known?"

She hung her head, if for no other reason than to avoid the hurt look on his face. He'd always been so open and honest with her. Layla was the shady one—the dealer of secrets and lies.

"Couple days," she said, voice barely audible.

He exhaled long and deep. If disappointment had a sound, Mateo's sigh would be it. He willingly forfeited the envelope. Her fingers reluctantly seized it. As much as she'd wanted the job, in the face of betraying Mateo, it no longer seemed worth it.

"You already know how I feel about that scene. But if this is what you want, it's not my place to stop you," he said.

"But it's not like that!" Layla gripped the envelope so tightly it crinkled in protest. "I'm doing it to honor Carlos, to shine a light on that dark, murky world, and so I—" She stalled. Finishing the thought meant revealing another secret, and she absolutely was not ready for that.

Though she'd had no problem revealing that secret to Ira. As soon as he'd asked why she wanted to win, she blurted out the truth about needing to find a way to pay for journalism school. The interview ended shortly after, and out of all the questions he'd asked, and there'd been quite a few, she knew that was the answer that clinched it.

But this was Mateo, and there was no good way to say: *Oh, and by the way, I have my heart set on journalism school in New York, and I'm hoping this job will cough up enough cash so I can move far away. And just so you know—you're not invited.*

How could she convey that to Mateo, of all people?

But from the length of her silence, she already had. Or at least she'd alarmed him enough to prompt him to ask, "So you can *what*, Layla?" His voice carried an edge, but his shoulders sank in defeat. "Is this about the prize money? Because you know I'd gladly give you whatever I have."

She gazed around her room, taking in the dark wood floors and white beach-board walls that matched the rest of the remodeled Venice Beach bungalow, the jumble of freshly laundered clothes in need of sorting, the stack of books she'd been meaning to get to as soon as she found some free time. She paused on the portrait her father had painted of her at age five. Her head thrown back, eyes shut tight, mouth stretched wide as she laughed at something she could no longer remember. It was probably the last time her life felt so uncomplicated, the last time she'd felt like a kid. Within a year her mom would be gone, and she and her dad would take the first tentative steps toward forging a new life without her.

Maybe her mom's abandonment had affected her more than she'd thought. Maybe a therapist would say it had something to do with her becoming the sort of perfection-ist who couldn't bear to disappoint anyone, lest they leave. All she knew for sure was she never wanted to disappoint Mateo—and yet, she knew she eventually would.

She gnawed her bottom lip, pulled the towel tighter around her. A quick glimpse of his face told her anything she said would be met with suspicion.

"The only reason I didn't tell you is because I knew you wouldn't approve, and I can't stand to upset you. . . ."

"I'm not upset." He shook his head, started again. "Okay, I'm upset that you hid it. But mostly I'm worried about you getting involved in that scene."

"You don't have to worry."

"Of course I do. I love you." He spoke as though it was really that simple—like there was no other way to reply. He shoved his hands deep into his pockets, causing his jeans to slip enticingly low. "And when will we see each other? You'll be working every night of the week."

"Just Thursday through Saturday. Oh, and we have a meeting every Sunday. And I'll need to work on strategy during the week, but otherwise, I'm totally yours. And you can always stop by the club to see me, you know."

He made a face, prompting her to say, "Or not. Just—" She forced herself to meet his gaze. "Just trust me. I promise there's no need to worry. You'll see."

He pulled his lips in and glanced out her bedroom window at the small yard beyond. "You sure this is what you want?"

What she really wanted was to rewind the morning, pull Mateo onto those soft rumpled sheets, and repeat all the delicious things they'd done to each other just a few hours before. But they needed to deal with this, so she nodded instead.

He frowned, swiped his shirt from the back of a chair, and pulled it over his head. The sight made her simultaneously panicked and relieved. Relieved for this to be over, and panicked at the thought he might never return.

"Listen, I'm not gonna lie, I really wish you'd rethink this. Doesn't change how I feel about you, but I need some time to process." He flipped a hand through his hair, grabbed his sunglasses and keys from the dresser, and made for the door.

"I'm sorry," she whispered, forcing the words past the lump in her throat, but Mateo was already gone, and her phone was chiming again.

# TEN

# MR. BRIGHTSIDE

When Layla walked into Lemonade, despite the trendy lunch crowd, Tommy spotted her immediately. He'd been 98 percent sure she wouldn't show. Now that she was here, he was nervous in a way he couldn't explain.

She slung her bag over the back of her chair and settled before him. "What's this about?" Her expression was as annoyed as her voice.

He fixed his gaze on hers and leaned closer. A move that had never failed him back home, but Layla was immune to his charms.

"Now that we're working together, I thought we could try to get to know each other."

She sighed, reached for her bag, and started to stand. "You are seriously wasting my time."

"Or—we could skip all that and go straight to talking strategy."

"Tommy—" She shot him a look like she was about to explain the truth about Santa and the Tooth Fairy all at once. "I know you're not from here, so I'm going to do you a favor and—"

"How do you know I'm not from here?" Tommy cut in.

"For one thing, you have an accent, even though you're convinced you don't. For another, you're way too languid to ever be confused for a native."

"What? Everyone knows Angelenos are laid-back."

She rolled her eyes. "It's all PR. You want to see the soul of the city, take your chance on the 405 freeway during rush hour and see how long it takes you to merge into the far left lane, and how many times they flip you the bird along the way."

Tommy fought back a grin. She was sarcastic and cute, but it was better to keep the thought to himself. "Okay, so it's a tough town, friends are in short supply—kind of remedial stuff, seeing as we covered all that at the interview. Clearly you mistake me for some dumb country hick with a clump of horseshit stuck to my boots."

Layla bit her lip, looking surprisingly chagrined.

"I know you're small-talk averse, but let's get one thing clear—yes, I'm from Tulsa, or more accurately, a small town just outside Tulsa that no one's ever heard of, so it's easier to say I'm from Tulsa. But, contrary to what you might think, I did *not* grow up drinking milk from my very own cow. I didn't do my business in an outhouse, and I do not make out with my cousins. My life so far has been normal, maybe a slightly different normal from yours, but that's more about geography than anything else. I'm not a stereotype. So please don't treat me like one."

She frowned and settled back in her seat.

"And I wasn't kidding about talking strategy." He rubbed a hand across a swath of carefully cultivated chin stubble. "I think we can help each other."

She folded her arms across her chest and glanced longingly toward the door. "We're on different teams. I'm meeting mine in an hour."

"Well, I just came from my second meeting with mine, and it was a total waste of time."

"So now you're trying to get back at them by wasting mine?"

He shook his head, refusing to acknowledge her words. "Way I see it, this entire contest is rigged to help Ira, not us."

"Um, yeah," Layla snapped, which was pretty much the verbal equivalent of rolling her eyes. "*Everything's* about Ira. The winner is a well-compensated afterthought."

"And yet one of us will be eliminated each week for not pulling our weight or whatever excuse Ira comes up with."

She allowed a cautious nod of her head. She was still with him, which was the most he could ask for.

"So, I don't know about you, but I don't have a lot of faith in my crew. And there's no way I'll share my better ideas so they can use them against me."

Layla squinted in confusion, which only made her look cuter. "So . . . you want to give *me* your better ideas so *I* can use them against you?"

"Yes." He grinned. "But not entirely . . ." He swiveled in his seat, surveyed the line at the counter, and without another word, got up and took his place at the end.

It was a trick he sometimes employed when he needed a moment to gather his thoughts. It also offered the added benefit of keeping the other person completely off balance, too busy wondering what was going on to build an argument against him.

When he returned a few minutes later with a cup of lemonade in each hand, he gave her first dibs. "Blood orange or mint?"

Layla flipped her hands on the table like she didn't care either way. "You want to get on my good side, always default to coffee. But fine, blood orange, whatever. Is there a point to all this?"

"Here's the thing—" He circled his hands at the base of his cup and leaned toward her. "Ira needs us more than we need him. After selling his Sunset Boulevard clubs last year, he's determined to make his mark on Hollywood Boulevard. Sunset was a no-brainer. It's been an established hangout for pretty much ever." He looked pointedly at Layla. "I may not be a native, but I did do my research. Anyway, Ira's sunk a ton of money into his attempt to revitalize the area and make it the new Sunset, money he can probably afford to lose if the whole thing blows up, since we all know Ira's richer than God, but Ira doesn't play to lose. Failure isn't an option. He's in it for the win. Always. And he'll do anything to get it."

"Sounds like you know an awful lot about Ira. What's that about?" Her brow rose as she did this adorable thing with her mouth that Tommy tried not to focus on.

He shrugged in reply. No use alerting her to just how obsessed he'd become. "I like to know who I work for. Anyway, from what I gather, the clubs are struggling. Sure, some industry players have dropped in, but Hollywood Boulevard's a tougher sell than Sunset, so they haven't gained any traction. That's where we come in. We're there to elevate his brand, make it sexy, exclusive, and most important in Hollywood—young. In the end it will come down to three of us. Well, ultimately one of us, but before that, three, since there's no way Ira will eliminate an entire club from the competition when there's money to be made. He'll pick us off one by one, just like he promised, but he'll be far more strategic than he lets on. Then he'll make us battle to the death, probably for his own amusement, because that's how Ira rolls."

Layla took a moment to consider. "Okay," she ventured. "So why me? Out of all the other contestants, why me, as opposed to, oh, I don't know, Gamer Boy, Goth Boy, Cowgirl, hell, even Queen Bitch Aster." Reading Tommy's expression, she explained, "I prefer nicknames to real names, and that last one is from an old David Bowie song."

"*Hunky Dory* album." He nodded appreciatively, enjoying her look of surprise. "What—you mistook me for a Directioner or a Belieber?"

"No—I—" She shook her head, gazed down at her drink. She was completely off balance, just how he wanted her.

"Listen—" He lowered his voice to a conspiratorial tone. "You seem like you have little tolerance for bullshit, and you don't seem overly starry-eyed where Ira's concerned."

She nodded. So far they agreed.

"But that's also what's going to cause most of your problems."

She narrowed her gaze, clearly not liking the sudden shift from flattery to problems she probably wasn't even aware that she had.

"From what I've seen, the locals tend to be a little needy. They work hard, putting as much effort into working out and looking good as they do at making money. They live for flattery, praise, and feeling important. They want to claim their place in the spotlight, and top every VIP list."

"Talk about stereotypes." Layla frowned. "There's over four million people living in this city. Clearly not everyone's the way you describe. . . ."

"Maybe not, but the ones who frequent Ira's nightclubs—"

She waited a beat before conceding. "Yeah, okay, guilty as charged."

"And correct me if I'm wrong, but you don't strike me as the group-hug-positive-affirmation-attaboy-go-get-'em-tiger-ass-kisser type."

She gnawed her lip, then immediately made herself stop.

"So, I'm offering to help you with your social skills, and in return, you're going to help me brainstorm some ideas. Everyone wins."

He hadn't even reached the end when Layla pushed away from the table, looking like she was seriously considering dumping the rest of her lemonade onto his head, but settled for grabbing her bag instead.

"Are you crazy?" She glared, not even attempting to lower her voice, as all the other tables turned briefly to look at them before returning to their own conversations.

He sipped his drink and continued to observe her. "I'm sorry if that seemed insulting. I only meant that I can help you smooth over some of your . . . rougher bits, and in turn—"

"And in turn I can give you all my ideas. Yeah, I'd say that's a really fair trade, a truly fantastic offer, and not the least bit insulting. Nope, not at all." She hitched her bag onto her shoulder and made to leave.

"Layla!" In a flash, he was up and racing behind her. "I like your no-bullshit attitude. Lets me know where I stand, which at the moment is clearly too close for your comfort."

She was already outside, squinting into the sun as she fumbled for her sunglasses.

"Look—I'm sorry . . ."

Her glasses firmly in place, she turned on her heel, narrowly dodging a yoga mom pushing twin boys in a stroller—one screaming, one placidly observing the world—and made her way down Abbot Kinney with Tommy rushing behind her.

"Layla—"

She whirled on him, nearly crashing into a girl in a bikini cradling a cat in her arms. "What, Tommy? What is it you're trying to say?"

"I'm assuming you've received Ira's list." He tried to peer past her lenses, but they were too dark to reveal much of anything. "You seem like the least likely person to fawn over a celebrity, which is pretty much a job requirement."

She swallowed, but otherwise stood perfectly still.

"And that's going to make it even harder to score Madison Brooks and Ryan Hawthorne, never mind Heather

Rollins and Sugar Mills."

She was shaking, actually shaking with rage—a reaction that seemed entirely disproportionate to the circumstances. Then again, he had no idea what had inspired her to join the contest in the first place. Clearly she had something at stake. He assumed all of them did. But he was only trying to help. And in helping her, he could help himself.

"Tommy—" Her voice was strained.

He sank his hands into his pockets, adopting a loose, easy stance, ready for whatever she threw at him.

"Do yourself a favor and delete my number." Her lips thinned, her back stiffened, her hands clenched—even her hair seemed to react. She was the most openly reactive girl Tommy had ever met.

"Guess it's not a good time to ask you what nickname you gave me?" he called after her, watching as she muttered an insult under her breath and shot across the street. So eager to put some distance between them she risked getting run over by some old dude in a Bentley making an illegal U-turn.

Their meeting had gone even worse than he'd feared, and yet, he couldn't help but grin when he replayed the memory loop in his head.

Layla wasn't his usual type. She could never be described as busty, and yet, every girl should be so lucky to rock a tank top like her. She was blond, which was a plus. But it

ALYSON NOËL

wasn't the kind of blond Tommy usually liked. It wasn't the glossy golden California blond the girls back home tried so hard to emulate. Funny to think he'd driven all the way to LA to be interested in a girl with hair the color of an Oklahoma wheat field.

Even though she clearly hated him, something about their meeting left him excited in a way he hadn't felt for a while.

*Delete my number,* she'd said. Not a chance. He'd back off for now. Give her some space. Though he was serious about them helping each other. He just hoped she'd make it through the first cut.

He thought about contacting Aster. She and Layla were the only ones he'd connected with at the interview, but he doubted he'd get very far. She had too much of that high-maintenance Madison Brooks vibe. She'd probably just laugh in his face. Besides, Tommy had nothing to offer a girl like Aster, and he doubted she had anything to offer him other than a fat contacts list filled with spoiled rich preps who wouldn't deign to step foot inside the Vesper.

*Or would they?*

Tommy watched as the male star of one of cable TVs biggest hits climbed out of a black convertible Porsche and ducked inside an organic café without notice. In Oklahoma, an actor of that caliber would've been mobbed. Yet in Venice, people were too cool to even acknowledge his presence.

LA operated on a whole other frequency, and if Tommy had any hope of making his mark, he'd have to find a way to tune in.

What if instead of trying to outwardly woo Madison—a task that was impossible at best—he concentrated on making the Vesper so hip, so illicit, so talked about, those rich preps got just curious enough to clamor for a walk on the wild side, Madison included. Kind of like the Los Feliz lifestyle tourists who used to come into Farrington's.

It could work.

It could absolutely, 100 percent work.

For the first time since he'd secured the gig, he had an actual working plan and a damn good one at that.

Of course he couldn't go it alone. He'd need Ira's consent. But what better way to impress the old man than coming up with an idea that just might save them both from failure?

# ELEVEN

## ROYALS

Aster Amirpour sat at the formal dining room table, pushing her food around on her plate and ignoring the incessant chiming of her phone like the good, well-mannered, obedient girl Nanny Mitra raised her to be. Eighteen years old and she was still watched over by the same nanny who'd changed her diapers as a baby. It was so beyond ridiculous it ventured into preposterous, outrageous, absurd, ludicrous—

"You gonna answer that?" Her younger brother, Javen, who looked very much like the boy version of Aster except, damn him, his eyelashes were even longer and thicker, tilted his fork toward her iPhone.

"Of course not. We're eating and that would be rude." Aster returned his look with one of her own, before letting her gaze drift among the display of fine Irish linens, gleaming silver flatware, and her mother's finest china place settings—fussy didn't even begin to describe it. Even in her parents' absence, her family's more stodgy traditions raged on.

"Then can you at least silence it?" Javen bit off the tip of his asparagus spear and closed his eyes while he chewed. When Nanny Mitra decided to cook, a task that was usually left to the family's personal chef, it was a rare and precious treat.

Aster silenced her phone and returned to the business of eating, or at least she pretended to eat. Her stomach was so jumpy with nerves and excitement it left no room for anything else. It was her first night on the job, and she had a plan that could put her in the lead. If Ira wanted the club packed with hot young bodies, then Aster would deliver everyone from her contacts list (and their contacts lists, and so on). Of course she didn't have a shot in hell of getting Madison Brooks, much less anyone else on Ira's list, but none of them did. It might have been premature, but she considered herself way ahead of the game.

Compared to the other contestants, she was the closest thing to Madison among them. They had so much in common, it was eerie. They were both girly girls, which meant people often overlooked their brains and ambition, they both had a healthy appreciation for the finer things in life (namely designer clothes and accessories), they both knew how to command the full attention of a room simply by entering, and they were both severely underestimated by people who refused to see them as anything more than a pretty face, and Aster couldn't help but wonder if Ira had underestimated her too.

During the interview he'd blatantly assessed her like she was a piece of fine art he hoped to sell for a steep return. Which was fine since it clinched the job, but Aster was determined to prove she was more than a pretty face to be used as Night for Night bait. She wasn't just playing to win—she was there to meet the kind of people who could boost her career, and yeah, as long as she was there, why not obliterate the rest of her competitors and leave her mark on the world?

"Aster, please—eat!" Nanny Mitra's voice nudged Aster away from her thoughts and back to the table. She motioned toward Aster's nearly full plate, her dark eyes narrowed, her perfectly lined and colored lips drooping into a frown. "You're too skinny," she scolded.

*This again.* Nanny wouldn't be happy until Aster had dimpled thighs and a major muffin top. According to Nanny, not only did Aster not eat enough—*too skinny!*—but her weekly routine of tennis lessons and dance classes were doing more harm than good—*too many muscles aren't good for a girl!* It was a never-ending battle Aster had no hope of winning.

Aster looked to Javen for support, but the smirk on his face made it worse. So she focused on picking at her lamb chops and pushing her potatoes around, but Nanny wasn't fooled.

"Nice Persian boys don't like skinny girls. You need to put some meat on your bones and fill out your curves."

Aster warned herself to keep quiet, to humor Nanny and take a few bites—what could it hurt? But something inside her, something so weary of being lectured on all the ways she needed to change in order to be more appealing to Persian boys, wouldn't be muzzled.

"So, let me get this straight—you're asking me to eat even though I'm not hungry, so some random boy I don't even know will find me pleasingly plump? And then what? He asks me to marry him, and I immediately say yes and forfeit all my dreams so I can produce a litter of babies and stay fat for him?" Her eyes met Nanny's. She loved her, loved her like she loved her own mother, but sometimes her ideas were beyond comprehension, and they needed to be challenged. "Seriously, Nanny." She tried to soften her voice and rein in her annoyance. "This isn't the old country. People in LA covet a whole other look, a whole other life. Girls don't eat to be more appealing to boys."

"Though sometimes they *refuse* to eat to be more appealing to boys," Javen piped in, causing Aster to laugh in spite of herself, and Nanny Mitra to fiddle with the gold locket at her neck that contained a picture of her long-deceased husband as she mumbled in Farsi under her breath.

"Too much skinny—too much skin always on display." Nanny Mitra's command of English, which was usually flawless, always faltered whenever she was confronted by a world moving too fast for her liking.

Aster rose from her seat. "We will agree to disagree, because I love you dearly despite all your crazy outdated ideas." She circled to her side of the table and bent to kiss the top of Nanny's head.

"Where are you going?" Nanny grasped her hand.

"I told you," Aster said, knowing she hadn't. "I'm going to Safi's to help her prepare for her party." She smiled brightly, made herself blink. Hadn't she read something about liars not blinking enough and it was a dead give-away? Or was it that they blinked too much? Crap. She couldn't remember. Though it wasn't like she was actually lying; she was stopping by Safi's, and Safi really was pre-paring for a party. It just happened to be Aster's Night for Night Full Moon party. The idea was genius. Foolproof. Now if she could get past Nanny Mitra, she could put it in motion.

"And she promised to drop me off at the mall on her way to Safi's." Javen flashed Aster his most dazzling grin. "I'm meeting some friends."

Aster glared at Javen. Driving him to the mall was never part of the plan. Clearly he was onto her, though she had no choice but to go along.

"Um, yeah," Aster said. "I mean, *yes*." She was quick to correct. Nanny had a major intolerance for slang, and Aster couldn't afford to take any chances. "I'm dropping Javen at the mall. But he's getting his own ride home, *right, Javen?*"

The look that passed between them—triumph on Javen's part, disbelief on Aster's—well, she couldn't believe Nanny missed it.

"You grow up too fast." Nanny removed the linen napkin from her lap and struggled to rise as Aster rushed to help, and Javen alerted the maid to start clearing the plates. "That's exactly what I will tell your parents when they call tonight and you are not here to speak with them."

Aster balked, fearing Nanny might say exactly that, with that same incriminating tone. But just as quickly it was over, and Nanny was good-humored again. "Now go. Live your lives. Enjoy. But I want you both home by eleven."

Now they both balked. "Nanny, Safi has a lot of planning to do, it might run later—"

"But not too much later?" Nanny's look was final, her tone nonnegotiable, leaving Aster no choice but to agree.

Then, as soon as Nanny was out of earshot, Aster grabbed hold of Javen's sleeve and said, "We need to talk."

\* \* \*

ALYSON NOËL

Aster peered into her rearview mirror as she backed her Mercedes out of the subterranean twelve-car garage. "Not cool." She glanced at her brother.

"You lied to Nanny." He playfully wagged a finger. "Besides, I know all about your party at Night for Night," he quipped, seemingly pleased with himself.

Aster frowned. She should've known he'd find out. Most of her friends had younger brothers and sisters around Javen's age.

"I can't wait to check it out. You know, as a reward for not telling Nanny."

"You're underage." She pulled up to the big iron gate at the end of the drive, hit the remote, and watched it swing open.

"We have fake IDs."

"Yeah?" Aster stole a look at him. "Twenty-one or eighteen?"

"What do you think?"

She pulled onto the street, passing a succession of mansions tucked behind big gates and taller hedges as she drove in the direction of Santa Monica Boulevard. "I think there's a big difference between fifteen and eighteen. Don't even get me started on twenty-one."

"I'll just show up then. It's not like you can stop me."

"And how are you getting there?"

"I have friends, Aster."

"Trust me, I know all about your friends." She stared through the windshield at the perfectly manicured streets, aware of her brother cringing beside her.

"Meaning?"

"I know about your male friends. I know you like boys better than girls. And I'm pretty sure that's not something you're willing to go public with. . . ."

She didn't have any real proof of what she was saying, but when she saw his eyes widen in fear as the color drained from his face, she felt like the worst sister ever for using her brother's sexuality as a bargaining tool.

"Javen, I'm sorry." She rushed to undo the damage. She couldn't care less if Javen was gay. But unfortunately, her parents and Nanny wouldn't see it that way. "You know I want you to live the life you're meant to, and I'm willing to help you do that—but you cannot bribe me in front of Nanny. We're a lot better off working together instead of outing each other."

Slowly the color returned to Javen's cheeks. "Does this mean you'll reconsider sneaking me into your club?"

"No." She frowned. "I'm new at this. I can't take any chances."

"But later?"

"Everything's negotiable," she said, knowing in that particular case it most certainly wasn't.

They drove the rest of the way in silence until she pulled

into the Grove parking lot, where his friend waited. "You'll cover for me tonight, right?" She needed a verbal so she'd have one less thing to worry about.

Javen nodded distractedly, his attention drawn to the cute boy waiting for him. "You know, when Mom and Dad told us they were spending the summer in Dubai, I knew it was destined to be the best summer ever. But then when they said Nanny was coming to stay, I thought my life was officially over."

Aster laughed. She'd felt the same way.

"But now that I know we've got each other's back, I'm pretty sure it's gonna be epic." He grinned in a way that left him looking so beautiful, so young and hopeful, Aster's heart clenched in response. Her brother was standing on the cusp of his life, about to experience all the undiluted joy and heartbreak the world had to offer, and there was nothing she could do to protect him from the darker moments that would surely find him. Though she'd do her best to protect him from Nanny Mitra and her parents.

He slid from his seat and loped toward his friend, while Aster, overcome by a surge of love and protectiveness, tapped the gold-and-diamond hamsa pendant that hung from her neck, said a silent prayer for Javen, and made her way to Safi's.

## TWELVE

# I WANNA BE SEDATED

Layla gazed around the nearly empty club and sighed. It was closing time at Jewel, but it was only slightly less crowded than it had been before. The crowd on the dance floor had been so sparse, even the DJ looked bored. Her first night on the job was a flop. And despite Karly's claim that her good friend's cousin's boyfriend's brother had once styled Madison's hair on a movie set so she'd probably be the first to snag her, Madison never appeared. Still, they had managed to pull in enough people to save the night from being a total disaster, no thanks to Layla.

While Layla had plenty of friends, none of them were big on clubbing. Had she been in charge of the Vesper, they might've shown, but soon as they heard she was promoting the slick, glitzy, upscale Jewel, they were quick to turn up their noses in that totally hypocritical, indie snobbery way that always amused and amazed her. When it came down to it, her friends' disdain of the mainstream and moneyed made them just as big snobs as the mainstream and moneyed snobs they disdained. Yet they could never quite see it that way. Whatever. She loved her friends. Loved them for the very reasons they wouldn't be caught dead at Jewel. But that didn't mean she didn't feel they'd abandoned her.

Hoping to secure some gets for the weekend, she made for a group of girls whose slinky, barely there dresses told her they were into being noticed.

"Hey!" She rushed toward them, ignoring their withering glares. "I was wondering if you wanted me to take your picture." She waved her cell phone in front of them, pegging them as way too vain to pass up the offer.

"Um, no, thanks." The tall blonde sneered as though Layla was some pathetic last-call letch.

"It's not for me," Layla raced to explain. For better or worse she'd started this mess, and she was determined to finish. "It's for the club. I'm one of the promoters." She paused, giving them ample time to act impressed, but they remained before her, arms crossed, brows raised. "I was going to post it on Twitter and Instagram. You know, under the Jewel account." She rubbed her lips together, hoping they were too clueless to know the club didn't have social network accounts. Ira thought his brand was too cool for all that, a major misstep she intended to fix.

She waited while they conferred with one another, acting like it was a much bigger deal than it was. Making Layla feel as weird and obtrusive as she had on her first day of junior high, when the popular girls physically ejected her when she'd accidentally sat at their lunch table.

"Okay," the blonde finally said. Every group had a leader, and she'd clearly been crowned. "But only if we get to approve the picture before you post it and you promise to tag us."

Layla blinked. This was one high-maintenance crowd. "Maybe I should run it by your agents first," she joked.

They stared blankly in return.

"Deal," she agreed, taking a series of shots and trying not to laugh as they all huddled together, making that bizarre *this is my sexy face* duck-lips expression she'd never understood. After collecting all of their Twitter and Insta handles, which she planned to use to lure them back, she called, "Bye!" as they made for the exit. She immediately regretted it when they all burst out laughing.

God. She was such a colossal dork. Mateo had no reason to worry. There was no way she'd get sucked into this world. Stupid Tommy was right—if she couldn't even get her friends to show up, and the duck-lips girls had taken her for a joke, then how in hell was she supposed to appeal to Madison Brooks? She needed to do something quick if she didn't want to be the first to flame out.

She climbed on her bike and made her way down the boulevard, vowing not to look when she passed Night for Night and the Vesper. It would only make her feel worse, yet the fierce competitor in her couldn't keep from sneaking a peek.

The LA private-school crowd lingered outside Night for Night, leaving Layla to wonder how many were regulars, and how many Aster and her team had lured in.

When she reached the Vesper, she revved the throttle, desperate to make it past the intersection before the light turned. Then she cursed her crummy luck when the car in front of her hit the brakes, forcing her to skid to a stop just a few feet from Tommy and some platinum blonde wearing fishnets, sky-high ankle boots, and a tiny black dress that just barely contained her.

Fortunately he was too busy flirting to notice she was there.

Or not.

"Layla!"

He called her name twice, as Layla focused hard on the light, willing it to turn. If it wasn't for the camera just waiting for her to make a run for it so it could photograph the evidence and deliver a ticket straight to her door, she would've been out of there.

"Layla—hey!"

*Crap.* She commanded the light to change, but it

remained a frustrating shade of red, as Tommy stood in the middle of the boulevard, tugging on the sleeve of her black leather jacket.

"What did I tell you last time I saw you?"

"You came to my hood. How rude would I be if I didn't say hey?" He grinned when he said it, as though he'd just recited a lovely bit of poetry.

"Do you think you could let go of my sleeve?" It was lame. But it was the best she could do now that she'd made the mistake of meeting his gaze.

His hand dropped to his side, but that dazzling grin remained fixed, along with those deep blue eyes.

The light changed, horns honked, and still she sat frozen, hating herself for every second that passed.

"How was your first night?" Tommy seemed immune to the chaos around them.

"Apparently not as good as yours." Layla nodded toward the girl, taking a series of cleavage-centric selfies as she waited for Tommy's return.

"Nothing to worry about," Tommy said. "She's just a friend."

"Worried?" Layla shot him her best *you need to wither and die now* face. "Don't flatter yourself."

He didn't react. Didn't even flinch. Just remained infuriatingly, sedately before her.

Layla glanced between the girl and Tommy. The sight left her incensed.

Must be because she missed Mateo. They rarely argued, and when they did, she always regretted it. Mostly because she was usually the one who started it.

"Let me know if you change your mind," Tommy said. Responding to her confusion, he added, "About sharing strategies."

She frowned. Ticket be damned. She'd pay any fine to get away from him and his stupid grin.

She gunned her bike and shot into the intersection just as the light began to turn red again. She needed to put some serious distance between them and the nagging truth that she should probably take him up on his offer to help, all the while knowing she wouldn't.

Something about him left her uneasy. It was like he saw right through her, right down to her crummier bits—the stuff Mateo either failed to notice or forgave far too easily—and he wasn't the least bit repelled. If anything, he seemed delighted by the discovery, because he shared the same crummy bits too.

She drove another few blocks, then pulled to the side of the road, where she fumbled for her phone, praying Mateo would still be up, and that he was willing to talk.

"You okay?" It was the first thing he said. Making her feel guilty for worrying him.

"I don't think I'm cut out for this job." Her voice sounded as tired as she felt. "I made a fool of myself."

"So quit."

Layla frowned. Quitting was never an option. She'd rather die trying than wave a white flag. He should've known that.

The silence lingered between them, until Mateo finally said, "Where are you?"

Layla watched a homeless man pee against a wall as another picked through a trash can, the entirety of his worldly belongings piled into the stolen shopping cart beside him.

"The glamour capital of the world."

"Why don't you come over?"

"Might take me a while to get there."

"I'm not going anywhere."

She didn't realize how tense she'd been until her shoulders sank in relief. Even if he didn't approve, Mateo would always be there for her. He didn't hold grudges. And he never veered from what truly mattered. Most of the time she had no idea why he loved her. She was just grateful he did.

Feeling better already, she slid her phone into her pocket and merged back onto the street. It would all be okay. She would not lose her way. She could have Mateo and her job. There was no reason to choose. Though if she didn't come up with some better ideas, Ira would choose for her.

# THIRTEEN

# EVERYBODY WANTS TO RULE THE WORLD

Aster stood beside the DJ booth and gazed upon the dispersing crowd like a queen surveying her subjects. Her first official night on the job and she was already a success. It was like all the recent graduates from LA's most exclusive private schools had shown up wearing metallic moon and star tattoos, transforming the Night for Night dance floor into a writhing, swirling constellation of the next wave of LA's movers and shakers.

"Nice turnout." Taylor stood alongside her.

Aster snuck a sideways glance at the pretty blonde. In her perforated leather minidress, she looked surprisingly chic and sexy for someone Aster had originally taken for a prep.

"Thanks!" She grinned. "It was so much bigger than I expected."

"Was it?" Taylor narrowed her gaze.

Aster looked away, refusing to engage in whatever game Taylor was playing. All that mattered was that it was past closing time and the mob was just starting to thin.

"I thought we were a team," Taylor said.

Aster continued to watch the dance floor, spotting her friend Safi and trying to make out the boy she was with before they faded into the crowd.

"You hijacked the night—made it all about you. You don't want to play on our team, no problem. We'll do just fine without you."

"Will you?" Aster returned the look, watching as Taylor mumbled under her breath and stormed off to where Diego and Ash waited.

First night of the competition and her team had already turned against her. It was just as well. What was the point of working together when only one person would win? Even though Aster didn't understand the rules, she figured she'd be better rewarded for breaking them than trying to follow them.

The night was a success, and nothing Taylor said could change that. The only immediate problems Aster faced were her throbbing feet and aching cheeks thanks to her four-inch heels and an overload of grinning and air-kissing. Party hostess injuries. Well, she'd better get used to it. If things continued like this, she'd sail through the first week and beyond.

"Aster." Ira came up behind her. "Got a moment?"

She followed him up the stairs and into an office that was strictly business, like Ira himself, not a single personal touch to be found. He gestured toward a chair, and Aster gratefully lowered herself onto the seat. Stifling a sigh of relief to finally be off her feet, she rubbed her aching calves while Ira rummaged through his desk.

"Those were decent numbers for a Thursday." He retrieved a white envelope bearing the red Unrivaled Nightlife logo, then leaned back in his seat.

Aster smiled sedately while a fist-pumping happy dance raged in her head.

"Mind telling me how you did it?"

"I created a party within the party. Told everyone on my list that a golden star or moon tattoo would gain them entry." She raised her wrist, displaying the one she wore. Then, feeling clumsy under the glare of his unblinking gaze, she dropped her hand to her lap. "Anyway, they had to go through me to get them, and I guess word spread." She shrugged, unwilling to admit she'd possibly stolen kids that were on her teammates' list.

"And?"

She shifted in her seat, unsure what he meant.

"They got some metallic tattoos—is that it? No free drinks? No discounts at the door?"

"I can do that?" she asked, wondering why she hadn't thought of it.

"Only if your gets are famous. Which none of them were."

She sank a little lower, not feeling quite as pleased with herself as she had a moment before. "I guess people like to feel like they're part of something cool."

Ira gave her a thoughtful look. "What works on a Thursday will fail on a Saturday. You need to aim higher."

She dropped her gaze to her lap.

"Anyway, I know you're tired, so here." He slid the envelope across the desk, and without even checking, Aster knew it was filled with a fat wad of cash.

She lifted her gaze to meet his, their eyes locking for a long, lingering moment that left Aster wondering what he might expect in return.

"Wow . . . thank you." She studied the envelope, wanting to believe it was a well-deserved prize, and not something shady that would leave her feeling dirty and compromised.

"I'm the one thanking you." Ira watched her from a set of dark-blue eyes that saw much and revealed nothing. "You'll find I can be very generous toward those who impress me." He nodded toward the envelope, while Aster scrambled for the perfect reply, but nothing came to mind. "Though I warn you . . ." His gaze deepened like he could see through her dress, right through her flesh. He was old enough to be her father, and yet, she couldn't help but wonder what it might be like to kiss him. Not that she wanted to. She didn't. Not even. But still, Ira made her string of former boyfriends seem like an embarrassing succession of underdeveloped, fumbling boys in comparison. "I'm rarely impressed by the same thing twice."

His voice jerked her away from her thoughts and not a moment too soon. She rubbed her lips together and tugged her dress closer to her knees, hoping she hadn't inadvertently revealed what she'd been thinking.

She nodded in reply, knowing she'd just played her one greatest hit on an otherwise empty playlist. First thing tomorrow she'd brainstorm—as soon as she got a decent night's sleep. She stifled a yawn. Waited to see if there was more. But when Ira rose from his chair, she was quick to stand too.

He came around the desk to offer his hand—a hand that practically swallowed hers, capable of crushing her fingers without any effort.

"Now go get some rest." He led her back into the nearly empty club, leaving Aster to wonder if he was going to walk her to her car. And if so, was it awkward, sexy, grotesque? Before she could decide, he told one of the bouncers, James, to escort her outside, leaving Aster to tuck the envelope into her bag and make her way to her Mercedes. She waited for James to leave before she opened the envelope and thumbed through the stash of twenties and hundreds that certainly added up to—a lot. It wasn't like she was dumb enough to

sit alone in her car on Hollywood Boulevard, counting her
fortune.

She tucked the envelope back into her bag and pulled
onto the street. Reveling in the fact that she'd managed to
gain Ira's notice for something more than her looks.

Now, if she could just manage to sneak past Nanny
Mitra, the night would be complete.

# FOURTEEN

## SEX AND CANDY

Tommy headed back inside the Vesper, aware of the girl following him—Serena, Savannah, Scarlet—he couldn't be sure.

How long was it since he'd last been with a girl? It was too depressing to calculate, but he did anyway. Amy. His ex-girlfriend from Oklahoma. Right before he broke the news of his move. After that, it'd been nothing but tears, recriminations, and . . . it was better not to think about. Point was, LA had proved to be a long and brutal dry spell. The locals loved to complain about the drought; well, Tommy was smack in the middle of his own personal famine, and if this girl with the name he couldn't remember was offering relief, who was he to turn it down?

He had nothing to feel guilty about. No one to answer

to. Besides, a man could only go so long without sustenance. Allowing his eyes to feast on the bounty before him—the perfect breasts (probably not real, but who cared?), the slim waist curving into a pair of plush hourglass hips—he looked right at her and said, "You should probably go."

She blinked, tilted a bit on those skyscraper heels. "You serious?" She looked like she couldn't believe he was turning down such a delectable offer. He could hardly believe it himself.

Still, tempting as she was, he didn't want to settle for a night with some hot girl he had nothing in common with. She had a groupie's knowledge of music, which he could forgive, but so far she'd agreed with everything he'd said, which had become really boring, really fast.

"Sorry," he said. "The club's closed."

"I can't believe this." She pouted adorably but made no move to leave.

"If it makes you feel better, neither can I." He shrugged.

"Is this because of your girlfriend?"

He squinted, having no idea what she was getting at.

"The girl on the bike." She hooked a thumb toward the door that led to the street.

She was offering a way out that would save face for them both, but not wanting to lie, he said, "It's complicated."

"Isn't it always." She shot him a lopsided grin and planted a kiss on his cheek, leaving him with the lingering scent of sweetness, promise, and girl, and it was all he could do not to race after her.

The bartenders were still cleaning up. The manager was somewhere in back. And since Tommy was too amped to return to his shithole apartment, he grabbed a spare guitar, took his place onstage, and started to play. So lost in his music, it wasn't until the second song ended that he noticed Ira Redman was watching.

Tommy lifted the guitar over his head and placed it against the stool, shrinking under the glare of Ira's harsh gaze.

"Needed to blow off some steam," Tommy said, feeling the need to explain, but wishing it hadn't come off so awkward.

"Funny you chose music over the girl."

Tommy stared. How much had Ira seen?

"How'd the first night go?"

Tommy shrugged. "You tell me."

"I'm more interested in how *you* think it went."

Unlike the rest of his team, he didn't have a big group of friends to pull in. So he'd had some cards made, passed them around his favorite record store, and made sure to leave some at the yoga studio down the street. As far as strategies went, it was far from genius; still, it had resulted in plenty of nonfamous gets and some smokin' hot yoga girls.

Ira stared at Tommy, waiting for an answer, but Tommy knew better than to boast, especially when there was nothing worth boasting about. Ira would only call him on it. Make him feel shakier than he already did. He was ruthless. The way he'd ditched Tommy's mom after learning she was pregnant was all the proof Tommy needed. Sure, he'd left her some cash—enough to cover the abortion. But he couldn't bother to stick around long enough to drive her to the clinic. Ira just assumed then, like he did now, that everyone would gladly do his bidding. It probably never occurred to him she'd use the money to buy diapers and a crib.

"Could've been better," Tommy finally admitted. "And it will be. I have an idea I'd like to discuss, if you have a minute." He stepped offstage, preferring to be on equal footing. "I want to take that back room and turn it into a private space."

Ira frowned. "It's already a private space."

"No, I mean *private* as in VIP access only."

"That's where the bands hang between sets."

"Exactly," Tommy said. "We've got a good summer lineup, and if we opened that room to a select group of people, gave it more of a lounge feel, we could increase our numbers and up our cool factor."

Ira looked him over but gave nothing away.

"And I want to run it and get credit for the gets, since

I'm the one who thought of it."

"What about your team?"

"What about them?" Tommy shrugged dismissively.

"And which VIPs can you deliver?"

"At the moment, none." No point in lying. "But soon, plenty. More than that room can handle."

Ira got up without a word and headed toward his office, calling over his shoulder to say, "For now, why don't you work out a plan that doesn't depend on my help."

Tommy glared at his back, wondering who he hated more in that moment, Ira or himself. It was a good idea—bordering on great—but his delivery had been a mess. It was simultaneously cocky and sloppy. No wonder Ira hadn't taken him seriously. Still, watch him steal the idea and deny Tommy the credit.

He snatched his leather jacket and banged outside to his wreck of a car. Screw it. He'd find another way to build his numbers and impress the old man in a way he'd have to acknowledge. He had an idea he'd been spinning as a backup, but he was hoping to put it off until later in the contest, in case he got desperate. It was risky as hell and could land the club in serious trouble. Still, he saw no reason to wait, as nothing good ever came from playing it safe. If nothing else, Ira would admire his drive. And if it worked, it would secure him the win. Tomorrow he'd test it. By Saturday, he'd have the kinks ironed out. By Sunday,

Ira would be rewarding him for a job well done.

He wondered if Layla would pull it together by then.

He grinned at the memory of Layla's face—that sweet urchin face with the pouty lips, clear, wide-set eyes, and a complexion pure as porcelain.

When it came to the kind of networking needed to succeed at this job, she was her own worst enemy. LA was a town of actors and storytellers, populated by those more comfortable playing an imaginary role than being themselves, and the prize always went to the one who faked it best.

Layla didn't know how to be anything *but* herself. Wouldn't be long before she came around and admitted he'd been right all along.

The Scarlet-Savannah-Serenas of the world had nothing on her. He'd waited this long to get with a girl; he figured he might as well hold out for the one who truly intrigued him.

# FIFTEEN

# YOUNG AND
# BEAUTIFUL

Luckily, Javen had silenced the house alarm, which allowed Aster to sneak into her room without alerting Nanny Mitra and fall into a deep, soundless sleep. Or at least it was deep and soundless until her phone chimed the next morning with a text from one of Ira's assistants, confirming Night for Night had brought in the biggest haul, thanks to Aster's efforts. Though there was complete silence from her team, which made her feel bad. Aster wasn't used to being hated.

What was that saying about success breeding contempt? Apparently it was true.

She leaned against her tufted silk headboard, fumbled through her bag for the envelope Ira gave her, and spread the contents across her crisp white Frette sheets. Despite her family's massive wealth, when it came to their kids, her parents kept a tight fist. She owned exactly two dresses she could wear to the club—one of which she'd worn for the interview, and the other last night. The rest of her wardrobe consisted of stuff her mother approved of, which meant buying more dresses, really sexy (but tasteful, not trashy) dresses was imperative. A few more stilettos would also be good. Maybe some jewelry as well—the trendy, costumey stuff—the kind of things that would make her mother faint if she ever caught Aster wearing them.

She transferred the money to her wallet, rang the maid to send up some coffee, and headed for the shower. She had a big day of shopping ahead.

Having grown up in Beverly Hills, Aster knew plenty of boutiques that would've worked, but she wanted a place with no connection to her mom. Luckily, her mom never set foot inside Neiman's (she was devoted to Saks), which was how Neiman's became Aster's first choice.

She left her car with the valet and headed up the escalator, where she perused the endless racks of dresses, perfectly content to browse for as long as it took. When it came to serious shopping, she preferred to go it alone. She'd yet to meet a salesperson who didn't try to impress their personal taste onto her.

She dragged her haul into a fitting room and breezed

through a pile of sexy bodycon dresses until she'd narrowed it down to one absolute fave and two backups. She was just about to change and head down to the shoe department when she overheard a girl in the next room say, "You'll never guess who's here! It's that guy from that TV show. You know, that one with the green eyes and jeez, I can't believe I forgot his name—he dates Madison Brooks."

Aster pressed against the door, her heart beating frantically. "Ryan Hawthorne," she whispered, waiting for the girl's friend to confirm it.

"Ryan Hawthorne?"

"Yes, and he's right downstairs. Probably buying something for Madison."

"If his show gets axed, that'll be his last gift to her in a while."

They both laughed.

"You have to see him. He's even cuter in person."

"On it. I don't want these jeans anyway. They give me mom butt."

Before Aster could hear any more, she was slipping out of her dressing room wearing the sexiest of the three dresses and heading downstairs. Unfortunately, the girl had failed to mention where Ryan was, but if he really was shopping for Madison, then he was either in cosmetics, handbags, or jewelry . . . which made for a lot of square footage to search.

She crept past the fragrance counter, made a detour past a pile of Prada bags, and was just veering toward a display case of statement necklaces when she realized the girl must've been wrong. With his signature tousled blond hair, tanned skin, and green eyes, Ryan Hawthorne was impossible to miss, and from what Aster could see, there wasn't a single guy in the store who could nail Ryan's golden-boy look. Though there were plenty who tried.

*It was too good to be true.* She cast a last look toward the jewelry counter as she made her way toward shoes, spotting a guy about Ryan's height with Ryan's tight build, wearing a black beanie and dark sunglasses. Of course Ryan wouldn't head out without some sort of disguise. Even in a store that was used to dealing with celebrities, there were bound to be a few tourists who wouldn't think twice about mobbing him. And yet, despite his attempt to go incognito, the longer Aster watched, the more she grew convinced it was him.

Even from a distance she could tell he really was cuter in person. But more important, he was wrapping up the transaction, which meant he could leave at any second. She had to act fast.

Grabbing the first Manolos within reach, she slid one onto her foot and stood before the mirror, angling her leg in a way that inched the dress higher, as she waited for Ryan Hawthorne to breeze past.

Only he didn't breeze past.

He stopped in his tracks and lifted his sunglasses high onto his head to admire the view. Not exactly a cool move for a guy who was known to be dating Hollywood's It Girl, but for Aster, it was a sign as good as any that she was on the right track.

The job, the dress, the shoes, it was all about to lead somewhere good. Ryan's blatant look of unadulterated male appreciation was enough for Aster to screw up enough courage to say, "Should I buy them?" She inched the dress higher.

"They've got my vote." Ryan's voice was throaty and tight, as he lost the battle to stifle the grin that took over his perfectly chiseled face.

She moved her gaze over his famously ripped and cut body, currently clad in jeans and a T-shirt. Her pulse thrummed, her hands started to shake, yet she still managed to look into the mirror and say, "Mmm . . . I don't know . . ." She swiveled her hips from side to side, all too aware of Ryan grinning like a fool who needed to move on but was completely unable to do so.

"I feel like I can't go until I see how this ends," he said, oblivious to the swarm of salespeople and shoppers beginning to gather, instinctively drawn to the scent of a scandal in the making.

The last thing she wanted was to get Ryan in trouble

with the press, much less Madison, who she desperately needed and pretty much worshipped. Still, she wasn't about to let the opportunity slip. Fate had put Ryan into her path; it was up to her to make the most of it.

"Well, you could always swing by Night for Night tomorrow night and see what I decide. If I buy them, I'll wear them. . . ." She swiveled again, flashed him her most seductive head-shot grin. Deciding it was better to leave him wanting more, she shot one last flirtatious look over her shoulder and headed for her dressing room. So taken by the excitement of what just occurred she could barely contain herself. It wasn't her first celebrity encounter, but it was the first one that mattered.

If she knew anything about men, especially spoiled, entitled men (and wasn't she practically an expert, having spent an entire lifetime surrounded by them?), she knew for a fact that theirs was an encounter he would not soon forget.

It was just a matter of time before he came to the club, and if he showed up with Madison, even better. Either way, victory was about to be hers.

# SIXTEEN

# BLURRED LINES

Madison Brooks lay curled on her side, sheltered by the shade of a large umbrella, enjoying the view of her infinity pool and the way it seemed to drop straight into the canyon beyond. After her luxurious closet, her backyard was her second favorite place on her property. As a child growing up thousands of miles from any piece of land capable of supporting a palm tree, her tropical paradise was yet another symbol of how far she'd come.

It was her first free day in . . . well, it'd been so long she couldn't remember when she'd last enjoyed a Saturday without at least one meeting, fitting, or script to read. But with the day stretching out before her like a delectable buffet with unlimited offerings, she was content to remain right there on the chaise, reveling in the fact that she had absolutely nothing to do and nowhere to be.

"Hey, babe."

At the sound of Ryan's voice, Blue, who'd been sleeping beside her, lifted his head, pinned back his ears, and let out a teeth-baring growl that had Madison toying with the idea of commanding him to attack. Of course she wouldn't do it, but that wasn't to say she wasn't tempted.

From a purely physical perspective, Ryan was as dreamy as they come. What with the way his sandy-blond hair caught the glinting rays of the sun, making it appear as though it'd been sprinkled with gold dust, the way his well-muscled legs strode purposefully toward her, the way his biceps popped under the strain of an arm loaded with Neiman Marcus shopping bags—it was easy to see why he'd single-handedly fueled the fantasies of so many teen girls (and most of their moms).

"You bring me a gift?" She lowered her sunglasses back to her nose. Sure, she was tired of him, but gifts were always appreciated and rarely returned.

He grinned his dazzling Ryan Hawthorne grin—the moneymaker, as he sometimes referred to it—and sorted through his collection of bags until he found the right one. "Did he just growl at me?" He cast a wary eye on Blue.

Madison watched as Blue leaped from the chair and trotted toward the house. Then she sat up straighter, crossed her legs at the shins, and dug through layers of soft white tissue before she unearthed a small square jewelry box at the bottom.

Hoops. Yet another pair of gold hoops. Only these were far prettier than most in her collection, mostly due to the little turquoise bits that adorned them. Madison traced her finger around the rims, approving of them far more than she'd let on.

She leaned in to plant a perfunctory kiss on his cheek, only to have him turn his head at the very last moment, claiming the kiss.

His lips parted, his tongue darted forward, as his hand rose to the back of her head and he buried his fingers deep in her hair, angling her face closer to his. "I missed you, babe." He breathed the words into her neck, her hair, before finding her lips once again.

He pulled her closer, and then closer still. And when his hand fell to her breast, his fingers about to ease beneath her bikini top, she pressed her palm firmly against his chest and pushed him away. "Easy, tiger." She kept her tone playful as she summoned all her will not to wipe her mouth on her towel. It wasn't that Ryan was a bad kisser, but every kiss was the wrong kiss when it came from a person you could just barely tolerate. "I want to try on my new earrings before you get carried away." She was hoping to distract him long enough that he'd forget where they'd left off.

Madison was convinced Ryan's heartthrob status was

due solely to the fact that not a single member of his adoring public would ever guess at the weird groans and embarrassing sex faces he made during the act. But Ryan's days as the reigning Teen King of prime-time TV were nearing an end. His show was on the verge of cancellation. The writers had run out of ideas, the plot had grown stale, and the ratings were falling—a death knell if she ever heard one. If Ryan's agent didn't book him something quick, preferably something bigger and better than the silly teen soap that had made him famous, he'd be officially declared a has-been by this time next year.

Aside from a handful of Teflon-coated, A-list elite who could survive a series of flops and still hold their fan base, the general rule in Hollywood was that you were only as good as your last project. The public was fickle—claiming their undying love and devotion one moment, while simultaneously looking for the next new face to adore.

The time was right to end things with Ryan. If the point of their relationship was to boost each other's images, then Ryan was about to become a serious detriment. She couldn't see a single reason to delay the inevitable.

"Gorgeous." His eyes appeared to sweep across her face, yet his attention clearly drifted. Like he was looking inward rather than outward, like someone else had claimed a place in his memory.

"So, what else did you get me?" She studied him

carefully, knowing there was nothing more. She was more interested in how he'd reply. Ryan was the kind of actor who relied heavily on the script. Improvisation was not one of his strengths.

His brows merged as though he'd forgotten where he was—or maybe who he was with?

Was it possible Ryan had grown as tired of her as she'd grown of him?

For the first time in a long time, he intrigued her.

"Uh, nothing," he said, his voice distracted as he struggled to return to the present. "The rest is just some basics I needed to replace. Been carrying 'em around in my car, figured I'd bring 'em inside in case I end up staying the night."

She nodded like she understood, and she did, just not in the way he intended. Ryan was hiding something. And while there was a part of her that couldn't care less, the other part, the part that kept a tight vigil on her image and anything that might threaten it, was on full, red-flag alert.

"I was thinking we should go out tonight." He acted as though the "going out" was a rare event, when they both knew it was the basis of their relationship. Being seen was imperative.

Instead of readily agreeing like she normally would, she leaned back, slowly, languidly, curling an arm around the back of her head, making her cleavage swell in a way he usually couldn't resist. When the move barely registered, she knew Ryan either had been, or was about to be, a very bad boy. "I don't know. . . ." She dragged out each word. "What did you have in mind?"

He rubbed his chin as though thinking it over, but his jiggling knee betrayed him. "Dinner at Nobu Malibu? We haven't been in a while."

Madison squinted, having no idea where he was leading. But there was something about the way he broached it, something so furtive and guilty, she knew right then she wouldn't end things today. For the first time in their relationship, she wondered if maybe she wasn't the only one playing this game.

"Hmmm . . . maybe . . ." She purred the words like a cat, uncrossed her legs slowly, seductively, before crossing them again, allowing one perfect thigh to slide against the other. Surely he'd see that. Surely he'd react.

"Whatever you want, babe." His voice adopted the deeper tone she knew all too well, as he trained his focus on her. "Dinner can wait—but this—" He traced the tip of his index finger over the peak of her ribs into the valley of her smooth, taut abdomen until it was nudging beneath the band of her bikini bottom. "This is all I can think about." He bent his head toward hers, as Madison closed her eyes, thought of a boy from a faraway place, and returned the kiss with the kind of fervor that surprised them both.

# SEVENTEEN

# GO HARD OR GO HOME

"Bro, you gonna set us up, or what?"

Tommy peered past the bouncer at the two punks he knew from Farrington's. He'd been called to the door to deal with them, and all he could think was, *How the hell did they find me?*

"We need to be on that list, bro!" one of them shouted. Was it Ethan? Tommy could never remember their names. Much less tell them apart.

He gazed past them. The line was long, filled with more important, age-appropriate gets.

"You know them?" The bouncer shot Tommy an impatient look.

He nodded reluctantly, knowing if he didn't, they'd make the kind of scene he couldn't afford.

"They eighteen?"

"Twenty-one, yo!" Ethan added a fist pump to go with it that made him look anything but.

"Eighteen." Tommy shot the kids a look of warning, knowing even that was a stretch.

"You say so." The bouncer was dubious, but lifted the rope anyway and granted them access.

*"Suh-weet!"* They burst into the darkened club, nodding their heads as they took in the graffiti-covered walls, the large stage, the crowded bar, and all the good-looking girls.

"What the hell is this? You guys stalking me?" Tommy grabbed them each by the sleeve and hauled them back toward him. He'd always been fonder of them than he liked to admit, but at the moment, he was pretty annoyed they had shown up.

"You wish." Ethan sneered and jerked out of his grasp. "This is so much better than your last gig," he said. "Glad we kept in touch."

"We didn't." Tommy shook his head, trying not to laugh. He didn't want to encourage them any more than he had.

"So when you gonna set us up with some of those black wristbands so we can get this party started?" This came from the other one, crap, what was his name? Colpher. That was it—some kind of last-name-as-first-name kind of thing.

Tommy stared between them. "How'd you hear about that?"

"Word's out, bro." They grinned in anticipation, as Tommy ran a hand over his chin, trying to decide if that was good news or bad.

It was only the second night of the trial, and apparently news had already spread to guitar stores and skate parks. His liberal use of the black wristbands, usually reserved for the twenty-one-and-over crowd, had given his numbers an even bigger bump than he'd anticipated. While he saw no harm in aging up certain eighteen-year-olds eager to get a three-year jump on the party, these two couldn't be more than fourteen tops, and Tommy refused to corrupt them any more than they already were.

"Listen—" He swiped a hand through his hair and looked toward the door, watching more of his gets filing in. "Hang out as long as you want. But don't cause any trouble, and don't even think about swiping a wristband."

Tommy watched as their faces fell in the kind of disappointment that was almost comical to watch. "You are the worst club promoter ever," Colpher said.

"Why you dissing us like that?" Ethan scowled.

"Yeah, yeah." Tommy laughed and ushered them to a spot near the stage he normally saved for VIPs. "Enjoy it while it lasts," he told them. "And pay attention to this next band—you might learn something. But remember, I'm watching you." He illustrated the point by aiming V fingers from his eyes to theirs. "You act like idiots, I won't hesitate to call your parents and tell them to come get you."

He watched them settle in, clearly pleased with themselves; then, ensuring the rest of his team wasn't looking, he slipped out the side door and made his way down the boulevard.

# EIGHTEEN

# THE POLITICS OF DANCING

In less than two hours the first week of competition would officially end. In less than twelve, Layla would be the first to get cut. She could only imagine the look on Queen Bitch Aster's face when Ira inevitably called Layla's name. She'd toss her glossy hair over her shoulder and cock a haughty brow in knowing disdain, watching from the plush seat of her throne as Layla left in disgrace, a metaphorical tail tucked between her legs.

The things that made her a successful blogger worked against her as a promoter. She might be whip smart, but she was a cynical loner at heart—more used to poking fun at celebrity culture than courting it. Her embarrassing attempts to lure people to Jewel—lame social media shout-outs and invites—had left her feeling like the world's biggest poseur.

Relying on her blog seemed sleazy and unprofessional, something that would ultimately work against her. But if by chance she got another week, she'd waste no time doing everything short of bribing her readers to get them to Jewel. Otherwise, there was no point continuing. Trying to balance her work at the club and her relationship with Mateo was stressing her out. While he didn't hold a grudge, he didn't exactly support her either. It felt like her world was split into two not-quite-equal jagged bits, neither one of them willing to adapt to the other.

Karly and Brandon walked by, slowing long enough to give her the stink eye, which she probably deserved, but it wasn't like it was her fault she lacked the right friends to succeed at this stuff. It was high school all over again. She was out of her element, didn't fit in. Only back then, she'd been a lot better at pretending not to care.

*Screw it. Screw them. Screw Ira. Screw all of it.* She headed for the bar, slipped around to the other side, and helped herself to a shot of top-shelf tequila. She'd failed in the most spectacular way—the least she could do was numb some of the pain.

"Last time I had one of those, I drank it straight out of a navel with a hit of lemon and salt, but I hear a glass is just as effective."

Tommy stood before her, his navy-blue eyes glinting on hers.

Layla scowled, tossed her head back, and drained the

tequila. "You shouldn't be here." She slammed the glass on the bar a little harder than intended. The alcohol was already slipping through her bloodstream, warming her from the inside and working its magic. The effect was so nice she reached for the bottle and poured herself another.

"You ever gonna cut me a break?" Tommy pressed his palms against the counter and leaned toward her, wearing a hopeful expression.

"Sure." She ran her finger along the rim. "Hold your breath and wait for it." She finished her drink and refilled her shot glass again.

"I like your honesty." He motioned to the bottle. "But in case you haven't heard—sharing is caring. I've got my own problems, you know."

Layla considered him for a long, intense moment. Her gaze lingered over the errant clump of light-brown hair that insisted on falling into his eyes, the worn Black Keys T-shirt that perfectly skimmed his lean, muscular frame, the faded jeans that hung low on his hips, the brown leather belt so worn she couldn't help but wonder how many girls had unbuckled it in a hurry. . . .

She tossed back her drink, poured herself another, and then filled a glass for him. If Tommy thought she was being "honest," then clearly he hadn't a clue what honesty looked like. Her annoyance with him wasn't for the reasons he thought. She was annoyed with him for being right, for showing up at her club just in time to catch her in a deeply shameful moment of failure and insecurity. For those stupid blue eyes.

She emptied her glass, poured another shot, downed it, then pushed her glass aside. It was time to stop playing games and get to the point. "What the hell are you doing here? Did Ira send you?"

He shook his head, grabbed the bottle, tipped a few more drops into his glass, and finished them off in a single toss. "I came to see you."

She rolled her eyes, tried to say something insulting, but the tequila was drowning her brain cells and she couldn't think of a single reply.

"Come on, dance with me." His fingers reached across the counter and circled her wrist.

"I don't dance." She yanked free of his grip, hating the way her wrist went from warm to cold the moment he released it.

"You serious?" Tommy's face creased like he was seconds away from howling with laughter.

"I know." Layla laughed in spite of herself. "I couldn't be worse suited for this job."

His gaze turned serious. "One dance. Then I'll head back to the Vesper so fast you'll forget I was here."

Layla studied him closely. Last she saw he'd been flirting with the kind of curvy blonde she could never compete with. She wondered if he'd gone home with her. She figured he had.

"Come on." His voice was gentle, his gaze sincere, or as sincere as it could get for a guy she hadn't decided to trust. She struggled to come up with one good reason not to go along, but her usually well-honed instincts were so diluted, next thing she knew she was following him onto the dance floor.

He pulled her deep into the throng, keeping a decent distance until the crowd surged around them, pushing them closer, and he slid a hand around the curve of her hip and pressed his lips to hers.

*I need to push him away. I need to stop this. I need to go to the bathroom and make myself vomit so I can get this tequila out of my system and stop doing things I'll only regret. . . .*

Ignoring the voice in her head, she rose onto her toes and kissed him right back.

Because she'd spent the last two years with Mateo, kissing Tommy felt foreign, illicit, and sexy in the way only bad things can be.

"Tommy . . . ," she murmured, not realizing she'd said it out loud, until he whispered her name in the same breathless way.

Despite his efforts to continue, despite her desire to let him, something about the sound of her name on his lips snapped her back to reality.

She released herself from his grip and pressed through the crowd, torn between relief and annoyance that he hadn't tried to follow. That he simply remained inside the circle of writhing bodies, silently watching her go.

# NINETEEN

# WICKED GAME

Madison Brooks leaned against her ice-blue velvet headboard, watching Ryan slip into a pair of dark skinny jeans before handing over the smoldering joint that dangled from his lips.

She passed the joint under her nose. The scent reminded her of childhood, strangely enough, but then Madison's childhood had been stranger than most.

"It's not an incense stick, Mad. You're supposed to smoke it, not sniff it." Ryan returned with outstretched fingers and an unbuttoned shirt, revealing the eight-pack abs he worked hard to maintain. He hated when she didn't partake, couldn't stand for anyone to be sober if he wasn't.

Madison gladly gave the joint back, musing on what else Ryan might hate about her. Just how long was his list? Was it longer than the list she'd made of things she hated about him? Oddly, the idea didn't disturb her.

She stretched her legs out and nudged her foot against the rumpled sheets, remembering how the party they'd started outside had eventually found its way in. He certainly hadn't hated her then. And, if she was going to be honest, she hadn't exactly hated him. It was totally warped, but there was something about this darker, secret-keeping side of Ryan that made her want to keep him around a bit longer.

Whether it was because she was just competitive enough to want to end the relationship as the one who got away (as opposed to the one who grew so monotonous and boring he couldn't wait for her to go), or because she had a fascination for secrets and the way they dictated how people lived and the decisions they made—she couldn't say for sure.

Maybe it was a combination of both.

Maybe it was neither.

It wasn't like she was going to run her case by a shrink to have it professionally analyzed.

Madison was one of the few in Hollywood who didn't see a therapist. Most everyone she knew, from the most elite star to the lowliest gofer, relied heavily on their weekly therapy sessions, along with the mood-enhancing drugs their therapists prescribed. Aside from a few well-vetted people, Madison's secrets belonged only to her. Her childhood story was well documented by the press, and that wholly fabricated lie was the only version she intended to share.

Ryan sat on the edge of the bed, the joint wedged between his lips, as he tugged on his boots.

"What would happen if I took a picture of you and posted it on the net?" She reached for her phone, feeling dangerous, risky, willing to push every boundary.

He pinched the joint between his fingers and took a deep drag. "You wouldn't." He spoke in that pot smokers' breath-holding way that never failed to get on her nerves.

"How can you be so sure you can trust me?" She snapped a series of pics until he pitched the joint and pounced, his clothed body landing on top of her naked one.

"Because that would hurt you as much as it would hurt me." His gaze was direct. A bit sleepy and bloodshot, but direct all the same. That single look telling her he was well aware of the game they both played.

He reached for the phone and she swung it high over her head, grinning in triumph when he abandoned the quest and settled for kissing first her neck before working his way farther down.

He refused to stop until Madison melted beneath him. Then, grasping the phone from her hand, he deleted the pictures and said, "You smell like sex. Good sex." He grinned and pushed away.

"You smell like someone who's not afraid to play dirty." She frowned at the phone he'd abandoned by her side.

"You sure you don't want to come?" He returned to the mirror, ran his hands through his hair.

She slipped onto her side and plumped a pillow under her head. "I'd rather hang here, maybe sneak in a bubble bath."

He grabbed his wallet and keys, came around for one last toke before carefully snuffing the joint. "I'll miss you, Mad." He headed for the door.

"I have no doubt," she whispered, watching him leave as her phone chimed with an incoming call from a number she hadn't seen in a very long while.

She'd barely gotten to hello, when a male voice said, "We have a problem."

# TWENTY

# LIPS LIKE SUGAR

A self-satisfied grin crept onto Aster's face as she headed up the stairs, well aware that Ryan Hawthorne would follow. Of course he'd follow. He'd basically followed her directly from the Neiman Marcus shoe department to the Night for Night dance floor. It was the perfect way to end the first week.

She'd spotted him the moment he walked into the club—well, she and every other girl in the vicinity. Though unlike the rest of them, Aster breezed past, pretending not to notice or care.

Guys like Ryan were used to girls fawning all over them—happy to bask in the glow of a big-name celebrity while requiring nothing in return. While it was probably an ego boost for the guys, it was degrading for the girls.

If they were after a quick hookup so they could brag to their friends, then whatever, carry on. But if they were hoping it would result in something more (and Aster suspected most of them were), then that was their first major mistake. Nobody in the history of relationships ever wanted to be with the person who was too easy to get—or at least not for long.

Aster had managed to remain a virgin for as long as she had, not because of her parents' expectations (that had little if anything to do with it, not to mention, her virginity was a technicality at best), but because she held herself in such high regard she'd yet to find someone worthy of sharing such an intimate part of herself. Not that she thought Ryan Hawthorne was that person. For one thing, he had a famous girlfriend. For another, Aster desperately needed to not upset that very famous girlfriend if she had any hope of getting Madison to the club.

Still, there was nothing wrong with a little harmless flirtation. And what better way to drive Ryan crazy than to ignore him?

She reached the top of the landing when a cool hand circled her wrist, pulled her behind a pillar, and said, "I lost sleep wondering how this mystery might end. Would she buy the shoes—would she not?"

She lifted her gaze to meet his. "Do I know you?" She watched as he threw his head back and laughed.

"Are you always this big of a tease?" He angled closer until his face was just inches from hers. She could make out the sheen of stubble on his chin, see the individual amber flecks in his eyes. But it was the lips that really struck her—those perfect, pouty, endlessly photographed lips. She wondered what they'd be like to kiss.

"Where's Madison?" Her tone was sharper than intended.

"So you do know who I am."

"I know who your girlfriend is, but you and I have never actually met."

His laugh came easily. "Ryan. Ryan Hawthorne." He offered a hand.

"Aster Amirpour." She took his hand in hers, then quickly pulled away.

"Actually, Mad decided to stay in." He raked his fingers through his hair.

"So, why didn't you join her?"

A slow grin crept over his face. "I tried to be a good boy, but the mystery of the shoes had to be solved."

Aster's mind ran wild with all the different ways she could play it. Ryan Hawthorne had access to the world she desperately wanted to join, but she needed to keep her head and play it smart. She'd string Ryan along—he seemed to enjoy it—but not to the point of risking Madison's wrath.

She was glad Madison had stayed home. Sure, she needed

the get, but she was so far ahead of the game, there was no way she'd get cut. Besides, she'd lured Ryan Hawthorne to Night for Night; wasn't that triumph enough? Maybe he didn't count for as many points as Madison, but he was still at the top of the list, and if she could spend a little more time with him, she knew she could convince him to return, maybe next time with Madison.

"Shit." Ryan stepped away from Aster, putting more of a platonic distance between them. "Fans. And even worse, fans with camera phones."

Sure enough, word of his arrival had spread, and Aster was horrified to find her old private-school friends acting decidedly uncool for kids who'd grown up rich and privileged in Beverly Hills, where celebrity sightings were not a big deal.

"Hey, Aster!" they called, looking pointedly at Ryan.

She frowned, grasped his hand in hers, and led him back down the stairs and over to the Riad, Night for Night's private VIP area.

"So, you work here." He settled into a tented cabana as Aster drew the filmy curtains around them. "And here I thought you were the newest Victoria's Secret Angel."

She rolled her eyes and groaned. "Did you use that line on Madison too?"

He reached for the bottle of champagne chilling on ice, popped the top, and poured them each a glass. "Madison and I were introduced by our agents—it was all very romantic, I assure you." He leaned back against the cushions as Aster fiddled with the stem of her glass, unsure how to respond.

She was surprised by his openness, his unexpected level of honesty, not to mention his obvious fatigue regarding all things Madison. While she knew better than to believe anything she read in the tabloids, especially when it came to Hollywood's most buzzed-about power couple (if they weren't claiming a breakup was imminent, they were breathlessly searching for a baby bump every time Madison wore a flowy top), she was still shocked to hear him refer to their meeting in such a bored way.

Was Ryan already over her?

And if so, did Madison know?

Was that why she'd chosen to stay home?

And, more importantly, what did it all mean for Aster? Would she have to rethink her whole strategy, or—

"You know, you seem a little obsessed with Madison. It's the second time you've mentioned her."

Aster lifted her glass to her lips. He was right about that. She'd done an exhaustive amount of research. Had even made a folder full of pictures and interview clippings documenting her rise to the top. Madison was living the life Aster longed for, and Aster would do everything she could to emulate her, but it wasn't like she'd share that with Ryan.

"Just want to make sure you're not headed for trouble," she said, trying to find the balance between flirty and demure. "You know, sitting alone in this cabana with me."

"So, this is purely out of concern?"

She hesitated. He was smarter than she'd expected. He'd know if she lied. "Not entirely," she admitted. "I'm thinking Madison would make for one scary enemy. I'm determined not to find out either way."

He took a swig of champagne, then leaned so close he had to rest his hand on her knee to keep from falling into her lap. "Tell you what, no more Madison talk, okay? I'm sorry for the smarmy line I ran by you earlier. I'm embarrassed I tried. I can see you're no overeager groupie who will pretend to be charmed by whatever I say. Truth is, you intrigue me. And trust me when I say I did my best to stay away. Even tried to persuade Mad to join me for a nice romantic dinner, hoping it would keep me from doing something there's no turning back from—"

Before he could continue, Aster lifted a hand between them, halting his words. She needed him to slow down, needed them both to take a step back.

"I'm eighteen years old. I come from an area of Beverly Hills you might know as Tehrangeles, and I'd be under permanent house arrest if my family knew I was here, wearing these clothes and talking to you. I dream of being an actress, but it's proven impossible to catch a break. So I took this job hoping it'll help me live the life of my dreams as opposed to the life my parents have dreamed for me. Ira wants us to fill up the clubs, but if we can bring in celebrities, it counts more toward the win. And I'm telling you this because I already know about you since you're famous, but also because you're saying all kinds of complimentary stuff, when you don't know the first thing about me. Also, I figured you'd find out eventually and I didn't want you to think I was stringing you along, even though, admittedly, in the beginning, I was." She took a deep breath and clamped her lips shut. Fearing she'd gone too far when he cocked his head and narrowed his eyes.

"So, you were stringing me along in the beginning, and now?"

She paused; she'd already said too much. But with his green eyes boring into hers, he was impossible to resist. "Now I'm doing something I'll no doubt regret." She heaved a deep exhale, hardly able to believe she'd veered so far from her earlier vow, which had made better sense. She steeled herself for any reply he might volley, but she was wholly unprepared for the unexpected gentleness of the kiss that followed.

It was just one kiss. Soft. Warm. Over almost as quickly as it started. But the impression lingered.

He drew away and ran his fingers along the curve of her jaw, looking at her as though she was something both fragile and wonderful. "I'll tell you what, Aster Amirpour of Tehrangeles." His gaze glinted on hers. "If it helps you secure the win and live the life of your dreams, then I'll return as often as I can. I'll even bring Madison. But you have to remember when you see us together that nothing in this town is ever quite what it seems."

# TWENTY-ONE

# SUNDAY
# BLOODY SUNDAY

Layla woke with a raging headache, a soul stained with regret, and her father sitting on the edge of her bed, wearing an old paint-splattered Neil Young concert tee, looking unshaven, scruffy, but still handsome, while peering at her with concern.

"You okay?" he asked, his silver-streaked hair flopping into his eyes.

He seemed sincere, but she couldn't bear to face him, so she grabbed the extra pillow and held it over her head.

"Come on. None of that. I got you a treat." He tossed the pillow aside and handed her a cup of coffee from her favorite place down the street.

"I don't deserve a treat." She inched up the wooden headboard and took a small sip.

"I added a couple shots of tequila, you know—little hair of the dog—"

"You didn't!" She pushed the cup away, but her dad just laughed and pushed it right back. "You know you're not supposed to joke about that stuff." She reached for the aspirin and water he'd left on her nightstand. "And you're not supposed to help me feel better." She swallowed the aspirin and chased it with a big gulp of water, before returning to the coffee.

"Wikipedia claims otherwise."

She started to laugh, then instantly regretted it when it increased the pounding in her head. "You're supposed to lecture me, steep me in shame."

"Figured I could skip that part. You usually handle that just fine on your own."

She closed her eyes and fell back against the pillows, wishing she could rewind the last week and start over. In addition to all her bad decisions, of which there were many, she'd gotten drunk on tequila and kissed a boy she had no business kissing. What a train wreck she'd become.

Did that mean she was just like her mom?

Was the propensity for betrayal genetic?

She sincerely hoped not.

"So what happened? You try to outdrink all your gets? Is this an occupational hazard of working in a nightclub?"

She rolled her eyes. "I didn't have any gets."

"So who's Tommy then?"

Her eyes flew open. How did he know that name? But an instant later the memory bitch-slapped her smack in the brain.

She'd bolted to the bathroom right after that kiss, only to exit and find Tommy waiting to warn her Ira was there. Then he hauled her outside before Ira could see her.

"Tommy is—" She shook her head and shrugged, having no idea how to explain.

"Well, he got you home safely, so he can't be all bad."

He'd insisted on driving her bike, and for the first half of the ride she'd made fun of the way he handled it. The second half she asked him to pull over so she could hurl into the gutter. By the time they got to her door, she fumbled for her keys for so long Tommy took his chances on ringing the bell.

"Sorry we woke you," she said. It was the least of a long list of things she felt sorry about.

"Who said you woke me?" Her dad sipped his coffee. "I was in the studio. Working."

Layla brightened. At least one of them was taking positive steps in his life. "When can I see it?"

"Soon." He nodded, took another sip.

"Really?"

He shrugged unconvincingly and gazed out the window. "When it's ready. Meanwhile, I've got some interest from one of the bigger galleries. This could be the one that changes everything. Or at least it better be."

His jaw tensed with worry, causing Layla to study him with concern. It'd been years since he'd last sold a piece. And while it had fetched a high price, surely the money was close to running out by now.

She was about to ask him about it, but before she could get to it, he grinned and ruffled her hair.

"Hey—watch the head!" She playfully batted his hand. "Feels like I'm hosting a heavy metal band in there."

"Metallica or Iron Maiden?" His gaze narrowed as though he was trying to decide which would be worse.

"It's a metalpalooza, featuring Metallica, Iron Maiden, Black Sabbath . . . who'd I leave out?"

He made an exaggerated grimace. "You know what you need?"

"A time machine?"

"Yes." He nodded sagely, his blue eyes crinkling at the sides. "But until then, how 'bout I take you to breakfast. Something big, greasy, and loaded with trans fats."

"See, now you've just gone from being too soft on me to enabling me. It's a slippery slope, Dad."

"We'll discuss over breakfast. You can fill me in on the correct way to proceed when your daughter stumbles home drunk with a boy who's not her boyfriend." His gaze met hers. It was even sharper than his words.

"Looks like you got it down after all." She smiled wanly. "But I'm sorry I can't join you. I need to head out to a meeting so Ira can fire me."

Layla pulled up to Night for Night, wondering why Ira didn't just send the bad news via messenger. It would serve as a sort of poetic bookend to how the whole mess began. Well, at least they weren't meeting at Jewel. In her mind, the entire club was one gigantic crime scene she hoped never to revisit.

By the time she walked into the Moroccan-themed club, most everyone was there. She was five minutes early—they were probably ten. Yet another example of how poorly suited she was for the job.

She risked a quick glance at Aster, as perfect and prissy as ever in her short white tennis dress and long, glossy ponytail, and purposely avoided meeting Tommy's gaze. Though a quick head count told her Goth Boy was missing, and she couldn't help but hope his failure to show would count as a forfeit, allow her one more week to make up for the last.

But who was she kidding? She'd already been pegged as the first to go. Probably why they all looked so smug and relaxed, texting on their cell phones, or in Tommy's case, sprawling on one of the sofas, feet propped on an ottoman, taking a nap.

She needed to find another way to get to journalism school. Now more than ever a move out of state was imperative.

As luck would have it, Goth Boy slipped in seconds before Ira's swarm of assistants took their place before the contestants.

Layla found a vacant chair and sank into the cushions, looking lazy, insubordinate, but she was beyond caring. She just hoped they'd hurry up and fire her so she could get back on her bike and go on a nice, long, head-clearing ride. Laguna might be nice. And she could invite Mateo to join her. He'd like the surf, and they needed to spend some time together. . . .

". . . not surprisingly, Thursday night was our slowest night of the week."

When had Ira started talking? Layla forced herself to sit up straighter.

"Though there's no question the Night for Night team pulled in the most heads, mostly thanks to Aster Amirpour."

Layla fought back a smirk. Of course, Queen Bitch Aster got all the credit. Why was life so stinkin' unfair?

"Numbers at all three clubs steadily increased, culminating in last night, which saw the biggest draw yet. Each club managed to bring in decent crowds, but some more decent than others." He took a moment to gaze leisurely among them. Stupid sadist was enjoying himself. He'd probably drag it out for as long as he could, like he was the host of some dumb reality TV show.

"As you may know, the Vesper is the smallest of the three clubs, while Jewel is the largest."

*Well, there you have it. I never stood a chance. I was destined to lose from day one.*

"So the winners are decided on a percentage basis—which is to say we calculate the percentage based on club capacity versus absolute numbers. With that in mind, the winner for Saturday night is . . ."

There it was, the long pause Layla had been waiting for. She was surprised there wasn't a drumroll. Ira was so freaking dramatic.

"The Vesper."

Layla tried not to scowl as the Vesper crowd all virtually high-fived from their various corners.

"You guys have a bit of an underdog vibe, as the size of your crowd bears a direct correlation to the popularity of the bands that come through. That said, we've managed to book some solid summer acts, so I expect to see bigger and better numbers from here. Night for Night, you're second. You were close, but close isn't first."

There were eight people in the room all breathing easier. Layla wasn't among them. Still, maybe she should just close her eyes and take a little catnap like Tommy had. Surely they'd wake her in time to get sacked.

"Jewel was last." Layla popped an eye open long enough to see Ira addressing the Jewel team with a stern face. "If you don't pick it up, you won't stand a chance in hell of winning this competition."

Layla cringed. She couldn't help it. She made up one-fourth of their group, but she took 100 percent responsibility for the failure.

"I don't know what happened, but I suggest you figure it out."

So there it was, they'd been properly chastised. Now on with the public beheading!

"The club with the highest totals this week is the Vesper."

"But—" Aster nearly leaped from her chair.

Ira quirked a brow.

"But I brought in Ryan Hawthorne!"

"Ryan's not Madison. The get wasn't enough to overcome the Vesper's numbers."

Aster frowned. "Next time I'll get Madison," she mumbled, sinking back to her seat.

"My advice to you"—he stole a quick look at Aster—"to all of you, is not to get too comfortable. Rules can change on a whim. You need to be ready for whatever I throw at you. Now, on to the cut—"

Layla uncrossed her legs and ran her hands down the front of her dark skinny jeans. She should've made more of an effort on her appearance so she wouldn't so closely resemble the loser she was.

"Layla Harrison?"

The moment had arrived. She'd soon be the dead girl walking. Ira would do his best to embarrass her, of that she was sure. But it couldn't be any worse than the numerous ways she'd embarrassed herself last night alone. As soon as it was over, she'd be on her way, never have to see these people again.

"How you feeling?"

She shrugged, painfully aware of everyone openly staring.

"You helped yourself to a sizable amount of top-shelf tequila last night."

Layla rubbed her lips together, refusing to confirm or deny.

"Nothing wrong with knocking back a few, but not in the club when you're under twenty-one."

She grabbed her bag, ready to bail, when Tommy rose from the couch and said, "That was me, not Layla."

Ira shot him a shrewd look, while Layla stared incredulously.

"I was checking out the competition, not that there was any." He stole a glance at Layla, before returning to Ira. "Guess I got carried away."

The way Tommy stood before Ira, Layla couldn't help

but notice there was something markedly different about him. He wasn't doing this for her. This was about challenging Ira, daring the boss to fire him, all the while sure that he wouldn't. The silent standoff lingering for so long, everyone started fidgeting and shifting—everyone except Tommy, who stood his ground, making whatever incomprehensible point he was determined to make.

"Don't let it happen again," Ira finally said, his voice sharp, gaze unwavering. But Tommy just nodded and returned to his seat, as Ira turned his focus to Ash.

"The impressive numbers at Night for Night were no thanks to you. You pulled in maybe ten people max. We won't stand for that."

With the heavy eye makeup he wore, it was impossible to tell what Goth Boy might be thinking.

"You have anything to say for yourself?"

"No, man, just—thanks for the opportunity." He leaped from his seat and made for the door as Layla stared in confusion. Not understanding how she'd managed to survive another week. If Ira knew about the tequila, then clearly he knew her numbers were even worse than Ash's.

Whatever. She'd accept the reprieve for the gift that it was. Last night had marked her very last screwup.

A few minutes later, Tommy headed for the door as Layla rushed to catch up. "What was that about?" she asked.

He swung the door open, forcing her to shield her eyes

from the glare. Sometimes the incessant brightness felt like an assault. The forced cheeriness of three hundred and thirty days of sun was downright annoying. She'd give anything for just one rainy day.

"That was about me saving you. *Again*."

Layla shrank under his piercing blue gaze. As much as she dreaded bringing it up, she needed him to know she considered their kiss a mistake she would never repeat.

"Tommy, about—" she started to explain, but he spoke right over her.

"Forget it. It'll be our little secret."

She stood awkwardly before him, wanting to believe it, not sure that she could.

"As for what happened in there—" He hooked a thumb toward the club. "I'll let you know when I'm ready to collect on the favor."

"Excuse me?" She ran after him. "I don't remember asking you to do that. I was ready to pay the price."

"Clearly." He shook his head. "You didn't even put up a fight. So I took a swing for you."

She was afraid of the answer, but forced herself to ask the question anyway. "Why?"

His gaze roamed hers, studying her for an uncomfortable moment before he finally conceded, "I have my reasons. And now, because of it, you have a second chance to decide what you really want out of life."

She watched him slide behind the wheel of his car, wanting to shout some nasty retort, knowing she should thank him instead, and settling on neither.

And now, she owed him. Great. She could only imagine what he'd ask in return.

# TWENTY-TWO

# GHOST IN THE MACHINE

"How did this happen?"

Madison sat in the passenger seat of a dark-green SUV, tugging at the brim of her worn baseball cap and staring out the windshield at a landscape marred by cargo ships, brightly colored rectangular containers, and tall working cranes. Everything about the meet was designed to go unnoticed. The car was ordinary. The San Pedro port was too busy for anyone to question them, and if they did, Paul had the credentials to make them go away. Then there was Paul himself and his utterly forgettable face. It was one of the things that made him so good at his job: no one ever remembered seeing him, and it was nearly impossible to describe him.

"You told me—no, correction, you *assured* me—that

everything from my past was sealed, locked up tight, and safely stored in a deeply buried vault with no key."

He nodded, his pale eyes scanning the harbor. "I've recently come to think otherwise."

She sighed. Sank so low in her seat she could barely see past the dashboard. She had obligations, loads of press, a movie to promote, an impending breakup with Ryan that would inevitably become very public no matter how hard she tried to keep it under wraps. She didn't have time for problems. Not of this magnitude.

"How do you know it's not just another bogus attempt to extort me? You know how fame attracts opportunists." She studied him closely. The face that had once rescued her, changed her life in ways she could never repay, was now delivering the worst news he possibly could.

"This is different." He pressed his lips together until they practically disappeared, making her wonder who this moment was harder for, him or her. Paul prided himself on meticulous attention to detail. But if he really did slip, the life Madison had worked so hard to create would burn as quickly as her previous life had.

"How different?" She shifted in her seat, taking in his beige hair, beige skin, thin pale lips, unobtrusive nose, and a small set of milky brown eyes. He certainly lived up to his nickname, the Ghost. Though she mostly called him Paul.

Without a word he handed her a photo of herself as a very young girl.

Madison gripped it by its edges, making a careful study of the tangled hair, the dirt-smudged face, the blaze of defiance burning in those bright, determined eyes. A long-lost *before* picture in a life meticulously cultivated to consist entirely of *afters*.

Until now.

Her hands trembled, as she tried to remember who'd taken it—how old she might've been. Talk about a ghost. It'd been years since she'd seen that version of herself.

"I thought everything was burned in the fire." She turned to him.

It was the tragic explanation used to defend Madison's lack of baby pictures, or any other remnant of a life before her parents' death. The story had been fed to the press so many times it'd become almost mythical. An eight-year-old girl who managed to escape a terrible fire with barely a scar, only to rise from the ashes like a phoenix, reborn, wiped clean, delivered into the next glorious phase of her life.

She absently ran the edge of the photo against the scar on her forearm, remembering that day when she'd grabbed a piece of smoldering wood and held it to her own flesh while Paul looked on in astonishment. "It's to make it more believable," she'd said, knowing even back then she'd be playing a part from that moment on.

"Everything *was* burned." His tone was grim. It was probably the worst thing he could've said.

If someone had pictures of her, there was no telling what else they might have.

"There's no mistaking it's me." She looked at Paul. For the first time in a long time, she feared for her life.

He sighed, gripped the wheel tighter. "Here's what you're going to do."

She waited for the formula that would make it go away, willing to do anything to put an end to the nightmare.

"You're going to go about your life, and alert me to the first sign of anything unusual."

She turned on him. So incensed she thought she might spontaneously combust in her seat. "Nothing about my life is usual. I wouldn't even know how to recognize *un*usual."

"You know what I mean."

She frowned. Up to this point, she'd trusted him implicitly, but even the Ghost had his limits. "What I know is I'm not going to sit around and wait for this to destroy me."

She shook the picture in his face, and he plucked it from her fingertips. "Have I ever failed you?"

She studied him a good long time. "You just did."

He squinted, stared at the quilt of scars covering his knuckles. "If you're worried about people letting you down, you should take another look at your boyfriend."

She gazed out the window, watching a crane load a container onto a ship. Maybe she should crawl inside one of those large metal boxes, sail away to some exotic port, start a new life under a new identity, and Madison Brooks would disappear off the face of the earth. She'd already played that card once, and it'd worked out far better than expected. But now, it was just another fantasy that would never be realized. There was nowhere to hide for someone as famous as her.

*Or was there?*

"Ryan's stepping out with a girl named Aster Amirpour." He reached into the backseat and handed over a fat dossier, detailing nearly everything about the poor dumb girl's life.

"I know all about it." Madison shrugged. Suddenly feeling sorry there wasn't a single person she could trust. "You're not the only one on my payroll," she said, reading the surprised look on his face.

She opened the door and started to head back to her car, when Paul called her by the name her parents had given her.

"Be careful out there."

She frowned, shaken by the sound of that name on his lips. "Just do your job and I won't have to," she said, slipping behind the wheel and driving away.

# TWENTY-THREE

# SUICIDE BLONDE

## BEAUTIFUL IDOLS

**Heartbreaker**

So you know that beautiful, truly sensitive soul* we all
fell for in last month's ten-hankie weeper? Turns out, he's
an idiot. I know, I'm just as shocked as you. At this very
moment I'm ripping his posters off my bedroom walls, and
when I'm done burning the pillowcase with his face on it, I'm
changing my Twitter icon back to a pic of my cat. Maybe
after reading this, you'll consider doing the same.

In a recent interview with a splashy mag this blogger
*j'adores*, this is how Prince Not-So-Charming described his
idea of the perfect girl:

*"A girl who will watch you play video games for four hours, and then have incredible sex with you—that's the girl you should date."*

For those of you thrilled to just sit back and watch while your boy fiddles with his joystick for hours on end, I've got just the guy for you!

For the rest of us with a brain, standards, and a desire to play our own game, let's all take a vow to stop making dumb people famous, k?

*The first ten peeps who correctly guess the name of this week's horny but clueless celebutard win a place on the guest list at Jewel this coming weekend. Spill it in the comments!

Layla frowned as she skimmed her post. The story was secondhand, gleaned from a fashion mag. Not the kind of writing she envisioned when she'd decided to strike out on her own. But how was she supposed to go after the celebrities who'd started frequenting Jewel? Now that she was writing for her own blog, she couldn't exactly trash them when she needed them to help her stay in the game.

As for the exposé she promised Mateo—the sordid nightclub scene he'd warned her about proved to be nothing more than a bunch of kids, some famous, some not, all trying to enjoy their weekends and have a good time. Not exactly a crime.

Her phone chimed as Mateo's gorgeous face appeared on the screen.

"Y'almostdone?" He spoke so quickly the words ran together.

"Still working." She sipped her latte and scowled at her laptop.

"We need to be at the restaurant in twenty."

Layla squinted, having no idea what he was talking about.

"Valentina's birthday," he said, addressing her silence. "I guess you forgot."

She closed her eyes. Guilty as charged.

When she failed to confirm either way, he said, "You're still going, right?"

She sighed, hating what she was about to say. "You know I have to be at Jewel."

"What I know is you promised Valentina you'd go to her party."

Had she really done that? Probably. From the moment she'd gotten drunk and kissed Tommy, she'd agreed to almost everything having to do with Mateo or his family.

"That was back when I thought I was getting fired," she admitted.

"Well, you explain that to Valentina. She's going to be crushed."

Layla rolled her eyes. She was getting tired of his guilt

trips. "Laying it on a little thick, don't you think? All her friends will be there—she won't even notice I'm missing."

"I'll notice. My mom will notice. And in case *you* haven't noticed, my sister idolizes you."

"Well, maybe that's her first mistake." Layla angrily crushed the sides of her still-half-full cup. She should apologize. Take it all back. But part of her was daring Mateo to call her on her crap. She certainly deserved it for bailing on Valentina, never mind for the things he didn't know about.

"You know, you're only a couple weeks into this job and it's already happening—you're changing and you can't even see it."

She frowned. "Pretty sure the blog I just wrote proves I'm hardly the celebrity worshipper you accuse me of being."

"Maybe not, but you're so focused on that world, you're losing sight of the people who matter."

"That's not true, I . . ."

Her voice faded. Madison Brooks had just walked up to the counter and was placing her order.

She'd heard Madison worked out at a nearby gym and often dropped in for a post-workout caffeine hit. Luckily, Layla's decision to change her writing venue and hang around long enough to down three lattes had paid off. It was better than joining the gym and stalking her in a spin class.

"I gotta go," she mumbled, ending the call as she stared

at the back of Madison's head, knowing she had to act fast.

So far, no one had been able to secure her as a get, mostly because she was so hard to reach. But as Layla watched Madison wait for her order, minus the usual entourage, bodyguards, and overall fuss that usually surrounded her, there was a good chance Layla might change all of that.

She shoved her laptop into her bag and pushed away from the table, watching as the barista called, "Iced skinny latte for Della!" and handed the drink to Madison as though she had no idea who her customer was.

Clutching the drink in one hand, and her wallet and keys in the other, Madison struggled to shoulder the door open as Layla jumped in to help her.

"Here, I got it," she said, as Madison shot her a cautious look. Her eyes widened in recognition—surprise?—Layla couldn't be sure. "Um—I couldn't help but hear her call you Della." Layla raced to catch up as Madison darted down the sidewalk. "But you're Madison, right? Madison Brooks?"

Madison shook her head, muttered something unintelligible under her breath.

"I mean, it's cool if you don't want to be noticed. I totally get it. It's just that—" Layla took a deep breath, struggled to keep pace. "I'm a huge fan," she lied, surprised when Madison stopped and fixed those bright violet eyes right on hers.

"Are you?" she asked, as though she knew better.

Layla watched as a yellow Lab trotted past, pulling a kid with matching hair riding a skateboard with a surfboard tucked under his arm. "Well, yeah." She cringed, knowing she didn't sound one bit convincing. Desperate to cover the flub, she said, "And I wanted to invite you to a party."

Madison shook her head, spun on her heel, and stormed down the street.

"Nothing creepy, I swear," Layla said, which only made it sound even creepier. God, she was totally blowing this. Why was she so freaking inept? "It's at Ira's. Ira Redman's."

Madison turned to face her. "If Ira wants to invite me to a party, he knows how to reach me."

Layla raised her hands in surrender. They'd gotten off to a bad start and she wanted, needed, to fix it before it got any worse. "Not at Ira's—at Jewel. One of Ira's clubs. I'm a promoter, and—"

Madison whirled on her, looking extremely annoyed. "Trust me, I know who you are. You're a small-time blogger who makes a living trashing celebrities." Her voice was raised. People were starting to gather.

"That's not true!" Layla called as Madison started moving again, racing past a succession of parking meters and palm trees, the usual LA landscape. "Well, maybe it's partly true, but—"

"Look—you need to back off!" Madison swung around

just as Layla tripped over an uneven slab of sidewalk, spilling what remained of her coffee down the front of Madison's white tank top.

"What the—" Madison stared down at the mess, then back at Layla, her violet eyes wide, her expression a mixture of disbelief and outrage.

"I'm so sorry— I—" Layla came at her with a crumbled napkin, wanting to help sop up the stain, but someone had already alerted security to the poor A-list celebrity being harassed by the crazy girl who wouldn't back off.

"There a problem here?" A big brick of a cop stepped out of a storefront and inserted himself right between them.

"What? No!" Layla cried.

At the same time, Madison claimed, "Yes. She's been following me for blocks. Won't leave me alone. And when I asked her to back off, she tossed her coffee on me."

The cop looked between the evidence dripping down the front of Madison's top, to the empty coffee cup in Layla's shaking hand.

"This true?"

"I wasn't stalking her!"

"Who said anything about stalking?" His eyes narrowed, as Layla shook her head and clamped her lips shut, refusing to say anything that might further incriminate her.

"You want to file a report?" The cop looked at Madison.

"Definitely." She turned those widened eyes on his, as

she clutched her hand to her heart like she somehow feared for her life. "You'll be hearing from my lawyers."

The cop nodded, watched her walk to her car. Once she was safely inside, he turned to Layla and said, "I'm going to need to see some ID."

# TWENTY-FOUR

# KNOW YOUR ENEMY

Madison grabbed her purse, slipped out of her car, and made for Night for Night, where she greeted the bouncer, James, and leaned in for a rare, sincere hug she reserved for a small list of people. She truly liked James. Sure, he was a little rough around the edges, but heck, there'd been a time when the same could be said of her. James was street-smart, a striver, not afraid to work hard by taking on a few extra assignments, and he was fiercely loyal to those who were fiercely loyal to him—all qualities Madison admired.

She tipped onto her toes and whispered into his ear. "Is she here?"

He nodded. "But so far, Ryan's a no-show."

"Oh, he'll show." Madison peered over his shoulder,

squinting to get a better look inside the club. "You'll alert me when he does?"

"You know it."

"Also, don't give her the credit for getting me here."

"Any preference?"

"Anyone but Aster." She kissed him on the cheek, discreetly slipped a wad of bills into his pocket, and made her way in. It was rare for her to go out alone, but her usual crowd would only distract her, and besides, she didn't plan to stay long.

She moved through the club. It was one of her favorites based on decor alone. She'd visited Marrakech once, and though the trip had been brief, she thought Ira had done a good job of capturing that exotic, luxe feel with all the copper lanterns, curved archways, and abundance of hand-painted tiles. Even the music they played was more languorous and mellow than most clubs, the slow, sexy beat just low enough so you didn't have to scream to have a conversation.

She looked all around, hoping Ira wasn't there. He'd waste no time trying to impress her with buckets of champagne and a spot at the best VIP table. He was always really gracious, bordering on ingratiating, and while she usually didn't mind, tonight she preferred to keep it low-key. She would've told James not to tell Ira she'd arrived, but she doubted he'd go along. She wasn't the only one he was fiercely loyal to.

Even though the club was crowded, Aster was easy to find. She was right there in the Riad, as Madison had figured. In spite of all the pictures she'd seen, she was still surprised to find the girl was exceedingly pretty. While there was no shortage of beautiful actresses in LA, Madison was convinced the intangible thing that made some more compelling than others had nothing to do with the tilt of a nose, or the sweep of cheekbones. It was the ability to inhabit a role so fully the flesh seemed to dissolve into the character's being.

For Madison, the ability to disappear was what drew her to the craft. And, ironically enough, the time had come for her to vanish for real. Paul would do what he could, but she no longer trusted him to keep her safe on his own, and she had no intention of sitting around, waiting for the threat to find her. Luckily, she'd delayed her breakup with Ryan. Turned out she needed him now more than ever.

Madison prided herself on possessing a level of insight that was rare for someone her age. Her ability to read beyond the lines in a script and get to the absolute motivation behind every word, every action, was her greatest gift. And at that moment, watching Aster flirt with a producer who really should've been home with his wife and new baby, Madison sensed Aster's desperation, the insatiable need to be the star of every scene. Not exactly rare for an actor; they were known to be a needy, neurotic, insecure bunch, but unlike Aster, Madison had learned to rid herself of her baser emotions (or at least appear to), and desperation was the first to go.

A wisp of a grin caught Madison's face. If it was attention the girl wanted, then Madison would gladly provide. Though it would come at a price Aster wouldn't expect.

Madison watched in amusement as Aster's face transitioned from her charming, flirty, party-hostess expression to one of the absolute shock of finding Madison Brooks standing before her.

"Madison—hi!" Her tone was friendly, bubbly. And with her flawless olive complexion, glossy dark hair, enormous brown eyes with lashes so thick they didn't seem real though they most likely were, and the lithe, sinuous body of someone who was no stranger to dance class, she was even prettier up close and in person.

"I like your Sophia Websters." Madison motioned to Aster's embellished stilettos. There was no better friendship starter than a mutual love of overpriced shoes. And though they'd never be actual friends, their fates were now tied together in ways Aster could never foresee.

"Can I get you a table?" Aster beamed as though she could barely contain her excitement.

Madison glanced at her usual cabana. "I see my favorite is taken. . . ."

Aster blinked, once, twice, probably calculating the

amount of fallout she'd face by evicting the current occu-
pants to make room for Madison. Wisely deciding against
it, she said, "I'm so sorry. Had I known you were stopping
by . . ."

Madison waved a hand in dismissal, favoring Aster with
a grin like they were long-lost friends. "How could you
have known?" The grin faded as she allowed the question
to linger between them.

For a few startled moments Aster truly did resemble the
cliché of a deer caught in headlights. Then just as quickly,
the panic eased from her face and she said, "I have another
great table I think you'll really like. And I can have your
favorite champagne sent right over. Dom Pérignon rosé,
right?"

Madison nodded. The girl had done her homework.
Though if anyone had ever bothered to observe a little
closer, they would've noticed Madison rarely drank from
the bottomless glasses of champagne the clubs continuously foisted on her. That was where her entourage came
in. They provided the perfect distraction to the sober truth
that Madison wasn't quite the partier she pretended to be.

She followed Aster to a table along the terrace's perim-
eter, all the while studying her like Aster was a character
she might someday portray. She'd already seen all of Aster's
vitals on paper—home address, family net worth, the private schools and country club memberships—but to truly

understand Aster, Madison needed to observe her in person. It was imperative to know exactly who she was dealing with if she was going to allow Aster to play such a big role in her life.

Hollywood breakups were tricky. They came second only to the breathless vigil the tabloids kept over baby bumps and celebrity weddings. A split between actors had the power to boost or destroy a career—it all depended on how the story was spun.

Usually, a cheating scandal looked very bad for the cheater. But there were definitely cases where the tabloids turned on the victim, painting him or her to be so awful the cheater was automatically forgiven the discretion. However it played, one thing was sure: if the other person worked outside the industry, then they usually wasted no time trying to elevate themselves by selling their side of the story, attempting to make the leap from a virtual nobody to a permanent place in the spotlight. Of course, once a new scandal came along, they were quickly forgotten—but that didn't stop them from trying.

When news of Ryan and Madison broke, there would be no shortage of magazines willing to cough up some cash to anyone with info on the split. And after seeing her in person, Madison was convinced Aster wouldn't hesitate to make a grab for whatever fleeting shot at fame she could get.

From everything she'd gleaned so far, Aster was raised to be a good girl, and a scandal like that would rock her whole family.

Then again, Aster's dream of fame and fortune was apparently so strong she was willing to take a job her parents most likely did not approve of.

Who knew what else she was capable of?

Or just how far she'd go to get what she wanted?

It was that bottomless hunger that Madison was counting on.

She watched as Aster expertly popped the cork and filled a glass she then placed before Madison. "Can I get you anything else?" She smiled expectantly.

Madison was about to reply, figuring it might be fun to send the girl on an impossible errand, when her phone buzzed with a text from James, alerting her that Ryan had just walked through the door.

Madison waved her hand distractedly. She waited for Aster to leave before she texted James a quick thanks and slipped out without being seen.

# TWENTY-FIVE

# SHADES OF COOL

When Madison Brooks walked into the Vesper, not a single person noticed. The lights were dim, the band was in the middle of a raucous set, and the crowd was so focused on the music, no one bothered to check out the high-profile celebrity who seemed perfectly content to lean against the back wall, completely unseen.

When the band left the stage for a break, Tommy edged through the crowd, taking a mental inventory of all the faces he recognized as his gets when he spotted an image so inexplicable his first thought was that it was some kind of joke. Maybe even a look-alike. But when Madison centered her gaze right on his, and her beautiful face curved into a slow, flirtatious grin, well, he'd seen enough magazine covers and billboards to recognize the real thing when it was standing before him.

He glanced around the room, searching for the other promoters, wanting to be sure they hadn't seen her, since it didn't even occur to him she might've been there because of them. Determining they hadn't, he closed the few steps between them, all the while wondering how to address her—*Madison? Ms. Brooks?*—before finally settling for a casual, "Hey."

She tilted her head, allowing her hair to sweep past her cheek as she inspected him from behind the veil of loose strands.

"What'd you think of the band?" He hooked a thumb toward the stage, desperate to engage her.

"From what little I heard, they were good." She pushed her hair back behind her ears, highlighting those magnificent cheekbones, the gold and turquoise hoops, but none of it could compete with those deep purple/blue eyes that roamed his.

"You just get here?" Surely he would've noticed had she arrived earlier. Then again, when he wasn't partying with his gets, he was dreaming of the day he'd be onstage. He could've easily missed her.

Her lips tugged at the sides, forming a sort of half smile that rendered her so unbearably beautiful he thought his heart would melt in his chest. She lifted her slim shoulders into a shrug, but otherwise stayed quiet. She also didn't try to leave, so he had that on his side.

"Can I get you a drink? Someplace to sit?" Instantly chiding himself the moment the words were out for sounding so overly eager to please. Then again, *Madison Brooks was standing directly before him!* It was amazing he could even form a sentence in her magical presence.

"Yes to both," she said, that simple statement enough to inspire a million fist pumps in Tommy's head. "But not tonight. Maybe some other time when it's not so crowded."

"It's usually pretty crowded." Tommy's face broke into a humble-brag grin. "We've got the best live acts in town. But I can reserve whatever table you want."

"I know about your contest."

Tommy gaped, unsure what to say.

"You're the only one who hasn't stalked me, either on Insta, Twitter, or even in person. That kind of thing usually brings out the worst in people, but not you."

Tommy shrugged, tried to play it cool. "Didn't seem like you'd respond to any of those things, so I focused on quantity instead."

"Looks like it's working." Her gaze bounced around the club before returning to him. "Too bad Layla and Aster didn't share your strategy. Those two are the worst. You can tell them I said so."

"I'll pass," Tommy said, suddenly glad he'd never strategized with Layla. Because of it, he'd scored Madison.

Madison's gaze softened, she lifted a hand to his cheek, and for one brief moment allowed her fingers to move over his skin as though discovering something, or maybe even remembering something, it was impossible to tell. If Madison Brooks wanted to wander into his club and fondle his cheek, it wasn't his place to question her motives.

Though she had a reputation for being a big-time party girl, her gaze was sober and clear, yet there was something about the depth of her focus that made it seem like she was looking right through him to some other place.

"You're not from here." Her hand fell from his cheek.

Tommy shook his head. He was mesmerized. She was everything he'd expected—poised, pretty, not at all getable— and the exact opposite of what he assumed—open, authentic, deep.

"Let me guess—you came here to chase your dream of fortune and fame?" She cocked her head as her eyes glinted mischievously.

Tommy shot her a sheepish look and buried his hands deep into the front pockets of his jeans, suddenly reduced to yet another LA cliché.

She looked around the room. "I like this place. No one gives a shit that I'm here. You have no idea what a relief that is."

"Oh, but I do." Tommy grinned. "I'm here every day and no one ever gives a shit."

She laughed in a way that made the joke seem funnier

than it was, leaving Tommy to wonder if she was serious, or maybe just acting. The whole thing was confusing as hell. All Tommy knew for sure was that he'd never seen anything more beautiful than Madison Brooks enjoying a spontaneous laugh, whatever the reason. From the moment it happened, Tommy was hers to command.

The band returned and began a new set. The sudden burst of sound prompted Tommy to look toward the stage, only to return to Madison and discover she'd left.

He chased after her, which was not at all cool, but it wasn't like that stopped him. "There's still another set!" he called, but she was already gone, leaving Tommy to make a frantic grab for his cell and snap a photo of her retreating form. He needed evidence to prove it really had happened, as much for Ira as for himself.

When he could no longer see her, he touched the place on his cheek where her fingers had been, wishing he'd at least taken the time to shave, while simultaneously feeling bad for having misjudged her as yet another high-maintenance bitch who was way out of his league.

She might be out of his league, but after having met her and actually spoken to her, he had the sense there was more to Madison Brooks than he'd thought. He imagined them kicking back with a beer, riffing on their individual philosophies of life. From what he'd seen, it seemed entirely possible.

# TWENTY-SIX

# SHOW ME WHAT I'M LOOKING FOR

Layla hovered near her most important table of gets, making sure they had plenty of drinks, cell phone chargers, and whatever else they might need. She'd basically been reduced to a professional party fluffer for low-level celebrities, but a few of them had made Ira's list, so there was that to consider.

One thing was sure—she could remove Madison Brooks from her list, since Madison wouldn't be stopping by anytime soon. Still, despite the cop's dire warnings, Madison had never gotten around to filing a complaint, which gave Layla free rein to go after her on her blog every chance she could get.

When she wasn't bashing Madison, she was using her blog to promote Jewel, and it had made all the difference.

She'd also contacted Hollywood's top managers and publicists, letting them know their clients had a permanent spot on her guest list, and her dad had a friend who owned a trendy boutique in Santa Monica who was willing to offer some nice tie-in discounts. The kind of stuff she should've done from the start.

With the colored lights swirling overhead, and the music seeming to pulse against her skin, it was like being inside a kaleidoscope. Funny how quickly she'd gone from hating everything about her job to looking forward to the time she spent at the club. If nothing else, her nights at Jewel provided a nice respite from the outside world and the more stressful parts of her life, namely the growing tension between her and Mateo.

"The models are here!" Zion brandished a bottle of top-shelf vodka, grinning in a way that made it hard to tell if he was gloating or sharing. Though where he was concerned, it was one and the same. He modeled part-time (when he wasn't at the club, or waiting tables), and he'd managed to cut a deal with his agency that brought in the hot, young demographic Ira was after. Good for Jewel, not necessarily good for her.

She smiled tightly and showed him the text that had just come through. Ryan Hawthorne was back at Night for Night. The constant updates from Ira's assistants were simultaneously annoying and addicting.

"Bitch." Zion scowled, as Layla quirked her brow.

"More like Queen Bitch," she snapped, watching Zion make for his table of thirsty models.

She lingered near the edge of the sleek, white leather sofas that gleamed in alternating, vibrant jewel tones cast from the colored lights overhead, waiting for just the right moment to pounce. It was amazing how careless those silly starlets became after a few drinks. The cell phones they left lying around had given Layla access to all manner of juicy photos and texts she had no problem exploiting.

Her insider access had already paid off in a major surge in ad revenue. If things continued, she could easily pay for journalism school through her blog profits alone. Sure, the comments section was getting a bit vitriolic, but who cared? The numbers were the only thing that mattered, and the numbers never lied.

She ran her hands down the front of her tight black leather minidress—a recent investment paid for with blog money. She'd never intended to spend it on anything as banal as clothes, but the best way to gain the confidence of her gets was to emulate them. At first it made her uncomfortable, and between the sexy new clothes and platinum-blond highlights, she felt like an imposter. But the new angled layers did give her hair an edgy feel that suited her, and weren't the clothes really just a slightly girlier version of her usual look? Whatever. There was no denying it worked.

"I think my phone charger's broken!" one of the starlets whined, acting like it was the worst thing that had ever happened, and maybe it was. Layla had never met a more entitled, spoiled group.

She tried to determine who out of the whole rotten crew had said it. Her gaze centered on Heather Rollins, a B-list TV star with a major fixation on all things Madison Brooks. She was glaring at Layla as though she was personally responsible. Which she was, but there was no way Heather could've known that Layla always switched off at least one of the chargers each night. It might have been overkill, but so far, it had worked. And as much as she disliked Heather (she was hands down the worst behaved of them all, which was really saying something), for whatever reason, tonight the dice had landed on her. Layla considered it a windfall.

She topped off Heather's drink and fumbled with the switch she'd turned off earlier as though trying to fix it.

"How long is this going to take? We all want to dance."

"I'll have it working by the time you get back."

Heather swung her long blond hair over her shoulder and glared. "It better be." She watched her friends leave, then purposely unlocked the screen. Her pink glossy lips widening into a conniving grin as she slid the phone toward Layla.

Layla glanced between Heather and the phone.

Was Heather onto her?

"There's some new pics you might like." Heather's brown eyes shot Layla a knowing look. "Also, be sure not to miss the latest text from my assistant." Layla stared, dumbfounded, watching her go, as Heather glanced over her shoulder and said, "I help you—you help me. Feel free to send yourself whatever you need."

She merged into the crowded dance floor, as Layla scrolled through the phone before it could return to lock mode. She counted so many photos of Madison it seemed kind of creepy. Especially since it was obvious Madison wasn't aware of being photographed. Still, she moved through them quickly, zeroing in on a series of Madison and Ryan in a restaurant. One with them both at the table with a strange middle-aged man taking pictures in the background, one with Madison walking away as that same man approached Ryan, and the next with the man getting what looked like an autograph from Ryan while staring after Madison. They were weird, sure, though she wasn't sure why Heather had bothered to keep them. Still, she sent them to herself anyway along with another one so incriminating, the blog post was practically writing itself.

The texts were next. The one from her assistant included a pic of Ryan and Aster.

*So that's how Aster did it.*

She forwarded the pic to herself and left the phone charging. Apparently Heather loathed Madison as much as Layla did. And now, thanks to her, Layla's blog was about to go viral.

# TWENTY-SEVEN

# BACK DOOR MAN

Ira sat behind his desk and pushed another cash-filled envelope toward her. "Seems like Ryan's becoming a regular." His brow lifted. "I'd say that deserves a reward, wouldn't you?"

Aster stared hard at the envelope, feeling hollow, shaky, and more than a little nauseated.

Madison knew about her and Ryan.

Not that there was anything to know, or at least not exactly, but one thing was clear—Madison Brooks was onto her.

The way Madison had looked at her and purposely sought her out—there was no other way to explain it.

Funny how she'd gotten everything she'd wanted, only to realize she was in way over her head.

"Heard Madison dropped by too. Strange how she left just when Ryan arrived. You know anything about that?"

Aster frowned and examined her nails.

"Anyway, keep it up and you'll have a real shot at winning this thing."

She smiled faintly, eager for the meeting to end.

"Not quite the reaction I expected."

She shook her head, hoping to clear it, but it proved an impossible task.

Would Madison go after her?

Get some kind of revenge for inadvertently stealing her guy?

The only thing she knew for sure was she needed to get out of her head and back in the room.

"I'm sorry. I guess I just spaced. . . ."

What was she thinking? No one spaces on Ira Redman!

"I mean, I don't consider it done until it's done," Aster said, returning to where she'd thought they'd left off. "Celebrities are fickle. They can turn on a dime. And we still have many weeks left."

*Celebrities are fickle. They can turn on a dime.*

She just hoped one celebrity in particular didn't turn on her.

Ira regarded her for a long, uncomfortable moment. Luckily, Aster knew better than to fill the silence with needless chatter, though she was never quite sure exactly what Ira expected. Whatever it was, she hoped it wasn't tied to the money he'd been giving her.

"Get some rest," he finally said. "Have James walk you to your car."

She nodded, pausing just shy of the door. "Ira—"

He glanced up from his phone.

"Thanks for the . . . recognition." She waved the envelope before him. "I really do appreciate your recognizing my hard work." She cringed at the redundancy, but she needed to make it clear that in her mind the money was a bonus for her efforts and nothing more was required of her.

He waved a hand in dismissal, and she made her way through the club, only to find Ryan waiting by the back door.

"I told you not to wait." She frowned in annoyance. Yes, he was gorgeous and famous and his attention was flattering. And yeah, there was a good chance she was starting to like him, but that was never part of the plan. He was supposed to help her make the right connections, maybe even win the competition, but lately, she'd drifted wildly off course.

Aster wasn't the kind of girl who went after another girl's guy, and the idea of stealing Madison Brooks's guy was completely unthinkable. Some girls might consider it a victory to score a famous guy away from an even more famous girl, but Aster didn't see it that way. It made her feel guilty. And the way Madison had looked at her made her feel skanky.

"I wanted to see you to your car." Ryan swiped a hand through his hair and flashed that irresistible grin.

"I have James for that." She sounded prim and spoiled in a way that reminded her of Madison. "Besides, you were with me all night." She stepped through the back door and pressed into the chilly night air, hugging her arms at her waist to keep from shivering.

"I wanted more."

She leaned against her car door, letting it support her. "And Madison?" She looked right at him.

"I heard she left. I have no idea why."

"You sure about that?" She wanted him to admit he'd gone too far, crossed a line. At the same time she hoped he'd convince her that all was well, that whatever she was worried about existed only in her own paranoid head.

He scratched at his jaw, watching a stream of cars driving up and down the boulevard. "I'm pretty sure Madison doesn't give a shit what I do."

Aster studied him closely. That was the last thing she'd expected. "So why are you still together?"

Ryan, frowned, glanced around the small, mostly vacant parking lot, then back at her. "It's . . . complicated."

"I don't do complicated." Her voice was drowsy, not just because of the late hour but also the confusing world she now occupied.

"I said Mad and I are complicated." He moved closer, so close she could feel his breath on her cheek. "There's nothing complicated about you and me." The smile that followed was impossible to resist. And when he leaned in to kiss her, she did nothing to stop him.

He'd kissed her before, but never like this. She could feel the depth of his reverence in the way he held her, the way his tongue slid against hers, the way his hands tenderly cupped her cheeks.

"Aster . . ." He pressed his forehead to hers. "I'll handle Madison. But you have to know you're driving me crazy. I can't stop thinking about you."

It was all the right words said in all the right ways, and when he reclaimed the kiss, his hands gripped her hips and crushed them hard against his. A low, rumbly sound came from deep in his throat as his fingers crawled along the inward curve of her waist, inching toward her breasts, which seemed to swell in his hands. His thumbs tracing delirious circles, his breath warm in her ear, he whispered, "Aster, come home with me, *please*."

"No." It took all her will, but she somehow managed to push him away. Flustered and breathless, she tapped the door handle, eager to escape, only it didn't unlock. *Damn!* She shoved a hand in her bag and fumbled for her key fob, all too aware of the way her breasts ached for his touch, the way her hips longed to melt against his. She hadn't meant to let things progress so quickly. But Ryan was so sexy, and sometimes being a virgin was a burden. Still, there was no way she was sleeping with him. Or at least not tonight.

"No?" He moved until she could feel him pressing hard at her back.

She took a steadying breath, located the key fob, and opened the door. "No." She pulled away, angled her body onto the seat, where she could finally catch her breath. "I know it's not a word you're used to hearing, especially when it comes to asking girls to have sex with you." Her eyes met his, might as well put it out there. "But I'm not going home with you. It's been a long night, and I just want to go to bed. My bed. Alone."

He knelt beside her, that face, those lips just inches from hers. "You're killing me, Aster!" He reached for her cheek, ran the tip of his finger around the curve of her ear.

"So you tell me." She pushed him away, overcome with relief when he smiled good-naturedly and leaped out of her way.

She closed the door between them and pulled onto the street, glancing into her rearview mirror to see he was still standing right where she'd left him, watching her go.

How much longer would he be willing to wait?

Would he last the summer?

Or would he burn out in a week and never return?

The choice was his. All she could do was wait and see.

# TWENTY-EIGHT

# WORK B**CH

Layla parked Mateo's Jeep just behind Aster's Mercedes, scrolling through the comments left on her blog, as she waited for Aster to finish admiring herself in her rearview mirror.

Just as expected, the story she'd written, based on one of Heather's photos of Madison's face hovering suspiciously close to a tabletop, was a hit. The comments section almost evenly divided between Madison worshippers who refused to believe it, and Madison haters who'd suspected all along. Though it was starting to lean toward the latter.

In the end, it didn't matter what the majority thought. The seed had been planted, and Madison deserved nothing less.

## BEAUTIFUL IDOLS
### Snow Angel

I don't know about you, but I can't think of anything sadder than the picture that follows. Either that tabletop is rocking an irresistible winter-fresh scent—Madison Brooks has a serious case of undiagnosed narcolepsy—or, more likely, America's sweetheart has just hoovered up a nostril full of nose candy. . . .

Aster's door closed with a *thunk*, prompting Layla to shove her phone in her bag and scramble out of the Jeep to catch up. Determined to reach Aster before she went inside Jewel, Layla called for her to stop, only to watch Aster roll her eyes and keep going.

"Heard you had a good night last night." Layla moved alongside her, knowing she'd clinched it when Aster paused, waiting for Tommy, Karly, and Brittany to wander inside before facing her.

"What do you want?" She placed a hand on her hip, tapped her foot against the sidewalk. Trying to come off as haughty and cool, but there was a crack in the veneer, and it was about to get worse.

"I'm ready to collect." Layla kept her tone friendly. No need to alarm her just yet. Watching as Aster shifted from cool to irritated in a handful of seconds. "Don't tell me you've already forgotten our deal. The one where you sold your soul for a chance to promote Night for Night."

"So you're confirming you really are Satan. I'm sure that will come as a surprise to absolutely no one." Aster shook her head and waited for Zion and Sydney to go in before she continued. "Look, can we settle this later?"

"I'm sure Ira won't mind if his prize pony's late." Layla studied Aster's perfectly made-up face, her shiny hair, her ridiculously long legs spilling out of a pair of pink shorts. She had that wealthy, privileged, well-tended look that Layla could never achieve even if she tried. And she wouldn't. But still.

"What's that supposed to mean?"

It wasn't meant to mean much of anything. But the way Aster's mouth twitched told Layla she'd hit a nerve she'd be sure to explore. "It means you're everyone's favorite, Ira included."

"Yeah, well, guess you wouldn't know about that. Seeing as how you have a gift for making enemies."

Layla grinned, deciding to humor her. It was one of the perks of having the upper hand. "Not everyone can be as popular and sought after as you."

Aster fiddled with the strap on her Louis Vuitton purse and gazed toward the door leading to Jewel. "Your point is?"

"I want you to bring Ryan Hawthorne to Jewel along with all his celebrity friends. And I want you to do it under my name."

"Um, okay." Aster tossed her hair over her shoulder and made for the club. "I'll get right on that!" She laughed as though Layla was joking.

"You can laugh, or you can consider."

"Reasonable requests will be considered. That request is beyond pathetic, even for you."

"Your choice." Layla shrugged, watching her go. "Guess I'll just have to send this pic of you and Ryan kissing to Perez Hilton, TMZ, Page Six, Gawker, Popsugar, Just Jared—have I missed anyone?"

Aster froze.

"Oh, of course!" Layla gave a cartoon slap to her forehead. "Madison Brooks! I bet she'd just love to know about this latest development."

Aster slowly faced Layla.

"Or, you can bring Ryan and his crew into Jewel and I'll forget I ever saw it."

"Where'd you get that?" Her face paled as she squinted at the image on Layla's phone. Starting to reach for it, when Layla yanked it away.

"Doesn't matter where I got it. Question is, what are you going to do about it?"

"This is blackmail." Aster's lips thinned into a tight, grim line.

Layla shrugged, watched as a group of tourists with a selfie stick posed with some old dude impersonating

Marilyn Monroe in a swingy white dress.

"And blackmail is illegal."

Layla grinned. "So sue me."

Aster rubbed her lips together, glanced longingly toward the door.

"You are a terrible person, you know that?"

Layla made for the door as Aster grabbed hold of her arm.

"Fine. I'll do what I can. But there's no guarantee."

"For your sake, there better be." Layla left the threat to dangle as she went inside and parked herself in the Vault next to Karly. She was relieved that Aster had fallen for the threat. Taking Madison down was one thing—she deserved it. And while Aster undoubtedly deserved it too, Layla felt queasy at the thought of going through with it.

Everyone was spread out among the white leather sofas, either napping or on their phones, though they all shared the same tired, stressed look. Two weeks into the competition and it was already taking a toll.

"Where's Ira?" Sydney got up from her seat and looked all around. "This is bullshit keeping us waiting."

"Shhh!" Brittney grimaced, as though Ira was listening, while Tommy remained with his eyes closed, catching some z's.

Annoyed, paranoid, and exhausted—Layla could relate to all three.

A moment later, when everyone's phones started to beep, Jin was the first to say, "It's Ira. He sent a video link."

"So now he fires us by video?" Sydney rolled her eyes.

"Fires you, not me." Karly smirked and hit Play the same time as Layla, watching Ira's face fill up the screen.

"I warned you I like to mix it up, which means today, two of you will get cut."

"But that'll cut the competition short!" Zion shouted, leaving Layla to wonder if he realized the video was pre-recorded.

"If you impress me next week, then maybe I'll make up for it by not firing anyone. Or maybe I'll fire three. Up to you whether or not you decide to impress me."

"Is he on a yacht?" Taylor brought her phone closer to her face, as Aster stared at her screen with a conflicted expression.

"I'm in a hurry, so let's make this quick," Ira said, his sunglasses reflecting a bikini-clad girl wielding the camera. "Vesper, you're in first place."

The Vesper crowd started to cheer, but they were quickly shut down by everyone else who wanted to hear.

"Night for Night second, which makes Jewel last. Again." He shook his head and frowned.

"No thanks to you," Karly muttered under her breath, glaring at Layla.

"Hey, I brought in Heather Rollins and her crew," Layla said in her defense.

"Did you bring her in, or hang by the door so you could claim her as yours?"

Layla rolled her eyes and focused on the video. "Diego, you scored Madison Brooks, well done."

"What?" Aster spun on her seat, shooting eye daggers at Diego, who looked momentarily stunned.

"Tommy, you too."

Aster looked like she was about to implode.

"Brandon and Jin—don't bother coming back. I doubt Jewel and the Vesper will miss you."

A second later, the screen went black.

No good-bye.

No *enjoy the rest of your weekend*.

Not even a gradual fade.

Layla had no idea why she had to show up for that, other than Ira was an asshole with serious control issues.

Still, he hadn't fired her, and now with Aster soon to deliver Ryan and his crew, she'd last another week for sure. After that, she'd have to come up with some other Hail Mary to save herself.

TWENTY-NINE

# GOLD ON THE CEILING

"Hey—" Tommy raced to catch up with Layla, who'd fled Jewel like the place was on fire. "Remember how you owe me that favor?"

Layla did a double take. It was like déjà vu, only this time she was on the receiving end. "Have you been talking to Aster?"

"What?" He squinted into the sun and walked alongside her.

She shook her head, slid on her sunglasses, and kept walking.

"I'm ready to collect."

She continued to ignore him.

"You know, this is how rumors get started," Tommy said. "Notice how no one's talking to each other anymore?

Freaks them out that we still are."

"You're the one talking. I'm just trying to get to my ride." Layla shook her head and made for the Jeep.

"Can't believe you already forgot about the time I saved your ass." Tommy looked at her.

"Can't believe you've forgotten you're not exactly innocent."

"Maybe so, but I handle it better." He regretted it the instant he said it, and quickly tried to recover. "Besides, you don't strike me as the type to go back on your word."

"I don't remember giving my word. You said, 'You owe me,' and I said nothing."

"You are seriously harsh."

"And this is news?"

"What does a guy have to do to get a ride home?"

"Well, for starters, you could just come out and ask as opposed to all this cryptic nonsense about deals we never struck." She propped open her door.

He laughed and climbed in beside her. "What happened to your bike?"

"My boyfriend and I made a trade."

So, she had a boyfriend. Not necessarily good news, but not exactly a roadblock either, considering the way she'd kissed him.

"He a surfer?"

"Why?" Layla pulled onto the street.

"'Cause the floorboards are coated in two feet of sand."

Layla shrugged and glanced in the rearview mirror. "So kick off your shoes and dream of Malibu. Meanwhile, where to?"

"Los Feliz." He dropped his backpack between his feet. "Though I warn you, my place is a dump."

"Well, it's not like I'm moving in."

He shook his head. She was feisty as hell, which was exactly why he liked her.

"So, will you play me your demo tape?"

Tommy looked at her in shock. He didn't remember mentioning his music.

"You are a musician, right?"

He nodded slowly.

Did he really look like some kind of wannabe rocker cliché?

Was he that pathetic?

"Can I hear it?"

Tommy hesitated. If she hated it, she'd tell him. But if she didn't hate it, the compliment would mean more than most.

"Just because I'm bad at charming people, as you say, doesn't mean I'm bad at reading them."

"I never said you—"

She waved it away. "The tape. I want to hear it. If for no other reason than it will save us from the slow, burning torture of small talk."

He slid the disc from his backpack and inserted it into the stereo. Holding his breath as the first strains of a six-string guitar filled the car. When his vocals kicked in, he thought he'd keel over from anxiety. Layla said nothing. And the few times he peeked, her expression was blank.

When the first song ended, she still hadn't spoken. Same went for the second and third. He was just about to beg her to put him out of his misery and give him the verdict—good or bad, either way he could take it—when she finally lowered the volume and said, "Your lyrics are amazing. Your voice is strong and distinctive. Your guitar playing—I'm assuming that's you on guitar?"

He nodded, barely able to breathe.

"You really slam that thing, which, I hope you take that as a compliment because it's meant as one."

"But . . ." There was always a *but*.

"But nothing." She shrugged, that simple statement bringing some of the sweetest relief he'd ever known. "It's all there. You've got a really strong foundation. It's like that car you drive. It's got all the makings of a classic; it just needs a little spit and polish and a fat wad of cash to push it over the edge."

He looked at her in wonder. It was a compliment delivered like a fact. Nothing effusive about it. No, *Ohmigod, Tommy—you are the most awesomeness!* like all the other girls had said, if only to get on his good side.

For that reason alone, Layla's compliment meant more to him than the opinions of anyone else who'd heard his music so far.

Ever since the contest began, his rock-star dream had taken a backseat as he became more and more determined to impress Ira through his business savvy. But as soon as it was over, he'd get back in the studio. Layla's comments confirmed it was a dream worth pursuing.

He could finally exhale.

When she cranked the volume and hit Repeat, choosing to spend the rest of the ride listening to his music, the compliment became even sweeter.

"Don't say I didn't warn you." Tommy paused before his front door, watching Layla roll her eyes in response. He was surprised she'd even agreed to come in. And though he wasn't sure what it meant, at the very least, he hoped they could find a way to be friends.

"I guarantee I've seen worse."

"Doubtful." He laughed but opened the door anyway. Trying to see his shithole apartment through Layla's eyes and cringing on her behalf.

She crossed the worn carpet to the other side of the room, aiming straight for his collection of vinyl stacked against the wall, where she promptly pulled *Led Zeppelin IV* from its sleeve, placed it on the turntable, and lowered the needle. She turned to Tommy with a grin when the opening strains of "Going to California" filled the small space.

"You a Zeppelin fan?" Tommy handed her a beer.

"Thanks to my dad, I was raised on this stuff." She clinked the neck of her bottle against his and took a sip. "Your music is reminiscent of Jimmy Page, and the lyrics remind me of you."

Tommy stood before her, rendered temporarily speechless. "Jimmy Page is one of my idols," he finally said. "As for the rest, well, thanks."

She lifted the beer to her lips, took a long swig, and glanced around his small but mostly tidy den. "It's not as bad as you pretend." She nodded. "I mean, there's no weird smell, you have an impressive collection of much-loved, well-read, waterlogged paperbacks, and who doesn't love a popcorn ceiling inexplicably speckled with gold bits?"

She flashed a wicked grin, then turned and headed straight for his bedroom as Tommy followed. It was his house, but she was in charge.

She stood next to the mattress on the floor and looked all around. "Candles. Decent sheets . . . how many girls have you brought here, Tommy?"

He opened his mouth to reply, then promptly shut it again. He wasn't sure how to answer. He wasn't sure he was willing to answer.

"Surely I'm not the first?"

"What if I said you were?" He watched her carefully, unsure where this was leading.

"Then I'd have no choice but to accuse you of lying."

"Well, okay then." He was more than willing to drop it. The sight of Layla in his bedroom was way too tempting. Their kiss had been brief, but he wouldn't forget it any-time soon. As much as he wanted to repeat it, he needed to focus on winning the contest, not chase after a girl who was constantly giving him mixed signals, despite having a boyfriend. Eager to return to more neutral ground, he led her out of his room and over to the couch.

"So how'd you score Madison Brooks?" She pulled her knees to her chest and wrapped her arms around them. "It doesn't seem like her kind of club."

Tommy sipped his beer. Layla ignored hers. "She just showed up," he said, unwilling to share anything more.

"But what was she like? I mean, you talked to her, right?"

The question was simple, but when Tommy started messing with his hair and scratching at his cheek, he knew she suspected him of hiding something. Like she said, she was good at reading people.

"She was nice." Tommy's voice was tentative. He wanted to say more but wasn't sure it was safe. His fingers played at the rim of his beer, as his gaze grew increas-ingly distant, lost in the memory of the night one of the most celebrated girls in the world decided to drop into his club. "I mean, we didn't really talk all that much, but she wasn't anything like I expected. She was almost like—" His voice faded, he shook his head, unable to put a word to it.

Layla leaned forward, urging him to continue.

He searched the room as though he expected to find the answer written on the wall with peeling paint, the carpet with the creepy dark stain, or maybe even the torn cover of the Hunter S. Thompson paperback. "Like some of the girls I used to know back home," he finally said.

Layla squinted, but he soon went on to explain.

"Not the kind I usually dated." A small smile broke onto his face. "She just seemed really normal. Uncomplicated. Not spoiled. Like she didn't belong in the glamorous life she'd found herself in. Like there was a part of her that was better suited to a much simpler existence in a much smaller place . . ."

His voice halted. From the incredulous look on Layla's face, he'd revealed far more than he should have.

"So, you come up with all *that*." She drew air circles with her finger. "And yet, you claim you 'didn't really talk all that much.'" She cocked her head, allowing her hair to flop into her eyes. "Sounds like you talked a lot more than you let on."

Tommy shifted uncomfortably, picked at a loose thread

on the cushion. "Maybe it's better if we don't talk about the competition."

"Why not?" She narrowed her gaze. "It's the only thing we have in common."

"We both like Zeppelin," he said. It was a pathetic attempt, but he was eager to return to a more peaceful state. He hated confrontation. Especially when he had no idea why he was being confronted. "What're you doing?" he asked, watching as she leaped from the couch and inexplicably made for the door.

"This was a bad idea." She ran a hand through her white-blond hair and frowned. "Competition and friendship don't mix."

"But—you barely drank any of your beer." He pointed stupidly at the mostly full bottle as though that was enough to convince her to stay.

"You finish it," she snapped, her mood shifting so quickly he could barely keep up. "Like you said, you handle it better."

Without another word, she let herself out. Leaving Tommy to wonder what the hell had just happened.

# THIRTY

# NOTHING ELSE
# MATTERS

Madison sat on the patio at Nobu gazing out at Malibu Beach, enjoying the feel of the soft breeze brushing over her cheek. Ever since she'd moved to LA, the ocean had become a welcome retreat. Watching the waves continuously lap at the shore was her favorite way to meditate. She'd thought about buying a place by the water, but with all the public access, beach houses were tough to safeguard. Besides, for the moment, all her dreams were on hold until her problem was handled.

"Was that James I just saw?" Ryan bent to give her a perfunctory kiss. "You know, the bouncer at Night for Night? Could've sworn I just saw him tipping the valet and collecting a sick matte-black CTS-V coupe." He shook his head. "Didn't know being a bouncer paid so well."

Madison shrugged like she had no idea what he was talking about. Ryan didn't need to know about her arrangement with James or anyone else on her payroll. What she was about to divulge was revealing enough. She could only hope he'd cooperate—that their time together hadn't resulted in complete animosity.

He claimed his seat reluctantly, wearing an expression of wary distrust. Well, they'd have to find a way around all that. Now more than ever they needed each other.

"So, what's this about?" He centered his green eyes on her, his voice surprisingly brusque.

She gazed out at the sea, watching the sun slice through glorious bands of purple and pink as it dove toward the glistening silver-blue water. "Remember that night when you wanted to come here for dinner but I chose to stay home, so you said you were going out with your friends but you really went to see Aster Amirpour at Night for Night?"

His eyes widened, but he soon got control of his face and switched into neutral.

"I was just wondering—exactly how serious are you about Aster?" She leaned back in her seat, observing him closely. Watching as he shook his head, clutched the sides of his chair. He was just about to bail when she reached toward him and said, "Please—no more games. Let's be straight for a change."

He flashed her a dubious look, shot a hand through his

tousled blond hair. The silence stretched between them until he finally relented. "I don't know." He splayed his hands on the smooth wood tabletop, studying his fingers as though trying to recall the lines that went with this scene. "I guess my interest lies somewhere between not very and very."

Madison nodded. "And what is it you see in her, aside from the obvious?"

He ran a hand over his face, gazed at the other diners, before returning to her. "Mad, come on." He flipped his hands on the table and frowned. "What's this about?"

"It's about getting to the truth."

"Jeez, I . . . this is really uncomfortable, okay?"

Madison nodded, encouraging him to continue.

"Fine." He focused on his fork, pressing the tines with the tips of his fingers. "According to my shrink—"

"You told your shrink?" She knew he saw a shrink, everyone did, but she didn't realize he actually confided in her. She figured he was just there for the medical marijuana prescription she'd written for him.

"I thought it was like confession—that I was supposed to confide all my sins." He shrugged. "Anyway, according to her, my attraction to Aster is about her needing me in ways you never could. She also says I'm acting out because of my show getting canceled. Trying to bolster my ego and feel important again." He looked away, as though it pained him to say it.

"And what if I said she was wrong?"

Madison observed him placidly, knowing she'd clinched it when he tilted his head, nodded for her to go on.

"What if I told you I do need you—more than you could ever guess?"

Ryan licked his lips and leaned toward her, clearly aware that a deal was about to be struck. "I'm listening."

"Good." Madison grinned, settled deeper into her seat. "Order us some drinks, and I'll explain everything. But first you have to promise not to tell your shrink, your priest, or anyone else what I'm about to tell you."

He nodded agreeably and flagged down a waiter. As the man approached, Ryan flashed Madison his best heart-throb grin and said, "And then later, you can tell me all about Della, your arrangement with James, and how you really got that scar on your arm."

# THIRTY-ONE

# DESTINATION UNKNOWN

Aster spun before her full-length mirror, making sure she appeared flawless from every angle. Ira was hosting an industry party at Night for Night and all the biggest players were invited, which meant she needed to look her absolute best.

She gazed at her Valentino heels and frowned. They went perfectly with her cream-colored vintage Alaïa minidress she'd recently picked up at Decades on Melrose. Normally she avoided used clothing; something about it seemed kind of icky. But the way the dress clung to her curves banished her worst germophobe fears. There was no doubt Ryan would love it. But to really pull it off, the shoes were imperative. Question was: How to get them down the stairs and out the door without Nanny Mitra noticing.

It was the final night of week three in the competition, and though she was managing to hold her own, the Vesper's numbers continually trumped hers, and Jewel was gaining traction, what with all the models and B-list celebs they were pulling in. Layla was crazy if she thought she could bribe Aster into sending Ryan Hawthorne her way.

When she'd first seen the pic, she was panicked. The thought of someone photographing what she thought was an intimate, private moment was disturbing at best. Last thing she needed was the pic to go viral, and yet she couldn't afford to let Layla win. She'd send Sugar Mills and whoever else she could wrangle from her agent, but that was the most she would do. Layla would just have to deal.

For now, she had bigger problems at stake, namely the shoes. Nanny was definitely onto her and Javen. Usually she was in bed by nine o'clock, nine thirty at the latest. But lately she'd taken to watching late-night TV, claiming to be a recent convert to Conan and company. Though they'd done their best to cover for each other, it was getting increasingly difficult with Nanny always poking around in their business.

She lifted her fingers to the gold-and-diamond hamsa pendant and begged whoever was in charge of such things to see her through another night, and, if it wasn't too much to ask, all the ones that followed. Despite outward appearances, Aster was starting to slip, mostly thanks to her friendship with Ryan.

While she'd managed to put him off, she couldn't help but wonder how much longer he'd be willing to settle for the few covert kisses they'd shared. Just the other night he'd accused her of being a tease. And though he'd smiled when he said it, there was an edge to his voice that left her uneasy.

She couldn't afford for him to lose interest. Not only was she becoming addicted to all the attention he showered on her—it was a rush unlike any she'd ever known—but she was also starting to believe he was actually serious about helping her break into Hollywood. He'd even promised to set up a meeting between her and his agent—a major upgrade from her own worthless agent. She knew he wouldn't let her down, but she also knew that eventually, he'd expect her to yield to more than just kissing.

From what Aster could piece together via the tabloids and blogs, Ryan and Madison were still together, but Ryan swore they were as good as over. She hoped he was telling the truth. She'd never intended to like him so much.

She slid her purse onto her lap and riffled through the contents—keys, lip gloss, driver's license, cash, and the condom she and her best friend, Safi, had bought one drunken night on a dare and that she'd carried around ever since just in case, were all there.

The only hitch in her plan was the shoes.

Going barefoot wasn't an option. But then neither was wearing the heels downstairs at ten o'clock at night in her robe while Nanny Mitra watched TV. Since she'd started the day faking a cold, if only to explain her exhaustion from staying up late and her subsequent need to sleep in, she figured she might as well play it out all the way. She slipped her robe over her dress, cinched it tightly at the waist, slid her window open, and tossed the shoes and purse onto the lawn two stories below. Cringing when the stilettos landed with a thud, she held her breath, hoping Nanny Mitra hadn't heard, and made for the stairs.

Arranging her hair to hang in her face, mostly to hide the fact that she was wearing foundation and blush (the eyes and lips she'd do in the car), she headed into the den, her eyes widening when she saw Javen lounging in one of the side chairs, pretending to read. Guess she wasn't the only one with big plans. He was playing his part, she was playing hers, the two of them working to keep Nanny subdued.

"Thought I'd come down and say good night," she said. "I just took some NyQuil and it's making me tired, so I think I'll turn in."

Nanny nodded and started to rise, but Aster raised a hand to ward her off.

"I might be contagious," she explained. "And I'd hate

for you to get sick. I'll see you in the morning."

She and Javen exchanged a complicit look, as Aster headed back to her room and waited for her brother to text her the moment Nanny fell asleep in her chair, which didn't take long. Then she snuck down the stairs in her robe, just in case Nanny unexpectedly woke, slipped out the front door, gathered her purse and shoes from the lawn, and raced toward a whole new life that was finally about to begin.

Aster stood in the Riad and glanced nervously around the club, hoping Ryan hadn't changed his mind about her just when she'd decided on him. He knew about the party. Knew how important it was to her. And tonight of all nights she needed him there. She checked the time again. It was unlike him to be late.

"*Aster.*"

A hand circled her wrist. Lips nudged her ear. She closed her eyes in relief and breathed in a cloud of Tom Ford Noir.

"You look amazing." He led her to the sofa and claimed the space beside her, his fingers cupping her knee, at first tentatively. Then seeing she didn't squirm or push him away, he ventured a few inches higher until his hand was resting near the hem of her dress.

"You came alone?" Her heart raced at the possibilities unfolding before her.

"You were expecting Madison?"

At the sound of her name, Aster instinctively recoiled, only to have Ryan pull her back to him. "Can't even remember the last time we spoke," he said between kisses.

"And yet, according to the tabloids, you guys are as hot and heavy as ever."

Ryan pulled away, buying a few moments' reprieve by pouring shots of chilled vodka. "It's in the works. I promise. I just hope you can be as patient with me as I've been with you." His gaze met hers, and she felt herself squirm. He had been patient. She had led him on. Or at least sort of. Not entirely. But yeah, maybe a little.

She leaned in for the kind of kiss she'd so far avoided. Her body pressed against his, she kissed him fully, deeply, and once she'd started she found it nearly impossible to stop. He buried a hand in her hair. Pulling away for a moment to gaze at her in wonder, before finding her lips once again. His fingers creeping steadily up her thigh, slipping under her dress, as she melted into his arms. Ryan adored her. She could hear it in his voice. Feel it in his touch. And as his fingers flirted with the edge of her thong, she wondered if it was actually possible to die of happiness.

His breath grew heated and quick, as he coaxed a finger under the lace, only to have her panic and push him away. "Aster, *please*," he moaned, his voice hoarse. "You have no idea what you're doing to me." He pulled her back to him, reclaiming her lips in a way that had her torn between ripping his clothes off and doing him right there in the Riad, and pulling the brake while she still could. Losing her virginity in public was never part of the plan.

"Ryan." She placed her palms on his shoulders and pushed him away until there was enough space between them for her to think clearly. "I can't do this—not here—not like this. . . ." She paused, unsure if she should mention he was about to be her first. Some guys liked that sort of thing, while others did their best to steer clear. She decided against it. The night was already more perfect than she'd imagined; she wouldn't allow anything to change that. "We need to slow down. Or at least I need to slow down." She took a deep breath, then rushed to explain. "I'm still at work. I can't exactly spend the whole night in here with you. Though that's not to say that later, after the club closes, we can't . . . finish what we started . . ." She flashed a flirtatious grin, aware of her heart pounding so loudly it was a wonder he couldn't hear it.

Ryan considered her for a long, thoughtful moment. Then, without another word, he rose to his feet, extended his hand, and shot her that world-famous smile that made a million hearts melt, hers included.

"Where we going?" she asked, afraid he was trying to lure her away, despite what she'd said.

"Dance with me, Aster. You're at least allowed to dance, right?"

She grasped his hand and let him lead her onto the dance floor.

"Though believe me, once you're off the clock, I have every intention of picking up exactly where we left off."

THIRTY-TWO

# THIS IS HOW A HEART BREAKS

Layla stood by the bar and checked the time on her phone. "You going to the party?" Zion asked, coming over to join her.

Layla took in his shaved head, gleaming brown skin, perfect bone structure, and bronze-colored eyes, and shrugged. Zion was ridiculously beautiful, and he knew how to work it. But somehow it wasn't nearly as annoying coming from him as it was from Aster Amirpour.

"Don't tell me you're going to pass up the chance to celebrate Queen Bitch Aster?" Zion goaded her.

"It's not about Aster," she reminded him. "It just happens to take place at Night for Night. Ira promised he'd rotate the parties."

"Well, don't tell Aster. She thinks it's her club. Just like she thinks it's her party."

Layla rolled her eyes. It was nice to share a common enemy. Not to mention Zion was the only one on her team still talking to her. Brandon was gone, and Karly had never warmed up. Though she often suspected it was probably because Zion didn't view her as a threat. Sure, she'd managed to bring in Heather Rollins, but Zion consistently filled up the club with so many insanely gorgeous models, it eclipsed her more modest gets.

Not like she cared. Thanks to Heather and all the Madison gossip she fed Layla, the blog was taking off. Still, in order to maintain her insider access, she needed to stay in the game, which made her just as determined as Zion.

"Is that your get?" Zion shook his head and made a disgusted face, as he nodded toward a man who could only be described as beige. "Honey, that's not even *normcore*, that's *borecore*. And it looks like mister tall, pale, and nondescript is heading your way. I'll leave you to it."

Layla watched as the man approached, the colorful overhead lights casting crazy shadows over his face. With his pleated khakis, tan walking shoes, and white golf shirt, he looked so out of place among the trendy young club kids, she wondered for a moment if he was somebody's dad.

"Are you Layla Harrison?" His pale gaze moved over her.

She nodded, watching in confusion as he reached into his back pocket and handed her a folded sheet of paper.

"What's this?" She squinted at the official-looking type-face.

"Restraining order."

She blinked and shook her head, sure she'd misheard.

"From this point on, you are not to go within fifty feet of Madison Brooks."

"Are you freaking kidding me?" Layla trembled with frustration and rage as her fingers crunched the paper into her fist. "I trip and spill my drink and now I'm a stalker? Is she for real?"

"Stalking charges are no joke. Neither are the slander-ous stories you post on your blog." His face was impassive, gave nothing away.

"It's not slander if it's true," Layla grumbled, before she could stop herself.

She shook her head and looked around the club, con-vinced Zion or Karly was playing some kind of prank. Until she looked at the tall, plain man again, saw the way his gaze narrowed on hers until his pale eyes nearly disap-peared.

"Who the hell are you?" she asked. His bland face looked vaguely familiar, though she had no idea why.

"I represent Madison Brooks. And it's in your best inter-est to take this seriously. We clear?"

"Crystal." She glared, watching as he turned and made for the exit.

As soon as he was gone, she ripped the document to shreds, deposited the pieces into the can behind the bar, dumped a load of ice cubes and lime wedges on top, and stormed out of Jewel.

When Madison had claimed Layla would be hearing from her lawyers, Layla assumed she was bluffing.

What kind of spoiled, entitled princess goes after someone for accidentally spilling some coffee?

*You are not to go within fifty feet of Madison,* he'd said. Like Madison got to dictate where Layla went. She shook her head and reached for her cell, about to call Mateo, if for no other reason than to share her outrage, only to press End before the call could go through. Last time she'd told him about her run-in with Madison, he was completely lacking in sympathy. She wouldn't give him a reason to say *I told you so.*

She climbed on her bike and headed down the boulevard to Night for Night. With the warm summer-night air rushing over her skin, she was tempted to keep going, maybe never return. She wondered if anyone would miss her besides her dad. Mateo would—at least in the beginning. But things had grown so tense between them it wouldn't take long before he realized he was better off without her.

But Layla wasn't a quitter. And so she left her bike at the curb and nodded at James as he unhooked the velvet rope and ushered her in.

The plan was to swing by Ira's table long enough to show her face and say a quick hello, then get the hell out of there. She was in no mood to party. All she wanted to do was climb into bed, pull the covers over her head, and never emerge.

She moved through the club, making her way toward Ira, when a fight broke out on the dance floor, scattering the crowd and leaving Layla to stare in disbelief to find Ryan Hawthorne, Madison Brooks, and Aster Amirpour at the center of the fight.

"How could you?" Madison cried, her lips trembling, cheeks glistening under the glow of the copper lanterns, as Aster gaped in shock, Ryan wiped his lips with the back of his hand, and Layla instinctively reached for her cell, set it to video, and edged closer.

Screw the restraining order. Layla was a professional, and this was too good to pass up.

Aster reached for Madison, attempting to calm her, only to have Madison lash out like an injured animal.

"Get away from me!" Madison yelled. "Don't you dare touch me!"

Ryan jumped between them, hands raised in surrender. "Mad—what are you doing?" His voice was incredulous, his gaze darting wildly, taking in the number of witnesses, before returning to his enraged A-list girlfriend.

"I stopped by, hoping to surprise you. It's been weeks

since we've seen each other, and now I know why!" She pointed an accusing finger at Aster, as Aster cringed behind Ryan, and Ryan moved to placate Madison, looking angry for sure, but not necessarily surprised.

Layla snuck closer, viewing the scene via her cell phone. Hardly able to believe she'd scored a front-row seat to what would be the most talked-about story for weeks—months if it turned out to be a slow summer for scandal. She centered her focus on Madison's eyes spilling fast tears, repeatedly asking Ryan *why*, as Aster stood awkwardly behind him.

It was the performance of a lifetime, that much was sure, and Layla continued to record it, following Madison as she raced for the door. Her head bent, arms wrapped tightly around her waist, she darted through a crowd that strangely allowed her to pass without incident, until she reached the place where Layla stood, lifted her chin, and looked right at her, almost as though Madison had expected to see Layla standing in that very spot.

Then again, it happened so fast, Layla couldn't be sure how much she'd made up in her head, thanks to her own panic at being discovered less than fifty feet away from the person who'd recently brought stalking charges against her.

When Ira stepped in to say a few words, Layla strained to hear, but the music muffled his voice. She was just about to stop recording when Madison reached the entrance at the same moment Tommy arrived. And Layla watched in shock as Tommy tossed a protective arm around Madison's shoulder, whispered into her ear, and led her out the door and into the night.

# THIRTY-THREE

# HOW TO SAVE A LIFE

Madison was shaking.

She also looked upset, like someone who'd just experienced something they wouldn't recover from anytime soon.

It had all happened so fast there was no time to think. One moment Tommy was entering the club, figuring he'd hang long enough for Ira to notice his presence, and the next Madison was barreling toward him, her face covered in tears. So Tommy did the only thing he could: he shouted at everyone to back the hell off, tossed his jacket over her shoulders, then walked her to her car, climbed behind the wheel, and drove around until he was sure they hadn't been tailed, before stopping at the Vesper and hiding her in one of the back rooms while waiting for the club to clear and it was safe for her to be there.

The most surprising thing was Madison's willingness to go along with his half-baked plan without a single word of protest. Then again, she'd barely spoken. It was like she was lost in her own little world, happy to let someone else take charge.

"You okay?" Tommy asked, once she was settled. Casting an anxious gaze at her beautiful face, noting how small and vulnerable she looked wearing his leather jacket. All the while repeating in his head, *She's just a girl—a girl in crisis. She needs peace, comfort, quiet, and a little support. You can handle it.*

Madison tugged the sleeves over her fingers and pressed them tightly to her lips for a moment, before dropping her hands to her lap as though surrendering a burden she'd carried too long. "God, I probably look terrible." She drew her shoulders in, gazing at him through bright, glossy eyes.

"Not possible." He claimed the seat across from her and offered a beer. He hoped she liked beer. From all the pictures he'd ever seen, she normally drank champagne. But the Vesper didn't serve champagne, and from the first day they'd met, he'd had the feeling Madison could kick back a cold one as good as any girl back home. From the way her fingers clutched at the frosty bottle, pressing it first to her cheek, then to her forehead, before taking a sip, he'd been right about that much at least.

"Thanks for getting me out of there." The look she gave him was far more grateful than such a small act deserved. "Very gallant of you." She tapped the neck of her bottle to his and took another sip.

"I do what I can." Tommy shrugged, wishing he'd said something cooler, not that he could think of anything cooler.

"How much did you see?" She set her bottle on the table, ran her index finger around the rim.

"Nothing." He picked at the label on his beer, though he had a good guess. "I'd just rolled up when I ran into you."

She lifted her chin, peered at him down the length of her elegant nose. "Doesn't seem like your kind of club."

"It's not. But I needed to make an appearance." Madison nodded, and Tommy was sure he'd never seen anything more heartbreakingly beautiful. With her mascara-smudged eyes, she seemed fragile, haunted, in need of protecting. He swallowed hard, fought to keep himself steady, even.

Madison blinked and gazed down at her hands, splaying her pale, delicate fingers against the scarred wood table. "I wonder if Aster will get credit for getting both me and Ryan to the club?"

It was Tommy's turn to blink. He didn't know Madison had heard the rumors swirling around about Aster and Ryan. Though he should've guessed. Madison seemed like the kind of girl who didn't allow much to slip past.

"What do you know about her?" She lifted her gaze and studied him closely. She'd know if he lied.

He tipped his head back and stared at the acoustically sound ceiling for a long, thoughtful moment. "Not much." He shrugged. It was the truth.

Madison nodded, took another sip of her beer, and sighed the sigh of someone grown weary beyond their years. What she needed most was a place to lay her head, and the promise of a new day. The refuge Tommy offered was temporary at best.

Still, despite the tears, she didn't come off as someone who'd just caught her guy with another girl. Tommy should know. He'd once had a girl dump an entire Big Gulp Slurpee on his head for flirting with her best friend. Though he didn't know her well, there was nothing about Madison that struck Tommy as docile, and yet she'd handled the news too easily, too matter-of-factly.

Then again, maybe Madison was just that good of an actress, able to keep her emotions in check.

If it didn't concern her, then it shouldn't concern him. He was better off shutting down his thoughts and focusing on finishing his beer.

"By tomorrow morning, the whole world will know—if they don't already." Her voice was distant, gaze far away. "But do me a favor, please don't ask for any of the details. Not that you have, and I appreciate that. It's just so nice to be with someone who's not necessarily a fan. Who probably doesn't know the first thing about me, and doesn't much care."

Tommy started to speak, about to protest the part about not being a fan, but then he thought better. He couldn't think of a single movie of hers that he'd watched. Then again, he wasn't much of a movie guy. Music pretty much ruled his life.

"Another beer?" He tipped his bottle toward hers.

She nodded, slid the empty toward him, and when he leaned in to take it, she clutched the front of his gray plaid shirt and kissed him with a need that surprised him. When she finally pulled away, Tommy had the distinctive feeling that a switch had been flipped—he'd been officially initiated into something he couldn't quite grasp, and yet there was no denying that from that point forward, there was no going back.

## THIRTY-FOUR

# LIKE A VIRGIN

After the awful scene between her, Ryan, and Madison, Aster was sure Ira would call a halt to the party. But Ira, always game to capitalize on a scandal, wasted no time escorting Aster and Ryan back to the Riad, ignoring Ryan when he told him they should probably call it a night.

"Don't be ridiculous." His tone was nonnegotiable. "Until things cool down, you're better off here than out there. When you're ready to leave, you can use the side door. I'll tell James to look after you. Trust me, no one will bother you with James around."

Aster remained silent, more than happy to let them work out the logistics. She needed to sort through her feelings. In light of what had happened, she figured she should be steeped in deep shame, or at the very least feel bad about all the upset she'd caused. She'd done the unthinkable, traumatized an A-list celebrity by stealing her boyfriend. Or at least that was how the press would play it, despite the fact that it was nowhere close to the truth.

Was she the only one who noticed how the whole scene seemed staged? When Madison had just appeared out of nowhere and started screaming, Aster had the distinct impression she'd spent the last week rehearsing the moment in front of her mirror. It was as though she'd purposely laid out a trap, and Aster, naive fool that she was, had blindly stepped in.

Only, she hadn't been all that naive. Or at least not entirely.

"One thing's sure . . ."

The sound of Ryan's voice pulled her away from her thoughts and back to the present. At some point Ira had left, leaving them with two flutes of champagne.

"You just took your first step toward making a name for yourself." Ryan looked her over appreciatively, while Aster picked at the hem of her dress. "Don't act so scandalized," he said. "It's the quickest route to fame I can think of, other than a sex tape."

She pulled away, ignoring the flute he pressed on her. "You act like I should be happy about it. Like you're happy about it."

He raised his glass and studied the bubbles. "Happy to

get my life back? Sure. Happy to be yelled at in a crowded nightclub while she cried adorably for her audience? Not in the least." He shrugged, took a sip, then quickly chased it with another. "But it's out there, Aster. For better or worse. Which means I have no choice but to find a way to play it to my advantage. And my advice to you, if you want to make it in this business, is to find your own angle to make sure it elevates you."

He abandoned his glass and leaned toward her, his hand returning to the place on her thigh that started the mess, even though it hadn't really started the mess. The mess got started that day in the Neiman Marcus shoe department, when Aster decided to flirt with another girl's guy in hopes of getting famous.

She swallowed hard, forced her gaze to meet his. His fingers were inching up her leg, her pulse quickening the higher they climbed.

"I guarantee by tomorrow your agent will be calling with all kinds of interview requests." He rubbed his lips together as though preparing to kiss her—a kiss that, despite everything, she still wanted.

"And I won't accept them." Her voice was indignant, angry, the logic of her mind completely at war with her heart. On the one hand, his touch was driving her mad. On the other, it was impossible to accept how glib he was acting after all that had happened.

"Good call. Don't talk to the press. Don't talk to any-one, not even your friends. You'd be amazed how quick they'll sell you out for a little cash and a few seconds of fame. Just go about your business, and when you do get ambushed, say, 'No comment,' and be on your way."

"*When* I get ambushed?" She pressed her legs together in an act of incredible will meant to keep his wandering fingers at bay.

"It's possible. But, babe, don't worry. I'll be with you the entire way."

He slid closer, pressed his thigh against hers. She wanted to believe him, but she needed to hear it again, needed to have it confirmed, leaving no doubt of the promise he'd made. "Will you?" She looked at him. "Will you really?"

"Only if you want me to."

His gaze bore into hers, leaving no doubt his word was good. Ryan offered everything she'd ever wanted—fame, fortune, nonstop media attention. Hers would be the name on everyone's lips, and all the cameras would be aimed at her face. Though she never dreamed it would happen like this.

He pressed a thumb to the underside of her chin, lifted her lips to meet his. His fingers gently eased her legs apart, reminding her of where they'd left off, and the places they still had to visit. "It's all good, Aster." He kissed her nose, her cheek, her forehead, her neck, before finding her lips once again. "You have no idea how good it's about to get. Will you trust me?"

She was alone in the Riad with Ryan Hawthorne.

By tomorrow morning she'd be famous, if she wasn't already.

It was pretty much everything she'd ever dreamed delivered straight to her door.

And there was no doubt that Ryan was entirely responsible for getting her there.

Ryan was rich, famous, connected, and more importantly, no longer Madison's boyfriend.

There was no reason for her to feel guilty.

Besides, she'd traveled so far from being a Perfect Persian Princess she might as well complete the journey.

She reached for her champagne, washed it down, and kissed him right back.

Her lips brushing against his ear, she said, "I just need to run to the restroom—meet me by the door?"

She kissed him fully, deeply, then pushed away and made her way through the club.

# THIRTY-FIVE

# JUST A GIRL

"Wow."

Tommy searched Madison's gaze and traced a finger across the curve of her cheek. The pulse of her kiss still alive on his lips, he was unaware he'd even spoken, until she smiled softly and repeated the word.

"Wow, indeed." She sighed contentedly and curled her fingers at the nape of his neck. "Country boys sure know how to kiss. I can't believe I'd forgotten that."

Tommy narrowed his gaze, detecting the slightest twang in her voice—something he'd never expected. So that was her secret, or at least one of them. Clearly Madison wasn't quite the East Coast prodigy she'd claimed to be, not that Tommy had ever believed that particular story.

There was something so accessible about her, which

seemed like such a ridiculous thing to say about a star of her caliber. Still, Tommy sensed she'd be more comfortable running across a freshly mowed lawn in bare feet than she was crossing a red carpet in designer heels.

The way she drank a beer, the way she kissed, the way her whole body relaxed when she was sure he was the only one looking, convinced him that if nothing else, he'd found a kindred spirit in the most unlikely of persons. It was like every other moment of her life was an act, while the moments they'd shared together were the real deal.

He wanted to ask her about the accent, really get in there and listen to every story she was willing to share, but he couldn't think of a single good way to approach it. Clearly it was something she'd worked hard to keep well under wraps; losing an accent like that was no easy feat.

"Madison—" He figured he'd start with a simple question and build from there. But before he could finish, her phone vibrated with an incoming text that had her face darkening the moment she read it.

"I have to go." She sprang to her feet and ran a hand through her hair, glancing around frantically for the purse Tommy handed her.

"You okay?" He stood beside her, sorry to see her go. She'd probably forget all about him. He knew he'd never forget about her.

"Yeah—I just—" She pressed her bag to her chest and

raced for the door, pausing on the threshold long enough to slip off his jacket and toss it to him. "Thanks." She looked at him as though there was so much more she wanted to say but no time to say it. She shook her head, blinked a few times, and the next thing he knew, she'd shot into the night.

"Madison!" He raced after her, his voice hoarse, breathless. "At least let me walk you to your car," he offered, anything to prolong his time with her.

But she was already gone.

Already running away from his life and back to her world of secrets and lies.

THIRTY-SIX

# BREAKING THE GIRL

Madison Brooks burst onto the sidewalk, aware of Tommy calling after her, his voice as perplexed as it was sincere. But Tommy had already helped more than he knew. Madison couldn't remember when she'd last felt so at peace—so accepted for her authentic self—as opposed to the girl everyone believed her to be.

Funny how she'd given up on Paul and decided to take matters into her own hands, only to receive his text at the most unfortunate time. A few more hours of drinking beers and kissing Tommy would've been nice, but Madison didn't fool herself about which held more importance.

She ducked her head low, arranged her scarf so it covered her head, and made a run for her car, only to grasp the handle and discover she'd left the keys in the jacket

Tommy had loaned her.

She glanced back at the Vesper, gazed down Hollywood Boulevard toward Night for Night, and decided to run for it, or rather walk really fast. A girl sprinting down the street with a scarf tossed over her head would attract too much attention. A girl walking quickly with a *back the hell off and stay out of my way* thousand-yard stare would make people think twice about messing with her.

Thanks to an unconventional childhood, Madison had been defending herself for as long as she could remember. Despite her pampered Hollywood life, she'd never forgotten how to take care of herself. Surely Paul would drive her home, which meant she could settle the key situation in the morning. If nothing else, it would give her an excuse to see Tommy, not that she needed one. From the way he'd kissed her, she was pretty sure he'd jump at the chance. The thought brought a smile to her face.

Her eyes scanned the palm-tree-lined boulevard, as the heels of her Gucci stilettos stabbed a succession of pink-and-gold Walk of Fame stars. Jennifer Aniston, Elvis Presley, Gwyneth Paltrow, Michael Jackson—she stormed past them all, including her own. Though she barely paused long enough to notice. The goal was accomplished, relegated to the past. Once Madison achieved something, she was immediately on to the next new thing. She made it a point to never look back.

Not a lot of cars on the road at this hour, but the freaks were out in full force. Must be later than she'd thought—certainly late enough for Night for Night to be closed—late enough for Ryan and Aster to have already moved on. She wondered vaguely what had happened after she'd left.

Was he upset with her for going overboard?

Had they gone home together?

Or was Aster still intent on playing her prim-and-proper game?

Either way, she wished Ryan well; the rest she'd read about soon enough. Funny how she'd put all that in motion only to have Paul come through at the very last moment, rendering the drama completely unnecessary.

Still, she couldn't think of a better ending. RyMad was dead, Ryan and Aster would get all the publicity they desired, and Madison was free to move on with her life without constantly looking over her shoulder, now that Paul had handled things for her.

She paused on the corner, checked both ways, then darted across the street, against the red light. The text had come in a good five minutes ago with instructions to hurry. Paul was a stickler for time. Madison would not disappoint.

From what she could tell, no one had managed to follow her and Tommy to the Vesper, which meant that no one was following her now as she returned to Night for Night. Though it wouldn't be long before the vultures came out in full force. Considering the scene she'd caused, she could expect nothing less.

She imagined how she might've looked under the glow of the lights—her face wet with tears, voice hoarse with accusation. There wasn't a girl in the crowd who wouldn't be on her side, other than her most ardent haters and Aster of course.

Her agent would have a fit. Her PR people would be in a snit. But Madison felt good about the decision, and if they couldn't get on board, she'd have to remind them exactly who they worked for. And if they still couldn't get on board, well, there were plenty more where they came from. Hollywood agents were like plastic surgeons and Starbucks—one on every corner.

She crept to the side door, punched the code James had given her into the keypad, and slipped inside the large darkened space. Her spiked heels echoing loudly through the empty club, she made her way up the stairs to the terrace, anxious to hear exactly how Paul had handled the threat.

# THIRTY-SEVEN

# BIGMOUTH STRIKES AGAIN

Layla carried her double espresso from the Nespresso maker in the kitchen to the cluttered desk in her bedroom. The pricey coffeemaker had been a little outside their usual household budget, but they regarded it as less of a splurge and more a necessity. Her father was known to spend a lot of caffeine-fueled nights holed up in his studio working on projects, and while Layla also wrote some of her best pieces at night, mostly she just liked really good coffee.

She'd always been a night owl, a trait she assumed she'd inherited from her dad, but it was nearly dawn and she refused to so much as look at her pillow until her story was written, polished, and ushered into the world.

Her fingers flew over the keyboard, fueled on the strongest beans Colombia offered and the insatiable rush of a shot at revenge. Queen Bitch Aster and Madison were going down, and they deserved nothing less. If Tommy got caught in the cross fire, oh well. He was the one who chose to rescue Madison.

She'd always figured Aster would go after Ira to secure the win. Maybe swing by his office after hours and flash a little thigh. And who was to say that she hadn't? Who was to say they hadn't hooked up—maybe, in fact, still were hooking up on a regular basis?

Either way, it was a wild card Layla wasn't willing to play.

The last person she wanted to make an enemy of was Ira Redman.

But Queen Bitch Aster Amirpour?

*Bring it.*

As for Madison . . .

Layla reviewed the video footage. Her stomach grew queasy as she watched the part where Tommy whisked her to safety like some gallant white knight in a pair of faded jeans, a black leather jacket, and trashed motorcycle boots.

Tommy was a fool. And Madison was an entitled brat who actively promoted her shallow, overindulged existence, inspiring legions of kids to emulate her, some who ended up dead like Carlos.

She read through the piece again, not entirely sure she should post it.

## BEAUTIFUL IDOLS
**RIP RyMad**

Dearly Beloved,

We gather here today to mourn the untimely demise
of one of Hollywood's greatest love stories—the not
so-conscious uncoupling of Madison Brooks and Ryan
Hawthorne.

Yes, readers, you read it here first:

RyMad is dead.

I know what you're thinking.

*How?*

And maybe even, *Why?*

And certainly, *Nooooo!*

Sadly, it's true. And as the Gods of Hollywood would
have it, yours truly was right there when it happened, and I
captured every ~~wretched~~ *wrenching* moment on video.

Though a word of warning before you hit Play:

Once you've seen this, you can never unsee it. The images
will be tattooed on your retinas for life eternal.

In lieu of flowers, feel free to pay your respects in the
comments.

The best journalists were fearless. Told the stories that
needed to be told. While it was debatable the Ryan-Madison-
Aster love triangle counted as a story that needed to be told,

maybe that wasn't for Layla to decide.

Whether it mattered in the big scheme of things wasn't the point. People would clamor to read every word. There was no greater pleasure than watching a celebrity's life go off the rails. It gave people a chance to choose sides, declare their loyalty (or lack of), and collectively shake their heads, smirk, and scoff at the idiocy of the rich and famous.

*How could he?*

*She should've known.*

*She looks like a gold-digging fame whore. . . .*

And if there were videos and stills to illustrate, even better.

Besides, it wasn't like Layla was blogging for some lofty intellectual news outlet. She had her own insatiable reader base and advertisers, and it was her responsibility to see they were properly fed in the way they'd come to expect.

For maximum impact (and maximum credit), she needed to publish the piece *ASAP*. Ensure hers was the story people read the moment they woke up and reached for their green juice.

She gnawed her bottom lip, crossed her fingers, took one last look at the stills with the snarky captions she'd added, and pressed Post. For better or worse, it was out there now, and there was no looking back.

# THIRTY-EIGHT

# ARE YOU HAPPY NOW?

Aster Amirpour rolled onto her side, bent her knees to her chest, and clutched her hands to the sides of a head that felt like a herd of elephants were stomping directly on top of it.

She didn't know which was worse, her parched and aching throat, or her killer headache. Until she forced herself into a sitting position, untangled her legs from the black satin sheets, pushed her soles against the white flokati rug, and tried to stand, only to fall back onto the bed. It was definitely the dizziness, followed by the nausea, with the headache and parched throat placing third and fourth respectively.

"Ryan," she groaned, in desperate need of some aspirin and a bottle of water that might hopefully kick-start the recuperative process. Unable to speak above a whisper, she rolled to his side of the bed and cracked an eye open, only to find it abandoned.

She thrust her arm out before her, ran her hand across the sheets. They were cold to the touch. As though he'd left a long time ago and hadn't bothered to return. But that wasn't possible, was it?

She bolted upright. Wincing against a surge of queasiness, she squinted through burning eyes at a bold and masculine space filled with modern, slightly oversize furniture. An enormous leather chaise, mirrored tables, and a king-size bed.

She dropped her head to her hands, unable to recall any details after leaving the club. The only thing she knew for sure was she was naked, alone, and she had no idea where she was.

Did the room belong to Ryan?

Was she in his apartment—or was it a fancy hotel suite?

She checked the bathroom and explored the adjoining den, finding more modern furnishings, more hard angles, sharp corners, and mirrored surfaces, but no Ryan. After a thorough check of each room, including the closets, it was clear he was gone, so she sent him a text that read: *Where R U?* When he failed to reply, she called, but it went straight into voice mail.

With the sun already peeking through the drapes,

sneaking home unseen would prove an impossible feat. Her car was still parked at Night for Night, and that stupid jerk who claimed to adore her enough to steal her virginity apparently couldn't be bothered to stick around long enough to drive her back to the club to retrieve it. There was no other way to read it. He hadn't even bothered to leave a note.

She dropped to her knees, dragged her purse from under the chaise, and went about collecting her belongings. Her bra and underwear were on opposite sides of the room, but they were torn, sticky, and so totally disgusting she couldn't bear to look at them, much less wear them. Her dress had been flung on the floor next to the couch in the den, and despite having once loved it more than any other dress she'd ever owned, now it seemed as trashy and contaminated as she currently felt. She wadded it into a ball with the undergarments and dumped the mess into the trash.

Though she drew a line at abandoning the Valentino stilettos. Ryan had taken enough. No way would she lose the shoes too.

In the bathroom, she ran some cool water over her face, but no matter how much she splashed and rubbed with the washcloth, she still looked like hell. Her eyes were bloodshot, her makeup smeared, and she bore the wild, abandoned look of someone staggering beneath a burdensome load of regret. Scraping her hair into a messy topknot, she rifled through the few pieces of clothing hanging in his closet and wondered if Ryan actually lived there. Still, there were jeans and a soft blue button-down shirt, and she didn't think twice about claiming them.

After rolling the jeans at the hem, she tucked the shirt halfway in, secured one of his belts at her waist, shoved her feet into the stilettos, swiped his dark sunglasses from the dresser on her way out the door, and began the long walk of shame home.

# THIRTY-NINE

# BULLET WITH BUTTERFLY WINGS

Tommy Phillips grasped the pillow next to his head and propped it over his cheek, reluctant to let in the light of a new day if it meant leaving the contented cocoon of his dreams.

His dream life—his waking life—they'd merged together so seamlessly there was no longer any boundary between them. It was like he'd spent the entire night kissing Madison Brooks—first in the Vesper, where she'd gazed at him through those exquisite violet eyes—only to carry the memory of her into his dreams, where she welcomed him into her arms once again.

Kissing her was insane! The kind of thing he never imagined would happen to him.

What was even more insane was the undeniable connection they'd shared. Tommy was sure he wasn't just a rebound, a convenient way for her to feel good about herself after discovering her boyfriend's betrayal. She was genuinely drawn to him. There was no disputing the evidence.

She'd trusted him to look after her, protect her, whisk her away from the gawkers and see her to safety.

Trusted him enough to see her as she really was, minus the veil of celebrity, just a real girl, drinking a beer, and kissing a boy she clearly had a crush on.

He sank deeper into the sheets, remembering the look in her eyes . . . the sweet wistfulness of her sigh . . . the play of her fingers at the nape of his neck . . . the intoxicating feel of her lips pressed against his . . . the regretful tinge in her voice when she'd left.

It was all the proof he needed to know she was as into him as he was into her.

And the best part was, Tommy had the pics to prove it.

He tossed the pillow, rolled onto his side, and reached for the phone he'd abandoned on the floor. He was about to check his camera roll when a long chain of texts popped onto the screen.

*How the hell—?*

He quickly scrolled through them, staring in disbelief at the numerous pics of the Ryan, Madison, and Aster drama. Including pictures of him with his arm secured around Madison as he led her through the Vesper's back door, shooting a cautious look over her shoulder as the door closed behind them, his expression promising serious consequences to anyone who dared follow.

But clearly someone had followed. And they'd made sure his hookup with Madison had gone viral.

He raced toward his grime-covered window, only to discover a swarm of photogs camped right outside. Most likely waiting for him to leave so they could shout their questions and insults and record his reactions.

He raked his fingers through his hair, unsure what to do. It wasn't exactly the way Tommy had hoped to make a name for himself, and yet he couldn't hide out in his apartment and wait for the vultures to move on to some other scandal.

Fact was, his fridge was empty, his cupboards were bare, and he had a serious need for coffee.

He shook his head, moved away from the window, and made for the shower. If he was going to make his tabloid debut, he might as well look his best.

FORTY

# WAKE ME UP WHEN SEPTEMBER ENDS

The driver pulled away with a loud crunch of gravel and a judgmental look (though she might have imagined that last part), as Aster punched the code for the electronic gate on the keypad and began the long walk up the driveway.

Her house loomed large in the distance. Probably because it was large, one of the largest on the block, which was really saying something, considering the high level of affluence in the neighborhood. But on that particular morning the Mediterranean manse seemed almost too large, sort of ominous and foreboding. Like the red-clay-tiled roof and sloping archways might turn on her at any second, become less of a luxurious sanctuary and more of a prison.

She wobbled uncertainly, her heels skidding against the uneven stones, until she slipped off her shoes and walked the rest of the way in bare feet. Her eyes darted wildly, looking for signs of Nanny Mitra, the maids and gardeners who came every day, anyone who might spot her lurking in her own front yard, looking as guilty as she'd surely be charged.

Normally she'd sneak into her house via the door in the garage that led straight to the back hall, but the remote to open the garage was in her car, and her car was no longer in the Night for Night parking lot. It'd either been stolen or towed. Either way she was screwed.

Sometimes, though, Javen left the French doors that led from the backyard into the den unlocked, mostly on the nights he snuck out. She could only hope he'd thought to do so again. Funny how their campaign to fool Nanny Mitra had made them closer than ever.

She crept around back, twisted the knob, and exhaled in relief when the door eased open and she stepped into a darkened den with the drapes still drawn. A good sign the maids had yet to arrive, which meant Nanny was probably still in her room, maybe even asleep. Aster slipped up the stairs, unable to so much as breathe until she'd made it safely to her room with the door closed behind her.

Tossing her shoes and bag toward the overstuffed chair in the corner, she sagged against her bed and stared at her reflection in the full-length mirror. She felt like crap. She looked even worse. And with the Sunday meeting scheduled for early afternoon, she doubted she'd make it, doubted she could pull it together by then, and had no plans to try. Despite what had happened—or maybe even because of it—she was still well in the lead, and there was no way Ira would take that away just because she failed to show at an obligatory event with a predetermined outcome.

What she wanted—no, actually *needed*—more than anything was a long, hot shower, if for no other reason than to scrub every remaining trace of Ryan Hawthorne from her flesh.

Scrubbing him from her memory was a whole other problem that wouldn't be remedied anytime soon.

She pulled the elastic from her hair and shook out the strands. After casting one last searing glance at her pathetic image in the mirror, she heaved herself off her bed and started to make for the bathroom, when her bedroom door sprang open, and her mother and father stood in the doorway.

# FORTY-ONE

# BLOW ME
# (ONE LAST KISS)

The last thing Layla wanted to do was attend Ira's Sunday meeting, but short of dropping out of the contest, what choice did she have? She made a list of things that were markedly worse. Things like: alligator wrestling, skydiving without a parachute, crime-scene cleanup—but compared to the prospect of facing Tommy, Aster, Ira, and the undeniable chaos she'd unleashed by posting their pics on her blog, suddenly all those things seemed not only more favorable but also maybe even downright pleasurable if she'd only give them a try.

The second she'd sent her post into the world, she was overcome with the dueling emotions of absolute triumph and overwhelming regret. Reader response was immediate—the number of hits escalated in a way Layla had never seen, and the comments section was overflowing. But once the reality of coming face-to-face with two of the people she'd turned into unsuspecting internet celebrities began to sink in, she couldn't help but wonder if she should've eased up on the tone.

Then again, as a Hollywood blogger, wasn't it her duty to report those kinds of stories?

She backed her bike from the garage, nearly jumping out of her skin when someone snuck up beside her and said, "Hey."

"Mateo! Omigod, you scared the crap out of me." She pressed her hand to her heart as though to keep it from breaking free of her chest.

He shoved his hands in the front pockets of his jeans and looked her over. "You're pretty jumpy."

"I had a late night. And a lot of caffeine." She cringed under the intensity of his gaze.

"Is that why you didn't answer my texts?"

She sighed and closed her eyes, wishing she could stay that way, block the world out. He was going to make her late, but mentioning that wouldn't go over well.

"I'm sorry. I was busy, and—" She directed the words to a spot just past his shoulder to avoid looking at him.

"Your blog. I know. Trust me, I read it." He continued to study her, as though daring her to meet his eyes.

His voice hinted at something she was sure she didn't

want to know, and yet she couldn't keep from asking, "And—what did you think?"

His features sharpened, as he gazed out at the house across the street—a recent remodel that resembled a two-story gift box with windows. "I think it's unlike you to be cruel," he finally said.

"It's not cruel if it's true," she snapped.

"But these are people you know—not public figures. There's a difference."

Inside she fumed. Mateo didn't know what he was talking about, but she wasn't going to stick around and enlighten him. "Listen," she said, trying to keep the edge from her voice. No matter how angry he made her, she hated when they fought, and lately it seemed like fighting had taken the place of everything else. "I have to go. We can discuss this later." She rolled her bike onto the street, trying to ignore the hurt look on Mateo's face.

She'd make it up to him later. But for now, she had a meeting to attend, and it had to come first.

She forced her mind to go blank as she made her way to the Vesper, but it was no use. Her hands were shaky, her heart was racing, and she knew it wasn't just the result of too much caffeine and too little sleep. This was about Mateo, and Mateo was wrong. The moment Aster had decided to steal Madison's boyfriend (not that Layla actually believed a person could be stolen, short of being kidnapped; people either went willingly or they didn't go at all—they weren't property one could swipe when no one was looking), she'd thrown herself into the ring. Same went for Tommy when he decided to rescue everyone's favorite celebrity. Layla had only done what any good journalist would do by reporting the story.

And yet, no matter how many times she replayed the words in her head, in the quiet of her soul she knew it wasn't entirely true. She'd acted from a dense, dark, and shadowy place. Forfeited her neutrality, the last remaining shreds of her journalistic integrity, and picked sides by choosing herself over everyone else. Anyone with a smidgen of insight could see Layla Harrison was far from innocent.

She paused before the ugly metal door and wondered if it wasn't too late to turn back. She could leave now, climb back in bed, and for a few blissful hours forget she'd ever allowed herself to get caught in this mess. She could—

"Layla?" The door opened before her as Ira Redman loomed on the threshold. "You joining us?"

She ducked her head low and slipped inside. The Vesper was the darkest of all Ira's clubs. Even with the lights turned up, it still resembled someone's hip, gritty dungeon.

"So, now that everyone's here—" Ira began.

Before he could finish, someone called from the back, "What about Aster?"

Ira lifted his gaze from his clipboard. His features

sharpening, he said, "Aster won't be joining us. Though I advise you to worry about your own survival, not hers."

From somewhere in back, someone snickered. Loudly, unmistakably, intended for Ira to hear.

Ira's steely gaze swept the room, though Layla sensed he knew exactly where it had come from. Ira claimed to know everything. Not to mention there were only eight suspects to choose from.

"If any of you have something to say, I suggest you do so. Passive-aggressive snickers, groans, eye rolls, and the like will not be tolerated."

The words were barely out before he had a taker. "Yeah, I have a comment."

Layla watched as Brittney rose from her seat, face flushed with anger. "How am I—how are any of us expected to compete when Aster and Tommy choose to pimp them-selves out to the top names on your list?" She tucked her blond hair behind her ear and glared hard at Tommy, who sank lower in his seat. "Don't pretend you don't know what I'm talking about." She folded her arms beneath her abun-dant chest and turned her focus to Ira. "Thanks to Layla, the whole freaking world read it. It's all anyone's talking about!"

Layla cringed and slipped toward the edge of her chair until she was hanging off the edge, wishing she could bend herself into tiny, unnoticeable, origami-like folds. The words she'd always dreamed of hearing—*the whole freaking world read it, it's all anyone's talking about*—were finally being applied to her, only it was for all the wrong reasons. Hardly the victory she'd dreamed it would be.

"We either need a new list, or . . ."

"Or?" Ira cocked his head, regarding her closely.

Brittney stood uncertainly before him, questioning her own convictions as she searched the room, desperate for takers to join her one-woman meltdown. But with everyone shifting uncomfortably, intent on avoiding her gaze, she was all on her own. Having talked herself into a hole, there was only one way out, continue or fold.

"I just—" Her voice cracked. She took a moment to clear it, harden her reserve. "I just don't see the point in continuing if the whole thing is rigged against me."

"So you're saying the contest is rigged against you?" Ira rubbed his chin in his usual theatrical way.

"I'm saying that it *feels* like it's rigged against me." Brittney's bottom lip trembled, her breath quickened.

"Interesting." Ira squinted, clearly finding it anything but. "Tell me—" His gaze moved among them. "At the start of this contest, did any of you have even the slightest connection to Madison Brooks or Ryan Hawthorne?"

Layla looked around and found herself shaking her head with the rest of them.

"Well, to my knowledge, which is quite extensive, I

assure you, neither did Aster or Tommy. You all began with an equal chance to claim victory. How you've decided to go about that was up to you."

"Well, excuse me for not prostituting myself." She mumbled the words, but Ira caught them all the same.

"And not once did anyone suggest that you do." He nodded to one of his assistants, then turned back to the group and called Layla's name.

Layla's head snapped up. There'd been so much drama surrounding Brittney's accusations, she hadn't been expecting him to call on her.

Her throat was parched, her tongue felt like a dried stump of wood shoved in her mouth, and her entire body had gone leaden with dread.

"Today's your lucky day."

She squinted, sure she'd misunderstood.

"Be sure to thank Brittney on her way out. Turns out she'll be leaving today instead of you."

Layla's eyes widened as she watched, as they all watched, Brittney mutter under her breath, gather her stuff, and storm out, with Ira's assistants close on her heels.

"But—" Finally able to access her voice, Layla glanced between the closed door and Ira. It had never once occurred to her she'd get cut. Her numbers were nowhere near Aster's or Tommy's, but she'd been holding her own—*hadn't she?*

Ira studied her. "But your numbers are decent? Is that

what you were going to say?"

She rubbed her lips together. It was what she'd been thinking, but saying it was no longer an option.

"This competition is about numbers, you're right. It's always been about numbers. But it's also about having what it takes to succeed, and how you go about answering the question: Just how far will you go to get what you want?" He held her gaze for a long, uncomfortable moment, leaving her to wonder if she was expected to answer. Before she could try, he went on to add, "Looks like you just got another week to determine that for yourself. And so—" He returned his attention to the rest of the group. "About that new list . . ." He motioned to his assistants, who passed around new lists containing a mix of some old names along with some new. Though it was interesting to see Heather Rollins had moved to one of the top five spots.

"Think of this as a guideline. What really interests me is how aggressive you are in building your numbers. Impress me. Dazzle me. Wow me. But whatever you do, do not disappoint me."

With that, he slipped out the back. Layla watched him go, wondering how the hell one went about *wowing* Ira Redman. She didn't even know where to begin.

She made her way outside, had just barely straddled her bike when Tommy appeared. "We need to talk."

Layla started her bike, refused to acknowledge him.

"I read your blog."

She studied him behind mirrored lenses, not saying a word.

"What I can't understand is why you would do that to me." He crossed his arms at his chest, looking truly perplexed.

Her fingers gripped the throttle. Running him over suddenly seemed like a viable option. Was he for real? How could she do that to *him*? Like she owed him special treatment because of one drunken kiss? Tommy Phillips seriously needed to get over himself.

She removed her glasses, wanting him to see the look in her eyes when she explained. "You made the choice to insert yourself in the drama. You chose to become part of the story. It was never about *you*, Tommy. Believe it or not, you are not the center of my universe."

"Is that what you tell yourself?"

She held his gaze, refusing to be the first to look away. "No, not just myself. I'm telling you too." She'd told him once not to mess with her. Not her fault he hadn't listened.

"I don't know what I did to piss you off, but clearly I must've done something for you to punish me for helping a traumatized girl who had no one else to look after her."

Layla's eyes widened, her jaw dropped, like some cartoon version of a shocked face. "Do you even hear yourself?" Her voice rang louder than intended. "You're completely delusional. *Madison Brooks had no one else to look after her? Is that the story you tell yourself?"* She rolled her eyes and lowered her glasses back onto her nose. "Don't act like you don't like the attention," she said, going for one final dig. "Isn't this exactly why you moved to LA—so people would talk about you? So your face would be in every tabloid, every blog? So you'd be inundated with interview requests? You should be thanking me, but I won't hold my breath."

She pushed her bike onto the street, a satisfied smirk sneaking to her lips when he scrambled out of her path.

"You don't get it, do you?" He followed alongside her. "Your blog's a hit, you're still in the contest, but none of that's a coincidence."

She should've moved on. Should've gunned her bike and gotten the hell out of there. But instead she stayed put, looking at Tommy, unsure what he meant.

"Ira Redman's a lot of things, but he's not an idiot. His fake attempts to ax you are all a big show. It was never gonna be you. What happened in there—" He hooked a thumb toward the Vesper, flicked his hair from his eyes. "That was Ira's way of challenging you to escalate the drama. The only question is: Will you? Will you throw us all under the bus for the win? Just how far will *you* go, Layla, to get what you want?"

The question hung heavy between them. Dissolving the

moment, Layla gripped the throttle and said, "I came here to win, same as you. And that's exactly what I intend to do." Then she sped onto the street without once looking back.

FORTY-TWO

# THE HAND THAT FEEDS

Tommy watched Layla speed away, his hands involuntarily clenched by his sides. She was smart, shrewd, and capable of reading people in a way that often surprised him. And yet, when it came to Ira Redman and the game he'd conned them all into playing, she was like a blind man slipping behind the wheel of a Ferrari, too caught up in the power and excitement to see the danger looming ahead.

Okay, maybe *conned* was an overstatement. They'd all gone into the interview with the clear goal of landing the job, and it wasn't that Ira hadn't made good on his word. But after observing him for the last several weeks, Tommy had learned Ira Redman was no altruist. He never invested in anyone or anything without expecting a sizable return.

He was challenging Layla to keep up the dirty work—to continue writing about the more salacious events at his club without fear of repercussions, or at least not from him.

No such thing as bad publicity—and in the world of nightclubs, the more scandalous and sordid the story the better.

Of course Tommy had no way to prove his suspicions, but then he didn't have to. It was Ira Freaking Redman—always scheming, always angling—an expert when it came to maneuvering every person, every situation, in a way that served him. Just like he'd done with Tommy's mom and the child he insisted she abort. He didn't want to be tied down, so he gave the order, moved on, and never looked back.

He treated life like a giant game of chess and the rest of the players were pawns. Where the contest was concerned, they were all puppets in his twisted theater, with Ira yanking the strings. There was virtually no limit to the metaphors Tommy could use to describe the situation he'd found himself in, and yet, clear as it was to him, Layla refused to see the truth.

"Tommy? Tommy Phillips?"

Tommy ducked his head low, shoved his hands deep in his pockets, and made for his car.

"Hey, Tommy—we were wondering if you might give us a word. . . ."

If nothing else, his brief experience in the spotlight had

taught him the paps always started off more or less pleasant, like potential friends in the making just looking to connect, only to turn in an instant. Dissing Madison, hurling insults—he'd learned that the hard way on his earlier foray into Starbucks.

"Go away." He glanced over his shoulder just in time to see a telephoto lens inches from his face. "I said fuck off!" He advanced on the guy, blocking the lens. He was over photogs, gossips, tabloids, and the rest of those bottom-feeding, low-life scumbags who made a living documenting other people's misery. Still the guy refused to give up.

"How's Madison?" he shouted. "Have you talked to her recently?"

Tommy narrowed his focus on the guy's nose, imagining how it might look smashed against his right cheek.

Deciding he might as well punch him to see whether the end result looked anything like the mental picture, he raised a fist, about to make contact, only to watch the asshole grin with the anticipation of filming the assault.

*Fuck it.* Tommy shook his head. *It's not worth it.* Without a word, he turned, aware of the photog chasing behind him, shouting insinuations, insults about his hookup with Madison, while Tommy struggled to maintain his cool, reminding himself he'd be out of there soon.

Or not.

He stood beside his car, staring in disbelief at the four

flattened tires—all of them slashed.

"What the—" Tommy whirled on the pap, who was busy photographing the damage. "You responsible for this?" He rushed him, fully committed to punching him in the nose after all, when a shiny, chauffeur-driven black Cadillac SUV pulled up alongside him, and Ira lowered the window and barked, "Get in."

Tommy shook his head. He wasn't interested in Ira. He had a trashed car and a photog inexplicably taking pictures of the damage. This was his mess to handle, and he would, if Ira would stay the hell out of his business.

"It wasn't a question." The door sprang open.

Tommy cursed under his breath, took one last lunge at the photog, if only to scare him, then reluctantly slid onto the seat beside Ira. He listened in stunned silence as Ira gave the driver Tommy's home address, reciting it from memory, before turning to him and handing over a fat envelope stuffed with what could only be cash.

"What's this?" Tommy glanced between the envelope and Ira.

"Originally, it was my way of thanking you for a job well done. Now it looks like you should think of it as payment toward a new set of wheels."

"You didn't have anything to do with that, did you?" Tommy turned to study Ira's profile. The words had come out before he'd had a chance to vet them, though he didn't necessarily regret them. For one thing, he wouldn't put it past Ira. For another, Tommy was in no mood to play games. The press was on his tail, his car had been vandalized, and despite the moments they'd shared, Madison Brooks had failed to reply to a single one of his texts.

He was worried about her. Sure she came off as tough and capable, but Tommy had seen a vulnerability most people would never suspect. He needed to know she was okay. Needed to know that whatever had shocked her into running hadn't gotten the best of her, or, God forbid, harmed her. If it turned out she'd decided she'd made a mistake by kissing him and that she never wanted to see him again, he'd deal. As long as she was all right, he'd handle it. It was the only thing that mattered.

"So how's Madison?" Ira asked, ignoring Tommy's question.

Tommy dropped his gaze to the envelope. Just how much of a thank-you was this? "How should I know?" He shrugged.

Ira continued to examine him. That was exactly what it felt like, being examined under a high-powered lens. "Considering you were the last to see her, I thought you might have some insight the others are lacking?"

Tommy watched Ira's mouth twitch at the side. Was it amusement? Contempt? At the moment, he didn't much care. He just sighed and squinted out the darkly tinted window to the sun-seared landscape beyond. Dead weeds, buckled sidewalks, sagging chain-link fences surrounding broken-down houses with peeling paint and bars covering the windows and doors. Other than a handful of manicured pockets they featured on the postcards, Tommy was surprised to discover the City of Angels mostly consisted of bleak urban sprawl.

"She's heartbroken," Tommy finally said. He needed to say something if he had any hope of getting Ira to stop scrutinizing him, never mind that it wasn't entirely true. Strange as it was, Madison hadn't seemed the least bit heartbroken. If anything, she seemed almost reborn, released, like a person who was standing on the precipice of a bright, shiny future. Though he wasn't about to share that with Ira.

"Heartbroken, huh?" Ira's voice betrayed a hint of amusement. "Who would've guessed?"

It was Tommy's turn to scrutinize Ira. He had no idea what he was getting at, but then Ira often spoke in riddles.

"Who would've thought she was a good enough actress to fool even you?" Ira's expression remained unreadable as Tommy sat speechless beside him. He hadn't even noticed the SUV had pulled up to the curb outside his apartment, until Ira said, "This is you, right?"

Tommy nodded, unsure what to do. Of course he needed to get out of the car and into his apartment before Ira could unnerve him even more. But suddenly the envelope felt too large and awkward in his hands. He needed the money more than ever, but nothing came from Ira without the expectation of some kind of repayment.

"Ira, I can't—" He started to return it, but Ira dismissed the gesture with a wave of his hand.

"Let's not play this game," he said. "I'll have your car towed and arrange for a loaner until it's fixed."

Tommy started to protest, but Ira cut in.

"This is LA, not . . . whatever small town you're from. Access to a working set of wheels is a matter of survival."

Tommy sighed, palmed the envelope, and slid out of the car before he had a chance to reconsider.

"And, Tommy," Ira called to him as the car pulled away. "I'm sure you'll find a way to repay me, if that's what you're worried about."

"That's exactly what I'm worried about," Tommy muttered, watching the SUV fade into the smog as he raced up the stairs to his shithole apartment before the paps could descend.

FORTY-THREE

# ANOTHER WAY TO DIE

"Mom . . . Dad . . . you're home!" Her mouth was moving, words were spoken, but Aster's body had otherwise completely shut down. Stunned, shell-shocked, stupefied—there was no single word to adequately describe the way she felt seeing her parents appear in her room. "I thought you were still in Dubai."

Her mother advanced, her mouth pinched with fury, eyes narrowed in scrutiny, as her father remained by the door, frozen with grief, and Nanny Mitra hovered in the background, fingering her locket and mumbling prayers of salvation under her breath.

"Where have you been?" Her mother's voice perfectly matched the stern expression she wore.

"Nowhere!" Aster closed her eyes. Damn, why had she

said that? It was the mantra of the guilty: *Nowhere—no one—nothing!* Still, her parents were the absolute last people she'd expected to see. They weren't due home for several more weeks. And yet, there they were, ambushing her in her very own room. "I mean, I was with a friend. I was with Safi—at Safi's." She cringed when she said it. She'd become so obsessed with her new job and her flirtation with Ryan she'd mostly blown off her friends, and yet, here she was, still using them as her go-to excuse.

"We've spoken to Safi." Her mother crossed her arms over the classic Chanel bouclé jacket Aster had once hoped to inherit. "Would you like to try again?"

Aster gulped, dropped her gaze to the floor. There was nowhere to go, nowhere to hide. She looked like crap, smelled like boy, and her mother was totally onto her.

"And what is that you're wearing?"

Aster rubbed her lips together, squinted at her clothes— or rather, Ryan Hawthorne's clothes. "It's just, you know, the 'borrowed from your boyfriend' look, that's all."

Her father let out a small cry of despair and rushed down the hall as though his daughter had just died and he couldn't bear to look at the corpse. But of course Nanny Mitra stayed put. She had absolutely no qualms about hanging around the crime scene.

"And who is this boyfriend you borrowed these from?" Her mother inched closer. Close enough to catch the scent of shame and despair surrounding her daughter.

"Mine." Javen pushed his way into her room and stood before their mom. "I mean, clearly I'm not her boyfriend, because—*gross!* But the clothes belong to me."

Their mother waved a hand in dismissal. "Javen, go to your room. You have nothing to do with this," she said, but Javen stayed put.

"You're wrong. I have everything to do with this. My sister raided my closet without my permission! I'd like to see her punished for *that*." He crossed his arms in defiance and arranged his face into the kind of angry expression he was unused to wearing.

It was a good attempt, and Aster loved him more in that moment than she probably ever had, but she wouldn't let him take the fall. Not like their mother was buying it. With a nod to Nanny Mitra, Javen was hauled out of the room by his arm, shouting in protest the whole way.

Too ashamed to face her mother, Aster stared down at her feet and studied her pedicure, sickened by the sight of the dark-red polish she'd chosen with the sole hope of gaining Ryan's approval. If she confided the truth that she didn't exactly have a boyfriend, but that for a few false moments she'd allowed herself to believe that she had, only to discover she'd been deflowered and discarded without a second glance—well, it was everything her mother had ever warned her about come true, in the most awful, most dramatic, most public way possible.

"There's no boyfriend," she whispered, eyes burning with tears.

"Then where did you get these clothes if there is no boyfriend to *borrow* them from?"

"Doesn't matter." She shook her head, wondering how it was possible for the night that had started so perfectly to end in such a nightmare.

"On the contrary." Her mother's voice rang as sharp as the verdict she would surely deliver. "You snuck out of the house, only to arrive home early in the morning wearing the clothes of a boy who isn't your boyfriend. I say it matters a great deal."

Aster forced herself to keep standing, keep breathing, but did nothing to stop the flow of tears that streamed down her face. She'd shamed herself, shamed her family. The only thing left was to wait for whatever punishment her mother deemed appropriate for the offense.

"All of which begs the question: If you're wearing his clothes, what happened to yours?"

Aster thought about the dress and undergarments she'd left in the trash. Stuff her mother had never seen and luckily never would—her one smart move in a long list of regrets.

"Does it matter?" She lifted her chin, her vision blurred by tears, as her mother stood stiff-backed before her. "Do you really give a shit about the current state of my clothes?"

Her mother's gaze hardened, as Aster awaited final judg-ment. Among her many crimes, she'd used foul language and spent the night with a boy who wasn't her boyfriend—a boy she would never marry—the ruling would undoubtedly be harsh.

"You're grounded until further notice."

Aster exhaled. She'd honestly thought she might be packed off to a brutal reform school for wayward girls, or excommunicated from the family. In the scheme of things, grounded wasn't so bad.

"You will not leave this house for any reason whatsoever outside of an emergency."

She nodded. That would certainly keep her out of the contest, but Ira Redman's competition no longer made the list of things she cared about. Besides, she didn't want to leave the house, possibly ever again.

"Okay." Her shoulders slumped in defeat as she headed for the shower, only to hear her mom call out from behind.

"You've disrespected yourself and brought great shame on this family. This is not something your father will recover from anytime soon."

Aster stopped, knowing she shouldn't say it, but she'd already fallen so far she figured she had nothing to lose. "And what about you?" She turned to face her mother. "How soon will you recover?"

She held her mother's gaze, the seconds seeming to

multiply before her mother shook her regal head, lifted a finger toward the bathroom, and said, "Go clean yourself up, Aster. Your father and I have had a very long trip. We are tired and in need of rest."

Without another word, she turned on her Ferragamo heels and closed the door behind her. Leaving Aster to stare after them, knowing she'd disappointed her family in a way *she* might never recover from.

# FORTY-FOUR

# THE SWEET ESCAPE

Layla wandered around the hotel meeting room. With its beige-and-white-patterned carpet, beige movable walls, and the lineup of beige chairs along the stage where Madison and her fellow actors would sit, the room elevated the neutral look to a ridiculous level. Still, the blandness of her surroundings did nothing to dampen her excitement at having fudged her way into her first press conference. She just hoped no one questioned her credentials. It would be embarrassing to get kicked out in front of a crowd she admired.

She moved among the other journalists, not sure whether to be relieved or annoyed when no one took much notice of her. Well, at least there was a coffee setup in the corner. She never turned down a chance at caffeine, no matter how bad the coffee might be.

"Late as always."

She gazed up at the woman who'd said it, about to defend herself, point out that she was actually early, when she realized the woman was referring to the event.

"Typical celebrity bullshit." She looked at Layla as though expecting her to agree.

"I know, right?" Layla said, immediately regretting it. It made her sound as young and inexperienced as she was. But the woman didn't seem to mind.

"Trena. Trena Moretti." She offered a hand, and Layla juggled her coffee in order to take it. "*LA Times* digital division." She shook her head, setting her wild bronze curls shimmering in a way that reminded Layla of fire season. "Still can't get used to saying that. I came over from the *Washington Post*."

Layla nodded. "Layla Harrison." She purposely omitted the name of her rag, mostly because it didn't exist. But when Trena leaned closer, eyes narrowed, trying to make out the name on her badge, she reluctantly said, "The *Independent*. Probably haven't heard of it, since we're new and . . . independent." Oh yeah, that was super convincing.

Trena shot her a knowing look. "First time at one of these?"

Layla was about to deny it, claim she'd been to many, but Trena was onto her. "That obvious?"

"You're drinking the coffee." Trena grinned. "Though it's good to see an excited new face. Reminds me why I was once drawn to this field."

"Why'd you leave the *Post*?" Layla asked, wondering if it was too invasive of a question for someone she'd just met, but weren't journalists supposed to dig deep? And besides, Trena could always plead the Fifth.

"A major career shift brought on by a cheating fiancé. Guess Madison and I have more in common than I thought." She laughed, prompting Layla to laugh too. With her smooth caramel complexion, and intense blue-green eyes, she was incredibly striking. "So, what's your interest in Madison?" Trena asked.

Layla shrugged. She didn't have a ready answer for that. "I guess I don't trust her," she said, deciding to answer honestly. "And I'm waiting for her to slip up, show us who she really is."

Trena tapped her water bottle against Layla's Styrofoam cup. "That makes two of us. You see that breakup video?"

Layla nodded vaguely. If there was ever a time to brag about her accomplishments, it was now. But her badge claimed she worked for a nonexistent rag.

Trena looked toward the stage. "Oh, finally," she said. "Shall we?"

Layla glanced in that direction. She'd planned to stay put, stick to the fifty-foot radius she'd been warned about.

ALYSON NOËL

But just as quickly she decided against it. She was a member of the press, and the press wouldn't be silenced.

She followed Trena, thrilled to have met someone who could possibly become a mentor. The two of them watched as Madison's costars took the stage one by one, leaving the chair in the middle, the one reserved for the star, empty, as the moderator took the mike and said, "We apologize for the delay."

"I'll bet." Trena rolled her eyes and shook her head.

"We're now ready to begin, but there's one caveat." He paused as though waiting for the situation to change within the next twenty seconds. When it didn't, he said, "It looks like Madison Brooks will not be joining us today."

That simple announcement was enough to set off an explosion of shouting as the reporters jockeyed for attention, yelling their questions.

*Where's Madison?*

*What explanation did she give?*

*Does this have something to do with the events at Night for Night?*

The moderator held up his hands. "I don't have answers to any of your questions, but if you'll all quiet down, we can proceed."

Trena glanced at Layla with an annoyed look on her face. "I don't know about you, but without Madison, I have no good reason to be here." She made for the door as Layla followed. "I'm not much for clubbing," she said, glancing over her shoulder. "But I'd love to talk with someone who was there. Something about that breakup feels wrong."

"I was there." Layla stopped short of the door, reluctant to leave her first press conference. With or without Madison, it was still worth attending.

"You don't strike me as the nightclub type." Trena studied her with renewed interest.

"I'm not." Layla shrugged. "Which is why I suck at my job as a promoter."

Trena fought to maintain a neutral face, but Layla caught the fleeting glimmer in her eye all the same.

"What do you say I buy you lunch, and in exchange, you tell me about your job as a promoter at Night for Night?"

"I promote Jewel. Another of Ira Redman's clubs."

"That works too." Trena pushed her way outside, assuming Layla would follow.

She gazed back at the stage, a bunch of *blah-blah* about how much fun they all had working together, when the truth was, they probably all hated one another. More Hollywood bullshit. The PR wheel never stopped spinning.

"Wait up!" she called, pausing long enough to toss her coffee in the trash before following Trena into the sun.

# FORTY-FIVE

# NOWHERE GIRL

## Was It Murder?

Following a very public breakup from former boyfriend Ryan Hawthorne after discovering his indiscretion with Aster Amirpour (a promoter for Ira Redman's Night for Night nightclub), America's Darling and tabloid staple Madison Brooks has seemingly fallen off the face of the earth.

Ms. Brooks is one of the world's most photographed celebrities, so the lack of sightings, along with the failure of the star to show up for scheduled appearances on *Ellen*, *Conan*, the *Today* show, and the press conference where she was first discovered missing, is troubling those closest to her, though the LAPD doesn't seem to share their concern.

"There are a variety of reasons why a person voluntarily disappears," claims Detective Sean Larsen. "Not all missing persons are victims of foul play. And being a voluntary missing person is not a crime in itself. We ask the press to keep that in mind. All of this wild speculation is probably only serving to drive her farther away. After all she's been through, the poor girl is probably just looking for some privacy."

Maybe so. But according to Madison's longtime assistant, Emily Shields, there's one thing Madison Brooks would never abandon. "Was Madison upset about what happened between her and Ryan? Of course, who wouldn't be? But even if she did decide to hide out for a while, she never would've left without Blue. That dog is her best friend in the world. He cries all day without her, like he senses something's wrong, and it's breaking my heart. If anyone out there knows what happened to Madison, please, please speak up. We need your help, since the police don't seem to care."

At what point will the LAPD wake up and realize what the dog knows?

Something's gone terribly wrong with Madison Brooks.

Trena Moretti skimmed the article she'd written, then adjusted the font until the screaming headline filled up the screen.

## Was It Murder?

Inflammatory? No doubt.

Attention-getting? Definitely.

But then, wasn't that the point?

It'd been days since anyone last saw Madison, and the usual rumors tossed around by the press had failed to satisfy her reporter's quest for the truth.

*Madison's on the set of a top secret project,* they'd said. Highly unlikely given that Madison herself had declared a hiatus, and from what Trena had gathered, Madison had done nothing to make her think otherwise.

*Madison's holed up at the Golden Door, overcoming "exhaustion."* The usual overused euphemism (along with *dehydration*) churned out by the Hollywood PR machine, which usually meant the star in question was suffering some sort of addiction, depressive episode, or maybe even an overdose—none of which applied to Madison. Not only had Trena contacted the Golden Door, but also Miraval, Mii amo, even the Ashram—a decidedly luxury-lacking starvation retreat inexplicably adored by A-list celebrities. Only the truly rich and spoiled would think nothing of spending thousands of dollars for a week of rigorous exercise, minuscule food portions, and austere rooms with shared bathrooms. And though Madison was undisputedly one of the most spoiled of all, according to Trena's sources, she hadn't checked into any of those places.

*Madison and Ryan are reconciling on a remote island*

*paradise.* Another unlikely scenario, considering Ryan
had become more visible than ever—there wasn't an interview he wasn't willing to grant. He basically repeated
the same unbelievable refrain, claiming he'd felt Madison
pulling away and so he'd hooked up with Aster Amirpour
in an attempt to make Madison jealous. It was undoubtedly immature—an act he deeply regretted. According to
*People, US Weekly,* and *OK!* magazines, not a day went
by when he didn't wish he'd handled it differently. More
than anything, he wanted Madison to return so he could
offer the apology she deserved. Though he entertained no
illusions about her taking him back, he was sure she was
off somewhere licking her wounds, wounds he'd undoubtedly caused, but she'd show up eventually. In the meantime,
after all she'd gone through, she deserved a little space and
privacy. He even went so far as to plead with the press to
back off the story and show some respect.

Trena had dutifully slogged through the interviews, and
as far as she was concerned, Ryan Hawthorne was giving
the performance of a lifetime.

There was something far darker at stake.

Madison wasn't quite the girl she pretended to be. She
worked hard to maintain her party image—yet she clearly
preferred her sobriety. She seemed to spend a lot of time
shopping—yet she spent very little of her own money,
since most of the clothes she wore were given to her by

the designers themselves. A single photograph of the right celebrity wearing the right dress was enough to boost a designer's profile, not to mention their profits, as it usually amounted to thousands of fans spending their hard-earned money to own the same thing. The result was an enormous return for a meager investment, and Madison was a willing participant in the game.

From what Trena could determine, Madison's house was her one major extravagance. Though the number of gates and security measures she'd taken made it seem more like a fortress.

Who was Madison so desperate to keep out?

Who was she afraid of?

For someone as famous as Madison, it was like hiding in plain sight.

Until now.

Trena tipped her stool forward, reached for the chai tea that'd grown cold, and read the headline again. She couldn't remember the last time she'd gotten so immersed in a story she'd lost track of time.

She was onto something good—she felt that deep stir of knowing that had never betrayed her. The story was so much bigger than it seemed on the surface, and she was sure that with a little more digging, she'd discover it went even deeper than anyone had yet to presume.

## Was It Murder?

Someone, somewhere, knew the answer. Though Trena sincerely hoped that it wasn't. As someone who'd grown up impoverished, forced to work for everything she'd ever achieved, she had little tolerance for privileged princesses like Madison. Yet the more Trena dug, the more Madison continued to surprise her. And though Trena was nowhere close to calling herself a fan, there was something strangely vulnerable about the girl that made Trena long to protect her. And yet, that wasn't her job. Her only responsibility was to report the facts. It was up to the police to safeguard the citizens. Though so far they'd hardly done much at all.

## Was It Murder?

If that didn't get the police moving, nothing would.

She pushed Publish, carried her mug to the sink, and tossed the contents.

Outside, the sun was starting to set, and when the sun disappeared, her most interesting subjects came out.

Trena had no plans to miss them.

# FORTY-SIX

# GLORY AND GORE

## Was It Murder?

The headline alone was enough to give Aster chills, but that didn't stop her from reading the corresponding article. Whoever this Trena Moretti person was—well, she seemed convinced that it was indeed murder. Or, if not murder, then something far darker than the *Madison is in rehab* rumor that had recently circulated.

But what was even worse than the thought of Madison being murdered—well, maybe not worse in a big picture sort of way, and certainly not worse for Madison, but definitely worse for Aster—was the implication that Ryan and Aster's now well-publicized tryst had somehow played a part in an A-list celebrity's disappearance.

An implication that was never brought to any real conclusion, but then that was never the intent. The seed had been planted. The worst-case scenario declared in bold headlines. The idea of an unthinkable tragedy released into the ether for anyone and everyone to speculate on and come to their own sordid conclusions.

Aster's phone buzzed with an incoming text, and she didn't so much as flinch, wasn't even tempted to glance at the screen. Her phone hadn't stopped buzzing since the day Layla Harrison's blog broke the story. The video, the stills from the video—they'd all been forwarded to her by "friends" who somehow thought she needed not only to know about all the horrible things being said about her, but also to read them firsthand.

Why they thought she needed access to the thousands of anonymous commenters calling her a whore, a bitch, and a slut—a few of them even threatening to kill her—was beyond her. What exactly did they expect her to do in return?

Aster had responded the only way she knew how—she'd obeyed her parents' orders and stayed sequestered in her room, musing on the slim divide between fame and infamy.

She'd wanted one—she'd gotten the other—and as luck would have it, they were inextricably linked.

Then again, from the moment she'd woken up alone at Ryan's apartment, nothing in her life had gone as planned.

The press had portrayed her as a slutty, conniving boy-friend stealer, only to fall for the lie Ryan had told them about trying to make Madison jealous. And yet, despite the numerous interviews he'd given, not once had he mentioned that Madison wasn't the only one who'd gone missing that night.

Her phone stopped chiming, allowing for a brief moment of peace, before it started again. Aster sighed, rolled her eyes, and thought about shutting it off. The calls and texts were relentless. A quick glance at the screen showed a caller ID reading *Blocked*.

She knew better than to answer it—willed it to go into voice mail. But after catching a glimpse of herself in the full-length mirror, something irreversible shifted inside her.

It'd been days since she'd last looked at herself. She was too ashamed, too afraid of what she might see. But after getting a glimpse, she found it nearly impossible to look away.

She moved toward the mirror and studied her face. Her hair hung loose and limp by her cheeks, her complexion was ashy and pale, and her eyes bore deep shadows, making her appear as bruised, hunted, and haunted as she felt.

What was it Ryan had said? Something like, *You just took your first step toward making a name for yourself.*

He'd also promised to remain right by her side.

*You have no idea how good it's about to get,* he'd told her. *Will you trust me?*

She had, only to never hear from him again.

The phone continued to ring.

She might look haunted, hunted, and bruised, but she was tired of hiding.

She dove for her cell. Clutching it with a shaky hand, she whispered a tentative greeting.

"Aster Amirpour?" The voice on the other end was deep, throaty, and rang with authority. "This is Detective Larsen with the Los Angeles Police Department. I was wondering if you might come down to the station to speak with us at your convenience. We have a few questions regarding the disappearance of Madison Brooks. Shouldn't take more than a few minutes."

She shifted her gaze to her laptop. *Score one for Trena Moretti.*

She shouldn't have answered, but now that she had, there was no turning back.

"Give me an hour," she said. "Two at the most." Tossing her phone on the bed, she made for her large walk-in closet. It was time to pack a bag.

She'd seen enough detective shows on TV to know better than to talk to a cop without a lawyer in tow. But all the lawyers she knew were either relatives or friends of her parents, and since she couldn't ask them, and since she had no money of her own, she really had no choice but to go it alone. Besides, it wasn't like she actually knew anything about what happened to Madison. The only thing she was guilty of was letting her ambition get in the way of her common sense by choosing to believe Ryan Hawthorne when he told her he cared about her. It might be embarrassing, but it wasn't illegal, and it was her truth to keep.

While everyone knew she'd played a part in the death of RyMad, she had nothing to do with the disappearance of Madison. Outside of Ryan, no one knew what had really happened between them, and since he'd yet to divulge that to the press, she figured her secret was safe.

She tossed some clothes in a bag, pulled her unwashed hair into a ponytail, swiped a little makeup on her face, took one last look around the room, and headed downstairs in search of her mother. Pausing in the kitchen doorway, Aster watched as her mother clipped the leaves off a dozen roses plucked from their garden before arranging them into a round, cut-crystal vase.

"I'm sorry I've upset you and Daddy." The words came out shakier than intended. "I'm sorry my actions disappointed and shamed you. But I refuse to be punished for making the kind of mistakes that aren't all that uncommon for someone my age. You may not agree with my choices, but I'm eighteen now, which means you no longer get a say in how I make my decisions." She pressed a hand to her fluttering belly, willing it to settle. All the while studying her mother's immaculately made-up face for even a trace of emotion, but her mother remained as cool and imperious as ever.

"And how do you plan to support yourself, Aster?" She set the curved, pink-handled pruning shears on the granite countertop and pulled nervously at her diamond-encrusted wedding band with perfectly manicured fingers. "You won't be able to access your trust for another seven years."

Aster closed her eyes. She'd been foolish enough to hope for a different reaction, maybe even a hug, but it was time to face the truth. Her mother had never been the warm and nurturing type. She was detached, wooden, regal, and cold, but Aster had loved her in spite of it. Her father was the dispenser of hugs and kind words—the one she ran to in moments of crisis. But her dad was no longer speaking to her, Javen wasn't home, and Nanny Mitra was the one who'd gotten her into this mess, by alerting her parents to trouble and encouraging them to return. It was hard not to feel bitter toward the woman who'd practically raised her. Still, this was her only chance at good-bye. It was time to speak her piece and move on.

"You can't hold me hostage." Aster pressed her hand to her cheek, about to wipe away the tears that had gathered, then decided against it. She refused to run from her emotions like her mother. She would allow them to surface—allow herself to feel them—no matter how much pain they might cause. "You can't turn this into some kind of tug-of-war over money. You can't control me that way anymore. If I don't want to live like this, I don't have to. And if you don't have it in your heart to release some of that money so I can adequately support myself, then I'll find another way."

"And what about school?" Her mother had gone from pulling at her wedding ring to fluffing the ends of her perfectly coiffed and colored shoulder-length hair—the only visible signs she might not feel as serene as she pretended.

"What about it?" Her mother's insistent focus on the practical was the single biggest tragedy of her family. Theirs was a house of repression, marred by the lies that resulted from living that way. Aster couldn't wait to break free. "I still plan on getting my degree, if that's what you're worried about." She shrugged, eager to wrap it up and be on her way. "I'll be back at some point for the rest of my stuff. So . . ." She moved to hug her mother good-bye, but it was like embracing a wall, so she quickly pulled away. Stealing a moment to send a quick text to Javen, promising she was only a phone call away. She felt guilty leaving him there on his own. There was no telling what her parents might do if they ever discovered he liked boys more than girls. And yet, how could she possibly protect him when she'd so epically failed to protect herself?

Without a single look back, she tossed her bag in the trunk of her car, settled inside, and headed down the driveway toward a new life.

# FORTY-SEVEN

# CALIFORNICATION

Tommy settled onto the hard metal chair and waited for the detective to bring him a mug filled with bottom-of-the-pot, end-of-the-day scorched coffee along with some of those little packets of powdered creamer. It was his first visit to the precinct, yet he was handling it like a regular.

He'd shown up without a lawyer, but he was pretty sure he didn't need one. He wasn't guilty of anything having to do with Madison's disappearance, and it was just a matter of time before they got that through their thick skulls and moved on to someone who might actually be involved. Until then, he'd committed to being as polite and cooperative as his mother had taught him. If he needed to amp up the simple-boy-from-the-country act, so be it. Whatever it took to get them off his tail and onto finding Madison.

There'd been a *shitstorm* of accusation, speculation, and downright hysteria, but Tommy refused to believe it. The memory of Madison was too fresh. Every time he closed his eyes he could feel her lips pulse against his. No way was she dead.

"You know why you're here?" Detective Larsen slid the mug of coffee toward Tommy and claimed the opposite seat.

Tommy pressed two of the creamer packets together, pinched off the corners, and dumped the contents into the cup. "I'm the last known person to be seen with Madison." He ventured a first sip and tried not to grimace—the first taste was always the worst, reminding him of just how far he'd fallen and how fast. His lifelong dream of gazing out at a crowd of hot girls screaming his name from the end of a stage had been replaced with the reality of a police interrogation and crazed Madison fans slashing his tires and sending him hate tweets.

Detective Larsen rested his beefy forearms on the table and hunched his shoulders forward. Regarding Tommy from under a lowered brow, he kept his voice quiet, conspiring, as though they were just two old buds enjoying an overdue conversation. "And how does that make you feel— knowing you were the last to see her alive?"

Tommy ran his fingers around the edge of the mug. *How does that make me feel? What is this, a therapy session?*

He lifted his gaze to the cop's red, scrub-brush hair clipped close to the scalp, his green eyes and pale, freckled skin losing the war against the relentless Los Angeles sun, his overtrained deltoids and pecs threatening to wage a hostile takeover of his neck. "Doesn't make me feel anything. I refuse to believe it."

Larsen pressed his fingertips together until they resembled thick, meaty sausage links. "You were the last known person to see her. There are pics of the two of you heading into the Vesper. A club you apparently had access to even after it had closed for the night. The evidence speaks for itself."

Tommy swallowed. At least they didn't know about the pics on his phone. The ones of Madison kicking back a beer, which were incriminating on two levels—one, because everyone knew Madison was three years shy of the legal drinking age, and two, because Tommy had yet to volunteer those particular photos. Short of arresting him, the cops would never know those pictures existed, and he was determined to keep it that way.

It was Layla's fault he was there, standing in as their number one suspect. Sure she wasn't the only witness, but she was definitely the first one to blog about it. Question was whether she'd done it on purpose, to get back at him for some unknown reason.

From the moment she uploaded that video, hers had become

the go-to blog for celebrity junkies. The Madison-Ryan-Aster-Tommy scandal was like catnip to them. They couldn't get enough. Then again, the scandal had also ensured that Ira's clubs remained a permanent fixture in the twenty-four-hour news cycle, with Night for Night and the Vesper becoming makeshift shrines to Madison as people traveled from far away to pay homage to the last known whereabouts of their favorite teen star.

Tommy returned his focus to Larsen. It was never a good idea to let the mind drift for too long. "I don't believe she's dead." He tried another sip of coffee. It was cold, brutally bitter, but the initial shock to the taste buds had faded, so he chased it with another. "And if she's not dead, then I couldn't possibly be the last person to have seen her."

"Huh. You make an interesting point." Detective Larsen gazed into the distance as though he was actually considering it, but Tommy recognized a con job when he saw one. "Still, in this modern age of Instagram, selfies, YouTube, cable news, and bloggers so hopped up on caffeine they no longer sleep, you'd think that if someone had seen Madison since you, we'd have some sort of photographic proof, wouldn't you? Wouldn't you think that?"

Tommy shrugged and swirled his coffee, watching the light-brown sludge run up and down the sides of his mug. "I told you what I think. My position stands."

"Well, then." Detective Larsen tipped back in his seat, his

chair rocking precariously. If he was trying to set Tommy off balance, he'd already failed. Tommy couldn't care less if he crashed and cracked his head. Tommy would make sure to finish his coffee; then maybe he'd consider calling for help. "You seem pretty confident about your position. Makes me think you might know more than you let on. What gives, Tommy? Is there something you haven't told us? Because if it's time you're worried about, I got all night. You keeping Madison alive somewhere?"

Tommy squinted in confusion. Did they honestly believe he was capable of kidnapping Madison Brooks and holding her hostage?

"Did you kiss her?" Larsen slammed the seat forward and leaned so far across the table his face was just inches from Tommy's. Close enough to take in a constellation of clogged pores and renegade eyebrow hairs.

Tommy winced and edged back in his seat. Larsen's breath stank of whatever foul thing he'd eaten for lunch, and he hated the way the detective's eyes went all beady on his. Like he wanted the details not just for the investigation but so he could store the mental image in his personal spank bank. Tommy shook his head, swiped a hand over his face. His body language was all wrong. Too fidgety. Made him look guilty. But he wasn't guilty. Why couldn't they see that? Why the hell was he still in this room?

"Did you kiss her? Did you take her to a back room and

try to have your way with her?"

"What the fu—" Tommy frowned. "What kind of perverted bullshit is this?" He finally pulled the brakes on his
tongue when he saw the way Larsen leered at him with
his crinkly eyes and puffed-out cheeks, looking as though
Tommy had just given him a beautiful gift, which he had.
He'd shown anger—enough to hint at a possible dark side.
Cops lived for those moments, and Tommy had walked
right into the trap.

"It's not bullshit," Larsen said. "So maybe you should
get serious and try answering the questions I ask you."

Tommy took a deep breath and focused on the large rectangular mirror before him, which, according to every cop
show he'd ever seen, allowed whoever stood on its other
side to study him without being seen. Speaking to that person, whoever they might be, he raised his voice, and said.
"Yeah, I kissed her."

"And . . ."

Larsen's brows wiggled in a way that made Tommy sick,
but determined not to show it, he said, "And . . . nothing."
He'd tried to keep it neutral, but his voice gave him away.
He was completely annoyed, and it was starting to show.
Still, what he'd experienced with Madison was far more
meaningful than some sloppy adolescent grope session. It
was . . .

"So tell me about the black wristbands."

Tommy snapped to attention. How the hell had he known about that?

"You know, I gotta admit, I was a late adapter when it came to the social networks. I mean, who wants to keep up with all the people you couldn't stand in high school, right?" He looked at Tommy as though waiting for him to agree, and when he didn't, he went on to say, "And yet, now that I've joined the modern world, I find them incredibly useful." He stared hard at Tommy, purposely pausing for a few awkward beats. "According to Instagram, you have a reputation for looking the other way when it comes to underage drinking."

Tommy relaxed. Luckily, he'd been smart enough to halt that particular practice just after Layla's story broke and the cops started snooping around. It was old news. Couldn't be proved. He had nothing to worry about.

"I'm hardly responsible for the crap people post on the net." He shrugged like he meant it.

"Maybe so . . . but those black wristbands are specific to the Vesper. Most of those kids taking selfies—is that what you're calling them—selfies?"

Tommy closed his eyes to keep from rolling them in plain sight. Larsen acted like he was a computer-illiterate octogenarian when he was probably somewhere in his mid- to late thirties. The whole thing was ridiculous.

"Anyway, most of these kids taking selfies with these

black wristbands are under twenty-one. And I'm telling you, there are hundreds of these pics, maybe even a thousand. I lost count. What I'm wondering is—were you aware of that?"

Tommy gulped. Surely he hadn't given away *that many*—had he? "I don't know what you're talking about." He struggled to keep his voice steady, even. He'd revealed too much already.

Larsen shrugged as though the topic was dead, but Tommy knew it was anything but. "Still, it's interesting how you've taken this terrible tragedy involving a girl you claim to care for and made it work for you. I like to keep up on celebrity culture by reading the blogs and the tabloids. Helps me do my job, seeing as most of those folks live in this town. From what I've gathered, you've managed to give a sizable number of interviews in a short time. You've spoken to *People*, TMZ, and *US Weekly*, to name a few. You moved to LA to break in as a musician, right?"

Tommy stared at him stone-faced, refusing to confirm or deny.

"Must've been disappointing to uproot yourself all the way from Oklahoma only to end up working at Farrington's Vintage Guitar, and even then you got fired. Luckily, you managed to rebound with this gig for Ira Redman, but really, how long do you expect that to last?"

"Yeah, I get it." Tommy met his gaze. "You did your

homework. You know all about me."

"Clearly I don't know *all* about you. Otherwise you wouldn't be here, would you? Still, it's impressive how quickly you've managed to position yourself."

Tommy was seething but kept it under wraps.

"I can tell you've done an ace job using your connection to Madison Brooks to lure in big crowds and get a leg up on your competitors. According to your interviews, you knew Madison far better than you let on. You spoke of her in almost lyrical terms, but when asked if you kissed her—what was it you said?" He leaned so close Tommy could feel Larsen's breath hit his check like a slap. "Real men don't tell." He pushed away, let out a loud, guttural laugh. "Real men don't tell." He slammed the desk, shook his head. "And they say chivalry is dead. I especially liked the way you shot the camera a look that hinted otherwise. Hit it outta the park. The fans, the haters, they can't get enough. Executed in true Hollywood fashion, wouldn't you agree?"

Tommy's shoulders slumped in shame. He'd done all those things, and worse. But what was he supposed to do? He was young and hungry, had no choice but to seize every opportunity. Besides, he'd tried avoiding the press and they only hounded him more. Giving them what they wanted was a win-win. They got the story, and he got the kind of exposure he wouldn't otherwise be offered. Besides, most of those interviews paid off in fat rolls of cash he was in no position to reject.

"You still pointing the finger at . . ." Larsen pretended to consult his notes, but it was just another tactic in an arsenal of many. "Layla Harrison? You still think she had something to do with Madison's disappearance?"

Tommy closed his eyes. Did he think Layla did it? Most likely no. Then again, he didn't know her as well as he'd wanted to, but that was all over now. He'd said it on the phone, back when the cops first called, mostly trying to lessen the heat on himself. Besides, it wasn't like Layla hesitated to push Tommy onto the proverbial tracks when she'd posted pics of him and Madison. All he knew for sure was that the girl had some unresolved anger issues. And yeah, maybe someone should take a closer look at her.

Tommy opened his eyes, fixed his gaze on Detective Larsen. "When it comes to Layla Harrison—let's just say I wouldn't put anything past her."

# FORTY-EIGHT

# SHAKE IT OFF

Aster Amirpour drove straight to the police station, pulled into a parking space, and rested her forehead on the leather-wrapped steering wheel. She was wired, shaky, and the fluttering in her belly when she'd left her house had upgraded to spasms. If she didn't get a grip before going inside, they'd misread her anxiety and peg her as guilty.

She took a series of deep, cleansing breaths, about to check her appearance in the rearview mirror, when her phone chimed with an incoming call and Ira Redman's name popped onto the screen.

She stared at her phone, unsure what to do. She wasn't in the habit of receiving calls from Ira, and she feared she might be in trouble for failing to show at the club and missing some meetings. After all he'd done for her, taking care of her after the Madison meltdown, not to mention the cash-filled envelopes—he'd believed in her and she'd let him down. If he was going to fire her, it was probably for the best. With her reputation as a slutty boyfriend stealer, she'd become a liability. The sooner they both put the whole mess behind them, the better.

She closed her eyes and cleared her throat, and then lifting the phone to her ear, she murmured hello.

"Aster, good." Ira's voice was hurried and deep, the sound of a busy man about to clear an unpleasant task from a list of things to conquer by noon. "You're alive. Up until now I was afraid Madison wasn't the only one who'd disappeared."

Aster cringed at the reference. "I left you a message," she murmured, hating how timid she sounded, but Ira always left her feeling nervous.

"Yeah, yeah, I got it." There was a muffled sound on the other end as he placed his hand over the receiver and spoke to someone in the background before he returned. "Still, that was one message, Aster. Your absence was a bit lengthier than expected."

She picked at a frayed spot on the jeans she'd bought at the Barneys denim bar. Funny to think how much she'd paid for pants that'd been purposely destroyed. If only she'd had enough foresight to buy a less-damaged pair. With her parents determined to cut off her finances, her shopping spree days were now a thing of the past. "Am I fired?" Her fingers instinctively reached for the hamsa pendant, despite any evidence it worked in her favor.

"What? No!" Ira's surprised voice boomed in her ear. "Where'd you get that idea?"

"Well, I just figured—"

"Don't figure. Don't ever try to second-guess me. You'll fail every time. I know you're getting a rough deal in the press and I wanted to check in and— You okay?"

She was crying. She hated herself for it, but she couldn't help it. She'd been unfairly ridiculed and shamed by both the press and her family. And now, because of it, she was penniless, homeless, and about as far from *okay* as she could possibly get—only to have Ira Redman, of all people, actually show some concern. It was too much to process in too short a time. And once she'd started crying, she found she couldn't stop.

"Aster—where are you? Tell me you're not driving." He sounded like a father—a concerned and caring father. Like the kind she used to have until she brought shame on her family and her dad could no longer bear to so much as look at her.

"I'm at the police station." The words were a whisper. She hung her head low, watching the tears spill onto her lap.

"What the hell are you doing there?"

Ira's alarm snapped her to attention. She peered in the mirror and wiped her hands furiously over each cheek. "They asked me to come down for questioning and—"

"And you decided to oblige them?"

She squirmed when he said it. The judgment in his tone rang loud and clear.

"You with a lawyer?"

She shook her head, and then realizing he couldn't actually see her, mumbled, "No."

"You talk to anyone?"

"Not yet." She looked over her shoulder, watched some cops climb into a squad car, neither of them exhibiting the slightest interest in her. "I'm still in the parking lot."

"Listen, start your car and get the hell out of there. Now. You hear me?"

A fresh flood of tears sprang to her eyes, and there was nothing she could do to stop the flow. Only this time she wasn't just crying, she was sobbing, with all the embarrassing snot-clogged sound effects to go with it.

"Aster?" Ira waited a beat, giving her a chance to calm down. "What's really going on here?"

She peered into the rearview mirror, scowled at her mess of a reflection, and jerked the mirror till it was facing the opposite way. "I have nowhere to go."

She could hear Ira breathing. And though it only lasted a moment, to Aster it felt like the silence would drag on forever. "Meet me in the lobby of the W in a half hour. It's on the corner of—"

"I know where it is."

"Fine. And, Aster—"

She was already starting the car, already starting to recover. Ira had a plan. Ira would take care of her. Or, at the very least, he would help her form a plan so she could take care of herself, which was even better. Either way, if she could think of this moment as rock bottom, then things could only get better

"Everything's going to be fine, you hear?"

"I know," she said, already starting to believe it. "See you soon."

# FORTY-NINE

# SHUT UP AND DANCE

Layla moved through the crowded club, the percussive techno beat throbbing in her head, as she took a mental tally of her gets before ultimately losing track and giving up. It was a lot. The most bodies she'd ever pulled in. And it was all thanks to her Beautiful Idols blog.

Not like she could compete with the kind of numbers they were scoring at Night for Night and the Vesper, but that was only because they'd turned into Madison shrines, and Jewel hadn't played an actual part in the drama, so there were fewer pop culture vultures dropping in. Though she was gaining a sizable list of publicity-starved B- and C-list celebrities. Including Sugar Mills, who Aster had sent over, as though that somehow made up for Ryan Hawthorne. Hardly. But she'd deal with that later.

"Can you even believe this?" she said to Zion, shouting to be heard over the music.

"Oh, like you can't?" He narrowed his dark eyes on hers, shaking his regal head as he made for his table of models.

Layla looked after him, unsure if the snub was because they were the last two standing at Jewel after Ira cut Karly, along with Taylor at Night for Night, last week, dropping the competitors to just six—because he knew her blog was mostly responsible for the kind of crowds Jewel was pulling in and it made him resent her—or if he was just being a bitch because he was clearly destined to lose and he refused to accept it.

Funny how gullible people were when it came to celebrities. Never realizing that nearly all pics of celebs frolicking at the beach in minuscule bikinis, or doing complicated yoga poses in the wild, were mostly staged by the celebrities themselves. And lately, Layla was so inundated with requests to catch them pretending to act spontaneously, between that and the club she had little time for anything else.

Sometimes she pretended to hate it, but it was mostly for Mateo's benefit. For someone who'd never fit in, who'd never been part of the popular crowd, she had to admit she actually kind of liked being in demand.

"Looks like you've been holding out on me."

Layla turned to find Heather Rollins standing behind

her, gripping a miserable-looking Mateo by the arm.

*What the—?*

Layla stared. Blinked. Stared again. Sure her eyes were deceiving her. Mateo had never once stopped by Jewel. He hated clubs. And yet there he was, hanging with Heather.

"Poor thing looked lost, so I figured I'd help him find his way. Where've you been hiding him, Layla?" She clutched Mateo's bicep with both hands, nudging her body against him as she grinned flirtatiously. "All this time I've been sharing my secrets, didn't realize you were still hiding yours." She pursed her lips and shot Layla a disapproving look.

"Not a secret, just my boyfriend," she said, watching as Mateo jerked free of Heather's grip and moved to stand beside her. Aware of the sudden rush of heat rising to her cheeks as she glanced between them, she felt nervous, inflamed. Must have something to do with her two worlds unexpectedly colliding. She worked hard to keep her life carefully compartmentalized. She wasn't one for surprises.

"Well, stop hiding him and start bringing him around." Heather's gaze lingered on Mateo, as he pressed a hand to the small of Layla's back and steered her away.

"Who the hell is that?" he asked, sounding as annoyed as Layla felt.

"She's not so bad," Layla said, unsure what frustrated her more—having to defend Heather Rollins, or Mateo showing up unannounced.

He looked around the club, seeming agitated, unnerved, totally unlike his usual self. "How do you know her?"

Layla closed her eyes and shook her head. Seriously? This was what he wanted to discuss when they'd barely seen each other all week? She took a steadying breath. "She's a regular fixture on my blog, which you clearly no longer read or you'd know that." She sighed, forced a more muted stance. "We hang out sometimes, that's all."

Mateo shot her a conflicted look, but Layla moved past it and took his hand in hers. "You can't blame her for hanging all over you." She inched closer, ran her fingers over the neck of his T-shirt. "Not when you come in here looking so amazing."

She cast an appreciative look at his dark jeans, charcoal V-neck tee, and black linen blazer—a far cry from his usual board shorts and wet suits. Clearly he'd made an effort, and she wanted him to know just how much she appreciated the gesture.

"C'mon." She grabbed hold of his lapels and pulled him closer. "Wanna drink?"

He shook his head.

"Wanna dance?"

He squinted. "You don't dance."

"I do with you."

He frowned and looked away. "How many of these kids

are messed up on Molly, or worse?"

Layla sighed. It took all her effort not to roll her eyes. "Not sure." She shrugged. "It's not like I took a survey."

"And it doesn't bother you that they might be?"

"Last I checked, I didn't work for the DEA, and neither did you." She let go of his jacket, crossed her arms over her chest, and stared at him. "What's really going on here?" she asked. Everything about him was grossly out of character.

"What's going on with you?" He rubbed his lips together, ran a hand through his hair.

"Can you be more specific?" She frowned.

"What happened to your blog and the inside story you were supposed to uncover?"

Layla looked at him, sensing that what he really wanted to ask was: *What happened to you?*

"Mateo, why did you come here?" she asked, ignoring the question. There was no good way to answer it that wouldn't just make everything worse.

When he met her gaze, the fight seemed to seep out of him. "To see you." He shook his head.

"Well, I'm here. Right in front of you. Asking you to dance. Question is: What are you going to do about it?"

Without hesitation, he grasped her hand, led her into the crowd, and pressed his lips against hers. The move reminded her of the time she'd danced with Tommy—a time she preferred to forget.

But maybe this kiss with Mateo could erase all of that. Or, at the very least, superimpose a better memory on top of the bad one.

She pushed closer, slowly grinding her hips against his. Relieved when Mateo anchored his hands at her waist and closed whatever space existed between them.

# FIFTY

# HIPS DON'T LIE

**Spotlight**

*Green-eyed teen heartthrob Ryan Hawthorne has been missing from the club circuit these days, and who could blame him? With a recent run of bad luck, including a canceled show; the embarrassing public breakup at Night for Night nightclub with his former A-lister girlfriend, Madison Brooks; and the rash of rumors in the wake of her disappearance, it's understandable he'd take a break from his party-boy ways. If there was ever a time for some serious self-reflection, it's now. As it turns out, that's exactly what Ryan's been up to, and we at Spotlight were thrilled when he took time out to answer our questions.*

**Spotlight:** *We're sure you're aware of the frenzy*

*following Madison's disappearance, but considering your former relationship with her, we're wondering—what are your theories?*

**Ryan:** *I don't have any theories. And I certainly don't buy into the conspiracy theories floating around. Look—I've said it before, and I'll say it again—I'm deeply sorry about the way things ended between me and Mad. I'd do anything to get her back. And I plan to do exactly that—if she'll have me. But for now, I respect her right to lie low, and I ask everyone else to grant her that too. She's had a rough go of it, mostly thanks to me. And while I can't rewrite the past, I can work on becoming the kind of boyfriend Madison deserves.*

**Spotlight:** *And what about Aster Amirpour?*

**Ryan:** *What about her? Getting involved with Aster is something I deeply regret. There's absolutely no excuse for my behavior and the way I betrayed Madison. Now I'm just eager to put that behind me as a lesson learned and do whatever it takes to try to redeem myself.*

**Spotlight:** *Well, everyone loves a good redemption story, so we're rooting for you, Ryan! But unlike certain news reports, you seem convinced that Madison Brooks is alive and well.*

**Ryan:** *Because she is alive and well. It's irresponsible* *to print things that suggest otherwise when there's absolutely no evidence to back it. But hey, I get it, sensationalism sells.*

**Spotlight:** *What would you like to say to Madison in case she's reading this?*

**Ryan:** *I want to tell her that I love her—that I'm sorry for my actions—and when she's ready to resurface, I hope she'll find it within herself to give me a second chance.*

Aster rolled her eyes and chucked the gossip mag to the other side of her room. *He loves her. He's sorry.* It was nothing but lies. But then Ryan was an accomplished liar. Look at all the lies he'd told Aster that she'd been dumb enough to believe.

Well, not anymore.

She shook away the thought and headed inside her walk-in closet, toes sinking into the plush ivory carpet as she tried to decide which of the two new dresses she should wear to the club. Funny how she'd started the week sobbing in the police station parking lot, with an empty wallet and nowhere to go, only to end it ensconced in a swanky penthouse apartment in the W hotel (thanks to Ira Redman, who owned the luxury pad), and her place in the competition intact.

Ira was right. The very thing she thought would lead

to her doom ended up being the best thing that had ever happened to her. Sure, her parents still weren't speaking to her, but she talked to Javen nearly every day, so at least she had that. And while she couldn't claim complete independence, seeing as she owed her current luxurious lifestyle to the generosity of Ira Redman, and while she wasn't exactly proud of the events that had spawned her good fortune, there was no denying Madison's disappearance and Aster's notoriety were directly responsible for the surge in numbers at all of Ira's clubs. Not to mention how she'd had her pick of interested agents, who'd already lined up a bunch of interviews and photo shoots.

A far cry from the day she'd left the police station, only to have Ira whisk her into the amazing apartment, where he'd settled her onto the sleek dove-gray leather couch with a cup of green tea while one of his many assistants arranged her belongings in her new room.

"You don't have to do this," she'd said, feeling small and overwhelmed in such a luxurious space. The floor-to-ceiling windows provided an amazing view of the city. The furnishings were modern, sleek, and of the highest quality. She could never repay him.

"Of course I don't." Ira had claimed the couch just opposite. "But I didn't get where I am by ignoring opportunities that have been handed to me, and you're smart and ambitious enough to understand what I mean."

She'd taken a tentative sip of her tea and waited for him to continue.

"Correct me if I'm wrong, but it was your ambition, first and foremost, that sent you into Ryan Hawthorne's arms?"

Aster had folded her knees to her chest, wrapped her arms around them, and hung her head in a way that encouraged her hair to fall over her face. More than anything, she wanted to cling to the belief that she'd truly cared about Ryan. She didn't want to think she'd willingly wasted her virginity on someone who'd cared as little for her as she did for him. But if Ira wasn't fooled, how much longer could she continue to fool herself?

"He was on the list." Ira's voice had remained neutral, just stating the facts as he saw them. It was the first time since the whole mess began that she hadn't felt the harsh sting of criticism. "And so you were determined to claim him as one of your gets, probably figuring where Ryan goes, Madison follows?"

She'd lifted her shoulders, unfolded her legs. She felt raw, exposed, incapable of hiding the truth. For the first time in days, she was ready to talk. "In the beginning—" She'd snuck a peek at Ira, seeking the strength to continue. "I liked the attention. He liked the attention, or at least he seemed to. But then . . ." She'd reached for her tea, holding the cup between her chest and her chin, trying to summon whatever it was she'd convinced herself she'd felt about

Ryan. "I thought he liked me. I truly believed the things that he said."

"Your first mistake," Ira had snapped, his entire demeanor displaying a distinct lack of sympathy. "Never, ever believe an actor. They're always acting. There's no off switch. You of all people should know that."

She'd frowned into her cup. "Please, I'm a failed actor."

"Are you?"

Her gaze met his.

"Or are you just failing yourself?"

Her shoulders had slumped. Her head felt too heavy for her neck to support. It was like whatever force had been holding her together had suddenly vacated, leaving her loose-limbed, limp, and desperately in need of guidance, and who better to direct her than Ira?

"After you finish your tea and pull yourself together, you're going to that police station. Failing to make good on your word will only annoy them, and that's something you don't want to do. But you won't go in as an emotional basket case with an overly sensitive tear trigger. You'll go in with a carefully crafted script that you absolutely will not deviate from. Once that's behind you, you will lose the victim mentality, stop hiding, and finally recognize your current predicament as the moment you've always dreamed of. And don't even try to pretend you don't know what I'm talking about, because we both know you've dreamed your whole life of having your picture in the tabloids and your name on everyone's lips. Maybe it didn't happen the way you'd envisioned, but now that it's here, it's your job to make the most of it. The very thing that makes you ashamed is the very thing that just might make you a star. Night for Night is still going strong, but it's got less to do with your fellow team member and more to do with the notoriety of all that went down. People love a good scandal, Aster. And, as it happens, you have the starring role in this particular story. Better embrace it, before something else happens and you fade into obscurity."

She'd hid her face in her hands, massaging her temples with her thumbs and taking a moment to process his words. "Ira, do you have kids?" She'd lifted her gaze to meet his.

He looked amused, but otherwise shook his head.

"That's too bad. I think you'd make a great dad."

Before she could finish, he was roaring with laughter. When he'd finally calmed down, he said, "I'm pretty sure that's the first time anyone has ever said that to me. I'm also sure it'll be the last. So—" He was back to business again. "You on board? Ready to take control of your life?"

Aster had glanced around the apartment. She could get used to living like that. "Yes," she said, voice filled with conviction. "I'm all in."

Ira nodded, seemingly satisfied. "Good, so here's what you're going to do. . . ." He'd leaned toward her and laid out the plan.

Still, nothing could've prepared her for the humiliation of sitting across from that creepy Detective Larsen, struggling not to focus on his leering face, as he'd asked her a series of demeaning questions that, thankfully, the attorney Ira assigned would not let her answer. She'd basically pleaded the Fifth, until Larsen gave up and told her to leave. She shuddered to think what might've happened if Ira hadn't saved her from going alone.

She shook off the memory and shimmied into the black lace minidress. She was just slipping into her shoes when she heard someone knock. Teetering on one Manolo, she opened the door to find one of the hotel staff delivering a small packet.

"Sorry to bother, it's marked 'urgent.'"

Aster stared at the envelope. There was no return address, which struck her as strange. Though she was already running late, she was intrigued enough to slip her index finger under the flap and dump the contents into her hand.

It was a homemade DVD in a clear plastic case with her name written in black.

Her belly churned, a wave of apprehension coursed through her, as her mind reeled with a thousand possibilities, none of them good. She stumbled toward the TV, unable to so much as breathe as the large flat-screen flickered to life and she collapsed on the couch.

Her worst fear had come true.

# FIFTY-ONE

# DON'T SAVE ME

Layla pushed free of the interrogation room and headed down the bleak hallway, which reeked of panic, dread, and burnt coffee. She was unsure if she'd just successfully cleared herself of suspicion or sealed her own disastrous fate. The fact that she wasn't wearing handcuffs and leg shackles was probably a good sign. Still, despite what seemed like hours spent protesting her innocence, between the restraining order and the Madison slams on her blog, Larsen seemed convinced that Layla had all the motive she needed to get rid of Madison Brooks. The only thing missing was evidence.

Desperate to put some distance between her and Detective Larsen, she made for her bike, thinking a nice long ride might clear her head. But considering the way her life was seriously spiraling out of control, she could circle the earth a handful of times and it probably wouldn't do any good.

Besides, now more than ever, she, Aster, and Tommy needed to talk. The fact that they'd been hauled into separate interrogation rooms around the same time was no accident. Clearly the detectives wanted them to see one another, probably hoping it would cause them to panic, confess to the kinds of things they'd previously chosen to omit.

Were Tommy or Aster guilty of harming Madison? Her first thought was to doubt it—doubt it in the way she'd doubt that anyone she knew was capable of something like that. But wasn't that really more of a naive, almost hopeful way of seeing the world? Wasn't it more likely that, given the right situation, the right circumstance, anyone was capable of just about anything?

Clearly Tommy viewed her as capable—or at least that was what he'd told Larsen. Or maybe he'd never even said that. Maybe Larsen was just maneuvering them to all turn on one another. All she knew for sure was she was growing increasingly uneasy with each passing day.

She kicked a rock with the toe of her boot, glanced between the time on her phone and the door to the station. Had he left before her? Short of marching back inside and asking, she had no way of knowing. She decided to wait a bit longer. Between the black wristbands he'd freely supplied to the under-twenty-one crowd and hooking up with Madison, she'd already seen the lengths he'd go to to win a contest—who knew how far he'd go now that his life was at stake?

An engine rumbled to life, prompting Layla to look up in time to see Tommy backing out of the lot. She darted toward him, shouting his name as he switched into drive, foot heavy on the accelerator, unsure if he failed to acknowledge her because his windows were closed and his music was loud, or if he was purposely ignoring her. It wasn't until she leaped right in front of him that she knew she'd finally been seen.

The brakes screeched, the car lurched forward, then back, missing her by a matter of inches, as Tommy leaned out the window and yelled, "Are you fuckin' crazy?"

She leaned on the hood and fought to catch her breath. At least she wasn't wrong about him not being a killer. He'd clearly chosen *not* to run her over when he very well could have and called it an accident.

"What the hell are you doing?" he shouted, his blue eyes narrowed in anger.

"We need to talk." Layla veered around the hood and stood beside his door. "You, me, and Aster. Can you convince her?"

"Do you think you've convinced me?" He shook his head, looked at her like she was insane.

She brushed her hair from her face. "I'm not spending my life in prison for something I didn't do, and neither should you. Meet me at Hollywood Forever in an hour." She went for her bike.

"The cemetery?" he called out from behind her.

She looked over her shoulder, centered her gaze on his. "Johnny Ramone's grave. I'm sure you know where it is. But don't worry—I have no plans to bury you. But if we don't find a way to get together and talk, they will." She hooked a thumb toward the precinct and pulled her helmet onto her head. She watched as Tommy shrugged and drove away, leaving Layla to hope he'd be smart enough to do what was needed.

# FIFTY-TWO

# PARANOID

Tommy Phillips pulled out of the precinct parking lot and drove a few random blocks, before stopping on a quiet residential street with Old Hollywood–style homes—the kind with red-tiled roofs, arched doorways, and spare, sloping lawns. Homes that harkened back to a different Hollywood, a less complicated time. Or maybe it hadn't been any less complicated then than it was now. Maybe things only seemed easier when viewed in reverse.

He stared out the windshield, needing a moment to process what had gone down, and, more important, what it might mean. First he got called into the station to go over the same shit he'd already been over, only to have Layla leapfrog onto the hood of his car, practically daring him to mow her down.

Who does that?

What the hell was she up to?

He rubbed his eyes with his knuckles, remembering the way Layla looked when she'd jumped out of nowhere. Serious. Determined. Convinced he wouldn't harm her. It was instinct that had forced his foot to the brake. Any decent person would've done the same. Still, it wasn't just an innate sense of morality that had kept him from hitting her. Truth was, he'd wanted to save her. Protect her. Probably because he felt guilty for pointing the finger at her.

Though that wasn't to say he trusted her. If nothing else, Madison's disappearance had permanently erased any hint of country boy naïveté that had managed to survive the trip from OK to LA. People were much more complex than they ever let on, making him wonder if it was ever really possible to truly know anyone—if he could ever truly know himself. When he'd first arrived in LA, he'd carried all kinds of bogus beliefs about who he was, where he was going, and exactly how he'd go about getting there. Only to find himself buffeted by the whims of circumstance, reacting in ways he never could've foreseen.

The ping of an incoming call interrupted his thoughts, as a picture of his mother bloomed on the screen. Thanks to her tabloid-reading neighbors, she called all the time. Claimed she didn't want him working for Ira, but whenever Tommy pressed for a reason, she changed the subject, begged him to come home, but that was no longer an option.

He let the call go to voice mail, promising himself he'd return it later, and scrolled for Aster's number. It was probably a mistake. But they could always leave if Layla proved to be as crazy as he suspected her of being. He turned the key in the ignition, once, twice. The engine sprang to life, and he squinted out the side-view mirror and merged onto the street.

"Layla wants to meet at Hollywood Forever, at Johnny Ramone's grave," he said, before Aster could speak.

"Who is this?" Her bitchy tone told him she knew exactly who it was.

He rolled his eyes, switched tracks on his playlist, and waited for her to stop playing games.

"The answer is no," she snapped. "No, scratch that, the answer is actually *hell no*."

Tommy stared at the bumper sticker on the Prius in front of him—a call for tolerance, unity, and world peace—too bad the owner drove like a tailgating asshole. "I think you should reconsider," he said.

"Oh, how you tempt me," she sang.

"Look—I have no freaking idea what this is about, but I'm on my way there. Maybe I'll see you."

"But more likely not." She ended the call before he had a chance to.

He tossed the phone on the passenger seat and made his

way to the cemetery he'd visited not long after he'd first arrived in LA. He'd wanted to check out the monument and statue of Johnny Ramone playing guitar that marked the place where his ashes lay. There'd been an abundance of flowers left in his memory and plenty of fans hanging around. Even in death it seemed Johnny was still living the dream.

Still, why would Layla choose to meet in a cemetery? Was it random, or did the choice have some deeper, symbolic meaning? It didn't make sense. But lately, not much did.

He hoped she wasn't dumb enough to try to manipulate him into admitting something he'd live to regret. Just in case, he resolved to record the conversation on his phone. Then he'd sit back and wait for either Layla or Aster to hang herself. If they chose to go down, he wouldn't go with them.

# FIFTY-THREE

# MISSING PIECES

The last thing Aster Amirpour wanted was to meet Layla and Tommy at some creepy cemetery filled with a bunch of dead Hollywood has-beens. Despite all its hipster movie screenings, themed parties, and reputation as a cool place to go on a date, she'd never felt the need to visit.

One cursory glance at the manicured lawns, the lake teeming with swans, and the elaborate mausoleums and grave markers honoring those who'd passed on was enough to convince her she'd be better off racing back to the comfort of her Mercedes and getting the hell out of there. Either Layla was planning a setup, or she was even more messed up than Aster had thought. Aster had told Tommy she wouldn't show—she should've honored her word.

Despite the blazing heat, Aster ran her hands over her

bare arms, warding off shivers, as she went in search of some dead rock star's grave. The crowds of tourists treating it like another place to visit between trips to Grauman's Chinese Theatre and Disneyland were annoying, as they clomped across the lawn, camera in one hand, five-dollar map in the other, searching for the final resting places of Jayne Mansfield, Rudolph Valentino, Cecil B. DeMille, and whoever else made their list. She rolled her eyes, seriously considering bailing on the plan, when Tommy found her and they agreed to find the monument together.

"You made it," he said.

She shrugged, still not sure why she hadn't stayed home.

"It's over in the Garden of Legends," he said. "Next to the lake with the swans."

"Let me guess—not your first visit?"

"He was an amazing guitarist. I wanted to pay my respects."

Aster eyeballed him from behind a pair of pink-tinted aviators it was almost too shady to wear, and tried not to judge. She'd been rude enough on the phone; maybe she should give him a break. "It would be really nice to know what this is about," she said, hoping she wasn't walking into a trap. Where Layla was concerned, it was entirely possible.

Tommy shrugged and walked in silence alongside her, the two of them approaching the gravesite where Layla watched from under the brim of a straw fedora that had seen better days.

"You came." She removed her sunglasses and regarded them with an expression that was simultaneously surprised and relieved.

Tommy shrugged. Aster folded her arms across her chest and stood beside him. Better to let Layla think they stood in solidarity against her. Whatever it took to keep Layla as off balance as Aster currently felt.

"I'm glad you did." She spoke in a voice that rang far more tentative than Aster expected. "We need to find a way to work together."

Aster frowned and looked all around. Sure, the lake was pretty, and the swans looked really peaceful, but she hated funerals, graveyards, anything to do with death, dying, and decay. She could never understand the fixation some people had with the dark side, the macabre, anything ghoulish or ghostly. Halloween was her least favorite holiday. Though of course Layla sat there looking perfectly at ease. With her dark skinny jeans and black leather moto jacket, she'd managed to nail cemetery chic, if there was such a thing.

"We're competing against each other, in case you've forgotten." Aster heaved her bag higher onto her shoulder, ready to leave. Better to head back to her luxury apartment, take a long, hot bubble bath, and try to forget she'd ever allowed herself to get dragged into this mess.

"It's not about the competition." Layla switched her focus between Aster and Tommy. "I'm talking about Madison's disappearance and how the cops are trying to pin it on us."

Aster sighed in defeat and sank onto the lawn. Tommy did the same, minus the sighing.

"Listen—" Layla leaned toward them, her tone hushed and hurried. "I'm sure we have our reasons for not trusting each other, but we need to find a way to save ourselves before the cops take us down."

Aster smirked.

Layla shrugged. Then turning her attention to Tommy, she said, "I know you pointed the finger at me."

Aster stared at Tommy in shock. It was the first she'd heard of it.

"If it wasn't for your stupid blog, none of this would've happened." He clenched his jaw, narrowed his gaze. "You are single-handedly responsible for this mess."

"Is that what you tell yourself?" Layla shook her head, tossed her hat on the ground beside her. "Are you seriously that naive?"

"Well, this is off to a really nice start," Aster grumbled. "Clearly we have some major trust issues that won't be resolved anytime soon, so can we just fast-forward and get to the point?"

Layla averted her gaze, taking a moment to steady herself before saying, "Aster's right." She pinched a blade of grass between her index finger and thumb, pausing to examine it before returning her focus to them. "I'm convinced we each know more than we're telling. And if we can set the animosity aside long enough to share what really happened that night, we might uncover something that'll point the finger elsewhere."

If it involved anyone other than the three of them, it might work. But no way was Aster agreeing to that. For all she knew, Layla was working for Larsen, maybe even wearing a wire.

"Fine," Layla said, when no one volunteered to take a turn. "It was my idea, so I'll start." She looked pointedly between them. "But first I want to see your phones."

"What—why?" Aster clutched her bag tighter, as though Layla might seize it.

"Because I don't want anyone taping this. I want us to speak freely, without fear of recrimination."

Layla tossed her phone in the center. Aster begrudgingly followed. And after fiddling with his for a bit, Tommy added his too.

"What?" He deflected their outraged looks. "You can't blame me for trying to protect myself."

Aster braced herself for Layla's response. Layla always defaulted to sarcasm, but this time, she somehow refrained. "Whatever. Here goes: I followed Tommy and Madison to the Vesper."

"How's that a secret?" Aster interrupted, not even trying to hide her frustration. "It was right there on your blog."

"Okay, so maybe I don't really have anything that hasn't already been documented and widely read. But here's the thing—my blog is not the best alibi, since it was posted several hours after I left the Vesper. Several hours after Madison left Tommy. And . . ." She paused, biting down on her lip as though debating whether to share something. "Madison filed a restraining order against me, which makes me just as big a suspect as you two."

"Why would she do that?" Tommy studied Layla as though it was the first time they'd met.

"Maybe she wasn't as nice as you think," Layla snapped, glaring at Tommy before shifting her focus to the lake, where the swans appeared to glide across a mirror of water.

Tommy pulled at the grass, his expression so unreadable, it reminded Aster of Ira. The silence lingered for so long, she figured she might as well go in his place.

It took guts for Layla to admit to the restraining order. Aster was surprised Madison hadn't filed one against her as well. And while she was no closer to liking Layla as a person, she definitely agreed that Madison wasn't nearly as nice as the image she portrayed. The girl had an edge. Aster had seen it the night she'd shown up at the club. Looking back, Aster could see Madison was doing reconnaissance, setting her up. For all she knew, Ryan was in on it too.

Whatever the case, like Layla, no way was she getting pinned for a crime she hadn't committed.

She tucked her hair behind her ears, cleared her throat, and said, "I don't remember anything after leaving the club."

"The amnesia defense? Always a classic." Tommy scrutinized her as Layla quickly shushed him.

"All I know is, after the whole Madison thing I wanted to leave, but Ira insisted on serving us champagne, telling us we were better off hanging out where he could look after us, which seemed a little weird—"

"Because it *is* weird," Tommy snapped, his harsh reaction prompting Aster and Layla to flinch. "What the hell was he thinking?" His lips pulled tight, as his darkened gaze moved over them.

"Oh, like you're above serving the underage?" Aster frowned, as annoyed with Tommy as she was with herself. She hadn't meant to cast suspicion on Ira. He'd been the only one on her side—the only person who'd volunteered to help. "The only reason no one turned you in is because it would shut down the club, get Ira in a load of trouble, and hurt all of our chances at winning the contest." She shook her head, still fuming inside, but forced herself to focus on the point she was determined to make, resolving not to get sidetracked. "I went home with Ryan. . . ." She took a deep breath, forced herself to look at them. Relieved to find it wasn't as bad as she'd thought. Where she'd expected judgment, she found encouragement. "And all I know is when I woke up the next morning in his ridiculously decorated cliché of a man cave, Ryan was gone."

Layla and Tommy both stared.

Aster nodded, swallowed past the lump in her throat. "I have no idea where he went. I never saw him again. I haven't told the cops. Haven't told anyone. It's too humiliating to admit. But then, the other day—" She lowered her head, needing a moment before she could divulge the worst part. "Someone delivered a video of me, doing disgusting things in Ryan's apartment."

She peeked through her long, angled bangs, trying to read their reactions. Layla looked angry, Tommy disturbed. Their lack of blame made it easier to continue.

"I just wish I could rewind my life and start over." She buried her face in her hands. It was out there now, no taking it back. Strangely, the confession didn't make her feel better, but it did make her feel lighter, maybe even more connected to Tommy and Layla, which probably wasn't such a bad thing, considering they were all in this together.

"You know—" Tommy turned to her, his tone much softer than it had been a few moments before. "Madison mentioned she'd been wanting to break it off but was afraid of how Ryan would react. When she caught him with you, she decided to take her chances and end it."

Aster was stunned by his words. Madison had always seemed so remote, not at all like a person who would share intimate stuff with someone she barely knew. "Sounds like she really opened up." She studied him closely. Just how much time had they spent together?

Tommy shrugged.

"What about that text she received?" Layla asked. "Can't the cops trace it?"

"They told me it was untraceable. Sent from a burner." He ran a hand through his hair, clenched and unclenched his jaw, clearly needing a moment to put his thoughts together. "Madison went to Night for Night," he finally said, his voice almost reduced to a whisper.

"How'd you—"

Before Layla could finish, Tommy said, "I know, because I followed her. I mean, not right away. At first I went back inside the club, but then . . . yeah, I went outside and headed in the same direction until I more or less caught up."

"Does Larsen know?" Aster leaned toward him. Finally, they were getting somewhere.

Tommy made a face. "You kidding? It's bad enough I'm the last known person to have seen her. If I told him I followed her, I'd be behind bars instead of sitting here, talking to you."

"But the club was closed." Layla squinted.

"She knew the code." Tommy glanced between them.

"Did you see anything?" Aster asked, trying to keep her voice soft, encouraging, free of the excitement that was building. He seemed jumpy, paranoid, not at all like Tommy, and she didn't want to scare him off by pushing him to reveal things when he didn't feel ready.

Tommy shook his head. "I tried to follow, but the door locked behind her, and by that time I was feeling pretty embarrassed for stalking her like that, so I bailed and went back to the Vesper. I was kind of keyed up, so I hung out for a while, had another beer. It wasn't until I was locking up that I discovered Madison's keys in my jacket. But when I went to move her car so it wouldn't get towed, it was gone."

"Who moved the car?" Layla asked.

Tommy shrugged.

"And the keys—you still have them?" Aster looked at him.

He dipped his head. "Yes."

"What's on them—anything of note?"

Tommy peered at Aster. "I don't know. They're just keys."

Aster fought to keep her face neutral. Why were guys so clueless when it came to girls and their things? "What I meant was, what kind of key chain are they on? How many keys are there? Are there little charms attached?"

"Does this really matter?" His blue eyes squinted against the fading rays of the sun.

"It might." Aster lifted her shoulders, rubbed her lips together. "I know it sounds like a long shot, but there could be something useful, some kind of reveal. I mean, keys are really personal, since they unlock your world."

"I hadn't thought of that." He stared into the distance as though trying to remember. Shaking his head, he said, "I'll take a look and let you know."

What Aster really wanted was for him to offer to let her take a look, since she had absolutely no faith in his detective skills when it came to deciphering girls, but she nodded instead.

"Well, I hope you hid them somewhere safe," Layla said. "If the cops discover you have them . . ." She left the threat unspoken.

"They're safe." His voice was tight, his expression guarded.

"So we know where everyone was except Ryan. Do you think Madison went to meet him?" Layla asked.

"Why would she do that after confessing she was afraid of him?" Aster felt dumb for jumping to the jerk's defense, but the question had to be asked.

"Well, she didn't actually say that, it was more implied. . . ." Tommy rubbed a hand over his jaw, looking increasingly discouraged, possibly second-guessing himself.

"Well, it makes sense considering Ryan's disappearing act. He probably used Aster as an alibi, figuring she was too wasted to notice he'd left." Layla looked at Aster and said, "No offense."

Aster shrugged. Lately, there was no shortage of offensive slurs directed her way. Layla's comment hardly qualified.

Tommy dug the heels of his boots into the earth and rested his arms on his knees. "Look, none of us have any answers. Only Madison knows where she went, and for the moment, she's not talking. I'm still not convinced it's as sinister as everyone says. I could be wrong about the car. I don't even know where she lives. Maybe she found a spare key and decided to get out of town for a bit."

Layla shook her head, completely undeterred. "Is there any way to determine what time Ryan left?"

Aster frowned. "The sheets were cold on his side, so feel free to draw your own conclusions." She sounded tired. She was tired. At first confessing felt liberating, but now it was beginning to yield just the opposite. By not telling the cops about Ryan, she could be implicated.

"And the tape?" Layla asked, almost before Aster had finished. "Is Ryan in it?"

Aster shook her head. "Nope, just me. I'm the star of the whole sleazy show."

"Is there a time and date stamp?"

Aster closed her eyes, wanting the whole thing to end. "It's not like I watched it that closely. Besides, you act like I'm going to hand it over for evidence, and there's no way that's happening. The cops don't even know I went home with Ryan, and I prefer to keep it that way."

"Unless you have to tell them," Layla coaxed.

"Not happening. You guys have no idea what this will do to my family. It's bad enough they suspect I had sex outside of marriage. If they see that tape, they'll completely disown me."

"What if it could get you off the hook?" Layla was relentless, and Aster had just reached her limit.

"Look, I didn't do it—okay? My only crime is sleeping with an asshole. No one sees the tape, and that's final. To be honest, I'm starting to regret my decision to tell you!"

"Aster—" Tommy grasped for her hand, trying to comfort, but Aster was too upset and jerked out of his reach.

Layla, on the other hand, had a one-track mind. She was the least nurturing person Aster had ever met. "What did you do with the video?"

"Why, so you can steal it?" Aster rolled her eyes, started to gather her things. This had gone on long enough.

"No, so no one else can. I hope you don't have it stashed in your room safe."

"What's that supposed to mean?" Aster rose to her feet. She was shaky, edgy, and deeply regretting her decision to meet.

"It means you live in a hotel. Which also means you're not the only one with a key to your room."

Aster shook her head, mumbled under her breath, so annoyed she wondered why she didn't just leave. Why did she allow Layla to taunt her?

"Look, I know you and Ira share some kind of special bond. . . ."

"What the hell are you implying?" Aster's eyes burned with anger, but what she really felt was fear. Did Layla know about the cash-stuffed envelopes Ira regularly slipped her? Just because she took them didn't mean she wasn't conflicted.

"Last I checked, you were the only one occupying one of his swanky penthouse apartments."

Aster sighed. Who was she kidding? She wasn't going anywhere. She sank back down beside Tommy.

"If we had to vote now, who would you finger as guilty?" Layla hunched her shoulders forward and tucked her blond hair behind her ears, revealing a pair of silver heart stud earrings that seemed wildly out of place. Aster would've expected skulls, daggers, or spikes. Must be some kind of ironic statement, she decided.

"The evidence is all pointing to Ryan, no?" Tommy looked between them. "He was probably really angry at Madison for making that scene."

"Mad enough to kill her?" Aster screwed up her face, unsure if her reluctance to believe it was because she couldn't bear to think she'd willingly gone home with a murderer. She had enough shame in her life. She didn't need to add that to the list.

"I'm not convinced she's dead." Tommy was adamant, but he had nothing to back it other than a potent combination of stubbornness and hope.

"Well, the fact that he disappeared in the middle of the night is pretty disturbing." Layla drove home the point.

"And it's not like he's not milking his role in the scandal." Aster rolled her eyes. Annoyed by the way Ryan had continually confessed his remorse, his undying love for Madison, and how he'd made Aster look like a convenient ego fluffer.

"The same could be said of you guys." Layla frowned, then looked at Tommy and said, "Is there anything she said, or did, that seemed unusual? Anything you saw that seemed out of place when you followed her?"

Tommy closed his eyes. When he opened them again, he said, "She spoke with an accent."

"What kind of accent?"

"Country. Mountain. She's definitely not East Coast, like she says."

Layla nodded excitedly, her blond bob swishing around her face. "I ran into her one day getting coffee. She went by the name Della. At first I didn't think much of it, since everyone uses aliases at Starbucks, but what if there's more to Madison's past than she admits? And what if Ryan discovered her secret and was blackmailing her or something?"

"Why would Ryan blackmail her?" Tommy asked.

"Because his show's getting canceled, he has nothing lined up, he lives an expensive, flashy life, and he's probably starting to panic. I'm just saying, it's a very real possibility. . . ."

"Okay, so we're all leaning toward Ryan, but what exactly do we do about it?" Aster said.

"Well, whatever we do, we can't afford to let the LAPD divide us. I'm not saying we need to be BFFs—but we don't have to depart as enemies either. Nothing good will come of that."

Tommy was the first to stand, but Aster was quick to follow. She'd heard enough for one day. She needed time to digest, work it out in her head. And though she didn't want to admit it, she was definitely second-guessing her hiding place for the video. She hoped Layla was wrong, but she was determined to get back to the W and confirm either way. Still, before she left, there was one last thing to get off her chest. Her words directed at Layla, she said, "If you so much as mention the sex tape or Ryan ditching me to Larsen or anyone else, so help me, I won't hesitate to take you down with me."

"Is that a threat?" Layla regarded her from under a quirked brow, as Tommy glanced anxiously between them.

"Most definitely." Aster lifted her chin, clutched her bag to her side.

"Noted. I meant what I said about us sticking together."

When Layla offered her hand, for a split second Aster nearly rejected it. But in a world where she no longer had any friends, she'd been touched to discover true compassion in the least likely place. She placed her hand on Layla's, and Tommy placed his on top. The three of them were united, for better or worse.

# FIFTY-FOUR

# RUNNIN' DOWN
# A DREAM

We need to talk—preferably somewhere private.

Trena Moretti stared at her cell phone and frowned. In another hour it would be too dark to run, and she didn't consider treadmills an option. She tossed the phone aside and returned to the business of lacing up her running shoes.

The phone chimed again.

I promise, you do not want to miss this. Text me.

Damn.

Trena glanced out the window and jumped to her feet. Running was her religion. It was sacred, necessary, and often illuminating. Some of her very best work occurred when she was pushing beyond her physical limits, gasping for breath and dripping with sweat.

She could use a little illumination. Her story had served

its purpose, effectively shaking the LAPD out of their iner-
tia and getting a lot of eyes to take note of her byline. But
lately, there'd been nothing juicy to report. Though all that
could change with Layla's text.

Still, forfeiting her run was unthinkable.

You a runner? she typed, putting herself through a series
of stretches while she waited for a reply.

You're joking, right?

Not a joke. Grab your sneakers and meet me at the Santa
Monica Pier ASAP.

It wasn't her favorite route, but it was easily accessible,
and it would have to suffice.

While Trena hadn't expected her to show—Layla struck
her as the type who'd spent her high school years thinking
deeply cynical thoughts and smoking menthol cigarettes—
she definitely hadn't expected her to wear a pair of old ratty
gym shorts, a gray tank top cut at the midriff, and a pair of
spanking-new trainers.

"You just run out and buy those?" Trena nodded toward
Layla's neon clad feet.

"A gift from my dad last summer when he envisioned us
waking up early to share a daily father-daughter jog."

"How'd that go?"

"First morning we jogged all the way to Intelligentsia
on Abbot Kinney. The second morning we slept in. Haven't
worn 'em since."

"Well, try to keep up. Run time is holy. I normally don't allow anyone to join me. And I definitely don't allow anyone to slow me down."

"Then I'll try to finish the story before I pass out," Layla said, joining Trena on the paved jogging path.

"Just so you know, this is my starting pace." Trena spared a look to the side. They'd only begun, and the girl looked like she was about to keel over. "Take it from someone who used to be an exercise avoider like you. All of this—" She jabbed a thumb toward Layla's slim legs and flat abs. "It's a gift. Enjoy it while you can, but know that from age twenty-five on, you gotta work to maintain it."

Layla nodded. "Is that it for the lecture?"

"Oh, there's more." Trena laughed. "But I'll spare you the ugly truth about the ravages of gravity, mostly because I'm eager to learn whatever it is you're willing to share before you conk out."

Layla narrowed her eyes and looked all around. "I've got a serious lead regarding Madison's disappearance."

Even though it went against the rules she'd already stated, Trena slowed her pace. "I'm listening. . . ."

"Okay, two things. One—" Layla paused. "I'm an anonymous source. You have to promise never to reveal where you got this."

"Scout's honor." Trena's voice betrayed a hint of sarcasm she instantly regretted. She was eager to get to the juice of the story but knew better than to show it. Especially now that she was about to hit pay dirt.

Layla nodded, seemingly okay with it, she said, "I've recently become privy to some surprising information the LAPD doesn't know. Or at least not in the way I'm about to relay. . . ."

"Layla, seriously. Trust me, okay?" Trena shook her head, watching as Layla struggled to fill her lungs with air before she continued.

"There's a very good chance Ryan Hawthorne knows more about Madison's disappearance than he lets on. He might even be responsible."

Trena nodded, fought to keep her face from appearing overly interested. "I'm listening. . . ."

"Apparently he has some unaccounted-for time during the early morning hours, probably around the same time Madison was last seen."

"Last seen by Tommy."

Layla was winded but had so far managed to keep pace. "From the time she left the Vesper to the time she was reported missing, no one's come forward admitting they've seen her. But my source tells me Ryan wasn't exactly where he said he was."

"Ryan claims he was at home. His doorman confirms it."

Layla frowned and stared straight ahead. "Doormen

ALYSON NOËL

can be bought. Someone needs to check the security tapes, if there are any."

Layla shook her head, was clearly losing steam. Was it the run that was getting to her, or was she shutting down, beginning to regret everything she'd confided thus far? It wasn't the first time Trena had seen someone second-guess their decision to share. She'd have to take a step back, be careful not to push, maybe even slow down her speed, if only a little. She focused on the run, switching her gaze between the colorful box-shaped houses on the right and the wide swath of golden sand and navy-blue ocean on the left. Allowing Layla all the space she needed before she decided it was safe to continue.

"Let's just say he's proved himself to be the asshole I've always suspected him of being," she finally admitted.

*Bingo.* Trena exhaled in relief.

She glanced at the girl. She was dripping wet, her cheeks were red, and yet, she refused to slow down. It was like she was punishing herself. Paying some kind of penance. But for what?

"The other thing the LAPD doesn't know is that when Madison left the Vesper, she went to Night for Night."

"Night for Night was closed for the night." Trena remained unimpressed.

"Madison knew the code. Seems like something you might want to look into, no?"

*Yes—most decidedly yes. Just as soon as I get my five miles in.*

But what she said was, "Is that it?"

Layla nodded, completely out of breath, her expression one of absolute agony. "And this is where I leave you." She spun on her heels and bolted the opposite way before Trena could thank her.

# FIFTY-FIVE

# PICTURES OF YOU

For the entire drive from Hollywood Forever Cemetery to the W hotel (which took far longer than it should have, thanks to the notorious LA traffic), Aster chided herself for confiding in Layla and Tommy when they'd given her absolutely no reason to do so. The stuff they'd confessed was nothing compared to the total humiliation of a sex tape.

She turned left against the red (again, thanks to LA traffic, she couldn't remember the last time she'd turned left on a green) and inched toward the hotel. Wanting more than anything to get up to her room and open her safe, if only to prove Layla wrong.

*The tape was safe. No one would go through her belongings. She had nothing to fear.*

But no matter how many times she repeated the mantra, her stomach continued to churn.

She pulled into the entrance at the same time her phone chimed with an incoming call. She glanced at the screen, half expecting it to be Layla, only to see it was Ira. Without even thinking, she pressed Decline.

He'd been good to her. Because of him she had much to be thankful for. But at the moment, she was too flustered to speak to anybody, much less Ira Redman.

Leaving her car with the valet, she raced for the elevator and repeatedly punched the Up button, until a voice behind her said, "Tell me, does that ever work?"

*Ira.*

Aster turned. Tried to look happy to see him, but the smile she'd forced to her lips faded when she saw Javen standing beside him.

"What happened?" She glanced between them, unable to think of a single valid reason for Javen to be hanging out with Ira Redman. Unless something had happened to her parents . . .

Ira nodded toward Javen, as her brother looked at her and said, "I want to move in with you."

The elevator rang. The doors slid open.

"I'll leave you to sort out the details." Ira started to turn. "Oh, and, Aster—"

She stepped inside the elevator, held the door with her hand.

"The next time I call you, don't hit Decline."

She blinked, released her grip on the door, and counted the seconds until it closed between them.

"Aster—" Javen started, but Aster lifted a hand and shook her head.

"Not here," she whispered, realizing just how paranoid she probably sounded, but it wasn't entirely unwarranted. "Whatever it is, it can wait until we get inside." She willed the elevator to climb faster—why was it moving so slowly? Now more than ever she needed to get inside her apartment. She wouldn't be able to relax and focus on her brother until she'd made sure the DVD was right where she'd left it.

Once inside, Javen raced for the floor-to-ceiling windows and took in the one-eighty view of the city as Aster made for the safe tucked away in the closet. Holding her breath, she punched in the code and swung the door open, only to exhale in relief to find that her jewelry, her Mac-Book Air, some cash Ira had given her, and the DVD were all there.

She sank to her knees. Dropped her head in her hands.

She wasn't crazy.

Her secret was safe.

It could only get better from here.

"You okay?" Javen stood in the doorway with a look of concern on his face.

"Yeah." She wiped a hand across each cheek and hurried to her feet. "Now tell me, what's going on? Why are you here? Not that I'm not happy to see you, because I am."

"Mom and Dad are crazy," he groaned, as she led him out of the closet and into the den.

"We already knew that." She ruffled his hair, deposited him on the couch, and made for the kitchen. She searched the fridge for something to serve him, but who was she kidding? She hadn't gone grocery shopping the entire time that she'd lived there.

"How do you feel about room service?" she asked.

"I say it's just another reason I want to live with you. You get to live in this sweet place and do whatever you want."

"Yeah, well, I'm three years ahead of you. I've earned the right. But don't be too impressed; none of this is mine, and the situation is temporary at best. No telling how long Ira will allow me to stay."

Javen's beautiful brown eyes glinted on hers, his thick dark lashes practically sweeping his cheeks each time he blinked. "What does he care? He practically owns this town. He'll let you stay as long as you want."

"It doesn't exactly work that way." Aster frowned, taking a moment to study her brother. Her heart surging with empathy for all the trials he'd yet to face but undoubtedly would. She'd been so focused on her own struggle with her parents' unrealistic expectations she hadn't stopped to consider his. He was an artist at heart—but they were actively pushing him toward a more rigid profession. He liked boys, but they were already on the lookout for a suitable wife. In their highly structured world, there was no room to wander. And despite his youth and good looks, Javen was already exhibiting the strain of the expectations they placed upon him. "I'll make you a deal," she said, wanting more than anything to help him but recognizing her own limitations. "If you promise to call Mom and Dad and tell them you're with me, then I'll let you stay. We'll order room service, watch movies, and stay up all night if you want. But tomorrow, you have to go home—sound good?"

Javen shot her a wary look. "Is this negotiable?"

"No." She tossed him the room service menu. "Order whatever you want. I'm taking a bath. After that, I'm yours."

Javen sank into the cushions, propped his feet on the coffee table, and immersed himself in the menu, while Aster made for the bathroom, where she went about filling the tub with heaping scoops of bath salts, before lowering herself in the water and resting her head against the tub pillow she'd bought her second day there. There was nothing like a nice hot bath to ease all her worries. For the first time in a long time she began to relax. She inched deeper, allowing the water to lap at her chin, soak the strands of hair all the way to her ears. It might not be the dream Jacuzzi she'd grown used to from her parents' house, but it served as a pretty good stand-in.

She had just closed her eyes, about to drift to a faraway place, when Javen knocked at the door and said, "This was just delivered." He tucked a plain manila envelope under the sill.

Same kind of envelope the DVD had arrived in.

The sight of it was enough to send a wave of panic coursing through her; she heaved herself from the tub. Water sloshing, feet skidding against the slick marble tile, she raced for the envelope, slid her index finger under the flap, wincing in pain when the edge sliced deeply into her flesh. She thrust the wound between her lips, her mouth filling with blood, as she dumped the contents onto the floor, gasping in shock when her gaze settled on a grainy picture of her naked, writhing self—a still from the video.

*No.*

*No!*

She yanked a towel from a hook, clutched it tightly against her, and stumbled toward her closet, needing to check the safe once again. Needing to verify the DVD was really still there. But that didn't mean it hadn't been removed at some point or that it had been the original DVD to begin with.

Had someone taken it, made a copy, and then returned it?

Or was there a duplicate already making the rounds?

At first glance it seemed just like she'd left it. But Aster was far more meticulous than most when it came to her belongings, and she distinctly remembered leaving the cash-filled envelope on the left side of the safe instead of the right, where it was currently placed. She'd been so relieved to confirm the presence of the DVD, she'd completely over-looked the fact that her things were rearranged.

She counted her money—it was all there. She flipped through her jewelry bag—it was just as she'd left it.

Still, someone had been there.

Someone had gone through her things.

She stashed the DVD in her bag. As soon as Javen left, she'd find a better hiding place

Her luxury pad might seem sweet like he'd said, but one thing was sure—she knew it never had been.

# FIFTY-SIX

# GOODBYE TO YOU

Mateo and Layla wandered through the gallery, checking out her dad's exhibit. It was his best work yet—vibrant, full of life, the vivid forms seeming to jump off the canvas—so why wasn't anyone buying?

"It's a good turnout." Mateo entwined his fingers with hers. "Maybe your dad can start to relax."

Layla frowned. "Forget the turnout, what we need are buyers."

She leaned against Mateo's shoulder, enjoying the dependable solidity of him. They needed more moments like this. Between the contest and all the drama surrounding Madison, they'd barely seen each other, and when they did, they acted overly cautious. Like the slightest misstep might derail their already fragile relationship. Even if it was just a date at her dad's show, Layla was happy to be with him.

She snuck a peek at her father. On the surface, he looked good, handsome as ever. But having recently come across some disturbing statements from banks and other unpaid creditors, Layla knew the stress he was under. If this show didn't result in the sale of at least one major piece, journalism school would have to wait. She'd need to stick around, use the money she'd earned from her blog to help save their house until they could figure something out. She was more than willing to do it—she'd do anything for him—but she hoped it wouldn't come to that. It would delay her dream and make him feel like a failure.

Her phone chimed with an incoming text, and Mateo's fingers instantly tensed. He'd tried his best to be patient, but he was reaching his limits. Still, she wasn't yet free of the contest, which meant she really needed to check it.

She clicked on the link Trena had sent and inhaled a quick breath as the words appeared on the screen:

*Blood Found on the Night for Night Terrace!*
*Possibly Belonging to Madison Brooks?*

Beneath the headline was a picture of Ryan Hawthorne surrounded by suits, his hand raised, shielding his face from the cameras, as he was escorted inside the police station.

Mateo peered over her shoulder, snaking an arm around her waist as he pulled her closer and said, "Good. It's over."

He tried to nuzzle her neck, but Layla batted him away. "And yet, you're still at it. . . ."

"Just—" She hated to upset him, but if he'd give her a second, she could give him her complete attention. "I just need to—"

Before she could finish, Mateo was shaking his head and heading for the bar. "I'm going to get us some drinks," he called. "When I return, maybe you can try ignoring that thing."

Layla frowned and skimmed the article again. Apparently Trena had nudged the police, and now, thanks to her, she, Tommy, and Aster were all off the hook. She could actually feel the weight of the burden melting away.

"Looks like you're not the only one receiving interesting texts."

Mateo held his phone before her as Layla squinted at a picture of her and Tommy kissing in the middle of the Jewel dance floor. It was time and date stamped.

She closed her eyes, wishing she could rewind time. When she opened them again, it was worse than before. Mateo looked as crushed as she felt. Difference was, he was the victim. She was the perpetrator. Their pain was hardly equal.

"I'm sorry," she said, cringing at the inadequacy of the words. She owed him far more than a shrug of the shoulders and an inept, though heartfelt, apology. "I don't even know what to say." Her mind swam with possibilities, centering on the horrifying truth that someone was spying on her. Someone had hated her enough to take a picture of her most regrettable mistake and use it against her.

She reached for Mateo, pressed her fingers to his flesh, but she'd already lost him.

"Who sent that?" She gripped so hard she was leaving red marks.

"Is that what you're worried about?" He pulled away. "I mean, that is you, isn't it?"

She closed her eyes and nodded. There was no point in lying.

"And the guy?"

"Tommy. Tommy Phillips." Her knees felt floppy, weak, as she struggled to steady herself. "He's one of the competitors, and that's the first, last, and only time that ever happened. I swear."

"This happened weeks ago, and I'm just now finding out about it? What else have you been hiding?"

She shook her head, gazed around the gallery. The timing couldn't have been worse. Not that there was ever a good time for something like that, but it was an important event for her father. She couldn't afford to make a scene.

"Mateo," she whispered, "I haven't been hiding anything. I swear. I think someone's setting me up!"

Mateo averted his gaze like he could no longer stand

looking at her. After the whole thing with Madison, he was sick of her conspiracy theories. But for the first time, she realized it might not end there. Maybe he was finally sick of her too.

"Doesn't look coerced to me." His gaze bore into hers.

She yanked the phone from his hand, but the number was blocked, probably sent from a burner.

"I don't understand. Why would someone do this?" she muttered to herself. Unfortunately, Mateo heard.

"Do you even hear yourself?" He was outraged. Well, outraged for someone who never got outraged. "This is all about what someone did to *you*? Never mind what you did to me, to us. Layla—"

She looked at him. Usually she loved the sound of her name on his lips. The way his voice lifted when he'd call to her after too long an absence—the way it dipped low and gravelly when he was caught by desire. She'd never once heard him address her like she was little more than a stranger, even back when she was.

Unlike most guys she'd dated, Mateo never hid behind a facade of forced manliness, never pretended the heart was just an overlooked muscle in an otherwise well-honed body. He was totally authentic. Mateo approached the world in such a genuine way, it left her in awe. But now, well, she couldn't help but wish he'd been better at stuffing his feelings like everyone else. If for no other reason than to spare her the sight of seeing him squinting in confusion, as though he was trying to find the best way to ingest a revelation that would inevitably upend everything he once thought he knew about her, about them.

Maybe he loved her too purely.

Maybe he loved her in a way she clearly didn't deserve.

And maybe his love for her had blinded him to the truth that Layla wasn't the wonderful person he believed her to be.

"I feel like I don't even know you anymore."

A single tear coursed down her cheek. She did nothing to stop it.

"I think we should take a break."

Her bottom lip trembled, her eyes burned; still, her gaze met his and she nodded in reply. There wasn't a single thing she could say that wouldn't just make it worse. She'd lied, withheld information, and no matter how much she loved him, and she did, probably always would, truth was, she'd had one foot out the door since the first night she'd met him.

Mateo could do better.

With any luck, she'd get what she deserved.

She watched him leave. Slipping away like a ghost.

Intangible.

Indiscernible.

No longer hers to hold.

She mashed the back of her hand against her cheeks, refusing to cry, or at least not in public. Her feelings could wait. Her dad needed this night to be a success.

She headed for the bar, grabbed a glass of red wine, and went in search of her dad. Her heart nearly stopped in her chest when she found him in a corner talking to Ira.

"I was just telling your father how much I admire his work." Ira grinned.

Layla forced a half smile and glanced all around. The gallery owner was making the rounds, talking up the work, but no one was biting.

"I'm thinking about expanding the Vesper. Adding a private VIP space. One of your dad's murals would really liven up the place. We were just negotiating the terms when you walked up."

Layla looked at her dad. He was playing it cool, but it was clear he really wanted the deal.

"My dad does great work. You won't be disappointed." She swallowed hard, shifted her gaze between them, feeling slightly dazed. As though she'd wandered inside one of her dad's paintings. Then, hugging her dad tightly, she said, "I'll leave you to it." Wishing she could say more—warn him not to go through with it—that there was most likely a whole web of strings attached to the project he wouldn't see coming until it was too late and he was completely entangled. But they were desperately in need of a savior, and if

Ira was willing to step in and deliver her dad from mounting debt and the prospect of homelessness, who was she to stop him?

Besides, there was a good chance she was being completely irrational. After what had just happened with Mateo, it was entirely possible.

She exited the gallery and made her way down the crowded summer sidewalk, making a mental list of all the reasons she should be happy.

*The temperature was a balmy seventy-five degrees, just how she liked it!*

But tomorrow would be hot, sunny, nearing triple digits.

*Her blog had surpassed her wildest expectations, had put her on the map, and was making her money!*

But all that would end as soon as she got booted from the contest and lost the access needed to keep it going.

*Ira commissioning a mural from her dad freed her up for journalism school in the fall!*

But she worried about her dad getting caught up in Ira's world.

*With Mateo now out of the picture, she no longer had to feel guilty about moving to New York!*

Mateo was out of the picture.

Who was she kidding? She sucked at positive thinking. For every good thought, she could easily find its much darker opposite.

It was only when she let herself into her room that she thought of one positive that didn't come with a dark side: *Thanks to her friendship with Trena, she was no longer a suspect in Madison's disappearance!*

And yet, without Mateo, even that failed to feel like a win.

# FIFTY-SEVEN

# BANG BANG

Tommy stood on the pink-and-gold-star-studded sidewalk just outside the Vesper, shielding his face from the relentless summer sun blazing high overhead like a cruel judging eye. It was another scorching-hot, zero-humidity day, and thanks to the drought and the Santa Ana winds, it seemed the whole city was burning. Griffith Park, La Cañada Flintridge, Angeles National Forest, and most recently, a brushfire was raging in Malibu. The air turned more acrid than usual and the sky darkened as though singed by flames, sending flecks of ash raining down, covering the city in a blanket of soot.

So far the expensive beachfront homes had been spared, but everyone knew if the fires didn't get 'em, the earthquakes eventually would.

Maybe it was the constant threat of impending Arma-geddon that gave Californians the reputation of being so open and friendly. Perhaps living on the edge of destruction and knowing the dream could end at any second gave their lives the kind of intensity other places lacked.

All Tommy knew for sure was that despite the grim faces on the local news channel, on Hollywood Boulevard it was business as usual. A stream of double-decker tour buses cruised past, as out-of-work actors dressed as Shrek, R2D2, and Superman hustled the tourists for pictures, and Aster reeled on Layla, her eyes blazing, body trembling, as she shook her phone in Layla's face.

"You did this, didn't you?"

Layla nodded, not so much as flinching at the sight of an enraged Aster looming before her, oblivious to the usual Hollywood Boulevard circus bustling all around.

"Even though you promised you wouldn't, you went straight to Trena Moretti and spilled all my secrets." Aster seethed, her anger so palpable Tommy was sure it was just a matter of seconds before he'd be forced to break them apart, and he wasn't entirely sure he was up for the task. The heat sapped his energy, made him lethargic, and the smoke-choked air made it a struggle to breath. Maybe the Hulk would be willing to help?

"Not exactly." Layla remained completely unfazed, which only added to Aster's rage. "I didn't divulge any personal details. I never told her how I got the info."

To Tommy's ears, it seemed sincere enough to end the fight. Which was good, since he was eager to escape the blistering heat and head inside the dark, windowless, air-conditioned club. But judging by Aster's clenched jaw and hate-filled stare, it didn't work. But then, just when he was about to intervene, he watched in astonishment as Aster seemed to melt right before him.

"I'm not sure whether I should thank you or curse you." She uncrossed her arms as the beginnings of a smile brightened her face. Leaving Tommy to question if he'd maybe imagined the whole thing. Surely what he'd witnessed had been no less than a brawl in the making?

One thing was sure, he was no closer to understanding the female species, and sincerely doubted he ever would. Though being a dedicated pacifist, he was mostly relieved he'd been spared a potentially violent scene between two people he was beginning to care about.

Layla nodded, seeming to take Aster's change of heart in stride. The Teflon expression she wore on her face gave nothing away. Tommy had seen that look before. It was the mask she wore when she was determined to deflect whatever chaos surrounded her. It was a shame things had gotten so weird between them. But with the contest winding down, and with the cops focusing on Ryan Hawthorne, maybe she'd learn to forgive him for pointing Larsen in her direction.

He looked at her with a hopeful expression, only to be met by a pair of rolling eyes and smirking lips that instantly reminded him exactly who he was dealing with. His chances of earning a pardon were slim. Though that wasn't to say he planned to give up. Even when she was hot, bothered, smelling of smoke, and misted with sweat he found her appealing in a way he couldn't shake.

"On the one hand"—Aster bent toward them, her voice lowered to a level that forced Tommy and Layla to lean in—"Ryan's involvement will undoubtedly result in more questions for me. I may even be considered an accessory for not admitting he left. But if Ryan really did harm Madison, then he deserves to be locked behind bars. But now that the mystery's solved, I have another, potentially worse one. Or at least worse for me." Her voice dropped even lower until it was just barely audible. "Remember that DVD I told you about?"

Tommy tensed, glancing between Aster and Layla, but before Aster could continue, the door swung open and Ira called them inside.

"Change of plans." His expression was as sharp as his tone, the opposite of what Tommy expected. Usually, Ira approached the Sunday meetings like a piece of performance art, all too happy to ramble and pontificate and waste their sweet time before finally getting to the point and firing the worst-performing contestant. But this time, after casting a wary gaze around the premises, scrutinizing the trash cans as though he expected to see someone leap out from behind them, he ushered them inside and motioned for them to sit at one of the tables. When he closed the door, it was like he'd shut out the world—leaving them at the mercy of Ira's agenda.

"I'm sure you've seen the headlines."

Ira's voice shook Tommy away from his thoughts and back to the present. There was no podium, no team of smokin'-hot nubile assistants, no formalities or hierarchy of any kind. The usual show was pared down to a casually dressed Ira, his shirtsleeves rolled to his elbows, his muscular forearms resting on the scarred wood table. It was a side of Ira Tommy hadn't seen, and it left him uneasy.

"Night for Night is shut down." His jaw tensed, his fingers drummed the worn wooden tabletop. "It's swarming with cops—been designated a crime scene until further notice—and there's no telling how long it will last. It's not like the LAPD is in the mood to cooperate." His face darkened, his gaze grew distant, hooded, effectively shielding his thoughts. "That said—" He splayed his hands on the table, taking a moment to study them, before returning his focus to them. "I think it's only fair we end the competition."

Beside him, Aster gasped, as Layla shrugged, not seeming to care either way, while Tommy felt the beginnings of dread. He needed the extra time to secure the top spot.

Thanks to the drama surrounding Madison, he'd been knocked off his game. Though their combined numbers were better than ever, after all they'd been through, it was like a limp to the finish. May the least wounded win.

"What about Zion, Sydney, and Diego?" Aster asked, glancing around the club as though she might've somehow missed them.

"I told them not to bother," Ira said, without further explanation. "I'd originally planned for an impressive cele-bration to mark the end, but we'll save it for another time." Ira's regret seemed genuine, but then he loved to put on a show, which made it hard to determine what was real and what was not. "You've all managed to surpass my expecta-tions. The lengths you've gone to were impressive. I knew you had it in you—that's why I hired you. And yet you never know what someone is truly capable of until they're put to the test. All three of you have been tested in ways you never could've foreseen, and you managed to stay focused, relentless, and willing to break a few rules along the way."

Tommy cringed beneath the lens of Ira's gaze. So he'd known about the black wristbands and did nothing to stop it? Pretty risky, considering the kind of trouble that could've caused. But then Ira was never one to shy away from a gamble, and neither was Tommy. Seems they had more in common than he'd originally thought.

"In some circles those are not considered estimable

qualities," Ira continued. "But in my world—they're some of the traits I most admire." He drew his brows together, fingered his tiger's-eye bracelet. "I'm sure you're all very anxious to learn the name of the winner, so without further delay—Layla Harrison—"

He centered his gaze on hers, as Tommy looked between them. No way would he announce her the winner. She was lucky to have made it this far.

"You were completely outmatched by these two." Ira wagged a finger between Tommy and Aster. "You were out of your element, and I should've canned you week one. But after a rough start, you managed to find your flow, and eventually you did a decent job of holding your own."

Layla nodded, her expression ready for whatever Ira was dealing.

"That said, today was the day you were going to be cut."

She was quick to concede the defeat. "I figured as much." She slanted her gaze first toward Aster, then Tommy.

"Aster Amirpour—"

At the mention of Aster's name, Tommy sat up straighter, his focus switching between Aster and Ira. She looked haunted, vulnerable, and yet it only seemed to enhance her beauty. Ira, as usual, gave nothing away.

"Your numbers were consistently good, and you scored some of the top names on my list. You also displayed a willingness to do whatever necessary to secure the win. . . ."

*Wait—* The dread Tommy felt at the start of the meeting had reached a steady hum. Was Aster getting fired? Because that didn't sound like the kind of thing you say to someone before you release the blade and shout, "Off with her head!"

It couldn't end this way. Now more than ever he needed the win. He had nothing else lined up, and he certainly hadn't traveled all the way from Oklahoma to craft customized coffee drinks for Starbucks's demanding clientele. Ira owed this to him—if there was ever a time for nepotism, it was now. Problem was, Tommy had never quite gotten around to revealing their connection, so how could Ira possibly know he owed the reward to his one and only son?

Maybe it was time for Tommy to make a reveal of his own.

"—and that's why you are undisputedly the winner of the Unrivaled Nightlife Competition."

Wait—who's the winner? Tommy looked from Ira to Aster, cursing himself for zoning out. But one look at Aster's beaming face was enough to confirm the worst.

Tommy shook his head, stared at the pockmarked table. After all the rules he'd broken . . . all the money he'd made for Ira . . . so he never managed to lure Ryan Hawthorne to the Vesper—so what? With the way things turned out, seemed like that should be celebrated, not mourned . . . and what the hell was going on between Ira and Aster anyway?

He should've seen it coming. Leave it to Ira to fuck him over, even though he clearly deserved the win. He'd earned it. And he'd be damned if Ira would take—

"Tommy Phillips—"

Tommy heaved a deep exhale. Forced his gaze to meet Ira's. Tempted to respond with a sarcastic, *Yes, Dad?* But he decided against it.

"You remind me of me at your age."

Well, there's a very good reason for that. . . .

"You're tenacious, hungry, a bit untamed, willing to try nearly anything. And while you didn't win the competition, I could really use someone like you on my team."

Tommy blinked, unsure what to say. Ira was tricky. Unless he spelled it out in clear, concise terms, there was no telling where he was leading.

"Which is why I'm offering you a job working for Unrivaled Nightlife. Actually, I'm extending the offer to both you and Layla. Think of it as a sort of consolation prize for a job well done."

Tommy peered at Layla—she looked as unsettled as he felt.

"Tommy, if you're interested, I'm offering you a chance to run that private room you approached me about. It's a sound idea. I'm willing to give it a try. And, Layla"—he turned toward her—"there's an opening in the Jewel marketing department. I think you'd do well there. And, Aster, of course, I invite you to stay on as a promoter. You'll receive a weekly cut of the heads you bring in, only this time it will be based on how much they spend. Oh, and in case you think I forgot . . ." He disappeared behind the bar, only to return with a new laptop for Layla, and for Tommy, the guitar he'd bought out from under him that fateful day at Farrington's. "Figured you'd put it to better use," he said, handing it over.

Tommy positioned the guitar in his arms and strummed a few strings. It needed tuning. Clearly Ira's lessons, if he'd ever really taken them, hadn't amounted to much. And yet, he was so overcome to finally have the twelve-string securely in his possession, he wasn't sure how to respond.

"And, Aster—I haven't forgotten you either." Ira slipped two fingers into his shirt pocket, retrieving a check he passed on to Aster.

Tommy leaned closer, straining to see the amount. He counted a whole lot of zeros that made Aster gasp and slap a hand over her mouth. "Thank you," she mumbled. "Omigod, thank you!" She spoke behind trembling fingers.

"Oh, and, Layla, it's not contest related, but since you're here—" He fished his fingers back into his pocket and handed her a check. "Will you pass this on to your dad? Can't wait to see what he comes up with."

Layla gazed at the check with widened eyes and a conflicted look, as Ira rubbed his hands together and said,

"What do you say we celebrate with champagne? Tommy, can you assist?"

Tommy hesitated. Surely Ira knew the Vesper didn't offer champagne. Theirs was a hard-drinking crowd.

Ira laughed—a seemingly genuine laugh, not practiced or forced, which made it all the more rare. "I managed to sneak a bottle out of Night for Night when the cops weren't looking. Seems the whole club is evidence."

Ira's casual mention of the crime struck Tommy as crass, especially after all they'd been through because of it. But then, Ira was hardly the sentimental type, and Tommy had better get used to it if he was going to continue to work for him.

Tommy reached onto the shelf, but there were no flutes, so beer mugs would have to suffice. Pinching the glasses between his fingers, he started to make for the tables, when Ira leaned toward him and said, "Just wanted you to know, you have nothing to worry about."

Tommy paused, not exactly following.

"They won't come after you. I've taken care of the evidence."

Tommy glanced at Layla and Aster, both of them lost in thought, before returning to Ira. "What evidence?"

"The security video showing you standing right outside Night for Night just seconds after Madison went in." Ira clutched the chilled bottle by the neck and held it between them. "It's handled. Luckily, I had enough time to delete that part before the cops seized it. Now they'll never know you were there."

"But I'm innocent!" Tommy's voice cracked. He sounded as frantic and perplexed as he felt. "I had nothing to do with it."

"Of course not." Ira shot him a look that wasn't at all convincing. "Look, I'm on your side. I think my actions prove that. Point is, now you won't have to defend yourself to anyone else."

So there it was—Ira being paternal and looking after his son without even realizing. Tommy was tempted to tell him and shock Ira as much as he'd just shocked Tommy. After all, Ira had destroyed evidence on his behalf. They were in this together.

"Ira," he started, but Ira was already heading back to the table, giving Tommy no choice but to follow.

"So—what do you say?" Ira's gaze moved among them. "Are you ready to officially join the Unrivaled Nightlife team?"

Layla was the first to accept, which struck Tommy as strange. He figured she'd tell him to stick it, or worse. He wondered if it had anything to do with the check.

Ira looked pointedly at Tommy, and, just like Layla, he reluctantly agreed. Glad he hadn't revealed himself. The day would come soon enough.

Aster was the last to respond. Tommy watched as her face played host to an array of emotions as she stared at the check in her hands. Maybe she was worried about being an accessory to Ryan's crime—maybe her reluctance had something to do with the DVD, and whatever it was she was about to reveal before Ira interrupted her and ushered them all inside—all Tommy knew for sure was she hesitated so long, Ira had to prod for the answer.

She curled the check until it fit snugly into her palm and folded her fingers around it. "Of course." She arranged her face into her head-shot grin. "Guess I'm a little flustered. I wasn't sure I'd win. Tommy was tough to beat." Her smile grew wider, a toothpaste commercial in the making. Though Tommy couldn't help but notice the way her gaze dimmed, her lips twitched, when her gaze met Ira's.

Had something happened between them? Before Tommy could ponder too long, the sudden pounding of fists slamming metal interrupted his thoughts.

"Open up—LAPD!" a voice boomed from the other side of the door.

Tommy froze, unsure what to do, but Ira remained as cool and composed as ever.

"What do you say we toss the drinks as I slowly make my way to the door?" He shot them each a look that had them racing behind the bar, pouring the expensive champagne down the drain, and shoving their glasses in the dishwasher, before rushing back to the table as though nothing had happened.

"What can I do for you?" Ira cracked the door.

Detective Larsen squinted past Ira's shoulder. "We're looking for Aster Amirpour."

Tommy instinctively reached for Aster. She'd gone cold, shaky, and totally unresponsive at the shock of hearing her name.

"What's this about?" Ira stood his ground, did his best to delay. Buying Aster just enough time to reach into her purse, retrieve a package, and thrust it at Tommy.

"Whatever happens, do *not* let them see this." Her face looked pained; the scent of smoke clung to her skin. "Not until you hear from me." Her lips trembled. She had trouble pronouncing the words, though her meaning was clear.

Tommy nodded, started to slip it under his T-shirt, then thought better of it and passed it to Layla, who frantically shoved it deep in her bag as Larsen fought to muscle inside.

"Don't mess with me, Redman," he barked. "If she's in there, it's in your best interest to turn her over. I don't care who you are; you try to keep her from us, we'll nail you for obstruction of justice."

Without another word, Ira swung the door wide, allowing a blast of heat and light to shoot into the room. His features sharp, gaze darkened, he seemed to almost fade into the shadows as a swarm of cops overtook Aster.

"What's this about?" Her eyes darted wildly from Ira to Larsen. "Why are you handcuffing me? I haven't done anything!"

"Aster Amirpour—" Larsen grinned, seeming to relish each and every word. "You are under arrest for the murder of Madison Brooks."

Aster's face drained of color as she bucked hard against the detective, an attempt to break free that was futile at best. "That's insane! I—"

"You have the right to remain silent," Larsen continued. "Anything you say can and will be used against you—"

"On what grounds? I had nothing to do with this! What did that creep Ryan Hawthorne tell you?"

"Ryan has a solid alibi."

"But that's not possible! I was with him that night—only he left and never returned!"

"You have the right to an attorney. If you cannot afford one, the court will assign one for you—"

"I was with him! I left the club with Ryan Hawthorne!"

"Ryan Hawthorne left the club with friends and returned to his place with those same friends. The doorman and video footage confirm it. There's no record of you."

*"But Ryan doesn't have a doorman!"* Aster screamed, recoiling in fear when Larsen thrust his face close to hers, his squinty eyes glinting with the anticipation of what he was about to reveal.

"Witnesses at Night for Night saw you leaving, but not with Ryan Hawthorne. We've uncovered the clothes you wore that night, and they're covered with Madison's blood."

Layla gasped, as Tommy instinctively reached for her hand. The two of them watched Aster crumble before them. Her body collapsing, folding in on itself, looking so lost and defeated she bore absolutely no resemblance to the strong, sexy, overconfident girl Tommy had known.

"That's impossible," she cried, her voice hoarse, reduced to a whisper. "I had nothing to do with it!" She lifted her chin, gazed around frantically until she found Ira. "Please," she cried. "Tell them! Call my lawyer and get me out of this!"

Her face lifted with hope as she watched him approach, only to crash in despair when he reached around her and removed the prize-winning check from her fingers.

"For safekeeping," he said. His gaze impenetrable, he returned it to his pocket. The cops pushed Aster out the door and through the throng of tourists and paparazzi already gathered like vultures, leading her away under the glare of falling ash and flashing lights.

# ACKNOWLEDGMENTS

This book has been so much fun to write, and it's all thanks to the following people: my lovely and amazing editors Katherine Tegen, Claudia Gabel, and Melissa Miller, who made this book possible; my wonderful agent, Bill Contardi, the perfect combination of humor and smarts; and, as always, my husband, Sandy, who showed me that all things are possible for those who believe.

Read on for an exclusive look at
the second book in **ALYSON NOËL'S**
**BEAUTIFUL IDOLS TRILOGY**

ABOUT *love,*

*death,*

AND THE *lies* IN BETWEEN.

# Blacklist

**Breaking News: Discovery of Blood-Soaked Dress Leads to Arrest of Night for Night Party Promoter!**

By Trena Moretti

Just in—Mere hours after teen heartthrob Ryan Hawthorne was called in for questioning regarding the disappearance of his former girlfriend, Hollywood A-lister Madison Brooks, Los Angeles police received an anonymous tip leading to a blood-soaked dress thought to belong to Night for Night party promoter Aster Amirpour.

While the official statement released by the LAPD states that tests are underway to determine the source of the blood, an LAPD insider assures us they've received confirmation that the blood on the dress is a match for the missing celebrity.

According to our sources, the dress was turned over to police when a W Hotel employee became suspicious.

"I was only doing my job, which requires me to double-check the number and type of clothes found in the guest's laundry bag with the number and type of clothes the guest logged onto the form," said the employee, who wishes to remain anonymous. "This is the same standard procedure we always follow before we send the laundry out to our vendor. You would not believe how many people don't know the difference between a chemise and a dress. Anyway, in the middle of checking I noticed that a black dress had been improperly marked as a blouse. When I looked closer, I saw that the dress was covered in large dark stains that struck me as suspicious. It was then that I alerted my boss and they took it from there. If it really is the blood of Madison Brooks, then all we can do is pray for that poor young girl, because it really was an awful lot of blood. The dress was completely covered in it."

At the time of writing, Aster Amirpour was being booked into LA County Jail. We'll have more as this story develops.

# ONE

# GIRL AFRAID

Madison Brooks grudgingly surrendered the fading remnants of her dream and blinked into the blackness before her. The room was soundless, still. The air hung weighty and stale. Despite the promise of sleep, her waking life remained a living hell.

While she had plenty of fears—fear of forgetting her lines during a live performance, fear of her secret past being revealed—a fear of the dark had never been among them. Even as a child she understood that the mythical monster dwelling under the bed could only pale in comparison to the all-too-real parental monsters getting high in the den.

And it was no different now.

She pushed away from the soiled mattress she'd slept on and crept toward the solid steel door, alerted to any hint of scent, sound—anything that might provide a clue as to who had taken her, where they had taken her, and why. Over thirty days spent in captivity, and Madison was no closer to answers than the night she'd been snatched. She'd gone over the incident countless times—the memory playing on a continuous loop as she searched frame by frame, hunting for revelations, some small but crucial detail she might've missed. Yet every viewing remained stubbornly the same.

She'd broken up with Ryan only to be rescued by Tommy, and after sharing a few beers (along with a few memorable kisses), she'd received a text from Paul instructing her to meet him at Night for Night, and she'd fled without question. Though she should've known the moment she arrived at the closed and empty club that something had gone terribly wrong. Paul was professional. Punctual. If he'd truly intended to meet her, he would've been there already. She'd walked straight into a trap, but that was all hindsight now. Yet another item to add to the long list of things she'd chosen to ignore until she found herself with nothing but time to second-guess and berate herself.

How could she have been so trusting? So naive?

Why had she continued to wait on the terrace, reminiscing about a past she was desperate to keep buried while ignoring her gut instinct that urged her to flee?

Last thing she remembered was a curl of wind at her back, the wisp of a scent she still couldn't place; then a hand was clasped firmly over her mouth and time folded in on itself.

And now, several weeks later, she remained locked in a windowless cell that offered little more than a sink, a toilet, a bare mattress tossed on the floor, and a succession of bland, lumpy meals served three times a day.

Not a single sign of her captor.

Not a clue as to why she'd been taken.

Her diamond-encrusted Piaget watch, the hoop earrings Ryan had given her, the Gucci stilettos she'd worn, and the cashmere wrap she now used as a blanket served as the only reminders of her former Hollywood It Girl status.

If it was money they were after, they would've stripped her of the luxuries long ago. Allowing her to keep them seemed almost cruel. Like they wanted her to remember who she'd once been, if only to show her how quickly they could strip it away.

She sprawled on the cold cement floor with her legs splayed before her, wondering, as she always did, what was happening outside the cinder-block walls. Surely the whole world knew of her disappearance. There was probably even a task force specifically assigned to her case. So why was it taking them so long to find her? And more importantly, why hadn't Paul directed them to her when he was the one who'd insisted on embedding the microchip tracker into her arm, just under the burn scar, in anticipation of this very thing?

Right on schedule, the lights switched on—sending the fluorescent bulbs flickering, humming, and washing the room in a garish green glow. A moment later, when the slot snapped open, Madison crouched right beside it, stretched her mouth wide, and screamed from the very depths of her belly.

But just like every other day, the tray of lumpy food shot past, the slot slammed shut, and Madison's cries for help languished hollow and unheard.

She kicked the food aside and glanced around the small room, searching for something she might've missed, something she could use to defend herself with. Paul had taught her how to see past the mundane. *Nearly everything has a dual purpose,* he'd told her. *Even the most ordinary item can be used as a defense.* But even if she could fashion her stiletto heel into a weapon, there was no opponent—no one to fight. She was trapped all alone in her cinder-block cell.

With a frustrated sigh, she turned her attention to the pictures of her eight-year-old self spread across the ceiling and walls. The repeating image was occasionally spliced by a random strip of mirror meant to reflect the sorry state she currently found herself in. In the photo, her hair was tangled, her feet dirty and bare, an old doll dangled from the tips of her fingers as she regarded the camera with a deep violet stare.

It was the same picture someone had sent Paul as an unspoken threat.

The one he'd assured her had burned long ago with everything else from her past.

In the ten years since the photo was taken she'd traveled such a great distance, rose to great heights, only to come full circle and find herself as powerless, desperate, and filthy as she'd been as a child.

Everything Paul had told her was a lie. Her past had never been erased. It had been there all along, patiently waiting for just the right moment to remind her of the sins she'd committed on her rise to the top.

Someone had connected the dots between the hopeless child she'd been to the triumphant star she'd become.

Someone had uncovered the darker truth of her journey— the lies she'd told, the people she'd betrayed—and now they were making her pay.

While she refused to believe Paul was behind it—he'd been protecting her for too long to turn on her now—she couldn't rule out the idea that maybe someone had gotten to him. Either way, it was clear she could no longer count on him to find her.

Absently, she ran a finger over the web of fresh scars that covered her knuckles and hands—a reminder of an earlier bid to escape that had resulted in a broken pinkie, a badly strained wrist, and the loss of three nails. She'd acted impulsively, allowed herself to be driven by fear. It was a mistake she would not make again. Her next attempt had to succeed. Failure was no longer an option.

She remained like that, staring at the wall and formulating a plan, the images of her past and present selves merging into one, until the last meal was delivered and the cell went dark once again.

# TWO

# HEART-SHAPED BOX

## BEAUTIFUL IDOLS
**Innocent Until Proven Guilty, Yo!**
By Layla Harrison

Warning: If you landed on this blog looking to revel in the usual sarcastic celebrity snark fest, then you might want to get out while you can and save your clicks and comments for Perez Hilton, Popsugar, or wherever you go to fuel up on your daily dose of Hollywood gossip when you're done reading me.

Don't even try to pretend we're monogamous.
I know you've been clicking around.

While I'm usually all too happy to provide the sort of low-level, derisive, Hollywood dirt you've come to crave, today

I'm afraid I'm ~~unable~~ unwilling to come out and play.

Unless you've been hiding under the proverbial rock, you're probably aware that Aster Amirpour has been arrested for the murder of Madison Brooks. A good source confirms the Bravado Channel even cut a very special *Real Housewives of Hades* episode in order to report the breaking story, and I think we can all agree that the willingness to preempt the daily digressions of everyone's favorite cloven-heeled, cleavage-enhanced, pitchfork-wielding blondes shows just how very serious this story is.

As it turns out, it is serious, and I was there when it happened. Which means I watched in horror as an innocent person was unfairly handcuffed and hauled away in a squad car in front of dozens of paparazzi.

Until you've watched someone being accused of a heinous crime you *know they did not commit*, then you probably won't have any empathy for what I'm going through now. Thing is, I know beyond a shadow of doubt—well beyond any and all reasonable doubt—that *Aster Amirpour is innocent*. Which means I will not write about her arrest in my usual way.

While I'm more than happy to continue to report on all manner of Hollywood debauchery, I cannot and will not use this blog to bring down an innocent or perpetuate a story that simply isn't true.

Also, as we so often seem to forget during times like these, allow me to remind you that our legal system works on a little thing called the *presumption of innocence*, which translates to mean: *the burden of proof is on the one who declares, not on the one who denies.*

Look it up:

http://legal-dictionary.thefreedictionary.com/
presumption+of+innocence

546 Comments:

**Anonymous**
Your a fucking idiot.

**MadisonFan101**
Your friend is a murderer and you're both going to hell.

**RyMadLives**
Aster Amirpour is a slut and a murderer and everyone knows it but you.

**StarLovR**
You're blog is as ugly and boring and basic as you are.

**CrzYLuVZomby38**
If the dress don't fit, you must acquit! But we all know it fits, so . . .

**AsterMustDie**
I hope you end up as dead as Madison.

Layla Harrison sat at her desk, mindlessly sipping her coffee and glaring at the comments section emblazoned across her computer screen. She was supposed to be working. Supposed to be making her mark by ensuring that the party to herald the launch of Ira Redman's new Unrivaled tequila label was the most hyped, most talked-about party of the season. Instead, she was using company time (along with the company computer) to read the comments a bunch of media-manipulated morons had left on her blog.

"Innocent or guilty?"

Layla looked up to find Emerson, the guy from a few cubicles over, standing too close for comfort and peering over her shoulder.

With a click, Layla minimized the tab along with the other pic on her screen—the one of a frightened and pale Aster being ushered into a police car, the headline above it screaming, *Party Promoter Aster Amirpour Arrested for the Murder of Madison Brooks!*

It wasn't like she needed to study it. She'd stood right beside Tommy Phillips and watched the whole sordid scene play out just one week before.

"Definitely, one hundred percent *not* guilty," Layla snapped. To Emerson the case was little more than a hot piece of gossip about a fellow Unrivaled employee. It wasn't personal for him like it was for her. She resented him using it as an icebreaker, and had no problem letting him know it.

"Not like it matters." Emerson regarded her through wide topaz-colored eyes that his thick lashes and perfectly groomed brows only seemed to enhance. It was Layla's first day on the job, and it was already the second time she'd been on the receiving end of his go-to condescending expression. Thankfully she'd started midweek, so there were only two more days left until the weekend.

The first was when she got lost in the maze of identical cubicles on her way back from the break room, and Emerson escorted her to her desk with an eye roll and an audible sigh. Layla had spent the next half hour silently fuming. How was she supposed to recognize hers when they all looked the same? When it came to designing his clubs, Ira Redman spared no expense. So why wouldn't she expect a cool millennial campus, brimming with espresso bars, basketball courts, spa rooms, and maybe even a yoga studio or meditation den? But the Unrivaled Nightlife corporate offices, which basically amounted to a study in greige with their matching wall-to-wall carpet and workstations, were so opposite of what she'd envisioned—so disappointingly bland—that when she'd first walked in, she was sure she'd arrived at an accounting firm.

The rest of the day was spent online, researching Madison Brooks's disappearance a little over one month before and the evidence the LAPD had managed to stack against Aster in the ensuing weeks, only to get caught slacking off by Emerson of all people.

"Cases like that are all about perception." Emerson was still standing too close, still peering over her shoulder even though there was nothing to see—her screen had gone blank. "And perception *always* drives results."

Layla allowed her gaze to roam the fine planes of his face—the high cheekbones, square jaw, finely sculpted chin, smooth dark skin—and found herself frozen, unable to breathe. Extreme beauty often had that effect—as did the paralyzing fear of getting fired on her first day of work. She could only hope Emerson wouldn't inform Ira of her less than stellar performance.

"Figured you would've known that," he said. "After all, isn't that what our department's all about? Manipulating public perception into believing Ira's clubs are the only worthy place to see and be seen, and that his tequila is the only brand worth drinking?"

Layla fidgeted, fingers picking at the strands of her platinum bob while swiveling back and forth in her seat. While she was beginning to resent Emerson's presence, even she had to admit there was truth in his words.

# JOIN THE
# Epic Reads
## COMMUNITY

**THE ULTIMATE YA DESTINATION**

### ◀ DISCOVER ▶
your next favorite read

### ◀ MEET ▶
new authors to love

### ◀ WIN ▶
free books

### ◀ SHARE ▶
infographics, playlists, quizzes, and more

### ◀ WATCH ▶
the latest videos